HEART OF GRIT

—

Shelli Sivert

ISBN: 979-8-35092-448-0 (print)
ISBN: 979-8-35092-449-7 (eBook)

For the ones who love me best: Bob, Jed, and Gunnar.

CHAPTER 1

Beatrice Brannon

Friday, March 16, 1860, Victory Hills, a silver mining boomtown near the Comstock Lode discovery in the Utah Territory of the Western United States

A saloon's no place for a lady of refinement. Mama had told me so. Da had agreed. And the Ellerby girls—the picture of social grace and elegance—had said it many times. No indeed, unless I wore red-hot rouge on my cheeks and a corset pinched tighter than a tourniquet, I best steer clear of those places altogether. Frightful pity, with all the hubbub of an announcement, not to mention a real discussion among *mostly* intelligent men regarding the well-being of our town. Truly a shame, for all that would happen there. For all I'd miss.

"Pan's sizzlin' now, Bea," Mama told me, prodding me back to the present. "That butter'll burn if you wait much longer."

She hummed a melody from her home state of Kentucky as she drew cornbread from the brick oven. I knelt beside the hearth and cracked an egg into the iron spider. The ooze danced and bubbled. I cracked another, while in my mind, contriving a way into that saloon meeting.

A fake message! I'll deliver it to Da and take my sweet time on the way out, secretly taking note of every word. No, it wouldn't work. They'd never talk freely with a female present. And seeing that I had no real message, Da would see right through it. *Concealment may be my only option.*

My brother JP burst through the door, carrying a pail of fresh milk.

"Jeremiah Peter," Mama said in her gentle voice, "you'll take care not to spill a drop."

I rushed over to catch the swaying bucket, as Mama had *just* mopped the floor.

"Wretched cow gave me hell," he said.

Mama gave a tsk-tsk at his cursing, which by now, wasn't likely to be curbed.

"Poor Flossie," Cobber mumbled from his cozy spot by the fire. "Maybe if you was gentler with that cow."

"Fine words from a lazy loafer," JP protested. "You ain't done a lick this morning."

"I got leg aches. Mama said I could take it easy."

"Leg aches! That's a right cock-and-bull story."

And so the bickering began, as it did every morning between my eleven-year-old brothers.

I stooped to flip the eggs. On the way back up, my corset shifted sideways, not cinched tight enough. At fifteen, I'd been wearing a corset well on a year now, but still hadn't quite mastered the right tightness. The hourglass shape I'd hoped for hadn't shown up yet, nor the height. Mama, plump and lovely herself, once told me I had a big spirit for someone who didn't take up much space.

Da emerged from his and Mama's bedroom, blazoned in his dark overcoat and sheriff's badge, his booming presence bigger than the sky. We all waited for his first exultation, as if delivering the opening line of a play. He drew in a deep breath and said in his Irish brogue, "Now *that's* the smell of a Brannon morning."

"Morning, Da," Cobber said, rising to be held.

"How's my littlest cub, now?" Da embraced the boy, lifted him up like a marionette, swung him around, and rested him back down, giggling and dizzy.

"We have a situation." JP spoke to Da as a deputy might speak to a sheriff. "This young man is dodging chores again. This time it's leg aches."

"That true, Jacob Erwin? You wouldn't lie to get out of a little work, would you?"

"No, sir," Cobber answered.

"Well, I'm apt to believe you, then. 'Cause, you know, Brannons don't lie." A sideways smile emerged. "Now, that's not to say we don't exaggerate now and again, and maybe we throw in a bit of sarcasm here and there, but lie? Never."

Cobber chuckled, which annoyed JP, who'd failed to enlist Da to his side.

"Keep the yolks runny," Da said to me. "The runnier, the better."

I wrinkled my nose. "Good thing I'm the chef, not you."

"On she goes, too big for her britches," he said, shaking his head. "Do you hear this, Ellen?"

Mama offered him a side glance, adding, "Where do you suppose she gets it?"

He wrapped his arm around Mama's waist and leaned in for a kiss, but she denied him, inspecting his face. "Your eyes are red. How long you been up?"

"Oh, long enough. Not to worry now." His vague reply meant he'd been up for hours and probably out at the silver mine. He often failed to disclose all the time he spent there, sometimes waking up at ungodly hours and slipping back into bed so Mama would be none the wiser. That horrible, slow-to-yield silver mine—Da's only mistress.

At last, every plate was set and every coffee mug filled. Mama said grace and we dug into our fried eggs and cornbread.

"Might I go into town with you today, Da?" I asked, hoping the flush in my cheeks wouldn't betray my true motive.

"And why, Honey Bea? What business have you there?"

"I . . . was hoping to meet the Ellerby girls. There's some new fabric arriving today. Silk from China, actually."

"China?" he raised a brow. "That's a long ride for the wee silkworms, is it not?" He elbowed JP, attempting to lighten the boy's mood. "All the way from China to Victory Hills, Nowhere."

"I'm certain the price will more than compensate for the journey," Mama added.

"And I suppose that's a better use of your time than goin' to school?" This he said with a pointed expression, the way he did back in the days when he knew what was best for me.

"I told you, Da, I've outgrown that little school."

Mama came to my aid. "She's long surpassed that teacher, Jeremiah. Truly, it's torture for her. Lots of the older ones have stopped goin'."

"Well, so long as you keep readin' your Shakespeare and your Milton and your . . . what's his name?"

"Dante Alighieri," I said, in my best Italian accent.

"That's the one. Now, as for you boys, until you reach your sister's scholarly heights, you'll still be goin'."

JP gave a sigh that edged on a grunt. "It's not gonna help me become a famous marksman."

"Your sister could help you with that too," Da said.

JP gave a vicious scowl. "I'm a better shot than she is!"

"Relax, JP," I said. "The role of 'family marksman' is all yours. I give it to you."

"That's right," Da said, "Beatrice is becomin' an elegant lady, right before our eyes."

Mama added, "Though it's not a bad idea for a lady to keep up her skills in this wild country."

Mama and Da nudged me toward ladyhood of one sort or another, though neither told me how to accomplish this. I myself hadn't a clue. My rough-and-tumble childhood was hardly that of a lady's, full of shooting guns, riding horses—not on a sidesaddle, mind you—and I regularly helped Da gut the trout from our fishing trips with nary a gag. But as my childhood came to a close, I looked to Dante's Beatrice for refinement, radiance, and intelligence, as well as to my friends, the Ellerbys.

"So . . . you're willing to take me with you?" I slipped it in again.

Da took his time replying. I waited, spinning a forkful of egg on my plate, wondering why the men held their meetings at the saloon anyhow. To keep the women out, I'd say, so they could chew their cud and smoke their cigars and swear like sailors without a peep from any woman.

"I don't see why not." Da gulped the last of his coffee and stood. "We've got to make life interesting, haven't we? Even if all we've got is China silk to entertain us. Alright, Honey Bea, you've got until the time it takes me to hitch up the wagon to ready yourself."

"Oh, I'm ready now." I removed my apron and smoothed out my dress. "And I can help you hitch up."

"It's a chilly morn," Mama threw in. "Wear your shawl."

I took my shawl off its peg by the door.

"And while you're there, ask the Ellerby girls if they need a dress order. I'm happy to oblige."

"Please no, Mama, I can't conduct business with my friends. It's humiliating. Can't you work it out with Mrs. Ellerby?"

"Nonsense! It'll save me a trip to their house."

I gave a sigh equal to my frustration. "If it comes up, I'll ask."

"If it comes up?" Da scoffed. "You'll be lookin' at fabrics, for goodness' sake. Are you not made of sterner stuff than that?"

Only he could elicit such instant self-reflection. "Well, when you put it like *that*."

"Wait! Can we hitch a ride?" JP pled, meeting us at the door with his schoolbooks.

"You'll be early. What'll you do with yourselves?" Mama reasoned.

"But it's so much better than walking. And poor Cobber—he's got sore legs."

We each froze and raised our eyes until the irony wouldn't hold. Da exploded into laughs, and the rest of us followed.

"That kind of brotherly love really warms my heart, JP." I lowered the brim of his hat over his eyes, which he slapped back.

We hitched up Thundercloud and Parsley to the wagon and climbed aboard, the boys in the back and I seated in the front beside Da.

While Da hurried back inside to fetch something he'd forgotten, probably his pipe, I turned toward the house. The image struck me. "Boys, look!" But they bickered back and forth.

A rose-coral sunrise bloomed across the sky. Our quaint little saltbox house, built by Da himself, billowed smoke out its chimney. It was tucked neatly in a thicket of cottonwood trees that murmured in the gentle wind. Many a night, we'd all sit on the porch and listen to Da play his tin whistle. Fifty acres of land we owned. Fifty acres of wonderful wilderness to explore.

We jostled along in the wagon and ere long reached the schoolhouse. Da halted only long enough for the boys to take a mighty leap out. As for me, I was happy to have Da all to myself for a little while.

"You'll do well, Bea, with your smarts and your learnin'. Do it the right way. Don't bet your money on foolishness or try to strike it rich. Keep steady."

His comments were odd. He knew well enough I had no money, and as a young woman, even fewer opportunities to 'strike it rich.' I suspected he spoke more to himself.

"Is everything alright?" I ventured.

"Of course, Honey Bea, never better."

These words gave me no comfort. When Da overstated something, there was a chance he meant the opposite.

"You'll not make the mistakes I've made—always followin' the money. Ever searchin' for the shiny counterfeit thing."

"Da, you've done very well. You have nothing to be ashamed of. We have everything we need. And we're happy. Aside from when JP torments us."

"I've not been wise," he returned. "It's not what I imagined when I came here."

Of this, he meant his journey from Ireland to America at fourteen years old, leaving behind everything, even his family.

"Do you ever wish to go back?"

"I suppose it'd be nice to visit the old country again. Pretty as a picture. Like nothin' you've ever seen. But we had some hard times. Very hard times." He spoke softly, delving back into the past. "I never intended to stay in America, you see. I was gonna make my fortune and return to my da with bags of gold and money, but, well, by the time I made any money at all—"

"The famine hit," I finished in a hushed whisper. The great potato famine, from which the people of Ireland had only recovered in the last decade. Da always spoke of it somberly. He'd lost both his parents to it.

"Lord-a-mercy, we were so poor even the rats shunned us. Our name wasn't treated with respect. If folks heard the name Brannon, they'd spit on the ground. They'd turn you out. As if the ragged clothes weren't enough." He sighed deeply. "I wanted to do my da proud."

"I think he'd be very proud. *I'm* enormously proud of you."

He was pained, dispirited. "But I couldn't rescue his name."

We quieted a little and I didn't attempt to say it wasn't so. This was a persistent matter for Da and one he'd mentioned before, but I wondered why he spoke of it today. Was something else weighing on him? Instead of words, I sidled beside him and rested my head on his shoulder.

Oliver Street was the heart of our charming little boomtown. An array of storefronts greeted us, some with balconies and tall pillars. Others had flat fronts and ornately painted signs. All of them had the backdrop of the hills, speckled with pinion pines and juniper trees.

Da brought the wagon around, close to the saloon where several horses were stalled. He pointed toward the general store. "Ah, there's the Ellerby girls now. On you go."

Seeing as I didn't scurry off right away, he said, "Well, that's what you came for, isn't it?"

Finally, I let it escape. "Da, couldn't I go to that meeting with you?"

"I knew it!" he said, amused. "First time I mentioned it, your ears perked up like a fox's."

"You said Mayor Torrence was unveiling a secret. Does it get more interesting than that?"

"He lures us with those traps every time. Once, he needed volunteers to dig a well."

"Couldn't you say that I'm making a study of the mechanics of the Socratic method as it applies to the debates of men in an informal, parochial setting?"

He burst into laughter. "I'm certain I've just been profaned. Alas, I'll need a dictionary to know for sure. Bea, you know it isn't proper. Your mother would sooner drink strychnine."

"Da, I don't understand. You say you want me to make my mark, but how can I do that if I'm uninformed?"

"Well, I don't want you corrupted! There's no chance I'm takin' you in there with me. But tell you what, I'll listen keenly and give you all the particulars. And *you* can tell me all about the China silk."

I pressed a hand to my forehead.

"Go on! Don't embarrass your mother and me, alright?" He went his own direction.

I huffed plenty as I stepped down.

The girls spotted me and met me halfway.

"Beatrice, so good to see you!" Delilah Ellerby said.

"Morning, Delilah, Daphne."

As usual, they were clothed in the finest dresses, cloaks, and bonnets. Their father had done well raising cattle, affording them with all the trimmings of a rich life. I tucked some stray hairs into my braided bun.

The girls engaged in small talk, while I fixed my eyes on a large black carriage coming toward us. "Who the devil is that?"

They were more shocked by my cursing than anything in the distance. Eventually, they turned to see.

The elegant carriage crept by like an enormous black widow. Its shiny black paint was graced with gold-embossed scrolls. It halted at the saloon, and a gentleman in a sleek suit and dignified beard stepped down. Mayor Torrence welcomed him with a handshake.

"He must be the gentleman who wrote to Papa," Delilah said.

"What did his letter say?" I shot back, craning my neck.

"Goodness, I don't know. It's hardly polite for me to ask Papa about his personal letters, let alone for you to ask me."

I ignored her slight rebuke.

"Something about a new type of mail service," Daphne, the younger of them, added.

"New, you say?" I was more intrigued than ever. "What particulars do you know?"

"Dear Beatrice," Delilah said, tilting her head, "there is nothing so impolite as to inquire after matters which are of no consequence to you."

"But what if they *are* of consequence?" I asked.

The girls quieted at my remark. Had I said something offensive? Impertinent? "I suppose we'll never know unless we ask . . . right?"

"But you've not been invited," Delilah said.

Across the street, Mr. Hobbs fixed the closed sign to his print shop door and hurried toward the throng. I could no longer contain myself.

"Ladies, carry on. I'll only be a moment."

"Why do you trouble yourself?" Delilah said. "A respectable lady—"

"Doesn't belong in there, I know," I finished, "but before they go inside, I'll at least find out who the gentleman is. It's worth a try."

Delilah sighed deeply, as though she'd lost all progress in making me a fitting companion.

I smiled, curtsied, and hurried down the lane. One by one, the men stepped inside. I quickened my pace. Just as I arrived, the last man stepped inside and shut the door. I gave a punctuated sigh.

The alleyway, dim and vacant, called to me like a siren. A cluster of memories sparked in me. Years ago, my old pal Charlie had shown me a secret spot with a view into the saloon. Oh, the dirt we'd collected on folks! But now? Here I was, trying ever so hard to attain civility and charm.

Delilah's words echoed. *There is nothing so impolite as to inquire after matters which are of no consequence to you.*

But in that moment, with no one on the open road to check me, I slinked into the alleyway, determined with my life to hear what the men had to say.

CHAPTER 2

Charlie Rye

Friday, March 16, 1860

EASY *does it. Breathe.* I flung the saddle onto Dandy's back, ran the strap through the buckle, and cinched it up good. *Steady, calm,* I told myself. But it was no use with all that banging and clattering from the house. A pair of trembling hands clenched the saddle horn. I lodged my foot in the stirrup and swung myself up on Dandy's back. Ready to ride. Ready to blast out of there like a shotgun, away from my good-for-nothing devil of a pa. *I ought to just ride and never look back,* I told myself.

Lord knows, I tried before. Lots of times. Lo and behold, I'd get a mile outside of town, and my conscience would start gnawing at me, saying, *He'll never survive alone.* And for reasons unknown to me, I didn't have the guts to make a clean break from my only blood kin.

Oh, the racket! That bear of a man was all hell-fired and cursing, breaking everything that wasn't already broke. *It's time.* I gave Dandy a yah-nudge and took off. The harder we galloped, the freer I felt. Chains bursting, ropes loosening. I even started to laugh. *I outsmarted the old jackass.*

The fiery morning sky matched the burn in my chest. The clouds swirled and clashed like men on a battlefield. Did that foretell good things or bad? Either way, maybe there was hope for me yet. I had to believe it.

My thoughts wandered further than was good for me. Had he beaten her too? How in the nation did she ever fall for him? My mother, God rest her soul, had been a woman of importance in her Cherokee tribe. What they called a Beloved Woman. They'd ask for her counsel, her wisdom. Curse me if she didn't go and leave all that behind to be with the white men. One in particular. The one I called Pa.

Sometimes I could've swore I felt her. When the wind pushed at my back. Or in a fresh snowfall. Or in the flicker of a candle. But I ain't never met her—not since they cut the cord—so it only made me sound crazy to say so.

I hopped down outside Hobbs's Print Shop and tied Dandy's rope to a post. *First, breathe.* It'd do no good to rile him up with my bad luck. I buoyed myself up like I'd gotten so good at.

The shop door gave a jangle, welcoming me like an old friend.

"Mornin', Charlie," the old man's voice squealed like a hinge. "Fine mornin', ain't it? Would ya look at that sunrise! Yessir, like a fire in the sky."

"Hope it means good fortune's comin'," I returned, attempting to shake off my shadows.

"Well, son, nobody deserves it more than you." I liked how Mr. Hobbs called me son—a whole different feeling than when Pa called me that.

"It's the dawn of a new day, Hobbs. Somethin' big's a-comin'. It has to."

"You've got a good nose for these things. You must be right."

Hobbs polished down his printing equipment with a greasy rag. He paused and took a hard gander at me through his spectacles. "I say, who you tryin' to impress in that getup?" He gestured toward my new buckskin leather fringe jacket and trousers to match.

"Oh, this?" I stood tall and puffed out my chest. "Won this from a game of three-card monte."

"Bless my soul! All you need now's a gun in that empty holster."

"Don't remind me," I said. Hobbs had been there when I lost my '51 Samuel Colt in a poker match.

"Goodness, kid, when you gonna come out ahead instead of breakin' even?"

"No such thing as breakin' even in gambling, Hobbs, or in life neither. It'll always take your soul."

"That's a grim view."

"But said with a smile," I noted.

His laugh sounded like a silly hiss.

I hoisted myself to sit on the counter, picked up his latest edition of the *Victory Hills Voice*, and read the headline: "Three Miners Claim Big Bonanza at Silver City. Son of a gun, Hobbs, so many miners gettin' their bonanzas. When's mine comin'?"

"First off, you ain't a miner. They work like dogs. You wanna get lost in the catacombs and sweat blood, go ahead."

"Maybe I will. I ain't picky about where it comes from."

"Second off, if you're only after money, you're settin' yourself up for trouble."

Even though I shrugged off the old man's guidance, I knew he was right. Money didn't solve every problem. All the same, it sure didn't make 'em any worse.

I glanced down at the article again. From the corner of my eye, I noticed Mr. Hobbs fold his arms and stare me down. He was about to give me a preaching-to.

"You know what you need, son? An endeavor. Somethin' bigger than cards. Somethin' that'll give you some pride in yourself."

"Beg your pardon! What's wrong with cards?"

His expression didn't budge an inch. And that was enough to make me surrender to the pure honesty of it. "I know, Hobbs. How long I been sayin' it? Nobody'd love to make a name for himself more than me, but what're my options?"

He raised an eyebrow, like he'd been waiting to answer that very question. "Say, why don't you come with me to that meetin' at the saloon? I've a hunch the subject might interest you."

"I got a better idea." I hopped down from the counter. "Why don't you tell me what it's about and save me the hassle?"

"I've been admonished not to breathe a word," he said, lowering his voice.

"You really ain't gonna tell me? Come on, how long've we known each other?"

"Come be there in person when they announce it. Won't be the same comin' from my squeaky ol' voice."

I walked to the window and peered out onto Oliver Street. The sunrise had faded some, leaving a rosy haze over our pretty little town.

"Nah, I can't go. Mayor Torrence would never let me be part of his private gathering. He don't like me. Never has. Called me all kinds of names to my face. He don't want my Cherokee blood around, I reckon."

The two unforgivable counts against me, according to the mayor, were being born of a Cherokee mother, God rest her soul, and a white father with the most shameful reputation in town.

"He's always been ignorant." The old man gently patted my back. "Loves to hear himself talk—even if it's ugly talk. You got talent that can't be overlooked. Now if you could just direct that talent toward a meaningful pursuit."

I sighed long and loud, getting far more than I'd bargained for visiting his shop that morning.

"How's about this?" Hobbs leaned toward my ear, whispering. "Come in late."

"To the meetin'?"

"Sure," he kept up the whisper. "Come in late and stand in the back, see. And once they get talkin' and opinions get flyin', nobody'll notice you come in. The Grim Reaper himself could float through the door and nobody'd notice."

After a while, I said, "Why are we whispering?"

"Effect," he whispered.

"Listen, I appreciate the gesture, but I best not. My pa's gonna be there, and I'm in no mood to be around him."

"*Your* pa?" he said, his voice even higher than its usual tone.

"Yep. Sheriff Brannon invited him. Can't tell ya why."

He stroked the white scruff of his chin. "Well, it's Sheriff Brannon—he must have a good reason. He does have an uncommon ability to believe the best in people."

"I'll agree with you there, but it's gonna take a lot more than belief to mend my pa from his ways. You know what he did this mornin'? Tried to steal my money. I watched him go for the spot. Thing is, I took out all the cash the night before and put it elsewhere. Shoulda seen his face. Mad as a pit of snakes. Then he tries to say *I* stole it from *him*. Next thing I know, he's knocked me to the ground. Well, I knocked him down harder. Ain't so easy beatin' your own kid when that kid gets strong enough to defend himself."

I snapped out of my thoughts. Maybe I said too much. Let too much of my hatred show.

Poor old man strived to crack the tension. "Your pa still drivin' the whiskey wagon?"

"Yep, when he's sober enough to do it."

"In the early days, Charlie, your pa was a real quality person. Just had a stroke of bad luck."

"A stroke of . . . what're you carryin' on about?"

He rightly quit that line of reasoning. Nobody was going to tell me that my pa was some saint down on his luck. It wasn't enough that my pa destroyed his own life, but he had to destroy mine too.

"It's a sad state of affairs sharing a name with that man," I said. And I did, in every sense. Charles Vincent Rye. He the senior, I the junior.

"Charlie, you don't have to carry on the way he does. Be a better man. Your life ain't over yet. How old are you again?"

"Sixteen."

"See there, your life's just beginnin'. You don't have to go down that road. You got your own."

"Thanks, Hobbs, I'll keep that in mind." Maybe he caught my disdain, maybe not.

It was generous of the old man to try to give me a boost, but I knew the truth. I'd lived it for the past sixteen years. No matter what I did to escape my pa's influence, it always found me. I was the town bastard—son of a drunk. My pa had set a course for me, and there was nothing I could do to reverse it. Accepting my fate was one of the best things I'd ever done for myself. At least I could lessen some of the misery and find casual pursuits to pass the time.

"Charlie, it was you who said somethin' big's on its way. Don't you believe it?"

"Course I do," I said, but wasn't so sure. "For other folks, maybe."

"Well, I think it's for you, and I got a feelin' it's gonna start right down there."

He pointed toward the saloon, but my attention was pulled in another direction. Miss Beatrice Brannon stood in front of the general store talking with the Ellerby girls. I used to call her Bea, but I didn't know what to call her these days. It'd been a while since we talked. Too long.

A snicker sounded in my ear. "Well, I got an inkling as to why you got the buckskin outfit."

I scowled at him. "Give it a rest, Hobbs. I ain't some child you can tease."

"Can't I? Ain't got no grandson."

Bea. What could be said of her? She was a bright light in this forlorn existence. She had dreams and ambitions. What's more, she had the means to reach them. She was smart as a whip and came from good stock. And I'd never know why, but she believed in me. Always said I'd do something big. Well, I didn't know what she thought of me no more. Not since she took up with the Ellerby girls.

If that mammoth-like sunrise wasn't enough to make this morning notable, along came a swanky black carriage, grand and full of itself. The glint off that paint could've blinded me.

Mr. Hobbs let a whistle sail through his teeth. "Well, I never!"

"Pity's sake, you didn't tell me King Midas was comin'."

"Didn't know."

"You have no idea who's in there?" I asked.

"None."

A couple more seconds of deliberation was all it took. "You know what, old man? I'll go to your meetin'. I might even pretend I belong there."

"That's the Charlie I know." He patted my back once again and posted the closed sign in his window. "I'll head over. You wait here. It won't take ten minutes to get the pot stirrin'."

He left in a devil of a hurry.

My attention went back to the girls. Bea's gaze flew back to the carriage twice, maybe three times, as it halted in front of the saloon. She gestured an excuse to her friends and, before long, took off in that same direction. I smiled to myself. Bea was never one to be left in the dark—a right busybody. Too bad they'd never let her in the saloon. What was her plan?

My day just got a whole lot more interesting, I thought. *She's gonna spy. And I'm gonna spy on her spying.*

CHAPTER 3

Beatrice Brannon

Friday, March 16, 1860

I crept into the shaded alley and crouched behind a plump barrel—the same one that had been there since Charlie and I were children. With my back pressed to the saloon wall, I could feel the jangle of the piano plunking the tune "Oh! Susanna" on the other side. The smell, as always, was of urine. That alley was a common spot for drinkers to relieve themselves. I hoped none of them would get such an urge during my eavesdropping.

Mama would disown me, I thought, but I rallied my courage and climbed on top of the barrel. At the top of the window, a gap in the curtains gave an ample view inside. Standing there was risky, but I figured if I was seen in the alley, I'd be just as guilty standing on the barrel as not.

All this was utterly reminiscent of Charlie. What fun we used to have, what mischief! I found myself smiling at the memories. How long had it been since we'd spoken, other than a civil hello in passing? Two years, perhaps?

A few men began to seat themselves around a table. That's when Da broke in. "Gentleman, have you no respect? The most *advanced* among us should be seated first." He gestured to Mayor Torrence. I smiled. Da was always telling me that the best kind of insults are masked as compliments. His use of the word *advanced* could've meant venerable and respected . . . or just plain old.

Mayor Torrence did take his seat first and the others followed. Da sat across from him as part of the inner circle. A deep pride rose in my chest. As town sheriff, he'd earned his spot at the prominent table. No seats were saved; the men simply adhered to an unspoken decree. To the mayor's right was George Ellerby, the father of my friends, and to his left sat the unnamed guest. Da's best friend, Deputy Hartley, sat beside Da. All the other men, twenty or so, stood surrounding the table.

Two painted ladies flounced across the floor like peacocks. Arms bare and bodices cut dangerously low, they paused at any man who paid them attention. Some men gave a smile, others, a wink, and some, a touch on the arm. Thankfully, Da only nodded. These women were paid some respect in this setting, but not outside of it. They were the whole reason everyone was up in arms about respectable ladies avoiding these places.

A haze of cigar smoke lingered over the table like a rain cloud. Mayor Torrence, with his narrow face and long fingers, sucked the last drag from his cigar and stubbed its nub into an ashtray. The odor traveled through the saloon's outer walls. At the cue of his cane striking the table, the chatter and music quieted down. "Let's come to order, gentlemen."

I pressed my ear to the wall. Mayor Torrence cleared his throat and spoke in his slow, self-assured Southern drawl. "I've called this small assembly here today to introduce a new and exciting enterprise."

"That's a relief!" Da spoke for all to hear. "I assumed this'd be an awkward chat about how to revive your wounded career." A chorus of laughter followed. Da may have been a member of the inner circle, but he never shied away from a good roast, especially aimed at Mayor Torrence. "Or was the fire bell supposed to do that?" Da added.

The men laughed because it was true. Folks had blamed Mayor Torrence for the Town Hall fire getting out of hand. He had no fire department in place, nor even a bucket brigade. His solution was to build a fifteen-foot bell tower to be rung at the first sign of a fire. A true monstrosity. Nobody questioned its usefulness publicly, until today.

"Leave it to an Irishman," Mayor said, "to mock all the fine ideas but offer none of his own. Scoff if you will, Jeremiah, but that bell is gonna save lives and shops."

"With all due respect, Mr. Mayor, nobody ever heard of a bell puttin' out a fire," Da said.

Mayor took the guffaws in stride and replied with his own jab, "And nobody ever heard of an Irishman sober enough to carry a bucket."

The volley had begun. First the jabs, then the laughs.

"I'm proud of my heritage. Our men may enjoy a stiff drink, but at least we don't wear racoons on our heads."

Mayor shifted his coonskin cap and said, "Ah yes, you mock the great American frontier. But what's Ireland's slogan? 'Come to Ireland where our women are like our potatoes. Blighted and shriveled, but with enough beer you won't know the difference.'"

"That's not a joke!" Da hushed all the laughter, as Mayor had clearly crossed a line. In his impeccable timing, Da added, "Whiskey's our drink."

There was hardly a thing Mayor Torrence could say to quiet the uproar, so he conceded. "I'll allow you the last word, Jeremiah, if only to move us along."

Da and the others scoffed at his poor excuse.

"I am undeterred," Mayor said. "Now to introduce my guest—"

"So what's this about a war comin'?" Old Man Hobbs said in a voice stretched thin from years of speaking his mind.

Mayor Torrence sighed in irritation. Most of the men groaned and shook their heads. Da, however, was entertained by the old man's interruption.

"You've spoken out of turn, Mr. Hobbs," Mayor Torrence chided. "Who in our present company wants to speak about some imaginary war brewing out East?"

The old man's voice became tighter in his offense. "I got the missive right here from my kinfolk out East. They say some of them Southern states is getting serious about splitting off. If'n that's true, we'll have ourselves a civil war, sure as shootin.'"

A din of men's voices rose again in protest.

"Hear me out," the old man said. "This rising politician, Abe Lincoln, is gettin' a lot of attention. He stands firm against slavery, and if he's elected president—"

"Elected president?" Mayor interrupted. "Check your facts, Mr. Hobbs. For a rising politician, as you call him, he's certainly had a lot of defeats. Man can't even get himself elected senator. A pox upon us if we elect such a loser. Rest assured: we won't. And there's no war comin' either. Pardon me for treading on your lofty profession, Mr. Hobbs, but one can't believe everything one reads in print."

The mystery guest finally spoke up. "If you'll permit me . . . This outspoken gentleman's not entirely out of line. East of the Mississippi, the political chatter is very much entrenched in talk of states' rights, the expansion of slavery into the territories, and, well, the possibility of war."

For a moment, the room was still as a graveyard. The men's voices then babbled until a groundswell of noise besieged the room.

A gasp caught in my throat, not because of the subject matter, though shocking. A newcomer had slipped in. My old friend Charlie. Sixteen years old! Only one year my senior, yet there he stood among the town's nobles, simply because he was male. Well, there was no way in creation I'd let him see me hiding like this. He'd crow about it till the end of time. Despite the risk, I kept to my secret spot, eyes behind the curtain, resolved to stay until my curiosity was satisfied.

"Quiet, men!" Mayor Torrence rapped his cane against the table. "How shall I convince you? There is no war coming. The Southern states have been threatenin' secession since the revolution. Why would any rational-thinkin' man take 'em serious now?" He looked at his honored guest. "Really, Mr. Russell, I never pegged you for an alarmist."

The debate continued, despite Mayor Torrence's efforts to quiet it.

Charlie squinted in my direction. Had he seen me? I slipped my head out of sight. When I dared peek again, there he stood, arms crossed, shaking his head, plainly scolding me.

Oh, the indignity! It seemed a hundred mirrors reflected my fraudulent ways back to me. *So much for my quest to be refined and graceful.*

What about that reproachful look he'd just given me? The last time I'd seen him look at me so smugly . . . As quick as a snap, my memory placed me in the exact scene of the last time we'd spoken: the Ellerbys' sitting room. The girls and I were seated at the tea table when Charlie entered in search of Mr. Ellerby. Charlie had been hired to help with the cows. Then I'd said *those words* and looked at him *that way. Mercy, how could I have been so rude?*

I forced my mind back to the present. Now that Charlie knew of my spot, I had no reason to hide—not from him, anyway.

Deputy Hartley spoke up. "Sheriff Brannon, why are you silent? I *know* you got an opinion on these politics. I've heard you speak 'em on more than one occasion."

A glance of unspoken awareness flashed between Da and Mayor Torrence as though the two of them knew something the others did not, maybe from an earlier conversation.

"We're reasonable men, all of us," Da said. "We have claim to our own opinions. War's a scourge, for certain, but if we bury our heads in the sand, we'd be caught unawares if it comes. I say we keep our minds open to all the news and take what we can from it."

Mayor Torrence clenched his jaw, bothered by the quietude Da's words produced. For the first time, I pondered the bleak prospect. Could the United States possibly be bound for a civil war?

"Now we know where Jeremiah stands," Mayor said, an edge of contempt in his voice. "On the side of fear and discontent."

"Fear and discontent, you say?" Da rose to his feet. "Isn't it fear that makes a man close his eyes to the truth?"

Torrence sprang up too. "It's madness to let yourself fall prey to every speculation. But I should expect nothing less from you."

A silent outrage formed between them, locked in a stare, as if they'd sprung daggers and waited for the next move. Could Torrence have meant the silver mine? That it had been mad speculation and now he meant to make my father look a fool? But there was something else. Both men stood the offender and the offended. What had Da done to offend our grand mayor?

"What's madness is comin' here, where different opinions are not welcome." Da stepped away from the table.

Deputy Hartley pressed a hand to Da's shoulder. "Don't go, Jeremiah." Others spoke their support for him to stay.

"To be outright disrespected," Da said, "I won't abide it."

"Jeremiah," Mayor said with a peacemaking air, "calm yourself. Of course you can speak your mind."

"Can I? About every subject?"

"Shall I introduce myself, then?" the guest spoke up. This served to ease the tension. Poor fellow had been waiting long enough. Da seated himself again. Anger was diffused for the moment.

"I'm very sorry, sir," Mayor Torrence said. "Gentlemen, I shall at last introduce our honored guest. This is Mr. William Russell. Lend him an ear. What he says may alter the course of your life."

"Thank you, sir." Mr. Russell nodded. "I've come to give you gentlemen firsthand knowledge about an enterprise that's going to change our modern world. It will change the very nature of communication. All the regions of this vast country of ours will be connected in a way that has never been done before. And I daresay it'll make history. We call it the Pony Express."

Silence shrouded the room. A sudden zeal struck me, humming in my ears—a curiosity, a significance that had yet to take effect in my life—as though all my senses were bidding me to pay attention.

Were the men as enamored as I was? I searched their faces for answers and landed on Charlie's. He didn't return my gaze this time. He set and reset his hat, staring off into some unknown place. Perhaps something was stirring in him as well.

Charlie's impressive nods and gestures made him look so clever and grown-up. I saw him through a new set of eyes, it seemed. Sixteen had treated him well. My former beanpole friend now claimed a broader chest and fuller arms. His coffee-colored hair was grown to his shoulders, which suited him. Back in his school days, he'd kept it short, he'd told me, to appear "less Indian" and avoid some of the teasing. Being half Cherokee had made him the target of bullies. None of that seemed to bother him anymore. I almost envied, but certainly admired, this act of claiming himself. His confidence and happy-go-lucky attitude gave him an undeniable swagger.

All my flattering thoughts must have floated to him. He broke from his trance and offered me a satisfied grin. *Perhaps he doesn't hate me,* I thought. *Suppose he doesn't even remember that little incident.*

Then he crossed his eyes and bared his teeth in an ugly, horse-toothed smile.

Alright, now he's just trying to give away my hiding spot!

To that, I shot back a quick, angry glare. I still couldn't let anybody else see me, least of all Da.

"Folks on both sides of the country are eager for faster mail," Mr. Russell said. "Since the California gold rush, we can't keep up with demand. Folks in the East want word from their relations in California. And, heaven forbid, if this country does go to war, then the Pony Express will be vital to the preservation of our Union. California is key, gentlemen. It's a free state now, but if the South claims better communication with 'em, they could swing 'em to slavery. If that happens, the Union would be lost."

"Alarmist," Mayor Torrence said with a cough, giving his comrade a shoulder nudge. It was lighthearted enough, but he still held resentment.

"So when you say faster mail, how fast we talkin'?" a man asked.

"The transit time will be ten days, east to west and—"

"Hold it there, Mr. Russell," the same man interrupted. "Ten days? How's that possible? The stagecoach time is close to a month."

"That's the genius of it, if you'll pardon my boldness. It'll be set up in a relay fashion from St. Joe, Missouri, to Sacramento, California. That's nearly two thousand miles to cover. The route will travel in both directions. We've got about two hundred stations, some being built as we speak, and some are already in place. We've even commissioned use of the military forts. The rider will pick up a fresh horse at each station, placed every ten miles or so across the route."

"Let's have the mochila," Mayor Torrence cut in, summoning the saddler, who'd crafted something special for the occasion.

I tried to get a look at this so-called mochila, but the men crowded around it and blocked my view.

"The mail goes in these pockets called cantinas," Mr. Russell said. "All four cantinas will be locked. Three of them will be unlocked by officials at the beginnings and ends of the routes and at military forts. The fourth will be unlocked by the station managers to record the arrival times. The mochila goes right on top of the saddle. The rider's weight holds it in place. It'll stay with him as he transfers from station to station. He'll just slap it on the next horse and ride on to the next relief station. At the end of his shift, he'll stop at a home station to rest and pass the mochila on to the next relief rider."

"Is it riders you're after?" Da asked.

"Yes, and only your best. We've got a station thirty miles southeast of here that needs filling. We'll take Victory Hills's top two riders."

"I suppose now's as good a time as any," Mayor said, "to announce a race happening next Saturday to determine who'll go. That gives you just over a week to prepare."

A clamor of voices arose. It was hard to regret eavesdropping now. I may have been an eavesdropper, but at least I was an informed one.

The piano man started up again, and the ladies released themselves into the crowd. A few men went to the bar for drinks.

Just as the thought came that I'd better get moving, I felt a tickle on my neck. When I reached up, a horrid thing with eight legs scrambled its way down my body. I slapped frantically, throwing off my balance. I tumbled from the barrel, landing hard on my side into a small puddle. I hoped to high heaven that puddle was from yesterday's rainstorm. Scrambling to my feet, I noticed the victorious spider crawling away from the scene like a bandit. I shivered.

A voice from the mouth of the alley gave me a start. "Well, if it ain't Miss Beatrice Brannon."

Charlie stood there, arms crossed, eyes heavy on me like doomsday. Apparently, he did remember my offense. I cowered, knowing I'd have to answer for what I'd done.

CHAPTER 4

Charlie Rye

—

Friday, March 16, 1860

BEATRICE jumped all startled-like when she saw me. Had to catch her breath. I caught that highfalutin girl, and she knew it. She'd have to account for her rudeness all them months ago. Now fate led us to this point of reckoning.

"Charlie Rye, you startled me."

"I can see that." Even in the shade of the alleyway, her face was red as a pickled beet.

"Is the meeting over?" she asked.

"I had to skip out early."

"Well, what else did they say about the Pony Express?"

"Nothin' you need to worry your purty little head about. And besides, you wouldn't want to hear it from me, a person of such low caliber."

"Charlie, if you're implying that I ever said such a thing about you—"

"But it's true, ain't it? I reckon there's a reason, short of me having the plague, that you won't talk to me no more."

She threw those innocent doe eyes at me. "It's unfair to accuse me of such unkindness. *You're* the one who quit going to school two years ago. That's why we never see each other anymore."

"Is that right?" With folded arms, I sauntered closer to her, maybe an arm's length away.

"Yes, that's right," she said, crossing her arms too.

"I did quit school," I admitted. "After eight long years, I decided I didn't need them tellin' me to stop dangling my participles and whatnot. I can read and write good as any scholar. Besides, word has it you quit goin' yourself."

"Yes." She swallowed. "Last Christmas, I found it necessary to cease my formal education."

"What's *your* reason?"

She sighed. "We got a new teacher and, well, I doubt she'd know a dangling participle from a dangling carrot."

I gave a side smile, then remembered my purpose.

"You see, Bea, I can't help but think you might be . . . dodging me."

"Dodging you?" she scoffed.

"No question. And what about that *occasion*?" I said it. There'd be no turning back now.

She gulped hard, and her eyes darted elsewhere. "I don't know what you're talking about."

"Nice try. I wonder if you'd be so quick to forget if it happened to you."

"Oh, you mean the incident with the, uh . . . cows?"

"Them two girls is your friends," I said. "You wanna call 'em cows, I won't disagree."

"That's not what I meant." Bea buried a laugh, I could tell, but collected herself and said, "That incident was a long time ago, Charlie. I didn't realize your feelings were so fragile."

I gave a slow, cool-as-a-cucumber nod. "Fine, if that's how you wanna play. It's plain as day you ain't gonna apologize for disowning me."

"Come now, I did *not* disown you."

"Cuss me if you didn't! I remember clear as a bell. I come into the parlor, in urgent need to find Mr. Ellerby, and you said, 'Those boots aren't fit for a barn.'"

"I beg you not to remind me," she cut in. I could see she was troubled by it. "I didn't disown you, Charlie, but I am sorry for making you feel that way."

"OK, not the weeping, wailing, gnashing of teeth-type apology I was going for, but it's more than I'd get from either of them good-for-nothin' Ellerby girls. Why are you friends with 'em anyhow? Have you forgotten how they teased and tormented you, all growing up, callin' you *waif child* and *stink bug*? Why you tryin' to be somebody you ain't?"

"Somebody I ain't?" She bit her lip, as if trying to hold back a true scolding. Perhaps I'd gone too far. "It's called growing up. You might try it, instead of insulting me at every turn. Have you considered that it might be *you* who's trying to be somebody *you ain't*? That outfit, for example." She gestured toward my new buckskin clothes.

The fringe swung as I made an easy circle around her. "Ah, you noticed. Figured you would. I been playing cards these days. Got me a right stash of money. These buttons"—I held out one for her to see—"are genuine silver."

She squinted to examine it. "Silver plated."

I scowled and said, "What about *your* outfit, missy? Did the Ellerbys get a new sister?"

She did look pretty, but I wouldn't tell her so, not right now when I was trying to make a point. Truth be told, Bea was always pretty, no matter what she wore. The peachy glow to her face. Twinkly hazel eyes. Hair the color of autumn wheat. And those perfect lips that I'd do anything to make smile. She may've been trying to fancify herself these days, but to me, she'd always be the gritty old farmgirl I loved so well.

"I'll take that as a compliment," she said.

"You should," I said, forgetting which thoughts I'd said out loud and which I'd kept to myself. "How 'bout you don't judge me for all my fringe if I don't judge you for all your frills?"

"Deal," she said, a chuckle emerging. I got a little ahead of myself, seeing her jovial side come out. That gave me a mind to make her laugh again.

"I mean, here you are eavesdropping in this piss-filled alley and I'm inside rubbin' shoulders with the bigwigs. Who's grown-up now?"

If there was a smile before, it vanished and got replaced by something hurt. Blazes, I'd gone too far! Touched a little too close to the truth, maybe.

She collected herself and nodded politely. "It's been swell talking to you. Let's do this again in another two years."

She brushed past me, and I caught her hand. "Wait, Bea, I'm sorry. I can tell you all about the meeting—anything you wanna know."

She eyed our touching hands, so I let go. I hoped my words weren't too harsh. I really didn't want another two years to pass without speaking.

"You didn't happen to get a look at that mochila, did you?" She couldn't help asking the question. The curiosity was too much.

"I did indeed," I said. "But it ain't nothin' too fancy. Just a glorified saddlebag. Anyhow, why you so curious? So much so that you'd stand on this old barrel like back in the day?" I walked to the barrel and hoisted myself to sit upon it. "Laws, this brings back memories."

"I'm not sure," she said. "I guess I just don't understand why it takes being a man—or in your case, a boy—to be informed around here."

"Hey, who you callin' a boy? I had to grow up fast. 'Sides, I paid my dues to get into that saloon, me bein' Cherokee. I had to win a lot of rounds of faro before anybody showed me respect. As for today's shindig, I snuck in late. Mayor Torrence never would've let me in. So I know all about not bein' welcome someplace."

"Yes, you did have a time proving yourself, but the only way *I* could ever walk into that saloon is if I was wearing frilled petticoats with my knees exposed."

I couldn't help but smirk.

"And mind you, stop picturing it," she said, reading my thoughts like a diviner.

"Listen, Bea, if you don't like something, why don't you change it?"

"Maybe I will."

"You should. Stop hiding in the alley and go do something! Matter of fact, you should enter that Pony Express race. I'd like *somebody* to give me a good run."

"Me? I don't think so! I hardly think it lives up to my latest quest."

"Quest?"

"Never mind." She waved the word away like she was ashamed. "I gather, then, that *you're* going to enter the race?"

"Wouldn't miss it. This is my big chance, Bea. I can feel it."

"It is perfect for you," she admitted, happy for me perhaps, but with a hint of disappointment, maybe envy. "You'll be able to have that exciting adventure you're so keen for, not to mention you'll be able to get away from your—" She stopped.

"My pa?"

"I'm sorry. I didn't mean to insult you . . . or your pa."

"It's alright. It's true. Can't wait to leave that ol' buzzard in the dust."

"You'll be a hero," she kept on. "Mr. Hobbs can write about you in the newspaper."

I shrugged even though my insides nearly burst at the thought. The name Charlie Rye in the newspaper, and not 'cause I done something bad. "I'll have to win the race first. I'll be going up against some tough competitors. But let's face it—it'll be right fun to dust 'em."

"Such humility," she said with that jesting smile.

"That's me," I said, hopping down from the barrel. As I got the feeling that our chat was winding down, I wrestled with something else I wanted to say. "So Bea, this quest you're on."

"Yes?" She had me locked in those eyes that could only prod honesty out of me.

I messed with the fringe on my jacket. "I hope whatever it is, it means we can still be friends."

Her face warmed into a smile so genuine, so bright, it seemed to light up the alley. I missed that smile something powerful. "Of course, Charlie," she said, then playfully held out her hand, palm down. Did she want me to kiss it? I raised my brows and, with little hesitation, bent forward and kissed her hand. We both burst into a fit of laughter.

"Beatrice?" a prim and proper voice said. "Is that you?"

The Ellerby girls stood at the edge of the alley, holding bundles of fabric. Delilah gave me a real puffed-up glare.

I tipped my hat and smiled. "Afternoon, ladies." The only way to beat them Ellerby girls was to kill 'em with kindness.

Bea stood there, caught between worlds. "I bid you good day, Miss Beatrice," I said, giving a gallant bow, followed by a quick wink just for her.

"Good day, kind sir," she said, curtsying.

I waited as she joined her friends. It was the way of a gentleman, I thought, to let her leave first.

By the time I collected Dandy from down the lane and mounted, I noticed the girls waiting by the wagons, near the busted fence. How fortunate! I nudged Dandy's sides, increasing his speed. We took a mighty leap over that fence. Daphne, the younger one, gave a startled shriek. One more gentlemanly nod for Bea and I trotted off. Dandy and me'd been practicing that one.

Mud kicked up onto my back as Dandy and me flew through a marshy field of sprouting alfalfa. I wanted him to be ready for that race next Saturday. I imagined myself out on the Pony Express trail, doing a noble and great service for my country. "Name's Charlie Rye," I'd tell all the newspaper reporters, "spelled R-Y-E."

Just as I was about to jump another fence, a thought came that slowed me to a sudden halt. Dandy stomped about, impatient that I never took him over. *Where's Pa? He never showed up to the meeting.*

When we arrived home, Flintlock, my pa's horse, was by the gate, reins hanging down, as if he got abandoned. A pit grew in my stomach. Pa, that old cuss, would blame me for everything. He'd say I made him too cross to go to any meeting. I did throw him down, but only after he'd done it to me. *I shouldn't have done that. Now I'm no better than him.*

After settling Dandy and Flintlock in the shed, I took a deep breath, squared my shoulders, and made for the house. The place was silent. Dark too, as always. A single candle burned from the kitchen table, where Pa had overturned the pot of gruel I made him.

"Pa?" I said into the darkness, knowing he had to be in there somewhere.

As I shuffled inside, my feet got caught and pitched me forward. I hit the floor hard, tripping over Pa's legs. My hat fell off and landed on the other side of the room. A groan escaped my pa's lips, as well as that yeasty breath I'd become so accustomed to.

"Shame's sake, what you doing on the floor, Pa? You near killed us both."

His only reply was another groan. I stood to get away from that smell and kicked a few bottles as I did. Trouble with this scene was that I never got used to seeing it, like picking the same scab over and over and it never really healing.

"You done me wrong, son." He choked on a cough.

"Did I?" I folded my arms.

"When you knocked me down, it messed up my back. I couldn't move. Had to take a little tonic to dull the pain."

It occurred to me that if he couldn't move, he wouldn't have been able to reach the liquor or tack up the horse, but I kept my mouth shut on those particulars.

"Help me up, son. Set me against the wall."

"What about your back? I reckon I ought to get the doctor."

"No, never mind that, just set me up over there and I'll be alright."

I tugged him up by the sweaty armpits and propped him against the wall, as he requested.

"Did Jeremiah Brannon stop by?" I asked him. "I thought you was supposed to go with him to the meeting."

"My back was hurtin' too bad."

"Did he come in here?" I begged that he'd say no, that Jeremiah Brannon didn't see him in this pitiful state. Not that he hadn't seen it before.

"I couldn't reach the door," he said.

Unfortunate that this happened on the very day I made amends with Bea, as if to remind everyone—mostly me—what low stock I came from.

In a rare show of accountability, my pa said, "I reckon I let him down."

In the dim light, his eyes looked hurt and brimmed with tears. This bear of a man was reduced to a mere cub. "He told me he was gonna make me part of somethin' big."

"Guess you'll miss out on whatever it is." I pretended not to know. The Pony Express was mine, and I wasn't going to let my pa ruin it.

"You'll need to go talk to Sheriff Brannon for me." His straightforwardness made me chuckle in a frustrated sort of way.

"You want *me* to talk to Sheriff Brannon? And tell him what? Sorry, my pa's made a jackass of himself again." I stepped back, conditioned for swift retaliation. But there was none. Just another cough from this supposedly penitent man slumped on the floor.

"For some wild reason, he likes you," he said. "Thinks you're a fine lad. Just go tell him I didn't mean to let him down. Go and be my advocate, boy. Tell him to give me another chance."

There was no question but to go. As much as I detested the idea of apologizing for my pa's slovenly behavior to a man I respected, I was obliged to go and clear the rubble.

"Alright, I'll go."

"And Charlie, remember I said I's gonna make myself respectable? See, I'm doing it."

The irony would've made me laugh if I wasn't so heartsick.

Before I left, I threw in some words he wouldn't want to hear. "I see you chucked the gruel. Maybe you ought to eat some real damn food."

I slammed the door before the old cuss told me I had no right to tell him what to do.

Standing outside, I squinted up at the sky. No more glorious sunrise. Dark clouds were billowing like a rainstorm a-rolling in just for me. Year after year, Pa kept telling me about his lofty plans to become an upstanding citizen, but every day he done something stupid. And that's when I'd feel the tugging—weights pressing down on my shoulders, heavy iron chains wrapping around my ankles, yanking me down. I held my breath and let it pass through me. One of these days, I wouldn't let this bother me no more.

None of this changed the fact that I needed to talk to Sheriff Brannon. Ah, but I sorely dreaded it. *Talk about a losing battle.*

Well, I wouldn't go just yet. I needed a distraction. First, I'd head back into town and see if any games were on. I could catch Sheriff Brannon later at his home. Why not take another chance to see Bea?

Once again, I'd have to throw on my jovial attitude. Nobody would ever know that my pa got to me. Brooding was a horrible weakness. I hated it in others and despised it in myself. So I set out, bearing in mind that there was no way of succeeding, but still considering myself duty bound to try.

CHAPTER 5

Beatrice Brannon

—

Friday, March 16, 1860

As I sliced carrots and onions for supper that evening, my mind was in a flurry. On the whole, my day had held some pleasant surprises, like making amends with Charlie and the announcement of the Pony Express. But there were also causes for alarm, like the possibility of war coming and the argument between Da and Mayor Torrence. The most troublesome of these was something the Ellerby girls had told me at the end of my visit with them. Now I'd need to break the news to Mama.

A sly hand reached around me and snatched a handful of carrots. The culprit darted across the room.

"Hey! Those are for the stew."

JP popped them into his mouth, cheeks bulging like a squirrel's. Mama wouldn't censure him, so most of the day-to-day sniping was left to me. This evening, though, I tried practicing complete mastery of my tongue.

"JP," I began sweetly, "if you're not going to help, could you at least not hinder?"

"I *am* helping," he said, carrot saliva drizzling down his chin. "Helping myself to a snack."

Cobber, splayed on the floor alongside his marbles, snickered at his brother's joke. One glare from me and he retreated under a blanket.

"JP, will you please stoke the fire?" Mama said.

"Mama, I can't do a thing. I'm starving to death!"

"JP, do as you're told," I ordered. "The quicker you do it, the quicker we can eat."

Hunger was a powerful motivator, so he picked up the fire iron and gave the embers a few jabs. Afterwards, JP joined Da outside.

"Cobber, you really shouldn't encourage him," I said to the fellow writhing beneath the blanket.

He peeped his head out. "Sorry, Bea."

Poor, sweet lamb was constantly jostling between loyalty to his brother and being a good boy too.

"I can't believe those two shared a womb," I mumbled.

Mama sighed. I suspected she didn't appreciate her womb being spoken of aloud.

At last, the onion juice got to me. I set down the knife and wiped my eyes on my sleeve.

"You alright, Bea?" Mama asked.

"Yes, it's just the onions."

"Aside from that?"

I opened my watery eyes to find Mama's loving, concerned face pointed my way. Everything about Mama bespoke kindness—from the softness of her upturned smile to the gentle curve of her brows to her light brown eyes that held no prejudgment. Her thick, chestnut hair was tied in a loose bun and proffered a relaxed, modest quality. She had the kind of effortless beauty that sought no glory for itself. The news I had would crush her.

"Thank you, Mama. I'm alright."

Later, I told myself. I took off my apron and curled into the rocking chair with my favorite epic poem, *Divine Comedy*. Dante spoke to me in a way no one else could. My favorite passages were about Beatrice, that luminous being of wisdom, beauty, refinement. She gave me something to aspire to. "The everlasting pleasure that on Beatrice shone, her fair countenance, my gladdened soul contented."

To my dismay, I felt truer to Shakespeare's Beatrice in *Much Ado About Nothing,* all quarrelsome and cynical. *One day I'll be worthy of poetry,* I thought.

My reverie was interrupted by a knock at the door. Mama answered.

"Evening, ma'am," his familiar voice said.

"Charlie!" Cobber ran to greet him as though Santa Claus himself had appeared. "Look at this fine shooter!" he said of his newest marble.

"Hello, Mr. Cobber. Look at that! Fancy as they come. My, my! Just like a cat's eye."

Our tall-backed rocking chair shielded me from our visitor. I scanned the page, but none of the words made it to my consciousness.

"Beatrice, Charlie's here," Mama announced.

I peeked my head past my fortress long enough to say hello.

"It was good to see you today, Miss Bea." Charlie always added the *Miss* in the presence of my family.

"You too," was all I said. I wished he'd say no more. Mama would ask where this conversation had taken place, and I'd sooner die than tell her it was in the alley of the saloon.

"Supper'll be ready soon," Mama said to him. "Why don't you pull up a chair with us?"

"No thank you, ma'am. I wouldn't want to impose. I'm here to speak with Sheriff Brannon if he's home."

"He's in the back."

"I'll go around," he said. "These boots aren't fit for a barn."

Charlie just evoked my exact quote from the cow incident. Why? To tease me and make a joke? If so, it was a little soon for that, considering how awful I still felt. But if he was willing to make a joke of it, maybe I could too. I peered around the rocking chair again. "Only shiny boots allowed here in the Brannon household." Nobody laughed though, and it ended up sounding rude.

Cobber followed Charlie outside. I exhaled when Mama closed the door. My agitation surprised me.

Mama bent down in a proximity most uncomfortable. She waited in silence, perplexed, until I glanced up from my book. "What?" I said, uneasy under her stare.

"That was rather cold, Honey Bea."

"Oh, that was a joke only he and I understand."

"Still, you hardly greeted him. I'm just surprised, is all. The two of you used to be . . ."

"I know," I cut her off. "We used to be . . ." But I didn't finish the sentence either.

"Well, what happened?"

"Nothing happened."

"I'm mighty relieved to hear it. I suspected you two had a falling out because of the Ellerby girls not approvin' of him."

"No, that's not it."

"Well, *do* they approve of him?"

"I'm sure they have no objections," I said, nearly choking on my lie.

"Good." She returned to the stewpot for a stir. "I'm glad the Ellerby girls are treatin' you better, but it seems they're still bent on puttin' themselves above others. I don't much care for it."

I didn't understand Mama sometimes. She allowed JP to behave in whatever ruffian manner he wanted, but me, she'd correct even the slightest lapse in character. I shut my book with a slap. "If you must know, Charlie's become quite rowdy these days. He gambles . . . at the *saloon*."

Motherly concern peeped through, for a child not even her own. "I'm surprised they let a boy his age in there."

"Exactly."

"Well, don't give up on him," she said. "He's had a rough lot."

She was right. I'd certainly never begrudge him that, but the unfairness of being barred from the meeting surfaced again and stung.

Da burst in the back door, JP and Cobber following, each carrying a bushel of radishes from the garden.

As we sat down for supper, I felt Mama's inquiry on the verge, and it came.

"How was town today, Bea? Was the China silk everything you imagined?"

"Exquisite, actually," I answered in full honesty. "Never seen or felt anything like it."

"Do the girls want me to make something with it? I've got some lovely ideas."

Sure enough, the truth would have to be told, whether or not I was prepared.

"Sorry, Mama, I meant to tell you. They said their mother found a new dressmaker. They won't be needing your services any longer."

Mama's face stiffened. "Ever again?"

"I don't know. They didn't say."

"That's very curious." But her shock disclosed more than curiosity.

"I thought it was strange too."

"Did they say why? Did I make any mistakes on the last batch?"

"They gave no details. I'm sorry, Mama."

She laid down her spoon and rested her elbows on the table. I could see her mind ruminating, trying to piece things together.

"I'll go and speak to Mrs. Ellerby tomorrow," she said. "I'd hate to think it was because I've done something wrong."

"Don't take it personally, Mama. Lots of new folks have moved here. She probably wants to give one of the new ladies a try just to be polite. You know how she is."

"I do take it personally. I've been sewing her girls' dresses since they were young'uns. I don't know of a single time when she's gone to somebody else."

"Load of shite!" Da said, slamming his fist on the table. All of us were shaken. Da plowed his hands through his hair. We waited, knowing well enough Da wouldn't be rushed when he grappled with something on his mind. "They're tryin' to snuff us out."

"Who is?" Mama asked.

"Torrence and Ellerby." He stood, the legs of his chair squealing. He paced wildly. "They're tryin' to make an example of me. And now they're goin' after you. I never thought they'd stoop this low."

"I don't understand," Mama said.

"There's a perfect explanation, my dear. Mayor Torrence is a miserable, self-important arse. And if he doesn't get his way, he throws a right tantrum. All because—" He stopped himself.

"All because what?" I asked.

Da was in no humor to tell us why. "I'll fix this. I swear on my life, I'll fix this. Torrence and Ellerby won't know what hit 'em. I'll show 'em that Jeremiah Brannon won't be trifled with."

Da strode to the mantel and took up his rifle. He scoured around for bullets.

"Jeremiah!" Mama stood. "What in heaven's name?"

"Land's sake, Ellen. I'm not doin' anything stupid. I'm blowin' off steam, is all. Shootin's the best way to do it."

Mama met him at the door and placed a hand at the crook of his arm. "Please let us know what's goin' on, Jeremiah. Don't leave us in the dark. We're your family. Whatever it is, we'll understand."

Da resigned a portion of his anger. "I'll talk to you later, Ellen. It's not for the children's ears."

"We can take it, Da," I said, also standing. "Don't coddle us. We're Brannons. You've taught us to be brave. And if it comes to keeping a secret, these boys will swear on their lives not to tell anyone, won't you, boys?"

Their terrified heads bobbed up and down.

Da regarded each of our faces in turn. He must've seen the evidence he sought, for he rested the rifle back in its place and returned to the table.

"As you know, the Peregrine mine hasn't been as . . . profitable as I'd hoped. Aside from those few promising silver veins we discovered early on, there's been nothin' more. The miners have gone and left for other schemes. You see, I borrowed the money to run it from George Ellerby. It takes money to operate, you know—the equipment, the workers, the mules. Now it's time to pay back the money, but there is none because the mine didn't pay out."

For a good, long while, I didn't know what to say. One thing was certain: nobody made any childish peeps. For that, I was proud of my brothers.

"The answer is simple," he said. "I've already got a solution to pay the debt."

Suddenly, that moment from my eavesdropping came back to me, that flash of insight when I'd heard those words. I said them aloud. "The Pony Express."

Da slanted his head, probably curious about how I'd heard. Frankly, I'd avoided the topic on our way back home. "How did you—"

"Word gets around," I said, thinking quickly.

"Pony Express?" Mama's confusion was evident in the way she overenunciated the words. They meant nothing to her. If women had been invited to the meeting, she'd have been rightly informed. Anyhow, my premonition had been right. The Pony Express *would* come to mean something to me, to my family.

Da stumbled over his explanation. "It's a way of . . . delivering the mail by . . . by horseback. They need riders. And it pays double what I earn as sheriff."

"It's a new mail system," I explained, "set up in a relay fashion from one side of the country to the other. Stations will be placed every ten miles or so from St. Joe to Sacramento. The riders will carry the mail in pouches called mochilas that are designed to transfer from one horse to another. Then when a rider completes a stretch, he'll transfer the mochila to the next horse and rider, thus delivering the mail across the country in ten days."

"Whoa!" JP said. Both boys applauded.

"Word gets around indeed," Da said, brows raised. "Yes, well, that's the size of it."

I couldn't help but feel illuminated being informed on this matter. "Of course, there will be a race to determine the riders," I added.

"There will," he said, "and I'll win it. Thundercloud's the fastest horse in town. Who's gonna beat me?"

It made me a little queasy to think of Da racing against Charlie. How humiliating if my father should be beaten by him. But then, the Pony Express would be hiring the *two* fastest riders. Perhaps they both could win the spots.

"Would you need to be away, Jeremiah? Leave your job?"

"If it goes right, I'll take a sabbatical. Hartley can cover for me while I'm gone. By the end of summer, I can pay it off."

Each of us sat in our discomfort of the news regarding the mine, but judging from the past, we were equally as confident in Da's ability to fix it.

Apparent by the drumming of her fingers, Mama still had a question, which she asked gently. "How does this explain the Ellerbys finding a new dressmaker?"

Da blinked a great deal. "It doesn't explain a thing. I'm sure the one has nothin' to do with the other. In fact, I'll see Ellerby tomorrow. I'll ask him about it. I'm sure there's been a misunderstanding."

I wasn't sure Da had divulged everything—nor was Mama, certainly. But maybe we'd heard enough for now.

"I'm not afraid to ask Mrs. Ellerby myself," Mama said.

"You're not afraid of anything, my dear, or you wouldn't have married me. Nevertheless, I'll see him anyway and I'll ask."

Da's mood had begun to turn. It always happened this way. Being in his presence had all the trappings of a Shakespearean play. He'd wring our hearts dry one minute only to entreat us with a delirious fit of laughter the next. Da was the source of everything. The rest of us drifted with the tide. We braved his dramatic outbursts, and in return, he gave us his whole heart and soul.

"Look at these forlorn faces! Gracious night, I've not seen the likes of these since Bea's performance of Lady Macbeth. 'Out, damned spot! Out I say!'"

None of us could resist cracking up.

"Let's cease all this talk of doom and gloom and enjoy a peaceful supper, shall we? You know, I told your mother when she married me that I'd never let her down. Haven't I kept my promise, Ellen?"

Mama smiled as Da regaled us with the oft-repeated tale of their meeting.

That night, I sunk into my feather tick, listening to Da play his tin whistle from the other room. His Irish tunes—joyful, tragic, and bewitching—brought all the day's troubles to a peaceful close. These matters were trivial. I was safe, content, and belonged to a family of good repute, thanks to Da. We weren't skittish or fearful. Da had taught me to have a heart of grit, and I refused to fall apart now. These problems were nothing we couldn't bear. We were the house of Brannon. It would take more than these to make us fall.

CHAPTER 6

Beatrice Brannon

—

Saturday, March 17, 1860

THE scent of Da's black coffee diffused through the house, settling above my bed, nudging me awake. Odd, there was no noise from the kitchen—no Da lumbering about, clanking his dishes. He must've arisen early and moved quietly. I threw off my blankets, chiding myself for missing that precious time with Da.

My feet touched the cold wooden floor. I padded out to the fireplace, nudged the embers with the fire iron, and rested another log on top. A note on the table caught my eye, written in Da's scribble-scrawl.

Honey Bea,

I figured you'd be up first. Flossie needs milking. It's JP's turn, but shall we risk her kicking the barn to flinders? You're much better at handling her wily ways. If you don't complain, I'll offer a small reward. A Brannon Expedition! Just you and me. Yesterday, I spied bobcat and coyote tracks in the foothills. Now I'm off to break the mayor's neck, er, I mean horse.

Love,
Da

Breaking a horse for Mayor Torrence, I mused, an uneasy chill creeping over me. During our conversation at supper, Da had said that Torrence and Ellerby wanted to "make an example of him." Was this horse-breaking affair somehow connected? Did Da mean to regain his pride? Had his status been lowered because of the failed mine? Was he looked down upon now?

The Ellerby girls, come to think of it, had made their superiority known when they'd told me about their mother hiring a new seamstress. Likely, they didn't want to be associated with us hereafter. It seemed unnecessarily cruel to blame us for something we couldn't control, but such was our society.

One thing was sure: I wouldn't miss it. But there was this pesky business about milking the cow . . .

I tiptoed into the boys' room and shook JP's shoulders. "It's your turn to milk the cow."

"Leave me alone," he grumbled.

"Hurry now, she's starting to bellow. You'll be in trouble if you don't."

"Did Da say that?"

I answered in a manner of technical honesty. "Da says it's your turn. I have it in writing."

He lifted his drowsy head, growling something fierce, and began dressing. Bait taken! I'd answer for my falsehood later. (And I was circumspect about removing Da's note from the table). Besides, it would do JP some good to handle Flossie's "wily ways" too.

I threw on my Saturday dress—lightweight cotton, cornflower blue, and for pity's sake, no corset. My old boots, though falling apart, were far superior in comfort to the tall-heeled ones Delilah Ellerby had given me. I sectioned my hair into three and braided it as hastily as my fingers could work. I wasn't fit to be seen in any drawing room or parlor, but no matter, there would be nobody to impress today.

A chill touched my cheeks when I opened the door, so I took my knitted shawl off the peg and gathered it around my shoulders. A cottony-white haze cloaked the trees and brush as far as I could see. Da must've ridden Thundercloud that morning before the fog had descended.

I enjoyed the otherworldly walk in the mist, imagining the shipyards of Cork Harbour where Da had worked as a boy. Oft had he spoken of the white horizon that blanketed the sea on the morning he embarked to America at fourteen years old. A small pack and his tin whistle were his only possessions. Though his departure was prompted by desperation, still his independent spirit inspired me.

When I neared Torrence's ranch, I heard the piercing squeal of a horse in distress. Da was always so gentle with horses. This horse must've been a feisty one.

A dozen or so men were gathered for the spectacle, their arms dangling over the corral posts. Da's pride was on the line, no doubt.

There stood the mayor himself in his creamy white suit and coonskin cap, overseeing all this like Caesar at his gladiatorial games. George Ellerby stood at Mayor's side, blithely conversing as if they hadn't a care in the world. Ellerby, stouter than his tall friend, had the markings of a wealthy gentleman, with his tailored suit and fancy felt hat, but he had signs enough of peasantry: the crust of dirt on his boots and his unkempt beard and moustache.

My father was amid the chaos, holding the horse's lead rope, attempting to calm him and gain his trust. I didn't imagine this horse had much trust to give. He certainly wasn't much to behold. His coat was patchy, and his mane was a mess of tangled knots. The beast raged, bucking and head-tossing, his cries sounding like a passel of hogs.

Deputy Hartley, Da's good friend, greeted me with his usual cool disposition. "Mornin' Beatrice." He was one of the few adults who treated me as a peer. I appreciated the respect, though I couldn't be as calm and nonchalant. Hartley noticed. "They call him Havoc," he spoke over the squeals.

"It fits him." I climbed up one rung and rested my arms over the fence the way the others were doing.

"How's your mother and brothers?" the deputy said.

"Good," I may have said, though my attention was on Da and that creature. I wondered how everyone could engage in small talk with those hell-raising squeals going on.

The deputy gave my shoulder a nudge to break my hawklike concentration. It didn't work.

"That horse doesn't look well," I told him. "Where did Mayor get him?"

"Poor devil was caught in one of his fences. Torrence thinks he strayed from the herd when them wealthy ranchers passed through here last fall. He has a mind to train him and sell him. He's a Thoroughbred."

I wasn't impressed. This whole scene made me uneasy. And I doubted Da was being paid for his service. As long as I was already fretting, I might as well get the answer to my question.

"So, Deputy, do you know anything about Mayor Torrence making an example out of Da?"

He pointed an intrigued frown at me. "Is that what he said?"

I nodded.

"No, I can't think of what he could mean," he answered.

"I suppose you know"—I trod lightly, speaking of this shameful thing aloud for the first time—"about the Peregrine mine?"

"I do," Hartley said, shaking his head. "Damn shame. It's been a long time coming, but we both knew it was headed that way. He held out hope for so long. We all did, but it wasn't to be. How's he holdin' up?"

"Determined as ever to fix things, but he'll be alright. The real shame for me is owing Ellerby money. Of all people, why did he have to borrow from Ellerby?" I tempered my voice, loud enough to be heard over the noise, but quiet enough not to be heard by anyone else.

"He was the only man with that kind of cash up front," Hartley said, also taking cue from my discretion. "I told him not to use the land as collateral, but he wouldn't listen. I says to him, 'Jeremiah, if you can't pay it back, you want Ellerby owning your land? Could you live with that?'"

"What land?" As if by reflex, I clutched his arm.

"His land. The land you live on. Your fifty acres. It's the only way Ellerby would loan him the cash. Did he not tell ya?"

I couldn't respond. I couldn't speak at all. Da had left out that detail. He'd used our fifty acres—house and all—as collateral in this mine deal. And now the deal had expired, and we, the Brannons, were squatters on the Ellerbys' land. At supper, Da had said, *Torrence and Ellerby won't know what hit 'em. I'll show 'em that Jeremiah Brannon won't be trifled with.* Indeed, this whole charade was meant to prove his worth. To put him back on the top shelf.

The loud shrieks brought me out of my thoughts. Hartley looked at me pitifully, and I gave the shortest answer I could muster. "It'll be OK."

Skillful and cautious, Da kept his eyes on the horse at all times. *Come on, Da. You can do this. Show them.*

"Eventually, he's gotta wear himself out," called Mayor Torrence from the other side.

"The horse maybe, but never Jeremiah," Deputy Hartley responded.

The men's laughter agitated the horse, causing Da to lose control of the rope. The horse took a wild run around the perimeter, flinging dirt clods in his wake. The monster snapped at me with his teeth. That rancid breath! I recoiled and fell onto my backside.

The deputy took my hand and helped me up. "You OK?"

I nodded, brushing off my dress. I shook off my shawl and hung it over the post.

"Would you all stop shouting?" I blurted, trying to use a voice that wouldn't offend the horse.

For the first time, Da noticed me there. At the next safe moment, he climbed out of the ring for a moment's respite. "Thought I told you to milk the cow, Honey Bea," he said, breathing heavily, arms on hips. "Or did you pass it off to your brother again?"

I swallowed my reply.

A smile broke through on his lips. Not just any smile. One that conveyed love and pride. "Look at you, defendin' me."

"Well, they were breaking your concentration."

"This gal's too much like me, Hartley." Da wrapped an arm around my shoulders and tugged me close. "I've passed on my Irish temperament to at least one of my young'uns."

"That horse makes me nervous, Da. He's pure evil."

"No such thing as an evil horse. He'll warm up to me. They always do. Besides, Mayor Torrence says it can't be done. Now I have to prove him wrong."

"There's no need to rush through it, OK?"

"I know what I'm doin', Honey Bea. Even if I have to outlast the sun, I'll do it." He offered an affable wink and hopped back into the corral.

Da's voice, calm and reassuring, quieted my anxiety. "Whoa . . . easy . . . whoa . . ."

Havoc held still, but for his nostrils showing labored breathing. He drew near to Da and gave him a loud sniff, then lowered his head and allowed Da to stroke the bridge of his nose. Perhaps this horse had a tractable fiber after all.

Once again, Da was doing the impossible. Deputy Hartley gave me a smile as though to say, "See?" I smiled back at him and sighed.

Beyond the fog, a killdeer released a plaintive cry, loud and shrill. Its call sent the horse kicking and twisting, leading with his legs. Da backed away. Not far enough. Not fast enough. The horse's hind leg struck Da's head. Da flung backward, landing like a fallen puppet to the ground.

I cupped a hand over my mouth and resisted the urge to shriek like that killdeer.

The men rushed the fence, Mr. Ellerby shuffling fast to the horse, trying to seize the rope. I climbed over and dropped to my knees beside my father. Blood drizzled from a deep gash on his forehead. I pressed my sleeve to it.

My hands were tingly, going numb. I could hardly speak or understand with my world spinning like that. I tried to keep my wits. "Da? Are you OK?"

Nobody had control of the horse, who bucked and thrashed, reacting to the chaos. The horse gave Hartley a blunt kick to the chest. He gasped for air.

"Beatrice, get out of here!" Mr. Ellerby shouted.

I ignored him. Men shouted, the horse stamped and whinnied, and my head was a cacophony of sights and sounds.

"Somebody get a gun and shoot that horse!" I added to the noise.

Mayor Torrence aimed his rifle at the moving target, but he didn't shoot.

"Do it, Mayor!" I shouted. "Squarely between the eyes."

"Somebody shut that girl up. I don't take orders from nobody. I give 'em."

But still he didn't shoot. I charged to Mayor, ripped the gun from him, and aimed it between the eyes of the beast.

"Beatrice, no!" shouted Mayor, trying to wrestle it back.

"I'm a good shot," I said.

But Mayor pried it away, saying, "I'll handle the horse. Get out of the corral!"

"Honey Bea," I heard Da say, his voice thin and crackling. I dropped to his side again. His gaze roamed in different directions, as though trying to think straight. Just above a whisper, he said, "I might not make it."

"Of course you'll make it. I'll get Dr. Pearl."

"Bea, supposin' I don't, you'll be the man of the house. You hear me? You take care of 'em."

"There's no need for that kind of talk. Your cut's not as bad as it looks. Will you try? Will you please not give up?"

"I failed you," he whispered. "I failed you all."

"That's not true. Listen, somebody's getting Dr. Pearl."

"You go," he said softly. "Don't leave it to them."

"OK." I nodded. "I'll hurry. Promise me you won't give up."

"I promise."

A line of men guarded my father from the unruly horse, or I wouldn't have dared leave. I gave Da's hand a squeeze.

As I ran hard, the shrill whinny of that horse wouldn't quit.

Somebody shoot that horse. Lord-a-mercy, somebody do it.

A loud BOOM rang out, followed by a murderous cry, more hideous than any sound I'd ever heard. Then silence.

Mercy! Finally somebody had the guts to shoot him. I would've done it myself had Mayor not stopped me. I supposed none of those men had ever heard a girl shouting such crassness as to shoot it between the eyes, but I swore I would've done it myself.

I ran through a field of cheatgrass and boulders, stumbling and gasping. The blanket of fog grew thicker in the field, all my landmarks vanishing. My panicked breaths quickened as the whiteness closed in on me.

God, help me.

One breath after another, so rapid, I began to feel lightheaded. I fell to my knees into a patch of prickly thorns. The pricks in my knees were nothing to the pangs in my stomach, not knowing where to run.

From afar off, I heard the howl of Dr. Pearl's foxhound. I stood and teetered toward the sound. "Sal!" I called to her through desperate tears. "Sal!"

The dog found me in the field, jumped on me, and licked my face. She turned and ran; I followed her. At last, the ghostly shape of a pitched roof appeared. I clambered to the doorstep and beat the door nearly off its hinges. The doctor appeared in his night clothes, not yet dressed for morning. His trained eye traveled to the blood on my sleeve.

Barely able to eke out words, I said, "My father . . . got struck in the head . . . he's . . . he's at Torrence's."

Dr. Pearl grabbed a few items with rehearsed swiftness and piled them into his medical bag. He shouldered on his overcoat and opened the door. Sal stood waiting. One glance at the fog and the doctor said, "We'll have to put all our faith in her olfactory senses. Come on. She'll follow the tracks you left on your way here." The doctor and I hurried across the field, behind Sal, hoping she'd lead us in the right direction.

As we reached the edge of the ranch, Mr. Ellerby stood, waiting for our return, his face blank, wiped of any emotion. "Inside," he said to the doctor, pointing to the house where they had moved Da. The doctor strode up the porch. I was ready to follow when Mr. Ellerby clutched my arm, holding me back.

"Beatrice, it's . . ."

I searched his face for any hint of meaning, since whatever he wanted to say wasn't coming out fast enough.

"I'm going to my Da," I said.

"I feel I should warn you, Beatrice. He . . . he . . ."

I shoved past Mr. Ellerby and ran into the house. The hallway pointed to an open bedroom door. I stepped inside. My father lay on a bed. His eyes were open, glassy, absent. Blood streaked across every line on his face and onto the pillow. Deputy Hartley sobbed into my father's chest. Dr. Pearl pressed his fingers to Da's neck and imparted the news that there was no pulse.

My God, it's not true! This is my father. He's not dead. This is all just pretend. An act. A play. A bizarre dream. A nightmare.

The faint sound of Da's tin whistle seemed to play in my mind. I knelt beside the bed where he lay. Hartley lifted his head and vacated his spot for me. I laid my head on Da's shoulder. "Don't go," I whispered. "Please don't go. You promised to outlast the sun." How could life go on if the very glue that held mine together was no more?

CHAPTER 7

Charlie Rye

Saturday, March 24, 1860

THERE was no way to prepare our town for the death of Jeremiah Brannon, or console it neither. They buried him mid-week in the foothills beyond their home. Mrs. Brannon said during this morning's graveside service that Jeremiah wouldn't have wanted a headstone, nor anything to disturb the land, so his grave was marked with a boulder where his family could pay their respects before setting off on a "Brannon Expedition." All the townsfolk closed their shops for the service. In fact, the race had been set for today but was postponed one week out of respect.

Beatrice took it hard, refusing to leave the house or talk to anybody. Twice, I visited her house, and both times she wasn't feeling up to seeing nobody, so the second time, I put daisies by the doorstep and left without fanfare. Just as well. How could I console her when my own heart grieved as it did? Jeremiah was the best of men. He lent me a hand on more than one occasion and gave me an example to look up to. He helped my pa too, when everybody else treated him with scorn. You'd have to be a saint to help a man like my pa.

Bea and her da were real close. I reckoned I'd lost her forever to the grief when, that afternoon, as I brushed Dandy's coat out in my shed, she appeared in the doorway. Seeing her face was like cool water to a lone and dusty traveler.

"Bea!"

For a good while, we stood with no other words between us. First thing I noticed, she wore trousers with the pant legs too short. Her usual Ellerby-looking frills were gone. She wore her da's wide-brimmed hat, and her shoulders sagged like willow branches. I wanted to wrap the girl up in my arms and tell her it'd be alright, but I held back, not certain why.

"Bea, it's good to see you out and about," I told her. "Come sit." I sat on the bench and patted the spot beside me.

She shuffled toward me, removed the hat, and sat down. Her hair was cropped down to a bunch of frayed ends. "I've done it," she said.

"You sure have. Pity's sake, you look like you been attacked by a badger."

She returned a gaze that could've soured milk.

"Laws, I don't know what's got into me." I rubbed my forehead, wondering why I'd let the jester side of me show up. "I'm just glad to see you, Bea. I was worried I'd never see you again, and that wouldn't do. What brings you here?" I was quick to add, "Not that you need a reason."

Her gaze went to the ground. "Sometimes, I leave the house to calm my thoughts. I do my best to drown out that shrieking in my head."

I knew she meant Mr. Torrence's horse.

She went on. "Would you miss me, Charlie, if I was gone?"

"Of course I would. No question. Why do you ask a thing like that?"

"Because I might have to go." She took the brush from me, stood, and began working at Dandy's coat. "We're in debt, Charlie, quite heavily. You've probably heard rumors that the Peregrine mine didn't pay out."

"I did hear." I stood alongside her and stroked Dandy's neck.

"Did you also know that . . ." She stopped brushing and paced. I waited while she mustered up courage. After a spell, she stopped and faced me. "Da borrowed the money from Mr. Ellerby."

"And . . ." I didn't see how this was such a bad thing. Money owed was money owed, far as I was concerned.

"My da used our land as collateral—our house, our fifty acres. As of right now, the Ellerbys own the very ground under my family's feet. The ground in which Da is buried."

I let this settle in. This must've stung her hard.

"Maybe I could bear the shame from the Ellerby girls," she said, "but my family will have to leave Victory Hills if we can't pay the debt. My mama's got a sister back East who'll give us room and board. And when I say room and board, it's barely a step above the poorhouse."

"Surely Mr. Ellerby won't hold you to it," I said.

"That's where you're mistaken. A lawyer came to the house today and showed us all the documents. Ellerby, of course, didn't have the guts to show his face, but he is, in fact, holding us to it. By the end of summer, if we don't pay the loan in full, we'll turn over all our land to him, a man who already owns hundreds of acres."

A slow burn crept from my chest to the top of my head. "Give me that brush," I said. She handed it to me; poor Dandy never had such a vigorous brush-down. "That's the damnedest thing I ever heard. Comin' after a widow's family for all they got—and on the same day as the service! Ain't he supposed to be a Christian man? Even *my pa* wouldn't do a thing like that." It was the worst insult I could think of, but true to the situation. "When the town hears about this, nobody'll speak to him again."

"A lot of folks know, Charlie, and they're standing by him. They're punishing Da for being foolish—even after his death."

I plunked backward onto the bench. The brush dropped from my hand. Obviously, I didn't know folks as well as I thought. Sure, a few foolish ones gave me a hard time for being half Cherokee, but I'd come to expect that, as much as I resented it. But this was Jeremiah Brannon. Everybody loved him, or so I thought. If he didn't measure up, how could anybody?

"Da used to say that you're only as good as your final act. Now this is how everyone will remember him. By putting all his money in some defunct mine and leaving his wife and children destitute. But that isn't the truth of who he was. He never should've gone out this way. He never should've gone out at all." She sat beside me again. Her eyes glossed over with tears. She nestled in close to my shoulder and let the tears fall on my sleeve.

"I haven't told you my crazy idea yet," she said, sniffling.

"Does it have anything to do with your chopped hair?"

She sat forward, trying to work out how to say it, but I'd already guessed.

"You're gonna enter that race, ain't you? For the Pony Express?" I said.

"Why shouldn't I?"

"You should."

"It's the only way to pay off the debt in time."

"I like it, Bea. So you gonna do it? You think this backward town'll let you join the race like a normal person?"

"If you're referring to the fact that I'm a girl, I take exception to you saying I'm not normal. However, I see your point that our town is backwards."

"Hence the hair?" I asked.

"Hence the hair," she confirmed. "Maybe from a distance, folks will think I'm JP. I'm slighter than he is, so I'll pad my clothes a bit. And I'll probably have to show up at the last second—right in time for the race to start—so nobody gets a good look at me."

"But if you win, won't people want to congratulate their winner? They'll get a good look at you then."

"If I win, they can't stop me. Don't you see? I will have already proven myself."

I grinned and nodded at this sharp-as-a-whip gal. "Sounds like a right decent plan. Only one snag. You're gonna have to beat me, and I ain't gonna take it easy on you."

"That's just it. We can take the top two spots. Who in this town wants this more than you and me?"

She was right.

"Has your mama seen your hair?"

Bea actually snickered. "She thinks I did it because I'm grief-stricken. I told her it's because I plan on selling it. Both are true. Every little bit helps. She doesn't know my plan to join, though. Nor will she find out, not until it's done."

"Your secret's safe with me," I said. Being part of Bea's life again warmed me from head to toe. This harked back to the days when we confided only in each other. "You always know a true friend by the number of secrets you keep for 'em," I added.

"That's true. I've got plenty on you. Never forget that I was the one who taught you how to read."

I shifted around, fidgety. "You gonna noose my neck with that till the end of time?"

"Now you'll have something to noose *my* neck with. We'll always have these weak spots that only we know about."

"Listen, Bea, I got plenty of noose on you without this. Mind the time you pissed your pants while we was drawing quadrilaterals?"

"We agreed never to speak of that again! Besides, it was your fault for making me laugh so hard."

"How else you s'posed to make quadrilaterals fun?"

"Only you could," she said.

"For the record," I said, "to this day, I never told a soul."

"Well, that incident notwithstanding, I knew you'd understand. This whole crazy endeavor, I knew I could tell you with perfect confidence." A glimmer of hope shone in her brightened eyes. *Sometimes a glimmer's all you get.*

CHAPTER 8

Charlie Rye

Saturday, March 31, 1860

HISTORY *is going to be made today,* I told myself. *And what a spectacle to make it in!* Every man, woman, dog, cat, and chicken came to watch the qualifying race. Victory Hills had never seen such a swarm. Ropes kept bystanders clear of the road for us riders. The brass band played "Yankee Doodle Dandy," and the balconies were draped with red-white-and-blue bunting even though it was a good three months till Independence Day. Mayor Torrence really decked out the down, always in prize of folks' good opinions.

Nothing less than first place would do. Sure, me and Bea had a plan to win the top two spots, but she'd have to settle for second. The notion of letting somebody beat me, even to boost their confidence, didn't exist. Bea'd have to fight for it, like I planned to. And she would.

The baker stood in front of his shop, handing out free powdered-sugar doughnuts to all the riders. Non-riders paid a nickel. I got in line and took one, but my stomach started sloshing, so I handed it to a little girl with pitiful eyes at the back of the line. No eating for me.

Dandy stayed cool like I needed him to be. I patted and stroked his neck. No sign of Bea yet. Our plan involved her arriving just in time, *not late*. The race was about to start. I couldn't help glancing up every so often, hoping to see her.

A dozen other riders were in the running. We tightened saddles, secured bridles and reins, and checked for proper shoeing—all to keep our hands busy. I could've outfidgeted them all.

Jim Tidwell had a decent amount of skill. A short, burly frame gave him a mean riding advantage. Some folks called him Little Paul Revere. Reputation or not, I wouldn't let him intimidate me.

"Howdy, Charlie," I heard from behind me. There stood JP, powdered sugar covering his mouth like an old man's beard.

"What in the nation are you doing here? You're s'posed to be home distracting your mama."

"Aw, come on. And miss the shindig? Not a chance!"

"You agreed to it," I said, lowering my voice. "Folks are s'posed to think Bea is *you*."

"Well, Mama started talking about coming, and it sort of went to heck after that."

"Your mama knows about the race?"

"'Course she does. She ain't stupid."

"Don't tell me she's here."

"She's over there," he said, pointing. Sure enough, there stood Mrs. Brannon in the doughnut line with Cobber.

I yanked off my hat and slid a sweaty hand through my hair. "You spoiled it for Bea. I mean, how's she s'posed to ride Thundercloud if he's hooked to your wagon?"

"Dr. Pearl brought us in *his* wagon."

"OK," I tempered down. "Just go find a hidin' spot for the race where nobody can see you."

After he ran off, Mrs. Brannon came this way with Cobber trailing along.

"Hello, Charlie. Bea never told us you were racing. How exciting! And to think I almost didn't come."

"That would've been a shame," I said through a false smile.

"In fact," she added, "Bea practically insisted that I stay home with her. She's feelin' a little under the weather."

"Oh, is she? Too bad."

"But the boys begged me so heartily."

"Did they indeed?" I said, eyeing Cobber, who stepped behind his mother.

"We best go if we want a good spot," she said. "We'll be cheerin' you on."

Mayor Torrence climbed the bell tower, ready to start the race. The sight of him! Looked like a downright ass, with the blinding white suit and fluffy hat, begging to be admired. And what kind of man named a city block after himself? Oliver Henry Walter Torrence—those were the very same names as the four streets of today's racetrack.

"Ready riders!" he called.

My saddle squealed as I situated myself on it. I untied a tangle in the reins. My eyes flicked toward Bea's road again, but she wasn't there. Maybe her sickness wasn't an act. Either way, I'd keep my head up and not spoil my own chances.

Torrence raised his pistol in hand, ready to bolt us into action.

We riders were packed in tight. Jim Tidwell's boot was wedged in its stirrup, inches from mine.

"You should stick to the card tables, Rye," Jim said. "You're out of your game here."

"Oh, that's right," I returned. "Drained you dry last time. Thanks for the reminder. I needed a little boost."

I hunkered low toward Dandy's ear. "This is our race," I told him. And by winning, I'd prove to myself and everybody else that I was of a different caliber than my father.

BOOM! The pistol fired. Dandy shot us forward, but I held tight. Cheers rang out from all sides. A mass of hooves pounded the dirt.

"Go, Charlie!" I heard the Brannons shout as I sailed past them.

Dandy powered us to the front of the pack. We led Jim by half a length. Ours was a decent speed, but we'd need more. Jim battled hard, judging by those whips to his horse. Dandy leaned into the first turn onto Henry. We kept a small lead.

The crowd got sparse. Most waited on Oliver Street for the finish. The cheers faded behind us, but the hoofbeats amplified. I focused like an owl on its prey, gaining a full length on Jim. That is until a man stepped forward, waving his hat, crying, "Take it, Charlie!"

Cuss him! It was Pa. Why did he choose now, of all times, to cheer me on? Probably to show up and take credit for my success. That or sneer if I lost. Jim inched up beside me. My grip on the lead slipped. Jim overtook me, and it didn't take long for the rest to follow. I fell into last place, rounding the second corner onto Walter. Those old imaginary anchors tugged at me hard. A silly race didn't matter. Not when he was there, reminding me of everything I hated. Reminding me that I was condemned from the start.

"Look alive, Charlie," I heard from behind. I glanced over my shoulder. Bea galloped hard toward me, a bandanna covering her mouth and nose. She and Thundercloud were gaining ground in a devilish hurry. That's all it took. I was back in this race. If Bea could catch up after a late start, then by stars, I still had a shot.

She sped up alongside me to the right. Clever. She'd get the inside track. She'd need it, 'cause I was about to show no mercy. The two of us barreled in tandem around the corner onto Torrence Street. Our view was a bunch of horse backsides. We'd have to stoke an inner fire to get out in front.

Bea gave me a side-eye that meant she and Thunder were about to unleash something wicked. They inched ahead of us. Dandy didn't like that at all. He gave a little more and edged out Thunder. This back-and-forth went on the whole stretch. But Bea knew, like I did, it wouldn't be enough. Our race wasn't against each other; it was against everybody else.

Jim had the lead as we turned the final bend onto Oliver Street. Bea and me trailed behind that tight cluster, unable to break through. Dust plumed in our faces. We'd need to go around it and only had half a city block to do it.

Dandy was ready to make his move. With all my power, I pushed him forward. Sweat poured from my temples. I took to the left of the pack while Bea found her window to the right. The finish line came into sight, but I still had some gaps to close. I lost track of Bea. My mind closed itself off to everything except the win. Dandy's legs churned in a fury as we moved right up alongside Jim. My arms and legs burned from pushing so hard. I couldn't remember ever going this fast before. That had to count for something. Mr. Ellerby stood beside the finish, holding a flag, watching the line. A roaring and whistling filled the air as I sailed across the finish line.

The ovation trickled down. Folks looked to the line judge for answers. It was too close to call. Bea and Thunder trotted up alongside me. We glanced at each other, both out of breath, waiting to hear the outcome.

"Who won?" somebody in the crowd shouted.

Mr. Ellerby squinted in our direction and shouted, "It's a tie between Charlie Rye and . . . *that feller*."

Bea's eyes grew wide as acorns. All decorum gone, she tossed her hat in the air and lowered her bandanna. "Charlie, we did it!"

We swooped down from our horses and hugged each other, bounding up and down. A small gathering formed around us, probably to get a good look at the winner who'd come from behind.

Mr. Ellerby approached us. The instant he recognized Bea, his face froze. "Beatrice?" His daughters stood behind him, parasols pointed in the air, every bit as stupefied as their father. It was golden!

"I knew it was you all along!" said Old Man Hobbs, clasping his wiry arms around us. "The minute I seen you stormin' in on Thundercloud, I says, 'That's Beatrice.' Mighty fine ridin', both of ya."

Mayor Torrence sauntered toward us with his cane tucked in the crook of his arm. He only used that cane as a tool of fashion and not because of any injury, not that it matched the rest of his getup. "Well, Charlie, fine riding, I must say." He offered me a handshake—for the first time ever.

Bea, with excitement a-bubbling over, took Mayor's hand and bounced it up and down in a one-sided handshake.

"That's, er, some quality riding, Beatrice," Torrence said, "You've . . . shocked us all."

"Thank you, sir."

Dr. Pearl came alive too. "Congratulations, Miss Brannon," he said in his proper British. "You rode remarkably well, young lady. Tremendous fortitude and skill! My hat's off to both of you. What fine ambassadors for Victory Hills you'll make."

"Thank you, doctor," she said, brighter than a ray of sunshine.

Bea and me grinned ear to ear. Dr. Pearl wasn't part of the setup, but he sure played right into it. The more we got congratulated, the harder it'd be for them to stop Bea from going.

"Can somebody tell me what's goin' on?" Jim Tidwell said with that pickle-sucking expression he always wore. "This here's Sheriff Brannon's daughter."

"Name's Beatrice," she corrected. "And I just won a spot on the Pony Express."

CHAPTER 9

Beatrice Brannon

Saturday, March 31, 1860

THE glory of my win faltered as the opinions came in, none louder than Jim's.

"Is this a joke?" he said to Mayor Torrence, but for all to hear. "We ain't sendin' *her*, are we?"

"I don't see why not," Charlie said, in haste to defend me. "She beat you fair and square. Them sour grapes don't look good on you, Jim."

"I ain't sour grapes. A girl can't ride for the Pony Express. She'd never make it."

"What's wrong, Tidwell?" Charlie went on. "Ain't had your morning constitutional?"

"Mr. Rye, there's no need for crassness," Mr. Ellerby said, "ladies present and all."

"Oh pardon. Ain't you had your morning shit?"

"Charlie!" Ellerby rebuked. Jim crossed his arms, tiring of this conversation.

"Well, I don't know what he's carryin' on about," Charlie said. "Me and Bea won the race. That's the end of it. He's just sore 'cause he got a measly third place and now he's makin' trouble."

"I ain't makin' trouble," Jim said. "Mayor, talk some sense into him. He thinks we can actually send a girl."

Mayor Torrence said in his slow, twangy voice, "I agree with Jim here. It'd be downright"—he paused to find the right politician's word—"*imprudent* to send a girl out on that trail. Think of the dangers out there."

The wind had been knocked from my chest. That's the only explanation I had for not adding my voice to the debate about . . . me. I simply couldn't catch my breath to do so.

"Wait a moment, sir," Dr. Pearl cut in. "It seems to me that the dangers of the job are not the relevant point. As the winner, Miss Brannon assumes the risk."

Mr. Ellerby, of course, jumped in. "Most of us agree that it's highly improper to send a young lady. Let's also remember the gal's a mere fifteen years of age."

I wanted to speak my mind, but the scant air occupying my lungs wouldn't allow for words. I had won! I had proven myself, yet they were trying to disqualify me.

Then Mama appeared, worsening my condition. Her fabled expressions spoke volumes without saying a word. She seemed to say, "You told me a falsehood."

My own expression answered back. "I'm sorry, Mama, but you wouldn't have given me permission."

She inspected my hair, seeming to say, "So *this* is why you cut your hair?"

All these nosy onlookers, eager for entertainment, watched this silent disagreement take place.

Mama left me with a silent, "I'll see you at home." I watched her go, taking her dignity, and mine, with her. My plan just got its toughest strike yet.

"You see that?" Jim said. "Her own mother don't even approve."

"I don't believe Mrs. Brannon actually expressed an opinion," Dr. Pearl said.

"Nonsense," Mr. Ellerby said. "We all saw that. If that ain't disapproval, I don't know what is."

"Besides, it was just luck she won the race," Jim said. "She rode Thundercloud. She's got no experience with other horses. The Pony Express has their own. Mustangs got their own temperament. She'd get pummeled just like—"

I gave him a biting glare, warning him not to finish that thought.

Charlie stepped toe-to-toe with him. "We've heard enough from you, Tidwell, so shut your mouth, 'less you want me to knock you into next week."

"You can flap your lips all you want, but nobody listens to a cheater at the card tables."

Charlie threw a fist, but Mayor Torrence grabbed his arm. Someone held Jim back. "Fellers, stop! No need to cause a fuss. I've got a solution that'll make everybody happy. Alright?"

Mayor excused himself, leaving two worked-up boys in his wake, and climbed his precious tower. "Ladies and gentlemen, a matter has come to my attention. As most of you know, our race today was tied. Our first-place winners are Miss Beatrice Brannon and Mr. Charlie Rye. Let's give them a round of applause. They certainly deserve it."

Folks did as they were told, then quieted hastily to hear the controversy. I swallowed hard, like a prisoner at my own trial. The verdict was about to come in.

"Our third-place winner, who also deserves our recognition, is Mr. Jim Tidwell."

More polite praise followed.

"So now we're faced with the thorny problem of who to send to the Pony Express. We've got two spots to fill. Charlie Rye will take one. There's no dispute there. The question becomes: Is it reasonable and proper to send Miss Brannon out into the rough wilderness? Housed in the same quarters with men? I'm not even certain the Pony Express hires girls. I am certain, however, that the dangers out on the trail are not befitting a young lady. Folks, I'm leaving it in your hands. We'll take a vote."

I whispered to Charlie, "I've got to leave. I can't abide it."

"Wait," he whispered back. "What if you win?"

I paused, still with a morsel of hope.

"We'll do this informally by a raise of hands," Mayor said. "But first, let me say, Miss Beatrice Brannon is fifteen years of age. Her mother doesn't approve of her going. And, simply put, the work wasn't made for a girl."

So much for impartiality, I thought. Charlie agreed, judging by the disdainful shaking of his head.

"Without further ado," Torrence continued, "we'll take our votes. All in favor of sending Jim Tidwell, please raise your hands."

A sea of hands went into the air. There couldn't have been many left to vote for me. Mrs. Ellerby and her daughters raised their hands. Charlie's pa voted for Jim too. Deputy Hartley surprised me the most. He'd been there by my side at Da's passing, and here he was, voting against me.

"All in favor of sending Miss Brannon, please raise your hands."

My own hand went up along with Charlie's, my brothers', Mr. Hobbs's, and Dr. Pearl's. Mama was nowhere in sight, not that she would've voted for me anyway. Six hands.

A finer blow had never been dealt to me on such a large scale, nor by so many people. I wanted to burst into a puddle of tears. Not yet. I begged myself to hold it in, needing my composure to make one last plea, face-to-face.

Charlie gave me a regretful, pained look. My disappointment was his too.

"Take Thunder," I said, handing Charlie the rope.

I snaked through the throng and landed at Mayor Torrence, just as he alighted from the tower. All my silence had been working up to this.

"Mayor Torrence, I beg of you to give me a chance. You know very well about the Peregrine mine. If my father were still here, he'd pay the debt. He'd rather walk through fire than not pay it. This was the solution my father had in mind. Please let me do it."

His expression was unyielding. "I appreciate your spunk, Miss Beatrice, but here's the spot I find myself in. One of my good friends is an owner in the Pony Express. Today, I'm sending him a letter with the winners' names on it. I feel a hefty responsibility that he entrusted this selection process to me. And ultimately, it does come down to me. Now do you think for a minute I'd write down the name Beatrice Brannon? Don't you think he'd have a few questions about that? About my sanity, frankly?"

I called on my courage to push back, for Da's sake. "My father died breaking your horse. Don't you owe it to him?"

He moved in close to my ear. "Maybe some bleeding heart would surrender to this kind of bullying, but I am unmoved. Your father was bent on breakin' that horse—wild for an exhibition. I gave him every chance to back out, but he forged ahead. He wanted to show me up. Teach me a lesson. We're not here 'cause of that horse. We're here 'cause your father made a damned fool of himself—with his money and everything else. Frankly, it disgusts me. I'm not the only one who thinks so, just the only one who dares say it."

With those poisonous words, he departed. The wounds from Da's death came on afresh. The hinges of my body locked up, and my eyes closed. I stood there for a good while, until at last, I found the strength to move.

Charlie had already made it halfway through the alfalfa field, towing Dandy and Thunder. I caught up with him, red-faced and tear-sodden.

"What happened?" he begged.

"Mayor Torrence is a self-important arse."

"Ain't that the truth. What'd he say?"

It would've been too painful to repeat Torrence's hateful words. Instead, I said, "I guess it was a lie."

"What was?"

"When I first heard about the Pony Express, something came alive inside me. It knew it would become part of my life somehow. All I want is to keep a roof over our heads—the roof my father built. Is that so outrageous? What do I have to do to prove myself?"

"You already proved yourself, Bea."

"A lot of good it did."

"Listen, Bea, true feelings don't lie."

"What do you mean?"

He deliberated over something, a thought that wanted out. He shifted around to delay his answer. "Come on, the river's not too far. These boys deserve a drink, don't they?"

We led Thundercloud and Dandy to an alcove shaded by cottonwood trees along the riverbank. The horses plodded in up to their knees. Charlie slogged in as well, while I watched from the side.

"Remember this place? I'm pretty sure that's the tree I fell out of when I sprained my ankle." He pointed upward.

I didn't say much. Charlie was trying to get my mind off what had just happened, but it was too fresh. He noticed.

"Bea, supposin' the answer is starin' us in the face."

"What answer?"

"Supposin' you go to the Pony Express without the sanction of our town leaders? What if you take my spot? On the ledgers, you'd be Charlie Rye. Nobody there'd know the difference. Except for Jim and he'd keep quiet."

I tramped through the river and squared myself across from him. "I can't do that. I won't take your spot."

"Bea." He tilted his head, the way he did when he wanted me to see things his way. "It's your spot. You said you were meant to do this."

"But not at your expense! We were supposed to go together. And what about you? You've always wanted a noble venture. What if this is a bridge you're meant to cross? Anyway, I know how much you'd love to go."

"I'll admit, I wanted it, but now I've got a stake in *you* going. Mayor Torrence needs some decent medicine, and you're gonna be the one to give it to him. And that, my dear, would be far more satisfyin' than going myself."

"I don't want to be that vile man's medicine or set his thinking right. I just want to pay off the debt and help my family."

"And so you would." Charlie brightened. "But wouldn't it be powerfully satisfyin' to defy Mayor at the same time? You know your da wouldn't object to that."

I was afraid of letting him talk me into it. All the same, I felt it happening. I could already picture myself out there. I possessed every ability the job required. If I could just allow myself permission to break this first rule.

"When you put it that way . . . ," I said.

His side grin turned into a full-blown smile. "And don't worry about me. If there's a bridge I'm meant to cross, I'll find it. It feels right to give you back the chance you already earned."

My arms flew around his neck. He lifted me up by the waist and whirled me around, then placed me back down in the gentle pull of the river.

Never before had we shared so small a space. I knew it wasn't proper to stand so close to a boy with his arms around me. If Mama had taught me anything, it was the impropriety of, well, everything. But I stayed because I'd never seen his face this close. His skin was pure and smooth like a river stone, and his eyes held a kaleidoscope of brown, amber, yellow, and gold. They told the truth, but in riddles. Riddles I had not solved.

I had to let the moment go so it wouldn't lose its beauty.

"Charlie, I hope this works."

"It will. The Pony Express—it's yours, sure as night follows day."

My face must've lit up. My heart certainly did. "That's Shakespeare."

He shrugged. "I ain't so backwoodsy as you might think."

The ache of having missed out on two years' worth of experiences with Charlie hit me hard. Nothing was worth that. "You're gold, Charlie. Pure gold."

CHAPTER 10

Beatrice Brannon

Sunday, April 1, 1860

I awoke in my bed, cold and wet like a glacier. The nightmare had come to me again, as it did nearly every night with harrowing punctuality. No matter how many times it played out, it never lost its sting. Every sensory element became exaggerated. The swirling fog thicker, the piercing squeal louder, the vision of the horse more terrifying with his angular muscles, sharp hooves, blood eyes. Da would move toward the horse, reaching out his hand in a calming gesture. The killdeer would shriek; the horse would kick, buck, and turn mad circles. And the impact. Gracious night, the impact would send a jolt through me like lightning striking my head.

After regaining my breath, I patted the runoff from my forehead and peered out my window. The earliest hint of daybreak peeked over the foothills. This nightmare would keep to its cage, at least until nightfall.

I tiptoed to my chest of drawers, peeled off my sweat-soaked nightgown, and withdrew my Pony Express outfit: a pair of Charlie's old trousers, a loose-fitting oatmeal-colored shirt with a button-up vest, and a jacket on top of that. Never mind a corset to emphasize my waist and growing breasts. Now I'd rely on layers to convey the opposite. I put on Da's wide-brimmed hat with a string that tightened up to my chin. *This'll have to do,* I thought, inspecting myself in the mirror.

I placed my note for Mama on the kitchen table, pondering which circle of Dante's hell was reserved for rebellious daughters who abandoned their mothers in their hour of need, without permission and without so much as a goodbye. And on Sunday too, when we usually attended church together. Well, Da had given me the charge to take care of the family. I'd have to do it my own way.

My knapsack was packed to the seams with extra clothing, stockings, and a small cube of lye soap. I tied a bedroll made of two woolen blankets to the knapsack. I considered taking Da's tin whistle with me to keep him close, but instead I left it for Cobber, who celebrated the sacredness of things more than I did.

The back door squeaked as I eased it open, then I set out on foot. Charlie had told me to meet Jim Tidwell at the post office flagpole. Jim would be taking his mule team and a wagon full of supplies to the Pony Express outpost where we'd be stationed. Jim would be expecting Charlie, not me. Somehow, I'd have to convince that stickler-for-the-rules to take me instead. I pushed that thought aside and opened myself up to the beauty of my surroundings.

Rays of sunlight shot through thin, feathery clouds. Juniper trees juiced their piquant sap, and my boots left deep prints in the soft clay earth. A gentle wind blew the scent of pure morning earth my way. I breathed in deeply and let the freshness settle in my lungs. This scene calmed my soul and melted away the coldness of the nightmare.

No one else occupied the stillness of the road, save a curious desert cottontail with perked ears, who hopped from rock to rock, trailing me at a distance, offering cautious companionship.

Mornings used to suit me not so long ago. I'd have traded anything in the world to set out on a Brannon Expedition with Da this morning. He'd spot animals in search of food, and we'd retreat to a hiding place. We even saw a black bear once. Four of them, actually. Da found a great viewing spot along a rocky ridge to observe the valley below. Da, the twins, and I watched a mother bear rise on her hind legs and growl at a male bear, warning him to keep away from her two cubs. The deep, ear-throbbing sound from that mother bear's throat made us quake to our very souls. But Da, aside from a slight quickening of his breath, was calm as a morning lake. He seemed beyond fear. Invincible.

I picked up my footpace. Charlie had said to be there at sunup, but when I arrived at the post office, an empty road greeted me. I hoped I hadn't missed my ride. I waited on the steps, rehearsing the grand oration that was sure to convince Jim to take me along. Sympathy would be my best ploy.

Afar off, I heard the muffled boom-blasts of the mining operations, their explosions digging ever deeper in the earth. I couldn't help but think of the failed Peregrine mine and all the effort Da put into it, now an empty cavern.

Oliver Street shone in the morning light. In just ten years' time, this place had sprung to life. First, as a refitting joint for the California gold-rushers, but upon discovery of the Comstock Lode some thirty miles south, most of the residents stayed put, including us. Oliver Torrence and George Ellerby, the founders, were relentlessly protective of the town, that it not fall into the lawlessness of other nearby boomtowns.

The first sign of life this morning was Old Man Hobbs in his print shop, next door to the post office. Through the window, I could see him down on all fours, scrubbing his floor. He paused to wipe sweat from his brow and continued. His shop door was ajar when I approached, so I entered without the bell ringing.

"Morning, Mr. Hobbs."

He didn't hear me. I moved closer to see him working at some spilled black ink. His delicate hair swooped into a spiral atop his head, like a soft white peak of cream. I touched his shoulder.

"Oh! Miss Beatrice. You got me."

"Sorry, I didn't mean to scare you."

He sat backward on the floor, wheezing some. "Well, that ain't likely to come clean with just soap and water."

"I'll take a turn." He handed me the rag, which I dipped into an oily solution and scrubbed hard at the nasty stain.

"This floor has seen some ink spills, but this is the first time it's 'cause of vandalism."

I stopped scrubbing and caught glances with him. "Vandalism? Who did this?"

"Don't know. They broke in this morning." The old man lengthened his back, stretching out the kinks.

"Mercy! Have you summoned the sheriff?" The term *sheriff* had come out with ease, but it stung to use it and *not* have it mean my father. The sheriff was Hartley now.

"Not yet," he said. "I thought I'd try to get the ink while it's fresh."

I stood to get a look at it from above. The ink had smeared some, but it seemed to be a kind of shape, rather than a random spill. "Is it a letter? It looks like a *V*."

"I don't know. Whoever it is must be tryin' to send a message."

"What could anybody have against *you*?"

"Plenty. Lots of folks are angered right now. Tensions are high about the war."

There was that word again. "Do you think that's where we're headed?"

"Good chance of it, I'd say, but folks don't want to hear it. No indeed."

I recalled the heated debate at the saloon. Da and Mr. Hobbs had said they believed war was a possibility. The Pony Express man had agreed. Everyone else had decried it as ridiculous, especially Mayor Torrence.

"Seems a bit ignorant," I said.

"True enough, but is it still ignorance if it's willful?"

Da would've never left Mr. Hobbs in this vulnerable state. The man lived alone, upstairs in his shop. Someone had entered while he slept. What if they came back to harm him?

"I'll get Sheriff Hartley," I said. "This makes me ill." The next part, I mumbled only to myself: "Da would have the culprit jailed by sundown. Let's see what Hartley can do."

Mr. Hobbs shook his head. "Miss Beatrice, I appreciate your watchful eye, but don't worry about me. I been livin' on my own some twenty years. I'll get the sheriff myself. Now be a dear and help me up."

I extended my hand, and he softly grunted when I pulled him to his feet. He dusted off his trousers and squinted at my pack sitting by the door, as if questioning his eyesight. "You goin' somewhere, miss?"

I had no answer prepared, so I said nothing.

"Never mind, miss." He winked. "You got your secrets, and I don't aim to expose 'em." He pointed out his window at Jim approaching in his wagon. "I reckon your ride's here."

"Thank you, Mr. Hobbs! If you could—"

"Tut-tut-tut," he interrupted. "I don't know a thing."

I stole a quick hug, slung my pack over my shoulder, and left the shop.

Jim rolled along with his team of mules and scowled down at me. "Oh, at first I thought you was Charlie."

"Good, that's kind of the idea. You see, we decided to send me instead." I hauled myself onto the seat beside him with my pack on my shoulder.

By the looks of him, he'd never faced such audacity. "Whoa, missy! Who decided this?"

"Me and Charlie. It's quite simple. He gave me his spot."

"You must be jokin'." He peered left and right, probably looking for some person of authority to back him up.

"So shouldn't we be . . . ," I said, hoping with all my might he'd get moving.

"You think I'm just gonna set off with the wrong person? You think I wasn't there when the whole town—"

"Voted against me?" I finished, hoping the harsh words would sting him too. They didn't.

"This is ridiculous. Get out."

"But Jim, this is something that I really need to do. It's important to my family."

"I'll say it one more time: *get out*."

Everything in his voice and countenance was unyielding, but I couldn't give up. I closed my eyes and tried to conjure up a speech worthy of Dante himself, but something far more cunning arose. "I understand my father did you a favor not long ago."

An immediate flush broke out on his otherwise pale cheeks, and he shifted in his seat. I'd struck gold with my little guess. Da had done a good turn for most folks in town, that much I knew, but *this* was more than I could've hoped for. It was obvious Da had kept a secret for him. Hubris got away with me. "You wouldn't want that secret getting out, would you?" Oh, how wicked I was.

"You blackmailing me?"

"No, not in the least. Just saying you might like the chance to pay him back."

"You're a real pest, Brannon." A moment of fretful silence prevailed. At last, he shook the reins with a "Yah!" I was fearful quiet so he wouldn't change his mind. We jounced along and were almost to the edge of Oliver Street when the sound of cantering hooves stole our attention. "There's Rye," Jim said. "He can clear all this up."

Charlie slowed Dandy to a stop on the side of the wagon closest to me. He tipped his hat. "Mornin', Bea. Jim."

Jim leaned back and rolled his eyes. "This pesky rat thinks she can stow away in my wagon, Rye. You in on this plan?"

Charlie had probably come to help plead my case. Now that the deed had been done, I hoped he wouldn't make it worse. I motioned to Charlie to keep his lips shut.

"I ain't here to interfere," Charlie said. "Just wanted to wish you farewell, Bea, and give you this. It's a packet they issued all the riders." He handed me a folded red shirt, a horn, and a small Bible. "There was supposed to be a six-shooter, but Jim got the last one."

I glanced at Jim's side where the six-shooter hung.

"The horn is for lettin' the next rider know you're comin'," Charlie added. "Go on. Tear it up!"

"Thanks, Charlie." I stacked the items in my lap and gave him a nod. How I wished we could've gone together.

Jim sighed. "Alright, let's get moving, shall we?"

Off we lurched on our way. Charlie waved me off until he became a speck on the horizon. A hollowness stretched the cavity of my soul as Victory Hills disappeared behind me. I faced the future, my safe world being swallowed up by the vast unknown. Never had I been out on my own, not even for a single night. Someone had always been there to take care of me, to guarantee my safety. Now I'd rely on myself alone. The bitter sting of my anxiety must've been as Dante's, approaching the gates of his Inferno: "Abandon all hope, ye who enter here."

CHAPTER 11

Beatrice Brannon

—

Sunday, April 1, 1860

VICTORY Hills was nestled in a high mountain valley. Leaving it meant traversing a jagged path downward amid tall pines and iron-rich boulders. We called it Rocky Pass. Jim's two mules handled it skillfully, but I found myself clutching the side of the wagon. At last, the land flattened into a vast plain of rolling hills and tufts of pale-green sagebrush. I held up the hand-scribbled map, but every time I attempted to help with navigation, Jim snapped, "I know where I'm goin'."

My mind and body were in a state of high alert. I tried light conversation to soothe my nerves and possibly loosen Jim up.

"Have you seen many wild animals?"

He glanced my way, then back to the trail ahead.

"Da and I used to go out spotting for interesting fauna. Out in the foothills behind my house, we've seen deer, coyotes, bald eagles—we even saw some black bears once."

"Son of a gun," he said with zero enthusiasm.

"One time, we saw a mother bear—"

"Fascinating," he interrupted.

I sat back and folded my hands in my lap. "I just thought you might want to hear the story."

"I know all I care to know about black bears, thanks."

"OK." This trip was, so far, insufferable.

"You might notice I ain't too happy about this arrangement," he said.

"Well, nobody's twisting your arm."

"You are, actually. Anyhow, I done my payback for Jeremiah, and we're square. The rest is up to you and your own merits. I just wanna make sure we have an understanding. I ain't part of this little scheme you and Charlie cooked up. Says in the Bible that lying lips are an abomination to the Lord."

"I don't have lying lips."

"Oh, no? Does your Mama know where you are right now?"

I turned and subtly slanted my hat to hide the truth-betraying flush of my cheeks.

"That's right. Who's squirming now? I saw your mama give you the eye after the race. She didn't even know you was gonna compete, did she? Just like she don't know you're sittin' here in this wagon."

"Well, not telling her isn't the same as lying," I rationalized. "I left a note." Still, I couldn't help picturing Mama waking up this morning, padding out to start breakfast, seeing my note, pressing her hand to her heart, and sitting down to take it in. Not until then did it occur to me that Mama would never accept my note and leave it be. She'd either send someone after me or come fetch me herself, if she knew where to go.

Jim bent forward to see my face and chuckled. "Some special daughter you are, taking off without sayin' a word, your pa not a month dead."

"Don't speak of my father." Now he'd crossed a line, and he knew it.

"Listen, even if your mama gave you her blessing, our employer ain't likely to. Pull out my copy of the oath we riders agreed to." He pointed to the knapsack by his feet. I took out the paper and read it aloud:

I . . . do hereby swear before the Great and Living God that during my engagement and while I am an employee of Russell, Majors, and Waddell I will under no circumstances use profane language, that I will drink no intoxicating liquors, that I will not quarrel or fight with any other employee of the firm and that in every respect I will conduct myself honestly, be faithful to my duties and so direct all my acts as to win the confidence of my employers, so help me God.

I paused for a moment. "Of course I can live by this oath."

"You're already in defiance of it, missy. Says to conduct yourself honestly. The Pony Express won't take kindly to being deceived by one of their own hirelings. And what a stupid, reckless idea. You wanna lie about being a boy—that's your affair, but don't drag me into it. When the goin' gets rough, don't ask me to take you home. What's more, I don't know who's gonna be at the station—but you and me ain't friends, OK?"

"OK," I said. His words cut me a little. I wasn't sure why. We'd never been friends, but we hadn't been enemies either.

"I never even *met* the likes a' you, got it?"

"I got it!" No, his words cut me straight to the quick. A hiccup in my throat threatened to bring tears, but I swallowed it back down. The distance between me and anyone who cared for me was ever widening. Was I so different from Da? Was I so undeserving of the respect he had garnered?

Jim whistled some of the way, out of tune mostly, which I endured with the greatest patience. I hoped there would be friendly fellows at the outpost. I'd have to earn their respect before Jim's bitterness toward me became infectious.

At about noon, we spotted a thicket of red willow trees that grew along the Carson River. A small, ramshackle cabin came into view, made of juniper logs and a lean-to roof. A stacked stone chimney made up the east wall and puffed smoke out the top. Above the doorway hung the skull of a steer.

A barn of the same rough-hewn quality was situated nearby, as well as a corral holding two mustangs.

Two men sat wide-legged on tree stumps in the shade of the lean-to. We lurched to a halt. I jumped down, eager to stretch my legs.

One of the men, broad-chested like a bison, held a rifle across his lap. His shirt was unbuttoned, revealing a chest of dark curls down to his navel. With a deep, raspy voice, he said, "Welcome to Buckland's." The welcome sounded more like a warning.

I nodded, avoiding speech for now.

Jim stepped down and shook hands with both of them.

"Name's Squires," the bison man said. "I'm the blacksmith-farrier. I'm in charge for now. This's Oscar. He's the horse caretaker."

Oscar must've been a couple years older than me. His hair was disheveled and greasy. Every point on him was punctuated with red—elbows, nose, knuckles. His long, gangly arms folded in front of him like a praying mantis. These two were a rough-looking pair, but Da and Mama had taught me not to judge a person's outsides. I'd certainly try.

All their eyes piled on me, waiting for me to say my name. The moment was upon me to try out my "boy voice." I nudged my courage and said, "Charlie Rye, rider." I held out my hand, first to Squires, who kept his hands on his rifle. He took hard inventory of me and didn't like what he saw. I held out my hand to Oscar next, but he followed Squires's lead. I couldn't place their disdain of me. Did they know my secret? I didn't think so or they wouldn't have hesitated to say it. Perhaps my anxiety communicated an overall uneasiness or weakness. I pushed back my shoulders and said, "You don't believe in handshakes here at Buckland's?"

Their stares seemed to ask me what right I had to be there.

"Who sent this scrawny little varmint?" Squires rasped. "A puff of wind'll knock him off his horse."

Oscar laughed at the man's rudeness. Perhaps my credentials would ease their concerns. "My town had a race to see who'd win the Pony Express spots, and I tied for first . . . didn't I, Jim?"

Jim didn't back me up, of course, but kept silent.

"Oh, I forgot," I mumbled. "You never met the likes of me."

"First thing you gotta know," Squires told Jim, "is to stay watchful here at Buckland's. We got ourselves a right Paiute camp not two miles from these diggins." He pointed northeast up the river, toward a thicket of pines where dozens of smoke trails rose skyward.

"But, uh, no need to worry," Squires continued, slapping the rifle. "They come near us, they'll answer to me. I'm an advocate of private retribution." The gleam in his eye sent a shiver through me.

"We ought to hear 'em comin' though," Oscar added, "wailing out their ghost dance and all." Oscar chanted a mocking tribal song. Squires's laugh turned to a wheezing cough.

This shameful display became personal. Charlie's childhood bullies came to mind. *So, is this how it's going to be?* I thought. Squires and Oscar would never be able to gain my good favor now. I hated them both from that instant.

Jim said in a serious tone, "Thanks for the warning." He didn't join in their merriment, which gave me a fraction more respect for him.

"If we leave them alone, I reckon they'll do the same for us." Though I muttered it under my breath, Squires bristled. I busied myself by helping Jim unload crates and sacks so I wouldn't have to endure that man's looks.

Jim went inside without unhitching his mules. The two creatures eyed me pitifully, so I did it myself.

The inside of the cabin offered tight quarters, not much taller than Squires's head. A single lantern hung from the low ceiling. The fireplace—a crude stone and mortar outcropping—offered some light as well.

Two bunks hugged one wall, and a single cot lined the other. The numbers were off. Four people. Three beds. Where would the fourth person sleep? The floor? The barn?

Squires slouched down on the cot, making sure we knew he'd claimed it. Jim wasted no time planting his things on the bottom bunk.

"Hey, that's my bunk!" Oscar whined.

"Oh, give it a rest, rattlebrain," Squires said. "It don't matter if you slept there last night. Jim gets his choice, on account of being a rider. You're a station hand. He outranks you. Take the top bunk."

"Pardon me," I said. "I believe that top bunk would be mine."

"*Pardon me,*" Oscar mocked. "How'd ya figure?"

"Mr. Squires just said a rider outranks a station hand. I'm a rider."

I made my way toward the bunk, but Oscar blocked me. "Not so fast. I killed a bat today, so it's mine."

"What does killing a bat have to do with it?"

"'Cause there was a bat in this corner when I got here. You owe me! If'n I didn't kill that varmint, it would've sucked out all your blood in your sleep."

"Except bats don't suck blood," I said.

His scholarly rebuttal consisted of, "Yuh-huh."

"No they don't—not the ones that live here. There's a bat in South America called *Desmodus rotundus,* also known as the vampire bat, that's been known to feed off the blood of cows, but the bats that live here are completely harmless to humans . . . and cows."

A dumbstruck Oscar blinked in quick succession. The words had come out of me as if I'd been reading straight from my book, *A Field Guide for Young Naturalists.* I hadn't meant to sound like a smarty. I'd just wanted to alert him to a common misconception.

The silence snapped as Oscar and Squires burst into laughter. Even Jim found some camaraderie with them this time.

"Ya hear that, fellers?" Oscar said. "Pipsqueak thinks he knows a thing 'r two."

"Guess we've got ourselves a right professor," Squires rasped.

"Think you're pretty smart, don't ya, Professor?" Oscar said. His next line was a whisper just for me. "I'll git you for makin' me look a fool. Go ahead and take the bunk. I dare you."

His sour face and decaying breath made me wither. Mostly, though, I knew the dispute was over. I wasn't willing to live under his threats. Jeers came from the victors as I made my exodus to the barn.

I climbed up to a hay loft and saw immediate possibilities. They were the losers in this bargain, I convinced myself. The ceiling allowed room to sit up, but not stand, so I crawled to the middle and placed my knapsack on one side and my hat on the other.

That evening, with only a wink of sunlight left, I took a stroll along the river, trying to think of ways to survive my new environment. The river offered some solace, trickling over rocks, carrying leaves and water striders. I followed it for a while, stepping from stone to stone. Out of nowhere, a thud hit the back of my head. I whipped around to see Oscar drop his arm. He'd thrown a rock at me.

"What's your problem? You got the bunk, OK? Leave me alone."

"You made a fool of me about them bats."

"You did a fine enough job of that yourself."

"Still smartin' off. I'll teach you better." He strode toward me. I dashed a couple yards away, but he was quick. He shoved my back hard, pitching me forward. I splashed in the river on all fours. He planted himself on top of me, flattening me, my face in the water. He kept me down, pressing his body on my back. I lifted my head for air, but he pushed it back down. *He's going to kill me,* I thought. I wriggled out of his grasp and stood, facing him. He punched my cheek hard. The shock and pain doubled me forward. I willed myself back to my feet.

Breathing like he'd sprinted a mile, he said, "I swear . . . you're gutless. You fight like a *girl*."

He was still raring to go. My mind whirled, searching for a way out of this. I couldn't outrun him. I couldn't outfight him. I had to let him know he had won. My brothers' tussles always ended with Cobber in tears. That was JP's signal that he'd won. Laws, I'd have to cry. I'd have to make him believe he'd waged an unfair fight. It hurt my pride to think of granting him more power, but I wouldn't die at the hands of this imbecile.

"Have pity on me!" I wailed. "I never been in a fight before."

"What in the name of Pete? What kind of kid's never been in a fight?" he said, fists still poised for more violence.

"My parents are Quakers. They taught me that fighting's an abomination, so I never learned." I continued sobbing, finding it all too easy to conjure up tears. I didn't know if Quakers truly believed that, but it seemed plausible. They did call themselves the Society of Friends.

Oscar hesitated, which was exactly what I needed. The more seconds that ticked by, the more his anger would cool.

"You gonna just give up?" a hoarse voice questioned. Squires was behind me, leaning against a tree, his pipe glowing in the dusky night. How long had he been there? Why hadn't he stopped Oscar? As the one in charge, he was supposed to keep order, not spur Oscar on.

Oscar's face held uncertainty. He'd taken the bait of my lie and didn't want to proceed with an unfair fight, but he also wanted to obey Squires.

"Come on, Oscar! Give the kid proper lesson." It became obvious that Squires had given him the order in the first place.

"You're the type that gets under my skin," Squires said to me. "The real saintly sort—come to enforce your priggish morals on the rest of us. No matter. I can change that. I see you got yourself some nice book learnin'. Now all's you need is some schoolin' in the ways of the world out here. First rule: don't cross me. Just do what you're told and shut that cocky mouth of yours, 'specially when it comes to the Paiutes."

All was clear. This wasn't about Oscar or our dispute about the bats. This was about Squires and his hatred of the Paiutes. My remark earlier—that if we left them alone, they'd leave us alone too—had festered in him.

Squires advanced toward me slowly. I didn't move, giving the impression that I stood my ground, when, in fact, I was petrified. He clutched my arm with the grip of a bear trap. "Are we clear on that?"

My nod was frantic, like a trapped rabbit. The second he released the trap, I ran, which made him laugh heartily. The only other time I'd heard someone outright laugh after being cruel to another person was when

Charlie had been bullied at school. *How could anyone,* I wondered, *derive pleasure from degrading others?*

On my path to the barn, I saw Jim carrying a load of firewood. "What happened?" he asked. I refused to answer. As if he hadn't heard the commotion! I'd lost all patience for Jim. He, too, was out of my good favor.

Almost no light inhabited the barn after I closed the door. At least there was a door between me and those brutes. My chest heaved with anxious breaths, my hands shook, every pound of flesh hurt, and to deepen my wounds, I'd branded myself as a weakling. Now they'd never leave me alone. This was all wrong. I couldn't stay, not another minute. But I also couldn't ask Jim to take me home. Or could I? Maybe if I confronted him, owning my faults, he'd agree to it. Or maybe I could pretend to contract pneumonia and call for a doctor.

This is hopeless! I collapsed to the ground and hugged my knees. A pool of water formed around me in the dirt. *The townsfolk were right. The Pony Express is no place for a girl,* I told myself. *At least not this girl.* The thought made me ill. I'd wanted to prove them wrong. All those narrow-minded, backward fools voting against me. All those hands going up. All those folks wagging their tongues about how Da had left us destitute. How I'd wanted to shut down all that talk. Yet here I was in a heap, cold and bruised, living proof they were right. Why had I come here in the first place? Nothing was worth this.

The best I could do with nightfall upon me would be to get some sleep and figure out a way home tomorrow. Even in my pain, maybe because of it, I grew tired. Rest would be a blessing.

A kerosene lantern hung by the barn door. I lit it and brought the horses and mules inside. I'd need their warmth. The sweet mules, Titus and Molly, as Jim had called them, lapped up any affection I gave them, as if starved for it. "Well," I told them, "you two may be the only friends I make out on this trail."

I climbed to the loft and fashioned a bird's nest out of the hay and laid out my bedroll. I took off all my layers of clothes down to my undergarments and threw on the red flannel shirt provided by the Pony Express. The arms were too long, but the cloth felt warm against my clammy arms.

When I shook out my jacket, a shiny thing sailed from the pocket. *For all that's holy . . . one of Charlie's silver-plated buttons!* How had he sneaked it into my pocket?

The good tidings didn't end there. A small white corner stuck out of the flannel shirt's pocket. I plucked it out. *BEA,* it said in all capitals. Charlie's handwriting. I sat up. Mercy from heaven! This was more timely than when I'd received a copy of Milton's *Paradise Lost* for my twelfth birthday. I unfolded the note and devoured the words.

Dear Bea,

Good luck in the pony express though you won't need it. You got more than luck on your side. You got smarts, probably more than any of the men there. Certainly more than Jim! Your smarts will git ya out of any trouble. And you got grit too. I never seen a grittier girl and don't let folks tell ya different. I still can't believe you came from behind and won the race. Tied for first that is. That's one for the books. Aw Bea I'm awfully glad we made up after all these years. It's been too long comin. Not havin you around was like a piece of me missin. I feel a bit blue writing this note cuz I'm jealous. You'll be a gen-YOU-ine American hero! And the money ain't bad neither I reckon. Remember all your stories so you can tell me. I'll be with ya in spirit.

Your fred for always,

C. Rye

PS I almost forgot. One of the runs from your station goes east and one goes west. Get the WEST one! It'll take ya to Carson City station. I'm goin there to get outta Victory Hills. We can meet up and you can gimme a roundup of your journey so far.

The splendor of Charlie's friendship enveloped me like a warm cocoon. It didn't matter what these ruffians thought of me—or even that they wanted me dead. I had a best "fred," to quote Charlie's spelling, and the world could be swallowed up in its meanness for all I cared. I bit off a length of twine and strung the button on it. This charm would give me hope to keep me going whenever I got tempted to quit. I looped it around my neck, tied it, and tucked it beneath my shirt.

My hand was on the lantern, ready to dim it, when Jim burst through the barn doors. The animals spooked at the sound. "I just heard about the scuffle. You OK?" At last, his conscience had gotten to him. He'd been clear that he didn't want to be my protector, but pretending to be ignorant of what had happened was inexcusable.

"Of course I'm OK."

"Oh, 'cause I finally got the truth outta Oscar. Said he taught you a lesson."

"I'm fine, Jim. I'm here to make money, not friends."

"Good. I was sure you was gonna beg me for passage back home. That would've angered me to no end."

"How little you know me," I said.

He kicked around at the dirt, wondering what to say next. "It's gonna get cold tonight. How you gonna manage without a fire?"

"Go to sleep, Jim. You need not worry about me. We ain't friends, remember?"

He regretted his words from earlier, I could tell. I delivered one final thought. "For the record, I have no earthly clue what my da did to save your sorry hide, but I'm certain you didn't deserve it. Now shut that door up good and tight."

CHAPTER 12

Charlie Rye

Monday, April 2, 1860, morning

A wild eagerness kept my hands moving and my mind racing. I packed my haversack to the seams, slung it over my shoulder, and skirted around the house to the shed. Dandy and me would leave for Carson City before the stars disappeared. Mr. Hobbs was right about me needing a new endeavor, but I'd make no promises about giving up cards.

The Victory Hillers couldn't see me kicking around here. They thought I joined the Pony Express and I wouldn't let a soul contend otherwise. I would've left the same morning as Bea, but I needed an extra day to get provisions. It hadn't been easy, dodging folks.

My mind kept going back to Bea. How was she settling in? How was her first night there? When would her first ride be?

After securing my saddlebags in place, I heard the curious hooting of an owl. Not an ordinary owl. This one sounded human.

I peered outside to see a clump of a person behind the elderberry bush. Too small to be JP. Had to be Cobber. I hooted back.

As I drew closer, he stepped into view.

"Now that's the biggest owl I've ever seen."

Normally, he'd snicker at my attempt at a joke, but his purpose was fixed. "I'm glad I caught you, Charlie, before you go."

"How did you . . . ?"

"I know about you and Bea changing places. It's all in the note Bea left. Listen, there ain't a lot of time. Mama's not doing too good."

"How do you mean?"

"She's just . . . shouting, crying. I never seen her this way."

"About Bea leaving?"

"It's a mix of things. She's finally having it out. At first, when she saw Bea's note, Mama washed her hands of it, saying if Bea wants to be a fool, she won't stop her. But now she's intent on sendin' the sheriff to bring Bea back home."

"No, Cobber. We can't get the sheriff involved. Bea has to do this."

"Mama keeps saying, 'She's all alone, she's all alone.'"

"Bea can handle herself."

"That's what I said, but Mama won't have it."

"Listen, Bea has a ride into Carson City. I'm headed up there too. Tell your Mama that I'll make sure she's in good company. Would that ease her mind?"

Cobber ignored my suggestion and embarked on a whole new problem. "The other thing is she's selling everything we own. She's having a sale today and says she'll only keep what we can fit in a wagon. Nothing's safe! Not even Bea's books. I rescued this one."

He held up a hefty thing that had been tucked under his arm. It didn't take a scholar to know which one. Dante. The one she loved best.

"Take it," he said.

I accepted the book as graciously as I could, though I didn't much want to be lugging that cumbersome thing around. My packs were chock-full already.

"You love her, right?" he said.

A grunt-cough fled my lungs, spoiling all sense of coolness.

"It's OK. You needn't be embarrassed. I won't tell anyone."

I stammered to dispute his claim. "Cobber, I—"

"Well, if I loved somebody," he continued, "then I'd try to understand her better. You know, read the books she reads and such. To her, this book is the crème de la crème, so if you read it, then the two of you could, I don't know, be bound by the poetry of Dante."

My mouth came to a full stop. I shifted my weight, mulling over what he said. Now I knew what Bea meant by calling him the Wise Philosopher. Where did all of this come from? And where in damnation did he get the idea that I loved Bea? I kept my feelings for her so buried, I hardly recognized them myself some days.

He gave a sigh, like he'd said his piece and could rest now.

"Crème de la crème?" I questioned. To that, he smiled. "Cobber, I think you've got the makings of a true romantic. Try not to break too many hearts." I gave his hair a tousle and forced the book into my saddlebag. "Your mama will be alright. When she calms down—and she will—you comfort her and tell her Bea's gonna be just fine."

"How do you know?"

"Because she was made for this."

He waved me off. All the while, I wondered how in this troublesome world I just got bested by an eleven-year-old.

CHAPTER 13

Charlie Rye

Monday, April 2, 1860, afternoon

CARSON City stood about a mile in the distance with wide-open arms. My chest puffed out like a bellows, ready to take on whatever this blessed day would bring. I dropped down from Dandy to put on my disguise, trading out my sweaty shirt for one with a high collar and cravat. On top of it, I put a gentleman's coat. I added spectacles and a tall hat. Boy, that charity bin I snatched these from didn't see me coming.

My new identity would be Professor Charles Vincent. Vincent, after all, was my middle name and I never had much use for it. Getting the fake moustache to stick was the trickiest part. Alas, a bit of pine gum did the trick. I took a deep breath. Time to spread my wings.

Downtown burst at the seams with folks, wagons, and shops. Whatever conveniences Victory Hills had, Carson City had more. Why, just a trot through town boasted three saloons, two gun shops, and more clothiers than I could imagine, selling hats and boots and everything in between.

I hitched Dandy up to a post and took a free-and-easy stroll through town. Two respectable ladies promenaded past me with arms linked. The prettiest of them wore a white dress speckled with red rosebuds. They smiled my way and paused in front of the hat shop. "Oh, pardon me," I said, realizing they waited for me, a gentleman, to open the door for them.

Sorely absent from my hip was a gun, so the gun shop would be my next stop. I browsed at a leisurely pace and decided upon an 1849 Colt Pocket Revolver. Best part was, the merchant took a trade: my leather fringe outfit for the gun plus two dollars, which gave me extra cash for lodging.

The Higby Hotel touted "low, low rates," so I ambled inside to inquire. On my way in, I passed by a stranger whose eyes followed me keenly. I grimaced at him. He did the same back. I chuckled, realizing it was no stranger, but a mirror. If I couldn't recognize myself, then my disguise must've been tolerable.

"Two night's stay, sir," I told the man behind the desk.

He glanced up from his ledgers, took a hard look at me, and said, "That'll be four dollars."

"Says here it's a dollar a night." I pointed to the sign on the desk, right there in plain sight.

"Rates are double this week," he said, eyeing me like I was a weasel in the garden.

This again, I thought. He could see I was Indian and would treat me according to his ignorance. I'd learned to temper my wrath, keep my fists to myself, and instead, dish out the unexpected.

"Outside, it says you've got low, low rates. Maybe just one *low* would do. Unless, of course, you're referring to the staff. In that case, definitely two *lows* are in order."

He leaned forward. "How many *lows* would it take to get you the hell outta my hotel?"

I couldn't let him have the last word. "Just one, actually. One *low* goes a long way in a dump like this."

On his chalkboard outside, I rubbed out a couple letters to make it read, "low, low rat."

Laws, now I'd need to find another place. I sauntered along until reaching the center of town. Another hotel appeared across the road from an establishment called Jolly Spirits Gambling House.

Well, well. Where God closes a door . . .

The innkeeper, a woman, gave me no trouble, and in fact, seemed pleased to have a gentleman staying at her place.

"There's fresh water in the basin upstairs." She smiled. "Well, mostly fresh."

"Mighty kind of you, ma'am." I made my way upstairs. The room may've been tiny, but it still boasted fineries I'd never called my own. White lace curtains covered the window. The bed's counterpane smelled a little musty, but no matter. Wedged between the bed and wall was a small nightstand with a kerosene lamp resting on a doily. With the slightest turn of its key, the lamp produced light at my command. *One dollar a night will get you all this,* I marveled.

As the innkeeper promised, a pitcher and washbasin sat on the windowsill, so I pushed the curtains aside to give my hands a wash. From there, I had a perfect view of Jolly Spirits. As I whistled and scrubbed, merrily awaiting a game of cards, I glanced up to a sight that gave me a start.

I narrowed my eyes for a better look at the man. *Well, cuss me.* I stepped behind the lace curtain. That cream-colored suit and coonskin cap were his hallmarks. He swung down from his horse onto those gangly legs, unhooked his cane, and used it to help him into the saloon.

Curses! A perfectly good night ruined! Perhaps my whole stay in Carson City. The whole reason I came here was to hide—and the man I most wanted to avoid showed up here. Did he follow me? Did he find out about Bea taking my place and now he'd come to give me a reckoning?

A minute later, Torrence reappeared outside, like he didn't find what he wanted inside. He took a gander right, left, and at his pocket watch—maybe late for some rendezvous. In time, a short man with a skinny build, wearing a gray suit, edged up next to him. They spoke a few minutes, gesturing here and there.

Torrence drew something out of his pocket and handed it to the other man, who secured it in his waistcoat. The small feller went back inside the saloon. Torrence, however, glanced up at the window. I ducked, unsure whether he saw me or not. I'd have to stay holed up in here until he was gone.

I settled down on the creaky bed and, with nothing else do to, cracked open Bea's book, *Divine Comedy*. If I was going to read poetry, it might as well be funny. Well, I didn't see no humor in the first few pages. In fact, I finished all of what was called Canto I without a single joke being told. Sakes alive! A man alone in a gloomy wood? A bitterness not far from death? Who could laugh at that? I snapped the book shut with a rising suspicion that the word *comedy* meant something besides funny.

Hours came and went with me stirring crazy. I needed to get out and play some cards. They called to me like stray kittens mewing outside the door. I glanced out the window. Torrence's horse was gone. Still, I couldn't be too careful. He could be around any corner.

That rendezvous between Torrence and that skinny feller—it made me think maybe his visit had nothing to do with me after all. I could wander over to the saloon and probably be OK. I checked the cracked mirror. My moustache needed a touch more pine gum. I donned the spectacles and tall hat and headed out the door as Professor Charles Vincent.

A shop owner lit a streetlamp as I passed. Nightlife was just beginning. Outside Jolly Spirits hung a sign: "Must be 18 years or older to play." I stretched myself tall and waltzed through the double doors like the king of my own castle. *Two years shy ain't bad.*

The place was packed, wall to wall. In that thick and humid air, a body could've got drunk off the exhales alone. A man sat hunched over a piano, his fingers racing over the keys. In all that sea of heads, however, that coonskin cap was nowhere to be seen.

One look at that faro table and my pulse quickened. Carson City was going to pay out big. The prickles on my neck told me so.

Two ladies weaved through the crowd, the same ones from the hat shop. They watched the game casually. What were they doing here? Proper ladies weren't allowed in saloons, so as to not sully their reputations. Then again, maybe that was another absurd notion from my backward town of

Victory Hills. The rules must've been different in Carson City and maybe a lady could go anyplace she wanted.

A vacant chair opened at the faro table, and I took it. I was anonymous no longer. I played my first bet on my lucky number nine and won. As the night progressed, my earnings were scant, but enough to keep me playing.

As the clock struck nine, I entered a supernatural stroke of luck, winning several rounds in a row. On the whole, I wasn't superstitious, only when it came to cards. I'd come to learn that my winning streaks only lasted one hour. If I could win this last game before the clock struck ten, then it would pay out big.

Three other men sat at the faro table. One gentleman, surly and greasy-haired, must've been desperate, because he pulled out a silver snuffbox the size of his palm and set it in front of him. A fancy bee was engraved on the lid. Imagine the luck! My eye was keen on it.

"How many chips can I get for this trinket?" the man asked the dealer.

The dealer shrugged. "Ten."

"Pish! I paid a hundred dollars for it."

"Back when you wasn't so down on your luck," the dealer scoffed.

"I'll play you for it," I said. "Winner of the next round takes it. I win, I get that box. You win and you take my chips."

A gleeful expression replaced all surliness, and he gave a nod. The crowd took notice and gathered around. The last bet of this round was upon us. Time to guess the order of the final three cards to be flipped over by the dealer. My luck was always best when I didn't overthink it. "Three, king, eight," I said.

The man took another swig of his whiskey and guessed the reverse. "Eight, king, three."

The clock was two minutes shy of ten. *I gotta stop being so superstitious,* I told myself. Everything rode on this bet. If I lost this one, I'd lose everything.

The dealer flipped the cards: "Three, king, eight,"

Cheering erupted. I knew it! I knew Carson City would pay me well. I collected my chips and that silver snuffbox and surveyed the treasure before me.

Some fellers heckled the other guy, saying, "Explain that one to your wife."

With no warning at all, a woman planted herself on my lap. The lady in the rosebud dress! Back home, I'd seen ladies give attention to big winners, but I never imagined it happening to me. She came close to my ear and whispered, "I can think of a hundred ways to spend that money. All on me, of course."

My own stupidity struck me on the head. Yessir, I was easier to fleece than a baby lamb. The rosebud fabric had fooled me. I swallowed. This was no highborn, respectable woman on my lap. She was a—how to say it?—woman of the night. A soiled dove. A painted lady. Her lips were deep red like chokecherries, and she smelled of evening primrose.

"Hello, Miss Rosebud," I said, my voice cracking like a shattered music box.

She drew back her head with a quizzical stare, maybe reacting to the name I'd just invented for her, but more likely suspicious of me. She inspected my face, removing my spectacles. "Are you old enough to play here?"

I didn't answer right away, fearing my voice would betray me again. She replaced my spectacles and touched my fake moustache. "Who are you hiding from?"

"This is the biggest win I ever had," I spoke low. "Just let me enjoy it a minute longer."

"Give me that silver snuffbox, and I'll do whatever you like."

"Not a chance," I said, offended that she'd want to keep my excellent prize for herself. I gave my answer too fast. I should've weighed her experience to my lack of it and realized I was no match.

"Suit yourself." Offering a coquettish look, she flailed to the ground with a high-pitched "OH!" acting as if I'd pushed her.

A gang of men surrounded me—had me by the arms. They grappled me to the ground and threw punches from every direction. Some of them struck. My hat got knocked off, and I knew I'd never see it again, not in one piece.

"She fell!" I kept saying, but nobody listened. A man swiped my Colt revolver right out of its holster and fired a couple wayward shots. The men helped Rosebud to her feet. I caught glimpses of fleeting images as the men hauled me toward the door. The gray-suited man, the one I'd seen with Torrence, sat at the bar, calmly downing his whiskey.

The men tossed me out. I rolled down the steps, hitting every one on the way down. I stood up, dusted myself off, and pressed my hand to an empty holster.

As I recovered my breath, trying to figure out what in blazes just happened, the man in the gray suit appeared. His movements were quick and shifty, like a rat. "Hey there. You gonna let her do that?"

I straightened my coat and cravat and tested out my jaw that just got smacked.

"Don't ya see what happened?" he said, peering up at me from his small frame. "That little hussy was part of the scheme."

"What scheme?"

"To get money outta you. It goes like this: you win the game, she gets you thrown out, your winnings get left on the table and into their pockets. Get the picture?"

I gave a whistle of defeat. "Are all the saloons here like that?"

"Enough that you need to keep your wits about you. This saloon is worse than the others, and I been waiting to catch 'em at their game. Now that I've got you as a witness, we can take it to the sheriff."

"I appreciate your concern, but I'll be on my way. My pride's been wounded. Let's leave it at that, shall we?"

"Have it your way, but you better take this." He lifted my gun out from being tucked into his trousers and held it out to me. In that brief second with his arm extended, the cuff of his sleeve pulled back and revealed a black-ink symbol on his wrist.

"Thank you, kindly. How'd you get it?"

"I have ways of showing loyalty for those who show it back."

Loyalty? I thought. I hadn't known him five minutes. Why was he helping me? What did he want? Before I could take a breath to ask some questions, he jumped in with his own.

"What type of work do you find yourself in?"

"Professor of literature," I answered, eager to flaunt my make-believe smarts.

"Impressive! Is that a lucrative business in this day and age?"

Strangers didn't often discuss money. What could he be driving at? Would he break into my hotel room and rob me blind?

"Just enough to keep up my gambling habits," I said.

He laughed. "I hear you there! You seem young for a professor. You got a family at home?"

His questions had a purpose, for certain, but I couldn't say what. "No family yet," I said. He nodded as though this were just the information he wanted to hear. I added, "Except for my brother, who's a hired assassin."

He chuckled, not falling for it. The next question baffled me most of all. "What're your political persuasions?"

"Political persuasions?" I said. "I've endured some questions in my time, but this seems like an inquisition."

"Beg your pardon, I only ask because I don't want you to be caught unawares. This town's got a lot of opposing politics, and I'd hate to see you at the mercy of the zealots."

None of this made sense. I needed to figure out what he was up to or cut him loose. "Seems I already been good and duped," I said. "Could I fare any worse?"

"Sorry to say, but, yes, there's all manner of trouble a man like you could find yourself in. I seen many a tenderfoot get taken for all they're worth. I could offer you some help in that regard."

He seemed to wait for an answer, but I didn't have much of one. "Uh . . . I'll trust to my own luck. But thanks, Mr. . . . ?"

"Pascoe," he answered.

"Thank you, Mr. Pascoe. I'll start by steerin' clear of the gambling houses. I bid you good evening," I said, in the way of a true gentleman.

"Evening," he said, extending his arm for a parting handshake. He kept a firm hold, waiting until I got a look at that black ink on his wrist. The figure was a coiled snake with an open mouth and pointed fangs. He must've known I was intrigued.

Pascoe watched me as I crossed the road and went inside the hotel. I felt his eyes on my back. When I got to my room, I didn't light the lamp. The door had no lock, so I moved the bed to block it. When I looked out into the street, the man Pascoe was gone.

Well, if that wasn't the oddest night of my dad-blamed life. I replayed every incident from seeing Torrence out my window to that saloon girl sitting on my lap to this strange Pascoe feller asking me questions. Even odder was the fact that I wasn't too cut up about losing all my winnings. Wasn't it worth all this excitement? The seed of suspicion got planted in me, and I'd never be able to leave it alone until I knew everything, even down to that snake tattoo on Pascoe's arm. I'd find a way to stay in Carson City a few more nights. Me and Bea would have plenty to talk about when I saw her next.

CHAPTER 14

Beatrice Brannon

Thursday, April 5, 1860

AN early morning wind whistled through cracks in the barn like a dismal chorus of harmonicas. I reached for the silver button at my neck and held it tight, picturing the faces of all my loved ones. I also thought of those who had spoken ill of Da, namely Mayor Torrence. *This is why I'm here,* I reminded myself. *I will make this right.*

"Professor! Git some coffee on!" Squires hollered as he beat the barn doors. This morning, like every morning at Buckland's so far, Squires wrenched me from sleep by barking orders. Not that I minded waking up so much. My nightmare still haunted me. The pain of the dream was worse than anything in reality, even being ordered around by Squires.

The eastbound rider would be coming out of California today. If I wanted to end up in Carson City, I'd have to let Jim take this one. My patience at this awful place would be tested further, as I'd need to wait a few more days for the westbound run. Jim wouldn't give me any trouble about it, since he was just as anxious to leave. We were all stirring crazy, yet Jim had the only ticket out of here.

I ignored Squires's demands to make coffee and tacked up one of the horses instead. I spent as much time as possible with the horses and mules. Their company was preferable to any of the humans. Squires would explode at me, I knew, but I couldn't get myself to face the storm.

Turns out, the wind brought with it more than just dust. The distinct sound of galloping hooves drew closer. The Pony Rider! I tugged at the door, and the wind flung it open.

Jim charged from the cabin, buttoning his shirt, shouting through a biscuit lodged in his teeth, "Oscar, get out here and tack the horse!"

Oscar trailed at a tired pace, rubbing his eyes. They both arrived at the barn doors to see Ranger, one of the mustangs, saddled and ready to go. Both their heads turned toward me.

"I figured the Pony would be coming soon, so I tacked him up," I said.

Jim winced at me, borne out of disgust or amazement.

"I'd rather have a thank-you than that scowl," I said.

He gave me a cautious "Thanks."

Jim led Ranger to the point of exchange. Squires stood at the open cabin door with his pocket watch in hand. The eastbound rider galloped toward us, bounding across the plain at a good clip, a trail of dust swirling in his wake. The Pony Express had actually worked, just like Mr. Russell said it would. Here he was, right on schedule.

"Incredible," I said. The vigor stirred my soul watching him ride in, the same feeling as when I'd first heard about the Pony Express. I couldn't wait for my turn.

The rider tugged his pony to a halt, dropped down, and switched the mail pouch to Ranger's back. So that was the infamous mochila: a shiny, tanned-leather saddlebag with four envelope-sized cantinas—two in front and two in back. Squires moved at an easy gait, pulled out a key, and asked the rider which pocket to unlock.

"Back left," he answered. Squires opened it, pulled out the ledger, recorded the time, and locked it back in. Jim swung himself aboard and dug in his spurs with a "yah!" I set aside my dislike for Jim and cheered. Even Squires and Oscar offered cheers as Jim sped away. In that moment, we were united in our cause. With all the chaos behind the scenes, still everything clicked into place at the right moment. We were part of an incredible venture that connected people hundreds of miles apart. Letters to loved ones, valuable missives, and bits of news would reach recipients in a matter of days. It was almost unfathomable. *Charlie would've loved this,* I thought.

The inbound rider lowered his bandanna, coughing madly. I waited for a pause to introduce myself, but he turned and walked toward the creek.

"Where you goin'?" Oscar asked. "What's your name?"

"Water first," he said, nearly choking. His cheeks were pudgy and round like a child's, yet he wore an impressive beard. He couldn't have been much older than me—maybe my same age. He wore a blue military coat, but he looked more pirate than soldier.

Oscar and I followed him into the red willow trees, where he knelt, plunged his face in the water, gulped down mouthfuls, and then flung his head up for air. He walked a few paces, unconcerned with the lack of privacy, opened his trousers, and squirted an arc into the weeds. I had to force nonchalance.

"You gonna tell us your name or what?" Oscar said.

"Jairus." The boy spoke low and quiet. He buttoned up his trousers and held his hand out to me, but I didn't shake it because, well, I'd seen my brothers' hands after they did their necessity.

"Welcome!" I said instead.

Oscar had no problems shaking his hand.

"What's it like out on the trail?" I asked him.

"The first couple miles are heavenly." He mumbled, hardly moving his lips when he spoke. "The next fifty will bleed you dry. Fifty miles of gal-dern alkali dust in your face. You forget your bandanna, you're a dead man."

My elation from his grand entrance fell flat.

"Got any grub or coffee?" he said, making for the cabin.

"Professor here's s'posed to make some coffee," Squires joined in. "But I got a different job for him. Oscar, you're on coffee now."

Oscar didn't groan at the news because he knew Squires always gave me the less desirable jobs. Oscar and Jairus went inside, while I wondered what agony lay in store for me.

Squires gestured me to follow him, which I did. He went behind the cabin where an axe hung. He picked it up and touched the blade, trying to scare me. After a good, phlegmy laugh, he handed it to me. "We need firewood." He pointed toward a copse of piñon pines in the vicinity of the Paiute village. "That's where you'll get 'em."

My stomach felt like a heavy stone dropped inside it. "Why not these?" I asked, motioning toward the red willow trees that grew along the creek at our camp.

"For somebody called Professor, you're none too smart. They're no good for burnin'. We're goin' through 'em too fast. At this rate, we'll spend all our time choppin' trees. Them piñons will keep us warm, and they'll burn slower. No more questions. Off with ya. There's a big cluster—"

"I see 'em." That interruption was my only defiance. With the axe, I went along, resentful, but glad to be rid of him for a short time.

Squires had given me the risky assignment because, to him, I was expendable. If I didn't return, there'd be no search party. Jim, who might've shown half a concern, was gone now, and Oscar was all for getting rid of me.

After a mile-long trek, I reached the designated thicket. The trees' scent was fresh and clean and reminded me of home. There was no foreseeable danger. The Paiute camp was farther away than it appeared from the cabin. I found a good tree with plenty of branches, drew up my axe, and began chipping away at the bark. Working up a considerable sweat, I twisted the last of it free from the trunk and stood back, satisfied with my accomplishment.

A shriek sounded, long and clear. I spun toward the sound. A girl sprinted toward me, arms flailing. She was Paiute. Pushing me aside, she knelt beside the tree, examining the damage. She looked up at me, wild-eyed.

"I'm sorry," I said by instinct, knowing there was a language difference.

She tossed the axe away. A pine cone had fallen from the tree. She picked it up and said, "Tuba-aka." She pointed to her mouth, gestured toward her village and back to the pine cone.

From this, I guessed that the pine nuts from these trees were a source of food for her tribe.

"I'm very sorry. I didn't know."

"Why do you come?" she said, getting eye level to me. I was stunned, not only because she spoke English, but because I had no answer to give. How could I explain that an evil man had sent me out on this errand and that none of this was my fault?

She repeated her question, this time pointing toward the station, and I realized she wasn't asking why I was there chopping trees, but why, as a station, we were there at all. It became my lot to give a feeble explanation.

Nobody else was with her, and it was clear she didn't intend to harm me. This girl was probably close to my age. Maybe I could speak to her in frankness, from one young person to another.

"Let me show you." I knelt and brushed away pebbles and weeds to create a small clearing in the dirt. In that space, I dotted pebbles, in twos, from one side to the other. One pebble in the pair would serve as the station, the other would be the rider. The shiniest pebble would signify the mochila. I set the Pony Express in motion by galloping the shiny pebble coupled with another rock. When it reached the first station, I transferred the shiny one to the next rock and continued galloping to the next, and the next, until it reached the other side. I looked up at her, trying to determine whether she understood my depiction of the Pony Express in stones. "We deliver the mail this way, from one side of the country to the other."

Her arms were crossed. She squatted beside me, peering at my stone display. "Which one is you?"

I tapped an arbitrary stone, wondering where she was going with this. She picked up that stone and hurled it as far as she could.

We met eyes and sustained a few moments of awkward stares. *Well, that backfired,* I thought.

Her stern countenance eased into a smile. Mama always told me that every friendship began with a smile, so I smiled back.

"Numu," she said.

"What is Numu?" I asked.

"Paiute," she answered.

She leaned back and sat on the ground. The roundness of her face contrasted her chiseled, muscular arms. Her hair was wrapped in a spiral of twine down her back, and she wore a deerskin dress with a rabbit-pelt shawl that covered her shoulders.

"I watch your camp," she said. "It's my duty to keep watch."

"We're not here to do any harm," I said. But my line of sight, and hers, was already fixed on the tree. The untruth of my statement couldn't have been plainer.

"Do the men beat you?" she asked. Her fingers lifted my chin to inspect my bruise. "The big, hairy one we call Paggootsoo. It means bison."

I chuckled at the funny coincidence of how I had coupled him with that imagery too. She continued, "The tall one we call Waa'tata'a. Grasshopper."

I took note of how she'd said "we" when discussing our names. Our camp seemed to hold no secrets from them. They were far more familiar with our goings-on than we were of theirs.

"What do you call me?" I asked.

"Paddoo," she answered. "Willow stick."

I smiled, seeing the humor. I supposed it was appropriate. "How did you learn to speak English?"

"I travel with my father for trade. I translate."

"What is your name?"

"I am Tso'apa. Butterfly."

This fierce defender I'd seen moments ago now showed a more butterfly side.

Apologizing for the tree felt inadequate, but I didn't know what else to say. "I'm very sorry about the tree. How can I repay you?"

She shook her head. I supposed she meant there was nothing I could do.

"You go," she said with a sudden urgency.

"Is someone coming?"

She ignored me and pointed to the tree. "Take this."

"But it's yours."

"Take it." The gesture was less for the purpose of goodwill, I thought, and more to remove the evidence of the crime. She added, "*But no more*."

These words could not have cut deeper. "No, of course not," I said, almost whispering.

"The trees are important to us. Sixty years for one to grow. Some live to be hundreds of years. There will be revenge if you take more." Her way of speaking was simple and blunt. The truth stung, but I respected her for telling it.

"I promise this won't happen again. I give you my word."

The slight upturn of her mouth could have been a smile. I smiled back just in case, hoping she understood the depth of my apology. I believed that she did and that she'd keep our interaction a secret. I would too. With that, she was gone.

I dragged the tree corpse and my murder weapon over shrubs and boulders, disturbing anthills and animal burrows on the way back to the cabin. My disgust for Squires grew with every step. The man himself sat upon his favorite stump, chewing on jerky, when I arrived. I laid the piñon at his feet, as well as the axe.

"Just one?" he sneered. "Next time, I'll send you with one of the mules."

I buoyed my courage. "There won't be a next time."

He quit chewing, swallowed, and stood on his massive legs. "That so?"

I couldn't speak, not only out of fear, but also because I didn't want him to know about the Paiute girl or that we'd become friends. His hatred would ruin it, just as it had ruined everything else at that station.

He waltzed around the tree until he stood close to me, his scent powerful like garlic. "Think you can tell me no? Think you can disrespect me?"

I had to say something, even if it was only a mumble. "The trees belong to the Paiutes."

"Come again?"

"The trees belong to the Paiutes," I said louder. "They'll retaliate if we take any more."

He burst into a hateful chuckle. "That right? And how might you know that, *Professor*? Had a run-in with 'em?"

"The trees are guarded around the clock," I mumbled.

He took it in, then said, "If they're guarded, as you say, how is it you got one?"

I swallowed. *No, I won't tell him about my friend.*

"Did you meet that little gal that's been pokin' around here spyin' on us?" he said with a gleeful grin.

Oh, mercy, he knows about her. He's seen her.

"No . . . two men stopped me," I said, "after I'd done too much damage to the tree. They told me to take it, as long as I'd give my word that we wouldn't come back."

His brows furrowed. "How'd you happen to communicate all this?"

"I speak a little bit of Paiute," I said, digging further into this lie. "There's a small village near the place where I live. That's how I learned."

My lies didn't seem to help my cause, for he diverted right back to the topic that interested him most.

"That gal's a quick one. One mornin', I raised my hand to give her a hello and she's halfway gone to Egypt. Tell you what, I'll let you off the hook for your disrespect if you can get her to come talk with me. Just a friendly chat. A man needs companionship, don't he?"

My revulsion couldn't hide itself. My nostrils flared when I breathed. I'd sooner have been turned into a pillar of salt than spend one more second in his presence. I didn't run this time; I walked. His laughter pealed as I got farther away. I stole behind the barn and shook out every limb, my arms prickling like chicken skin.

Squires's laughter was a ruse; he was not joking. He was downright dangerous—the lowest kind of life-form to inhabit the earth. He was *that kind* of man. The kind to force himself on a woman or even a girl. Mama had warned me to steer clear of this kind, yet here I'd wandered into the wolf's den. That night, I slept with a pitchfork at my side and a steadfast determination to keep my secret.

CHAPTER 15

Beatrice Brannon

Wednesday, April 11, 1860

A man had arrived at Buckland's during the night. He'd corralled his horse and was, at this moment, inside with the men. I wondered if he'd be just as hateful as Squires and Oscar. All I knew was that if this coffee wasn't done soon, I'd miss breakfast entirely.

Using a cloth, I picked up the coffee pot by its handle and made my way inside. I much preferred cooking on the open fire. The men hovered around a pot of cornmeal porridge, spooning it into their mouths. I set the pot at the table. "It's late," Squires said, with a mouthful. I ignored him.

The stranger sat apart from the others at his own roughly cut desk that he'd brought with him. He busily scrawled away with a pen and paper when he took notice of me. He rose and, to my surprise, extended his hand. "Pascoe, station manager." When our hands clasped, he diverted his eyes with a nervous tension. Despite his unease, I was willing to give him the benefit of the doubt.

"The men started calling me Professor and it stuck," I said.

His politeness wouldn't last. "So you're the impertinent one they told me about."

I hardly knew what to say. Jairus, the new boy, spoke up, even if it was only a mumble. "It wasn't me who said it."

Squires glared at me while Oscar smiled to himself, both gestures claiming responsibility. It didn't matter what they thought of me, as long as I could have something to eat.

I squeezed my way into the circle and picked up a spoon.

Squires seized my wrist. "I don't think so."

"Why not?"

"I told ya. 'Cause the coffee was late."

"Late for what? Nobody's going anywhere."

"See what I mean?" rasped Squires to the new station manager.

"Even if it's late, you can't starve me," I said.

I'd misspoken. His grin told me he'd enjoy the challenge. He slid the pot away from me.

On cue, my stomach grumbled for all to hear. The men laughed. I left, defeated. Maybe I'd given up too soon, but I wasn't in the mood to fight for basic necessities.

The westbound rider was expected today, and it couldn't be soon enough. As I walked the horses around the corral, Jairus appeared, holding something small wrapped in a cloth. He leaned over on the fence and held it out to me. "It's just hardtack," he said in his low timbre. "Had some in my pack."

"You're a saint." I let go of the ropes and took the gift. I sucked on a corner of the hardtack to loosen it up. "You're aiding the enemy right now. They're sure to punish you for it."

He shrugged. "Ain't right to starve a body."

I wondered why Squires and Oscar left Jairus alone yet gave me such trouble.

After I'd made short work of the hardtack, Jairus climbed over the fence and walked alongside me. "You're taking the ride to Carson, ain't you?"

"Yes," I said. "The sooner the better."

"Then I better wise you up. That's where my brothers are stationed. They're a handful."

"Mercy, don't tell me they're bullies too."

"They are," he mumbled, "but a different kind. Their problem is they've been raised by my father. He's a military man, and he wants us to be military men too, so he treats us like his soldiers. My brothers don't handle it too good, so they act up. They pull pranks and the like."

I sighed. "What kind of pranks?"

"Aw, who knows how their brains come up with 'em. Just be on your guard. Remember that their weakness is my father. They address him as the Colonel. They live in fear of him. Only time they act up is when he ain't there. If you say you're gonna tell the Colonel, they'll straighten up."

"OK. Anything else?"

"Never, under any circumstances, agree to a shooting competition with 'em. They'll skin you alive."

"That's easy," I said. "I have no intentions of competing for anything."

"Well, they may try to trick you into it, just to humiliate you."

"Thanks for the warning," I said. This was far and away the most talkative I'd seen Jairus. He'd acted aloof every time I'd tried to strike up a conversation. In hopes of keeping it going, I said, "What's your mother like?"

"Don't mention it. She's in New York. Has been for a long while now."

"What's she doing there?"

He stared off into some sad place in his memory. "She's a member of a loud-mouthed women's group fightin' for women's suffrage."

"Women suffer plenty, seems to me," I said.

"Don't you know what *suffrage* means? It's the right to vote."

I must've turned red. I blamed my spotty education on living in an isolated town.

"Of course I've heard of it," I mumbled. "I just forgot what it was called."

"Well, she says she'll come back when they have it. Hope she ain't on a fool's errand."

"Are you saying women shouldn't have the right to vote?" I said, honestly wanting to know his opinion. I'd never considered the notion until that moment. Neither men nor women in the territories voted in national elections, not unless they crossed into a state.

"It don't matter what I think," he said. "It's a hopeless cause. Folks in this country are just too bullheaded."

"Maybe," I said, remembering how it had felt to be voted down, all because I was a girl. "But still, what if she feels like she's been called to it? You can't fault her for that, right?"

"I reckon I can," he said in a biting tone.

This signaled me to change the subject. "It sounds like your upbringing has been rather unconventional."

He gave a scoffing chuckle. "That's one way of puttin' it." Then he said something completely out of the blue. "The whole thing's got me afraid of girls."

This made me snicker, but it didn't seem to ruffle him.

"I could never talk like this to a girl," he continued. "I'm determined to be rich so some woman will marry me on account of my money and ignore the fact that I can't look her in the eyes when I'm talkin' to her."

"Talking to girls is nothing. You just ask her about herself and let her take it from there."

"That's all fine and well," he said in his low bumble. "But how do you deal with the armpit sweat?"

Jairus went on this way for minutes on end, educating me on his melancholy views about females and the world at large.

"I suppose nature calls," he said, rising. "Oh, and the Pony Express is comin.'"

I listened closely. Sure enough, hoofbeats sounded from afar off. "It's here. This is my run!"

Jairus helped me tack up a horse, and we took him out to the spot of exchange. Having forgotten my knapsack, I dashed to the barn, clambered up the loft, and swiped it. Jim rode up, alighted, and swung the mochila onto my mustang.

I scurried back, mounted, and was about to charge away when the cabin door burst open, and a loud whistle sounded. My pony got startled, so I tugged back the reins.

Pascoe strode my way, his hands full of papers.

"Get down," he ordered.

"Why?" I asked, hoping he wasn't taking my ride away from me.

"I reckon he needs to record the time," Jairus answered for him. In my eagerness to leave, I'd forgotten. Still, I wasn't sure why I needed to dismount during the process, but I did as he asked.

Using a key he withdrew from his pocket, Pascoe unlocked the cantina that held the ledger, filled in the time, and locked it back up. I readied myself to mount again, but he said, "Excuse me," and kept working. He snagged another key from his pocket, opened a different cantina, and rifled through the letters, removing some and stuffing in some of his own documents. He did the same thing with all the cantinas. Jairus and I shared a questioning glance but remained silent. It was a break in protocol, to be sure, but Pascoe did all this with such ease and none of his usual jitters.

"Pay no mind," he said. "Pony Express business."

Elated that I'd still get to take my ride and ditch this place, I mounted, jabbed my pony's sides, and kissed the air. We tore off with a quick start, and at last, Buckland's station was behind me.

My mustang huffed as steady as a steam locomotive across the dusty landscape. Tufts of green sagebrush and greasewood jutted up for miles. I followed the wagon trail marked by two dirt paths that snaked alongside each other. I could scarcely believe it. I'd actually done it. Here I was, riding for the Pony Express!

The cool wind in my face perfectly balanced the warm sun on my back. An unstoppable current charged every limb. Neither foe nor folly could stop me. A warmth enveloped my soul, as though for one perfect moment I was in the right place at the right time. But how strange, when minutes ago, I'd been oppressed by Squires. Now I was free, and I could ride the wind and conquer the world.

CHAPTER 16

Beatrice Brannon

—

Wednesday, April 11–Thursday, April 12, 1860

STIFF, saddle-sore, and worn-out. That's how I arrived at Carson City home station. Except for short breaks at the relay stations, I'd spent four continuous hours in the saddle. Now I craved rest. I couldn't help but wonder, though, what lunacy would I find at this station?

My dismount was more like a collapse. A man in military dress, who I assumed to be the Colonel, caught me. "You alright, son?" His tone suggested more irritation than concern. Trail etiquette, I began to see, didn't tolerate weakness, not in the smallest degree.

"Never better," I replied, though my unsteady feet and dizziness spoke contrary.

The Colonel unlocked the cantina, recorded my arrival time of 5:15 p.m., and locked it back up. He chucked the mochila on his saddle, ready to ride when I threw in a question. "Is this a military fort?"

His scowl told me that I was eating up precious time. "No, this is a regular relief station."

"So you won't be unlocking the other cantinas and taking things out?"

Since I'd left Buckland's, I'd been trying to figure out why Pascoe had unlocked all the cantinas and done his rifling act. None of the other station managers on my route had done that, but for some reason, I thought they'd do it here. Apparently, not.

"Take things out?" The Colonel must've thought I was delirious, with me tripping over my feet and saying loopy things.

"No, I don't steal from my employer, if that's what you're asking."

"Oh . . ." I faltered, "I didn't mean . . ."

"Private," he summoned one of the boys standing by.

"Yes, sir." The boy's reply was loud and clipped.

"Make sure this greenhorn gets some sleep," the Colonel said. "He could use it."

"Yes, sir."

"Corporal," he called to the other boy.

"Yes, sir."

"No tricks. Understand?"

"Yes, sir. Of course not, sir."

I stared at them, biting my lip. They weren't playing. This was the actual way they spoke to each other, father and sons. Without Jairus's warning, I would've been sure I'd come to the wrong place. They stood at attention as their father kicked off and began his first ride for the Pony Express.

"And there he goes," Private said. "May God grant him a safe journey."

Corporal added, "And keep him detained as long as humanly possible."

They burst into a chuckle, arms draped around each other's shoulders, and watched in glee as their father disappeared.

"Shall I break out the celebratory libations, Corporal?"

"I do believe we've had a successful mission, Private, and a small offering to the libation gods would not be unwelcome."

"How about you, soldier?" Private said to me. "Care to imbibe a little something on behalf of life becoming bearable once again?"

Before I could answer, Corporal cut in, "No, no, no. I got a fifth of Scotch stolen from the finest saloon in town and I ain't wastin' it on some tenderfoot. Oh, and soldier, never stammer in the presence of my father."

They lumbered inside the station, and I stood alone to take in the surroundings of Carson City. Unlike Buckland's, this station was placed in the center of town, plenty of shops and amenities nearby. The prospects looked enticing, not to mention that Charlie may've been there at that very moment. I longed to wander and see the sights, but I could barely stand on my two legs. I'd sleep first and explore later.

The station was built of stone, stacked and mortared, with an enormous wooden door, tall and wide enough for horses to go through. In fact, that was the point. The horses were stalled inside the cabin with the humans, separated by a thin wall. The manure smell didn't bother me; sleeping in the barn at Buckland's had gotten me used to it. Anyway, with an actual bed to sleep in, warmed by a fire, I had no complaints. As the boys got shamelessly drunk, I fell into a sound sleep.

In the morning, the bright sun streamed onto my face. The boys had opened the shutters, welcoming flies and other pests. I sat up and stretched my arms wide.

The boys lounged on the bed opposite me, semiclothed in union suit underwear that sagged like loose bandages. Corporal was the eldest, if height and rank were any indicator, possibly eighteen years old. His appearance mirrored the Colonel's, with dark hair slicked back to the nape of his neck, a full moustache, and a neatly trimmed beard.

"Morning, soldier. Must've been one hell of a ride. It's past ten. To outsleep us on a night like last night, well, that takes some doin'. What's the time on that, Private?"

"Fifteen hours," Private said, his back against the stone wall, lightly strumming a banjo. His beard was long and frizzled, not tidy like his elder brother's. "What's your excuse, soldier?"

"I must've been really behind in my sleep," I said.

"NO EXCUSES!" they both shouted in unison, followed by more snickering.

I could hardly believe I'd slept fifteen hours straight.

"Jairus said things were strict here," I said, "but I had no idea."

"Jairus is a fool," Corporal said.

"And he can't shoot worth a penny," the banjo-wielding boy added, "which makes him a double fool."

"So do you fellers have actual names or just military ranks?" I asked.

"I'm Corporal Abram Riley," the older one said.

"And I'm Private Elias Riley. And you?"

"They called me Professor at the last station."

"Professor! Sounds neat," Corporal Abram said. "You smart or somethin'?"

"Sure am," I said with no hesitation. "You better be on your guard too, 'cause you never know when some clever turn of thought is going to tumble out of me, and you'll be up all night trying to work it out."

"Whoa!" they said, jeering.

"Go ahead, ask me anything." I wasn't afraid of not knowing the answer. I could make up anything that sounded smart, and these boys would believe me.

"Oh, I got one," Abram said. "What color was Washington's white horse?"

Private Elias let out a snort of amusement, then added, "And what year was the War of 1812?"

They slapped each other, doubled over, impressed with their own hilarity.

"The War of 1812," I said, clearing my throat, "was fought between the years of 1812 and 1815. Its primary causes dealt with trade between the United States and Britain. This war is sometimes referred to as the second American Revolution."

Elias began plucking "Yankee Doodle" on his banjo while making a show of his wonderment.

"As for Washington's white horse," I invented, "his name was Lightning, and it was fabled that they lit up the streets when they charged through town."

"Well, if you ain't the smarty-est boy in all the West," Elias said. "I reckon that warrants a song. How's about a welcome song, Professor?" Without any reply from me, Elias strummed a simple two-chord melody and sang:

Professor, Professor, there's nothing he lacks.
He'll take you to task with historical facts.
As far as his brains, there is none to compare,
But you won't find his nose, for it's stuck in the air.

Abram applauded his brother's wit. I smiled good-naturedly. Having a small penchant for rhyming schemes myself, I thought of a ditty of my own and asked Elias to play the refrain again while I sang.

Oh, Abram, Elias, they're never apart.
They're trusty good soldiers, but just kids at heart.
They're silly and sloppy and full of good cheer,
But they'll stand and salute when their papa is near.

Elias's strumming halted, and he glared at me like I was the devil at his door. "You think we're afraid of our pa?"

"I was just playing along," I said.

"I was just playing along," Elias repeated in a snooty tone. "Well, guess what, Professor? You're absolutely right. He makes our blood run cold."

They fell right back into their laughter.

When the sunlight struck Elias just right, I saw a glint of something shiny through the strands of his beard. My hands went to my neck to feel for my silver button. Gone. "Hey, that's mine!"

Elias sat upright. "What's yours?"

"That silver button. You stole it right off my neck."

"I did nothin' of the sort! I found this outside in the dirt. Abram can attest to it."

Abram nodded vigorously in defense of his brother.

"Well, if you didn't steal it, you'll have no trouble giving it back to me, now that you know it's mine."

Elias's forehead creased, as though I'd handed him a real dilemma. He reached back to untie the twine when Abram said, "Hold up now! How do we know this kid's tellin' the truth? There's a lot of folks who wouldn't hesitate to get their hands on a real silver button."

"It's merely silver-plated," I reasoned. "Pretty much worthless in the real world. I keep it for sentimental reasons—a good-luck charm, if you must know."

"Did your sweetheart from back home give it to you?" Abram scoffed.

"Come again?" I said.

"You know," Abram said, cultivating a spiteful grin, "maybe it's from Bea."

I swallowed and felt the very temperature of my head rise at least three degrees.

"Look at that flush!" Elias said. "Ruddy as a radish."

"Oh, we're onto something," Abram said. "And we ain't giving up till we hear it all."

"There's nothing to hear," I said, trying my best to maintain my cover. At least they still referred to me as *he*.

"Don't try to pull the wool over us. We been trained in the ways of warfare and espionage," Abram said.

"We know about a girl named Bea who weaseled her way into the Pony Express," Elias said, "and that you're gonna meet her here in town."

My mind jumped from source to source of where they might've heard this. Had Mayor Torrence sent out a notice? Had Mama come looking for me?

"For a smart feller," Elias said, "you could work on your spelling a bit. Even *we* know how to spell the word *friend*."

My eyes flitted toward my knapsack on the floor, where the strap had been loosened. They'd tampered with it. I released a tense chuckle. Mayor Torrence wasn't after me. Abram and Elias had read my note from Charlie. Dense as they were, they thought *I* had written it. They didn't suspect *me* of being Bea, even though the note was in my possession. Still, I had to contain this.

"Listen, fellers, you got me. I have a girl back home named Bea, alright? And I wrote her that note, but I haven't got the guts to send it to her."

"I knew it!" Abram exclaimed. Both rose to their feet and danced in circles, linking arms. The most loathsome behavior came when they hounded me with an onslaught of sordid questions about this girl of mine and what her physical features consisted of, during which I remained silent. They must've still believed I was a boy or they wouldn't have spoken to me that way.

I got out of bed, picked up my knapsack, and said, in the most boyish way possible, "Alright, fellers, I can overlook the fact that you were rummaging through my personal effects if you'll kindly return the button and the note." I held out my hand to receive them, knowing all the while it wouldn't be that easy.

"I'm afraid it might cost you," Abram said.

I closed my eyes and sighed deeply, weary of being teased, disrespected, and bullied everyplace I went. The degree was lesser here than at Buckland's, but still a far cry from being among friends.

Abram drew the note from the access hatch of his union suit. I tried not to appear aghast that he'd kept it in *that place*. "I'm just saying," he said, "the *Gold & Silver Gazette* was lookin' for good stories, that's all."

"The *Gold & Silver Gazette?*"

"One of the newspapers here in town. They was askin' if we had any good material. Newspapers love a good conspiracy. Who's this Bea character, anyhow? Where could she be hiding in the Pony Express?"

"It could be a weekly column!" Elias piped in. "We could invent other letters to go with it. Think of what they'd pay for that! We'd call it 'To Bea or Not to Bea.' Get it?"

I needed to shut this down quick. "That's a fine little play on words, Elias, but I really don't think it's a good idea."

"Why not?"

"Well, because . . ." I stalled, trying to invent a worthy excuse. But the truth, I supposed, was worthy enough. "Bea would suffer for it, that's why not. Her family's buried in debts, and she's just trying to help 'em out. Her disguise was the only way she could do it. You wouldn't be so heartless as to expose her, would you?"

"This wouldn't exactly expose her," Elias said. "We wouldn't say which station she's at. By the by, which station *is* she at?"

"I don't know," I said, scratching a sudden itch on my head.

"Not to worry," Abram said. "We'd wanna keep her a secret too. If there's no mystery, there's no article."

Pacing the floor became necessary. "Alright, how do I get it back?"

They grinned at each other, and Abram said, "How good a shot are you?"

And there it was. The proposition, just like Jairus had warned.

"Decent, but a bit rusty," I said. "What does this have to do with my note and my button?"

"Well, how about a friendly contest?" Abram suggested.

"Are you saying I have to win *my own things* back?"

Elias tapped the side of the banjo, as if drumming up a response. "Yep, I reckon that's it."

Abram added, "And the promise that we won't sell the story to the *Gazette*."

"Well, if you do that," I tried to scheme, "I might just have to mention the stolen libations to the Colonel. I don't think he'd think too fondly of that. Looks like we're at an impasse."

"We ain't at no impasse," Abram said.

"What's an impasse?" Elias mumbled but was ignored.

"First off, you got no proof," Abram said.

"Hey, that's a good pun—proof." Elias chuckled to himself, never far from a joke regarding alcohol.

"Second off, the Colonel is miles away and ain't expected back for several days."

"And when he does come back," the younger added, "the story will already be sold."

They had me good. As Charlie would've put it, they "held all the cards." I sat down to collect myself, drumming my fingers. Jairus had warned me about this, and I'd had every intention of heeding it. But that was before they'd gotten possession of my things—and my story. A skewed version of it, anyway. Enough to get me found out.

I stood wearily, resigned. "Alright, I'll compete."

Both of them nodded, satisfied, possibly even gleeful.

"On one condition," I said. "I'll need to practice beforehand."

"Sure, we'll give you that," Abram said.

"And seeing as I have no firearm, I'll need to borrow one from you. I'd prefer to practice with the same one I use."

"All reasonable requests," Abram said, pleased. "Let's have it Sunday."

"Why Sunday?" I asked, suspicious of any motive.

"Ease up," Abram said. "Sunday's the slowest day around here. Most shops are closed and there's nothin' else to do. Let's say . . . high noon."

Elias stood, fiddling with *my* silver button between his fingers. Then we all shook on it, Jairus's warning fresh in my ears.

I had so very much to tell Charlie. Finding him became of paramount importance.

CHAPTER 17

Beatrice Brannon

Thursday, April 12, 1860

As I sauntered out onto Carson Street in search of Charlie, both my boots flapped open wide in front like frog mouths. I hadn't noticed how worn they'd gotten. I couldn't compete in these. My confidence waned just looking at them. Maybe Charlie would lend me his boots, just for the competition. All signs pointed to the fact that I'd gotten myself into a predicament, but it was too late to back out now. He might heckle me for it, but it didn't matter. I'd welcome the jeers if only to see his friendly face.

Saloons and gambling houses—I'd start there. The first one I noticed was called Jolly Spirits. I stood outside the door, ready to cross a boundary I'd never crossed. I pushed the door open and walked the circumference of the room. Not much activity at this time of day, nor very eventful. The barkeep glanced my way but didn't challenge my being there.

A hotel across the street would be my next guess. I took a walk through the lobby and didn't see him. I strolled in and out of shops, becoming more doubtful as the morning wore on. Perhaps Charlie never made it here. Could somebody have stopped him? Discovered our secret?

The sign above the nearest door read Tucker's Printing. Through the window, I saw a woman, whose back was to me, operating the printing machinery with all the ease of a bird in flight. *What a fine thing for a woman to engage in,* I thought. Normally, such work was done by men.

The gritty smell of fresh ink emanated from the door, just like at Old Man Hobbs's shop, giving me the smallest inkling of home. A bell chimed as I stepped inside. The young woman turned around to fetch something, and we caught glances.

"Good day to you, young man," she said. "The morning edition won't be ready for another hour, I'm afraid."

Still I said nothing, unsure of why I'd come in.

"Young man, are you OK? Haven't you ever seen a Negro woman running her own shop?"

In fact, I hadn't, but I didn't want to say so. "Good day," I said, curtsying, then inwardly chiding myself, forgetful of the role I was playing.

"Come here." She motioned, seemingly amused by my strange behavior. Her spectacles rested low on her nose, and her hair was parted in the middle and pulled back into a bun. She wore a dress of clover green with the sleeves rolled up to her elbows and an ink-stained pinafore.

I went to her and took hold of a lever, which she instructed me to pull. The lever stamped the contraption down onto a large sheet of paper. She used a different handle to roll out the frame. She told me to reverse the lever, which I did, after which she lifted the frame and peeled the paper slowly off the press. The newspaper title loomed large: *Statesman & Sentry*, and the first story was titled, "Easter Sunbay Brawl."

"Fie on it!" She set her spectacles up to her eyes. "I used the lowercase *b* instead of the *d* in *Sunday*. One could go cuckoo trying to get all the letters right. I hate to waste paper, but it'll have to be redone. You get your fingers going fast. Sometimes your brain just doesn't keep up."

The young woman sifted through a small drawer and pulled out a small piece of metal. "There you are, little rascal." She plucked out the erroneous letter and set in the right one. "Folks always say, 'Mind your p's and q's,' but it's the lowercase *b*'s and *d*'s that get me every time. A lesser professional would let it go, but am I one of those?"

I shook my head.

She smiled and took a closer look at me. "You're not a Carsonite, are you? What's your business here?"

"I . . . ride for the Pony Express," I said, shrinking a little, always wondering whether folks could see right through me.

"Ah! One of our illustrious American heroes, no less gallant than General Washington crossing the Delaware." She spoke with an air of sophistication tinged with sarcasm, and her dimpled smile was engaging and approachable. "Fortuity at its best! Why, only a fortnight ago, I thought up the idea to write a story about you young riders, and then one happens to stumble into my shop like the ass-headed Nick Bottom."

Bereft of words was I at this young woman, maybe twenty years old, referencing salty Shakespeare and running her own shop. And I wasn't certain, but she might've thrown in an insult as well.

"You run all this equipment?" I took a gander at all the wrought iron machinery, more than Mr. Hobbs had by far.

"That's the easy part. The trick is drumming up material folks want to read—original, fresh, salacious enough, but doesn't cross a line—and there's something to be said for a writer-reporter to maintain some semblance of integrity."

"A writer-reporter-printer," I mused aloud, "and a woman too."

She pointed to some fine print on the defective copy. "See there. Mabel Tucker, Editor."

I noticed another name above hers: Benjamin Tucker, Managing Editor. "Who's this?"

"My father—decidedly the finest man alive."

Here was something besides Shakespeare we had in common: she thought the world of her father.

She gasped as though remembering something unpleasant. "Oh, dear! Tell me you haven't promised your story to the *Gold & Silver Gazette*."

"No," I said.

"Good. You'd regret it. Slanderers! Well, that's another matter. Alright, I'll pencil you in. I'm busy today. Shall we say next week?"

"Certainly . . . if I'm here. I'm at the mercy of the mail."

"'At the mercy of the mail,'" she repeated. "I can use that. What's your name?"

"It's more of a handle. They call me Professor."

"My, my! Brains and bravery?"

I gave a wry smile. "I'm questioning both of those things about myself at the moment."

She laughed and made her hands busy again, smoothing out another blank paper on the contraption.

"May I take a look around?"

"Please." She nodded.

"I imagine you're fairly busy these days, with all the politics," I said, waltzing through the shop, pausing at trays of tiny metal letters and examining printed materials draped over rods attached to the ceiling.

"Indeed. Folks can't help but feel something brewing." She then paused before offering an oration, possibly the words of another. "It is not light that we need, but fire; it is not the gentle shower, but thunder. We need the storm, the whirlwind, and the earthquake."

The words hummed along the neck of my spine. "Who said that?"

"Frederick Douglass," she said. And though she'd answered my question, she seemed to speak mostly to herself. "There is awesome power in the printed word. The responsibility can be overwhelming."

I lingered at a table stacked with current issues of newspapers and magazines from around the country. One called *Harper's Weekly* caught my attention, upon which a man with deep-set eyes and prominent cheekbones graced the front page. Mabel noticed what had drawn me in and said, "That's Abe Lincoln. Have you heard of him?"

"Yes," I said, remembering vaguely the conversation I'd overheard at the saloon. "He's a rising politician." Mayor Torrence had been quick to discredit this man, yet here he was on the cover of a magazine.

"When the time's right, we'll endorse a presidential candidate. I've got a close watch on this Lincoln."

"I thought newspapers were supposed to remain neutral."

She chuckled. "Tell that to the *Gold & Silver Gazette*. They're about as Southern-leaning as they come. All their articles are about expanding slavery into the West and seceding from the Union and all this. There isn't a neutral hair on any of their heads."

"So your paper must be Northern," I said.

"Well, yes, if it must be something. The North doesn't want slavery and they don't want to return slaves who escape."

"Is our country going to war?" I asked.

"That's the big question. Tensions are simmering, to be sure." Mabel tapped the paper. "Lincoln here says, 'A house divided against itself cannot stand.' Then what's a young nation to do? Should America go to war if it means keeping the Union together?"

"War is a necessary evil," I parroted back a phrase I'd heard Da say.

"Do you think slavery should be abolished?" she pressed further.

"Of course. Folks should be paid for a job well done."

Something I said was not quite right. She yanked off her spectacles and placed them on her work desk. "You think that's what slavery is? A lack of wages?"

I opened my mouth to defend my puny argument, but something told me she was about to set me straight.

"Do you know how Negroes are treated out on the plantations? Atrocity would be an understatement. They have no rights, no voice, no self. They belong to the masters they're forced to serve—bought, sold, and traded like cattle. Slavery makes them property. Have you ever wondered what it would be like not to own your own life? Now I ask you, if the

Constitution says that 'all men are created equal,' how can slavery then exist?"

Being ignorant in the political affairs of the day was a far worse humiliation than wearing worn-out boots on my feet.

"Surely you've heard of Stowe's book," she continued. "It's fiction by a white woman, but a sympathetic view about the crimes against my people."

My blank stare told her I knew nothing of Stowe's book. Now I was truly sick. Being ignorant in politics was one thing, but in literature, my shortcoming was unbearable.

"Harriet Beecher Stowe," she clarified. "*Uncle Tom's Cabin.*"

"I've read Shakespeare and Milton and Dante," I said, dropping all the literary names at my fingertips. "But, regrettably, never Stowe. You wouldn't have a copy I could borrow, would you? I so love to read—and to be informed."

"Sorry, boy, my copy's signed by the author herself. I couldn't possibly let it out of my keep. Besides, where would you put it, riding for the Pony Express? You'd get it all . . . dusty."

"True," I said, not bothering to tell her the immaculate treatment my books received.

"Well, it's not too late," she said.

"For what?"

"To become an abolitionist," she said in a reverent whisper. "It's a dangerous business standing up for what's right. Why, folks who disagree get bricks thrown at them, spat upon, their establishments burned to the ground. But no matter. If one can't stand on a principle, then one needn't stand at all."

"I couldn't agree more," I said. "I'd love to become an abolitionist. How do I . . . make it official?"

"It starts in here," she whispered, pressing a hand over her heart. "And then, be willing to speak up when the occasion warrants. You'll know when the time is right."

I nodded, feeling conviction enter my heart. I had swum in safe waters too long, saying only things that pleased others. Time to leave the shoal. Dante, for one, had a fierce reckoning for all those locked in the vestibule of hell, owning up to nothing, standing for nothing, speaking out against nothing. It was one of the most tragic sins of all in his *Inferno*, as far as I was concerned. My ignorance, I decided, would no longer suit me.

Mabel lowered her voice, saying, "Might I put a question to you that requires some discretion?"

My answer must've been evident in my eyes that failed to blink.

"In your travels, have you ever come upon this?" She picked up a pen and dipped it in her inkwell. On a scrap of paper, she drew a sideways *V*, which became the mouth of a serpent with fangs. Its body coiled downward into a P-shape.

"No," I answered. "What is it?"

"Never mind, I shouldn't have said anything."

"Where did you see it? You've got me more than a little curious."

"Truly, I best not say another word, for your safety and mine."

Getting the first part of a secret, but not the second was the worst kind of punishment. "If I come across this symbol, what should I do?"

"The only thing I can tell you is to be vigilant. Whoever is behind this symbol is unquestionably no friend of mine."

My thoughts turned to the ink stain on Hobbs's shop floor. Could it have been the same one? I dismissed this thought almost instantly. What were the odds that the same person who'd harassed poor Hobbs would harass this woman too? Victory Hills seemed eons away.

The chime rang, and the door opened. A stream of people shuffled in and offered greetings. "Morning, Miss Mabel," they said in turn.

"Good morning," she replied. "Father's upstairs preparing his message. I'll be up shortly."

The first person to enter was a young woman, Black like Mabel, cuddling an infant to her chest. A man, presumably her husband, was close behind, with a tender hand on the woman's back. An elderly couple followed, white and probably of considerable wealth, trimmed in fine luxuries. In all, about twenty-five people entered and proceeded upstairs. Such a diverse group of individuals I had never seen before in one place. Even some young people my age were there.

"Well, I'm sure you've got Pony Express matters to tend to," she said, attempting to scoot me along. "Keep reading, Professor. It'll only do you good. Why, one day, you may come across William Wells Brown and your world will be forever changed."

"I hope so," I said.

"Say," she said, lowering her gaze to my feet, "couldn't the Pony Express scare up a decent pair of boots for you?"

I exhaled, laughing. "I came with what I had."

"Shame to have one of our celebrated American heroes in such a pitiful pair of boots."

I stared down at them, my stockinged toes peeping through. "Maybe they're symbolic," I said, coming to a new realization.

"How so?"

"If I'm counted among the heroes, as you say, then a proper pair of boots would never do. Were not the feet of Washington's men shod thus pitifully as they crossed the icy river that December night? What greatness was ever achieved in a strapping pair of boots?"

Mabel nodded slowly, pondering my words. "I like a debate that stretches my ideals, and I can appreciate your logic," she said. "Although I wonder . . . what kind of boots did Washington himself wear? I bet they were strapping."

"Well, I'm no Washington."

"Not Washington?" She mused. "Perhaps more of a newcomer . . . Lafayette?"

"Definitely Lafayette," I nodded.

We held the silence for a spell before bursting into laughter. This easy conversation almost made me forget my false identity.

Her attention was drawn out the window. "Lord-a-mercy, what are those CBBs up to now?"

Outside, Abram and Elias marched like toy soldiers, toting guns down Main Street.

"Those are the Riley boys, aren't they?" I said, wondering what she meant by CBBs.

"Yes, it stands for Cold-Blooded Boys. Folks call them that 'cause they're mighty good shooters. They could shoot the stinger off a mosquito. A rowdy pair, to be sure. Don't tell me you're bunked with those ruffians."

I gave a nervous smile and nodded.

"Then I must warn you not to go up against them in a shooting contest. They're always trying to hoodwink some greenhorn . . ." Her words faded once she noticed my petrified face. She clicked her tongue. "My, my, Lafayette! We are a newcomer, aren't we? Did you bet any money?"

"No, only a few trinkets," I said to simplify the matter.

"Good. When does this take place?"

"Sunday at noon."

"Oooh!" she said, as though taking a hit.

"They chose the time. Is it a bad one?"

"That's when everybody's letting out of church, and they'll get their biggest audience."

"Audience?" I swallowed. "They're going to humiliate me in front of the whole town, aren't they?"

"Well, there's always the chance they're liquored up," she said to comfort me, but added, "No, even then I'm afraid you're doomed."

"I can't cancel now. We already shook on it."

"Cancelling's out of the question. You're right about that," she said, "but maybe we could use this to our advantage."

"We?"

"The abolitionists," she said, "the folks who went upstairs."

"What do the abolitionists have to do with a shooting contest?"

"Oh, for heaven's sake, come with me." She seized my hand and flung both of us up the stairs.

The abolitionists sat on benches, chatting, when Mabel broke in. "Father, might I take a moment?"

"Of course. Who is this young man?" Mr. Tucker wore a long coat that emphasized his towering height. A white cravat plumed out of the coat, and he held an open Bible in his hands. He had the exact same set of dimples as his daughter. By this time, the small crowd had hushed to hear my introduction.

"As you know, Mabel," Mr. Tucker said, "only abolitionists are allowed up here."

"I know, Father. He's new to our ranks."

A delighted gasp fluttered though the group.

"I see," Mr. Tucker said, extending his hand to me. "It's always a pleasure to see a young person take an active part in the political affairs of the day."

I shook his hand and nodded.

"My dear friends," Mabel said, addressing the group, "I'll get right to the point. This boy is soon to go up against the CBBs."

Another gasp arose, this time with disapproval.

"That's right, he unwittingly waltzed into their trap. Let us help him rise to the occasion. Everyone'll be cheering for the CBBs. He'll need some folks cheering for him. Can't that be us?"

The room filled with sentiments such as, "It can," "Aye," and "Hear, hear."

"Those sneaky boys scheduled the contest for Sunday at noon," she continued.

They all groaned, as if the notion were so predictable.

"The only problem I see is the boots," she said. "Look at those boots. They're barely staying on his feet."

"Bless me," Mr. Tucker said, "those things look like a pair of crusty old dinner rolls. Surely we can do better than that."

"That's exactly my thinking, Father. But where in the world would we get such finery?"

Everyone's eyes fell upon the wealthy couple, the man wearing a sleek pair of black leather boots with a fold just below the knee. "I suppose you all mean me?" the man said, exasperated, and in an Irish brogue.

"I wouldn't dream of taking anyone's boots!" I said.

"Mr. Gallagher is only teasing about being annoyed," Mabel said. "Of course he'll lend you the boots. Just for the competition. Won't you, sir?"

"I'll do more than that," he said. "For a fellow abolitionist, I'll surrender them entirely. Go and make it a win for our cause." Mr. Gallagher began removing his boots.

Now I wanted to run. I couldn't be the symbol for their cause. My shooting ability wasn't worthy of that. And I positively couldn't take the boots from this gentleman's feet for my own.

"Truly, I appreciate the gesture, but I couldn't."

"Come now," Mabel said, "don't stop a man from acting in the Christian way. You can give them back after the competition."

"But I can't shoot on behalf of the abolitionists. What if I—"

"Nobody's expecting you to win, silly," Mabel said. "Just go, stand proud, and do your best."

They all spoke in favor of this—in favor of me—but I still felt like withering away.

The wealthy wife, Mrs. Gallagher, spoke up. "Dear lad, just put on the boots and see how you feel."

At this point, I felt I had no choice in the matter. I would shoot on behalf of the abolitionists while wearing the sleek black boots.

Mr. Gallagher, now stocking-footed, held them out to me. The congregants clapped when I took them. I sat, removed my old boots, and put on the shiny ones. They bid me to tuck in my trouser legs, which I did. I stood and peered down. Their fit was too big, but not as far off as I thought they'd be, Mr. Gallagher being small in stature. I took a few steps in them.

"There now," Mabel said. "Won't you give 'em hell in those?"

CHAPTER 18

Charlie Rye

—

Sunday, April 15, 1860

I woke up Sunday morning with Bea's book open across my chest. Some strange dreams did that *Inferno* bring about, to be sure. Murmuring monsters, tortured souls, three-headed dogs with blood-spilling fangs. I was never so glad to wake up, even if the racket outside did jar me out of my sleep. A body hollered from the street about some-or-other Cold-Blooded Boys doing a shooting exposition. I never heard of these boys, but I figured I better see what the fuss was about.

By sheer luck, my stay in Carson City got stretched to nearly two weeks now, even after all my money got stolen that first night. I found a new saloon—this one called Aces—and I only saw that Rosebud woman one more time. Whilst I pillaged the faro table, she watched, all coy-like, probably wishing she hadn't fleeced me, and then she retreated to friendlier turf.

Bea hadn't shown up yet. It troubled me. Word had it that the westbound rider arrived three days ago, but every time I inquired at the station, she wasn't there. The fellers there were a bunch of scamps and wouldn't tell me a thing. I thought about leaving her a note, but I knew it wouldn't make it to her. If I didn't see her by noon, I'd start a more thorough inquiry. No need to raise suspicion.

I put my disguise back in place and readied myself for another day in Carson City. Neither Torrence nor the man Pascoe turned up again, so I felt freer than ever. I strolled out of my hotel room, about to descend the stairs, when, down in the lobby, who should appear but the lady siren from the saloon. She spotted me and gave the cunningest look I ever did see. The night she stole my money, I wasn't cross, but seeing her again made me buzz with a sudden fury. She slinked through a maze of sofas and tables and caught me when I reached the last stair. "Hello, Mr. Vincent."

"How'd you know my name? I don't recall givin' you that."

"Word gets around," she said.

"It does indeed. Just like it gets around about that operation you got runnin' over at the saloon."

"Operation? I don't know what you're talking about." She glanced around, mindful of prying ears.

"I'll tell you, miss, I'm only a fool once. I can sniff out lying like a bloodhound, and my nose is burnin' from all the falsehoods. That was quite a show—you tumblin' to the ground like I pushed ya. What's the idea? I pride myself on being a gentleman, and I won't have some wax doll ruin my reputation. Why, I never felt such indignation. That's right, *indignation*. Professors can use pretty words like that."

"I'm very sorry, Mr. Vincent. I've waited in this lobby all mornin' just to come and tell you so."

"You waited, did you? Surprised you didn't invite yourself upstairs. I reckon you know your way around up there like a dream."

Something was hidden in the lady's looks, like she kept her offense in check and painted on a pretty smile. "Forgiveness is another pretty word," she said. "And how about mercy and compassion?"

"Step aside, miss, if you please. I'm gonna see what all the ruckus is about."

"Let me come with you!" she said, bursting with excitement. "I'm eager to see some fine shootin' today."

"Gimme one good reason why I should."

"I'd like the chance to start fresh, Mr. Vincent. Truly, I am sorry."

"Sorry don't get me my money back," I said.

Laws, she was pretty. Her flaming red locks were pulled back with ribbons and curls like a goddess of the Roman variety. The pink rouge bloomed like roses on her cheeks. She wore a shimmering green dress, and her eyes shone like the sun through an amber glass of whiskey.

"How about this as restitution?" She reached into a rose-embroidered purse, pulled out the silver snuffbox, and held it out in her gloved hands. The streaming sunlight glinted off it and nearly blinded me.

"How'd you get that?" I asked.

"I grabbed it in all the confusion."

"Which you caused," I reminded her.

"Listen, I'm convinced we have somethin' in common," she said, still not owning up to what she done. "Walk with me to the shootin' exposition, and if you haven't found a reason to befriend me by the time we get there, why, you can turn me loose and never speak to me again."

Once again, I found myself negotiating with my principles. How suitable could it be to have a woman of the night clung to my arm? Then again, what harm could be done? I never cared what folks thought. Even if I did, nobody knew the real me in this town. And there was that silver snuff box. I took it and stowed it in my pocket. "Aw, fine, but no more pranks or I'll take my grievances about that operation to the sheriff."

"I promise," she said. I took it as an admission of guilt.

"Shall we?" I offered the crook of my arm, and she took it.

A stream of folks came pouring out of a tall church at the end of the street, headed toward the opposite end. We joined up like a tributary flows into a river.

"These Cold-Blooded Boys deliver quite a spectacle," she said. "There's a showground down here where they like to compete. Every week or so, they trick some poor fool to compete against them. They've already swindled all the locals."

"So they found some out-of-towner?"

"Appears so. And what a time! Just when everybody's gettin' out of church. Look there, even the pastor's comin' this way."

A man in a long black cloak passed, giving us *the eye*. A few others did too, kind of like they were on the lookout for sin, and if they found it, they were to stare it down until it buckled under the weight.

"Just look at this pious lot," she said. "To them, I've fallen so far from grace, I might as well get a floggin' in the town square."

"If you can't stand their judgment, why don't you get out of it? Nobody's forcing you into your . . . way of life."

"Oh, I plan to. I'll need a man to do it, though, and one with some elegance. Not some poor fellow with no prospects. I'm teachin' myself French, you see."

"French? What's that got to do with it?"

"All the finest gentlemen speak French or German. *Je parle Français.*" She stumbled over the words. "What do you think?"

"I don't know beans about the words, but you could work on the accent."

She laughed and tugged tighter at my arm. "Don't you speak another language, being a professor and all?"

"I do. It's called poetry."

"Ooh, well that's impressive," she said. "Which kind of poetry?"

"The kind that's poetic."

"You know what I mean."

"You ever heard of Dante?" I said.

"Oh! He wrote about that inferno business, didn't he? I'd love to read Dante. Tell me what it's about."

"Why? So you can use it to trap some scholar?"

"Maybe," she said, chuckling. "But I'm not the only one playing a part, now am I?"

I kept walking, maybe even a bit faster, but not on purpose.

"Mr. Vincent, if that's really your name, please don't think I'm so stupid as to believe you're really a professor."

I stopped. "Why wouldn't I be? You sayin' I ain't got the smarts for it?"

"*Ain't got the smarts?*" she repeated, throwing my ignorant speech back at me. "Alright, Professor Vincent, give me a roundup of your much-studied Dante. What's it about?"

"Alright." I swallowed. "This man, Dante, wakes up in a dark wood and finds himself walkin' through hell. He sees all these tortured souls, sufferin' for the sins they committed."

"Oh dear! Maybe I'd rather not read it. Why indulge in condemnation?"

"You ain't jokin'," I said. "But then, some of these punishments—you never heard of the like. Makes you wonder if Dante believed that's what hell's really like or if he meant something more by it. There's a word for it. What is it?"

"Confusing?" she offered. "Grandiose? Boring?"

"It's definitely those things," I said, "but there's a word for it. It's a story that's meant to teach you somethin' else. It reminds me of *Pilgrim's Progress*. That's the very last thing I learned at grammar school before I—"

I stopped myself, but she finished for me, saying, "Quit going?"

"Anyhow, it's one of them stories that you have to look deeper. It's got lots of layers to it."

"Like an onion?" she said.

"Yes, and the deeper you get to the center, the more you wanna cry."

She laughed. "Pity's sake, perhaps you left grammar school a bit too early. You could have a real future in this."

"You're just tryin' to turn me into the feller who's gonna whisk you away from your life someday."

"I hadn't thought of that, but now that you say it . . ."

We both chuckled. "Nah, truth is I don't really have the smarts for it, but that's OK, 'cause I need a little more adventure in my life. I wanna do somethin' heroic and noble. That or notorious and bad. Either way, I'll make a name for myself."

She nodded to every word. "Well, if that isn't somethin' we have in common, I don't know what is."

A smile came through, sideways at first, as much as I wished it away. "Allegory!" I blurted the second it came to me. She eyed me carefully. "It's called an allegory! A story that's meant to teach you somethin' more than face value. I can't believe I remembered."

"I think *you're* an allegory," she said, smirking. "There's certainly more to *you* than face value."

"I'll take that as a compliment. And I'll even raise you one. You ain't your typical whore."

She didn't laugh, which I felt bad about 'cause I meant it as a joke, even a compliment. Instead, she leveled this at me: "Tell me, how many do you know?"

There I went, taking my jesting too far, like I did so often. "Sorry, miss, truly I didn't mean to offend." I felt I should throw in something sweet to lessen the bite. "I'm a lucky feller, walkin' the street with the purtiest lady in town."

"Don't toy with me," she said. "I've seen flattery in all its forms."

The moment I got false with her, she knew it. I decided to show her the same courtesy.

"The last thing I'd wanna do is toy with you, miss, which is why I should tell you: I'm sixteen years old. And not only that, but I got myself a girl. One that means the sun, moon, and stars to me."

She tried to make me think she didn't care, but the biting of her lip told me different.

"Sakes alive, Miss Rosebud, why would this bother you? If you only want a friend, as you say."

She mulled this over like she was gathering courage to tell me something, even closing her eyes and taking a deep breath. "Come get me in five years."

I choked on my own spit. "Miss?"

"That's right. I'll be here. I ain't going nowhere. Remove me from this life. I swear, I'll leave all this behind if you'll take me away and build me a life. We could go all kinds of places and put on airs and eat delicacies and drink brandies and do whatever we please."

It took a lot to shock me, but at that moment, my speech was plumb gone.

"In five years, you'll be twenty-one," she kept on, "and I'll be twenty-six. Our different ages won't seem so stark then. That's plenty enough time for me to finish up the life I got here and for you to grow up and make your fortune."

I found my speech again. "I'm sorry, miss. I got big plans—well, different plans from you and . . . I'm just saying, don't get your hopes up."

"My father was right." She sighed. "I'm a disappointment in every way. Maybe if he'd shown me a little kindness growing up, I would've turned out more 'to his liking.' He's got himself to blame, you know. He's the one who raised me. He's ashamed of me, and I him. Not just any shame. A bitter loathing. Do you have any idea what that's like?"

"There's almost nothing I know better," I said.

"At last, I think we've touched on the thing that unites us."

I gave her a skeptical look, though she was probably right. Maybe we were living the same life, but in different worlds.

"Anyhow, I've made peace with my wretched upbringing," she said.

"How do you make peace with something like that?" I asked, because, well, maybe she had some useful advice.

She cast an eye out into the unknown and said, "I decided that God's the only one who can judge hearts, but he's *not* the only one who can exact justice."

Not only did she not make sense, but she scared me a little. I raised my brows in surprise.

"Yes, in case you were wondering, a woman like me is still allowed to speak of God. If he's only God to the saintly, what kind of God would he be? Anyhow, there's another way I've made my peace with it, and it's the best of all: I'll outshine him."

"God?" I asked.

"No, my father."

"No offense, miss, but how would you—"

"You just leave that up to me," she said.

Somebody in the crowd shouted, "Ladies and gentlemen, I give you the Cold-Blooded Boys."

Miss Rosebud and me had walked the whole stretch of the road and landed at the shooting competition about to start. A boy dressed in military blues was pitted against . . . I narrowed my eyes for a closer look at the boy. *Could that be . . . ?* I shook free of Miss Rosebud's arm. "Blazing stars! Let go of me, miss. I can't be seen with you!"

"I declare! Now you're high and mighty?" She looked like a wounded child.

"It's just temporary. I promise. Ain't nothin' wrong with you. I'll explain later."

"If I give you the chance!" She stormed off to another part of the crowd and seethed, probably conjuring up revenge. My heart felt for the woman, but I couldn't have her arm tucked in mine just now.

Sure as the sun, there stood my Bea, a contender in the shooting contest. It did my heart real pleasure to see her. She made it! She made her first ride of the Pony Express all in one piece. Wasn't she afraid of being discovered, calling attention to herself? I knew she'd succeed, but I had no idea she'd eat it up like this. Now I knew for certain I done the right thing giving her my spot. I only hoped Miss Rosebud wouldn't make more trouble for me.

CHAPTER 19

Beatrice Brannon

—

Sunday, April 15, 1860

TIN cans were spaced evenly on the fence. Standing a hundred feet away, I could see them peppered with bullet holes. They were twisted and bent, the same way I felt with this crowd staring at me.

"Ladies and gentlemen," announced one of their devotees, "I give you the Cold-Blooded Boys!"

Uproarious applause followed. Folks were placing their bets . . . against me. Negotiations were taking place. *This again,* I thought.

"Here ya go," Elias said, handing me the rifle. I hefted it and put it up to my shoulder. It felt heavier somehow, even though it was the same gun I'd practiced with. "Newcomer goes first. Remember the rules. Whoever shoots the most targets with five bullets wins."

The relaxed shift of his weight, the way he spoke with no quiver to his voice, and how he seemed so natural in this environment—all of it shook my confidence. Something else too: the sinister glances he shared with his brother.

"Waitin' for the Rapture?" he chided, earning a chuckle from the people standing closest. I attempted to ignore them and control my breathing the way Da had taught me.

"Come on, Lafayette!" I heard Mabel shout. "Tall and proud now."

"Remember what you're shootin' for," Mr. Gallagher added. I wasn't sure what I was shooting for. The abolitionists? My family? Myself? Regardless, these boys may have tricked me into this spectacle, but I wouldn't get rattled.

I took aim at the first can. I sighted down the barrel, breathed as motionless as I could, and pulled the trigger. The recoil shoved my shoulder, sending me backward a couple steps. This peccadillo gave the townsfolk something to laugh at. Not a hit. That hadn't happened during my practice. Was I letting this crowd get to me? I wedged the stock more firmly in my shoulder.

"No shame in it!" one of my supporters said. "Keep your composure. You can do it."

The voices of Mabel and her group of abolitionists were so quiet compared to those who sided with the Cold-Blooded Boys, but their presence helped me feel less alone.

The crowd hushed, anticipating my next shot. Stance solid, I pulled the trigger. Another miss. The crowd uttered a collective "Oh!" which sounded more like delight than dismay. I needed to drown them out. Two misses in a row was no great failing, but I must take care with this third.

This time, I waited with added patience for the moment when I could trust all my senses to make the shot—breathing calmed, rifle steadied, aim true. I knew I had it now. I pulled the trigger. The recoil didn't faze my balance, but still, that pesky can remained. Something was not right. I'd felt sure about that one.

"I'm puuurty sure it's over now, boy," an admirer of theirs said. A string of jeers followed.

My eyes focused on a large elm tree thirty feet ahead, a short distance from the fence. A knobby pattern in the bark gave me an idea. Folks must've wondered what I was doing, aiming at a tree, but I allowed their voices to disappear. I adjusted the muzzle and took aim directly in the center of the knot. I exhaled and squeezed the trigger. My shot landed somewhere in the knot.

"That one counts," Abram said.

Folks outright laughed. If they were confused by my shooting at a tree, they must've been more so when I left my place and took the long walk to examine the dent my shot had made. My fingers traced along the wood. High and slightly to the right from the spot of my aim.

I stalked back to my place, pulled the lever back, took aim, this time adjusting for the fault in the gun's sights. Aiming slightly down and to the left, I waited for my moment and fired. The can flew off the fence. Mabel's crew gave me hearty applause. I exhaled, regaining confidence, and lowered the gun. I was right.

Elias took the rifle from me, saying, "Well, you managed to get one shot. Sure it wasn't just luck?"

Such audacity to talk like that, fully aware of his own dishonor. I wondered about the others who'd lost to them. Did the Rileys always provide the guns? They must've insisted every time, telling their competitors they'd be amiss not to use the latest "Henry rifle," when all the while, these boys had tampered with the aim.

Abram handed the rifle to Elias, who took his stance, aimed, and popped the first can off the fence. He waited for the cheers to die down, then took another shot. Hit. He took three more shots in succession, hitting every single one, left to right.

Across the throng, everyone lost their minds, shouting, cheering, and waving their hats.

Abram said, "Don't be so hard on yourself. The Henry rifle ain't for kids. Takes a man to handle it."

Unreal, I thought. *All this fuss for a pair of cheaters.*

Taking advantage of the noise, I took a private tête-à-tête with Abram. "Give me my button and note."

He grimaced at my outstretched hand, as if he hadn't the time.

"You don't think I know what this is?" I said.

His intrigue shone through, as if willing to entertain the idea that I was onto them, but still unyielding.

"That's right. Hand them over, soldier. Oh, and I give you permission to sell the Bea story, 'cause I've got a better one. Here's the headline: 'Colonel's Sons Are Lousy Cheats.'"

His demeanor bled into full-blown panic. While Elias still basked in the praise, unaware of our private conversation, Abram fished the note and button from his pocket and handed them to me. I secured them in my own. My indignation gave birth to a whole new me. A sense of my purpose drove me to do something rash. I was there to earn money, not make friends. The gun itself could serve as proof. Any gunsmith would be able to confirm my allegation.

"He says it takes a man to handle the Henry rifle," I blurted loud enough for all to hear. "Shooting a target that doesn't move? Where's the challenge in that?"

Folks jeered at my hubris. After all, what right did I have to taunt him after I'd clearly lost the match? Nobody could've been more shocked than me.

"I can shoot moving targets easy enough," Elias said, offended, as though I'd slapped him in the face.

"Let's see you then," I said. "How confident are you? Can you shoot a target thrown in the air?"

"Confident enough to outshoot you . . . again."

"Wait, Elias," his elder brother said. "You already beat him. Let's call it an afternoon."

"Doesn't sound like confidence to me," I said. "Clearly, you can shoot cans off a fence lined up in a neat little row, but maybe you've done this trick a few too many times. Maybe the Cold-Blooded Boys need to add a little variety to their show."

Whoops and hollers arose, especially from Mabel and her clan. Everybody was engaged now. The folks who had bet on their Cold-Blooded

Boys got their winnings. But the show was still going. With the accounts settled, could their loyalty switch?

Amid the crowd, one particular face stopped me cold, a motionless gentleman with his gaze fixed on me. He was an odd mix of youth and maturity, like his dapper clothing didn't quite fit his youth.

Upon my word, that's Charlie Rye. I fought the urge to smile. He tried the same but failed.

We were able to communicate with no words. "Good to see you," he nodded. "You too," I nodded back. He made a quick glance over at the tree, telling me that he knew why I'd gone to examine it. "Them boys is cheating," he must've been saying, to which I responded, "I know, and I won't let them get away with it." He replied by ever-so-slyly showing me the pistol on his hip. I nodded, saying, "I know exactly what to do."

"Quit now, Elias," Abram said. "He's tryin' to catch you in some snare."

"This kid's challenged my skill," Elias said. "I can't leave it at that."

"You already proved your skill!" his brother reminded him.

"How about we make this fun?" I said. "How about the Cold-Blooded Boys get a true test of their mettle?"

"What do you have in mind?" Elias asked.

"We're riders of the Pony Express," I told the crowd. "I'm willing to bet my first round of pay that I can shoot moving targets better than they can." I said to Elias, "Are you willing to make that bet?"

At last, Abram was on board. He must've seen it would be a loss of honor to back out now. He nodded to his brother to proceed.

"I'll take that challenge," Elias said, shaking my hand. All I could think was, *For all that's holy, he's going for it. I've got to make this count.*

"There's just one thing," I said. "That gun doesn't feel quite right to me. Maybe I'm not fit for such newfangled equipment. What would you say if I used a smaller gun?"

It was like I'd spoken a foreign language. I turned my attention on the crowd. "Does anybody have a pistol I could borrow?"

"I've got one, young man," Charlie called, stepping forward. All eyes went on him as he meandered through the crowd. Now we stood face-to-face. The urge to jump out of my skin had never been stronger.

Charlie held out the gun. "It ain't much, but I know the aim is true."

When I took hold of the gun, our fingers touched for the smallest moment.

"It's loaded, all ready to go," he said.

"Thank you, sir."

After a small discussion arose about who should throw the bottles, we settled on the town blacksmith.

"I'll go first." My mouth was way ahead of my confidence, which brought ovations from Mabel Tucker's group.

Abram gave one last jab to try to take me down, saying to the crowd, "It seems this kid ain't had enough humiliation for the day."

"It'll be his downfall!" someone shouted.

"Make him pay, Elias," said another man.

The blacksmith readied the bottle. I thought about everything Da had taught me. *Wait for the zenith,* he'd said. That brief pause before the target made its descent—that was the time to shoot.

On the count of three, the blacksmith chucked it sky-high. I brought the pistol upward, followed the target, waited for the zenith, and fired.

Directly after taking the shot, I closed my eyes, refusing to see if I got it. Mabel and her group went wild. Everyone else stood in bewildered silence. I'd shattered the bottle.

"If you ain't the luckiest kid," Elias said. "Gimme that pistol. Nothing's as easy as a handgun."

I was about to tell him to use his own gun but thought, *Why not? All that needs to happen now is for him to miss.*

The blacksmith counted to three. He pitched the bottle into the air, same height as my throw. Abram shot the pistol. The bottle plummeted to the dirt, unhit.

A collective groan rippled through the crowd, nobody louder than Abram. As for me, my mind went blank, all sound muffled in the haze of my disbelief. I had just won.

The so-called Cold-Blooded Boys took their guns and their blistering scowls and headed back to the cabin, full of shame and, hopefully, regret.

"Lafayette!" Mabel shouted, weaving through the crowd and wrapping her arms around me. "You've done us proud."

After my congratulators departed, Charlie approached, smiling without restraint.

I handed him back his gun. "Thank you, sir. That's a fine specimen."

"You're a fine specimen," he said, "as a shooter, I mean."

I shook his hand and whispered, "Meet me behind the tall church in twenty minutes." He winked, and I knew he'd be there. I longed to speak to him again, not under any guises. Around Charlie, I could be myself, more so than with any other person in the world, and I hadn't realized that until this very moment.

CHAPTER 20

Charlie Rye

—

Sunday, April 15, 1860

BEA'S win set me on fire. It righted so many wrongs for both me and her. Life had treated her cruel and unfair of late, but times like these seemed to settle the score a little.

I relived the whole event—every shot, every comment, every glance as I paced to and fro, waiting for Bea behind that church at the end of the lane.

"Charlie!" She appeared. We grasped each other tight. I closed my eyes and breathed her in. My girl was finally with me, in my arms, letting me be close to her. My blood was fired up, but my soul was soothed. Bea didn't let go for a long while. When she did, I saw genuine tears rolling down her cheeks. Tears clouded up my own eyes too. My pa would've been sick at me showing so much emotion, but I knew Bea wouldn't judge me that way.

"I'm so happy," she said. "I've never been so happy to see anybody in my entire life."

"Ain't that the truth." We embraced again. "Aw, darlin', I never been prouder of you." I called her a sweet name, but she didn't protest. For some of the finest minutes of my life, this hugging, happy, tearful reunion went on, and I did nothing to stop it. Shame's sake, I wasn't gonna be the one to bring us down from the clouds.

"How'd you do it, Charlie?"

"How'd *I* do it? You was the one to beat the Cold-Blooded Boys at their own game."

"No, this." The thing glimmered from a piece of twine around her neck. Every hair on my body stood on end. A rush of wind flew at me, it seemed, but nothing else around was affected by it. "You found my silver button!"

"Oh, stop. You can't fool me. You planted this in my pocket the morning we said goodbye. I'm starting to think you're some kind of magician."

"True as steel, the last time I saw that button, it was fastened to my jacket. I lost it on the day of the race. Never seen it since."

"You're teasing me. You slipped it in my pocket."

"I didn't, Bea. I swear."

"On your mother's grave?"

"I swear on my mother's grave. Come to think of it, I first noticed it missing right after the river. Maybe it fell off and right into your pocket."

She studied me skeptically. Perhaps she didn't know what I meant by "after the river." I stepped in to clarify. "Remember the time we—"

"I remember," she finished.

I let the silence hold until we both giggled like children. "That rascally silver button must have a mind of its own."

We flattened a spot in the tall weeds and sat on the ground, resting our backs against the church wall. An organist inside piped out a faithful old hymn that flowed through us to our bones. A flock of geese flew in perfect formation across downy clouds set against the bluest sky anybody ever saw. The hills before us were covered in thousands of pines and oaks. I never seen a prettier scene, not even in a painting.

Bea's hands rested at her sides. I looked down at the hand closest to me and wondered if, perchance, she'd let me hold it. Ere long, the geese passed by, as I knew the moment soon would too. I rested my hand on hers ever so gently. She beamed with surprise. So much so, that she crossed her other hand over and placed it on top of mine. I leaned toward her and breathed a kiss onto her soft cheek. She placed a kiss of her own on my cheek, then rested her head on my shoulder, our hands still clinging like cockleburs to a wool sock.

This moment with Bea was healing for my soul. I could almost feel my broken pieces being mended one by one.

She started snickering, and I did too, not knowing why. "What's so funny?"

"Nothing, it's just your fake moustache tickled my cheek."

"Oh, that? It's my cover. I'm a professor of literature. How does it suit me?"

"Really? I thought you'd choose more of a ruffian's character. Infamous card player or train-robbing bandit."

"Oh, I'm a card player, alright. But I wanted the respect of a professor. In fact, my disguise is so good that—" I bolted upright, remembering the crazy thing I needed to tell her. "Bea, I almost forgot. Mayor Torrence was here."

"In Carson City?" She sat up straight too. "Mercy, did he see you? Did he come here to fetch you? Does he know about me taking your spot?"

"At first, I thought so, but Bea, you never seen such an odd performance, sneakin' around like a tomcat. He's into something devious, sure as stars. Just imagine the heroes we'll be when we expose him."

"Tell me everything," she said.

"See, there's this feller Pascoe. He was—"

"Pascoe?" Bea clutched my arm. "Short man, skittery, wears a gray suit?"

"That's the one!"

"He's the station manager at Buckland's. How do you know him?"

"This Mr. Pascoe and our own Mayor Torrence got some scheme goin' on. Half this stuff played out right outside my hotel window. Mayor handed something to Pascoe. I couldn't see what it was. Small though, 'cause it went from one pocket to the next."

"Charlie, could it have been a key? Pascoe used a key to unlock the pouches. It was strange because—"

"Well, hello," a voice broke in, stopping us cold. Standing to our far right was Miss Rosebud, hands on hips, angry as a wasp. Bea and me stood up fast, sort of guilty-like.

"Miss Rosebud!" I said. "Didn't expect to see you here."

"Of course you didn't, but I found you just the same." Miss Rosebud drew closer, eyeing Bea like she planned on eating her alive. "So this is the sun, moon, and stars. Rather plain if you ask me, for a boy or a girl."

"You're out of turn, Miss Rosebud. I've a mind to—"

"Spare me your threats! You want to know why I was so interested in finding out about you? Because somebody was asking."

I swallowed.

"That's right," she said. "A man called Torrence came through here and started asking questions. Told me he'd give me twenty dollars for any tidbits I could provide."

"I knew it! I knew you wasn't after my friendship."

"That's just it. As we walked the street together, I changed my mind. I wasn't going to give him any tidbits at all. I felt I had a friend, but lo and behold, who drops *me* at the slightest test?"

"Pardon me," Bea asked me, rather calm-like, "who is this?"

Miss Rosebud answered for herself. "I'm the harlot who's been keeping your man occupied."

"You little minx!" I said. "That ain't true."

"It was true when I was sitting on your lap, wasn't it?"

"You're giving a false impression and you know it. Bea, don't listen to her."

"Her name's Bea, is it?"

I slapped a hand to my forehead. Where did all my caution go?

"Fine, I'll pay you a filthy twenty dollars," I said. "Is that what it'll take to keep you quiet?"

"Never mind the twenty dollars," she said. "I want something else."

"I told you, miss, I ain't comin' back for you in—"

"There's another way I need you," she interrupted. "You're gonna help me make someone jealous. Meet me at Jolly Spirits at eleven sharp. And don't bring this one with you." She flung a finger at Bea, then left as quickly as she came.

Bea and me exchanged wide-eyed glances until I thought of some way to explain. "She ain't bein' truthful, sayin' she's keepin' me busy and all that. You heard what kind of woman she is—one who takes bribes and does anything to get what she wants."

"She knows who we are," Bea said. "She's gonna tell Mayor Torrence. I think we just shot ourselves in the foot. You should've been more careful. I think my time in the Pony Express is done."

"No, it can't be. I'll fix this."

"How? By doing heaven-knows-what with that woman just to make some man jealous?"

"Listen, I'm not gonna let down my principles. I'll just see what she wants me to do. Maybe it ain't so bad. Maybe all she wants is a peck on the cheek." Right as it came out my mouth, I regretted it. "No, I—" My mouth clamped shut.

That look of hurt on Bea's face seared my soul like a branding iron. For how dumbstruck I was, I didn't know if I'd ever be able to speak again. How could I tell her that the moment we just shared was finer than all my finest moments put together?

"I need to go, Charlie. I better get back to the station."

Bea rounded the church and strode nearly halfway down the street before I found my voice. "I'll fix this, I swear," I called to her. "I swear it on my mother's grave!"

CHAPTER 21

Beatrice Brannon

Sunday, April 15, 1860

I'M a fool. I'm a fool. I'm a fool. I said it a hundred times in my head. *How could I let my emotions get away from me like that? How could I let Charlie hold my hand and kiss my cheek? And give him a kiss of my own? Where is my good sense? It surely meant nothing to him.*

A deeper question surfaced. Why did I care who Charlie kept company with? I'd never cared before. He was a card-playing, rabble-rousing saloon dweller. His goal in life was a reputation. How could I expect any more from him? I knew very well he ogled at the saloon girls. That's probably why he frequented those places: for the leggy, bosomy views! Why should I assume he'd never flirted with any of them?

I fiddled with the twine of my necklace until the knot came loose. The button I'd just worked so hard to reclaim, I hurled into a patch of weeds.

A tempest raged in my mind, and I could neither walk fast enough nor breathe heavily enough to calm the storm. A thought that had kept itself hidden in the corners of my mind now sprang forward: Did Charlie love me? In a sweetheart kind of way? What a strange thought to have after he'd made me feel so ordinary. But this was not typical for him—not at all. Charlie was always saying sweet things and putting my desires above his own.

Then in the river. We'd stood so close. He'd taken every opportunity to hold me, to make me laugh, to smell my hair, for heaven's sake. I'd felt completely at ease, even lighthearted.

A far more threatening thought came: Did I love Charlie? Every thought of Charlie had some all-encompassing feeling attached to it, never lukewarm. My feelings were like a weather vane at the mercy of the wind, pointing toward bliss one moment and fury the next.

All these things—were they proof of something? The note he'd given me had been an instant healing tonic. And moments ago, when he'd held my hand and kissed my cheek, emotions had awakened in me that I'd never felt before—a physical reaction to his presence.

Love is for the dimwitted, I thought, *a snare for the unsuspecting.* Only moments after allowing it to crawl into my hands, it bit and stung me. Thus jilted, I found comfort as the fox in the fable of the sour grapes. *I'm Beatrice. I deserve a Dante. A scholar, an intellectual, a poet. Any other sort would never appreciate me, my literary citations, my clever quips. All that would be lost on Charlie.*

No, that wasn't true. Charlie was cleverer than most. He knew different things than I did, but he was no less clever. *He* was the one with clever quips.

Heaven help me! I seized my head. Any conclusions on the subject could not be debated right now. I had a job to do. I needed to prepare for my next grueling ride. Dear me, I'd have to return to that wasteland, Buckland's. I almost welcomed the thought, if only to ride my feelings away.

Would it be worth it to stay in the Pony Express? Today's exhibition had made me fifty dollars richer, which I knew would help Mama a great deal. But it was still only a fraction of the whole debt, which seemed to be waiting like a vulture to gobble us up at the end of summer. And we'd be forced out.

This Rosebud woman. Who was she? What did she know? Enough to throw me out of my post, that was certain. If I were to stay, she'd have to be placated. Charlie was right. But what would she make him do? And what if Charlie did everything she asked but she still revealed my secret?

If she was the kind of person to take bribes, she'd surely spill secrets too. Perhaps my mere presence in the Pony Express was causing too many problems.

Why did you do this to us, Da? Why did you leave us in this terrible lurch? How could you have bargained with our precious land? Well, I'll fix your mess!

Guilt washed over me for thinking that way. I was no better than the judgmental townsfolk. *I'm sorry, Da. I know you did your best to take care of us. I don't blame you. I'll make it right. You'll get the respect you deserve.*

The street had quieted down considerably. I stood alone in the middle of the road. The few passersby didn't recognize me as the winner of the shooting exposition. All the people who'd cheered for me—and against me—were gone. It was just as well. I didn't crave recognition. And Charlie, well, I'd just lost him, maybe forever. This Rosebud woman was beautiful, alluring, and everything suited to the life Charlie wanted. He'd fall for her in an instant—if he hadn't already. A simple life in Victory Hills with a best friend like me would never suit him again. Not after the enticements of Carson City.

I calmed my breaths. Despite my unrest, I'd keep going. I'd stay in the Pony Express until somebody dragged me away.

CHAPTER 22

Charlie Rye

Sunday, April 15, 1860, evening

Curses! *I'm a fool and a scoundrel,* I told myself. *Every time Bea gets close to me, I chase her away with my antics. I'll fix this situation with Miss Rosebud.* No way could Bea leave the Pony Express on account of me. Now that I knew Miss Rosebud's game, I could play it. I'd get her to swear to secrecy. And contrary to what Bea thought, I could do it and keep my principles.

Moustache and spectacles in place and gun at my hip, I left my hotel room and slipped out into the night. Not many souls prowled the streets at this hour. Perhaps a few stragglers here and there. Most were either inside the saloons or gone home. Miss Rosebud's corseted shape leaned against the lamppost, wearing her white rosebud-print gown. I knew she was playing a role, but I didn't know which one. I'd soon find out.

When her eyes found me, she gave an impatient sigh. "You're late."

"And good evening to you too, miss."

"You'd be well not to keep me waiting in the future."

"First off, I ain't late. I'm squarely on time. Second off, there won't be a future. This'll be the last time I ever associate with you and then we're done."

"You speak very confidently for somebody in the wrong."

"In the wrong! Why you—" But I stopped myself before cussing her out. Instead, I said, "I agreed to this only so you won't squeal on me and my girl, but I'm doin' this by my own set of rules."

"Your own set of rules, you say? You think you're the one in charge? Amuse me, what are these rules?"

"I have two," I said, squaring my shoulders and straightening out my vest. "First, I won't do nothin' that'll break my girl's heart."

"How very honorable." She rolled her eyes.

"And second, you'll gimme your word that you won't squeal on me or my girl to Mr. Torrence or anybody else."

"Fine," she said, waving a dismissive hand.

"I want your unequivocal word."

"Unequivocal? That's fancy."

"Well, that's what I want," I said.

"Then that's what you have. Now for mine. If the gentleman I seek doesn't leave with an interest in seeing me again, all bets are off."

"If you don't mind my being frank, ain't this sort of your specialty? Ain't you been doing this for some time? Why do you need me?"

"I don't want him for a bedfellow," she said, which made me cough suddenly. "I want him for a husband, or at least for something more lasting."

"Oh, boy," I said with some hopelessness.

"This one's different," she went on. "He doesn't want a hussy. He wants a lady of elegance and education."

"Don't speak French to him." It was the least offensive joke that popped in my head. She wasn't amused. This woman was plain crazy, thinking she could entangle this man in her nets by deceit. Then again, what did I care? Long as she held up her end of the bargain. "OK, what's the plan?"

"His name's Baron von Klein. He's sinfully wealthy, and he's sitting at the faro table right now. I want you to play a few rounds with him."

"Sounds simple enough. Do you want me to win or lose?" I said this in cocky way, as if I could veer the game to my liking. Most times, I could.

"I don't care. Just keep him sitting at that table long enough for me to do my job."

"Which is what?"

"You'll see. Just play along. Oh, and be sure to look at me as though I'm the most desirable specimen you ever did see."

"I'll try," I said, clearing my throat, almost choking on my words. "How do we know each other?"

"You and I were engaged to be married, but you changed your mind and rejected me."

"Tragic. Now why'd I do that?"

"Because I'm too smart and ambitious. I have a mind of my own. Your mother doesn't approve of me. She wants you to find a woman who'll keep a house for you and be your servant all your days. You decided to comply with her wishes, though you're heartbroken over it. You've come to the saloon tonight to take your mind off your sorrows. You'll keep your Charles Vincent name. You teach literature at some uppish place, and you're in town on holiday. Your father died when you were, say, six years old, leaving your mother far too protective of you, but now she wants you to find a proper wife."

Finally, she stopped talking, and I said, "What's my dog's name?"

She tilted her head at me wasting precious time.

"Well, it's almost like you don't care about the details," I said, teasing her.

"Get in there," she said. "When the timing's right, I'll join you. And by the by, you don't have a dog. Your mother wouldn't approve."

I gave her a mock salute and waltzed in the door. A couple men surrounded the faro table, watching a game in the works. Custom said to wait for the next round to join the game. This gave me a chance to observe my opponent.

Baron von Klein shone like a show pony in a parade. The others were dusty, grimy peasants next to him, with their crushed hats and dirty fingernails. He had a trimmed beard and moustache, and a well-filled belly. A golden pocket watch chain was tucked into a red silk vest, and a white cravat plunged over it like a waterfall. If that didn't do it, he wore a velvet overcoat with a heavy collar. If intimidation determined the winner, he'd walk away with a second fortune.

The baron won the final round. Another man cashed in his chips and left. I took the vacancy. The baron nodded toward me, and I nodded back. Two other men played, plus the dealer. We each placed our bets, and the game began. I had a strategy to play small in the beginning and big at the end when the odds were better. As time whittled on, I got caught up in the game and forgot all about Miss Rosebud. My concentration paid off 'cause I won my first round. Delight came to my face until I remembered: *I'm supposed to be miserable.*

Another game started and still no Rosebud. I kept playing my best. Another feller won the next round. The baron shifted, as though he was antsy for another win. I decided to place bogus numbers to let the baron take that one. He won that game, seemed pleased, and kept playing. I slyly glanced around, but Miss Rosebud was nowhere to be found.

The baron played his chips like they were no more than biscuits. In the next round, the baron played big, so I played big too. My luck made up for what I lacked in money, and I took that round. When I scooped up my hefty pile of chips, the baron said in a German accent, "You have a special knack for this game, don't you?"

Now if it was *me* playing, I'd make some snide comment, but it was *Professor Charles Vincent,* so I answered with a humble, "Thank you, sir. As do you."

"It comes with much practice," he said. "Possibly too much."

All the men chortled. We all knew the craving.

"Are you a nobleman?" I asked.

"Yes, I'm Baron von Klein."

"Professor Charles Vincent. Pleased to meet you."

"Likewise."

"I wish I could be as jovial as you," I said, lamenting my poor acting skills. "I might be celebrating if I wasn't so . . . downtrodden."

Nobody asked why I was downtrodden, and I couldn't think of how to make them, so I told my story whether or not they wanted to hear it. "My heart's plumb broken, gentlemen. I can't be with the woman I love." Talking this way made me overly conscious of my age, my disguise, and every lie I was telling. I had no idea if I was duping them or not. "I broke her heart, true, but I broke my own in the process."

"Get this poor man a drink," the German said.

"No." I waved a hand. "I can't drown my sorrows in a glass tonight. I'm determined to feel this one as keenly as I can. She's worth at least that. You should see her. Her beauty alone would shame the brightest star. But that's not all. She's clever too. That's the problem."

The banker, certainly onto me, kept the game going even though I buried my head down on the table.

"Charles!" a shriek came from the doorway, and I knew the leading lady just took the stage. Rosebud entered with another female by her side, the friend I saw her with the first day. This woman, I guessed, was supposed to play the role of chaperone. They both hastened to the tables, their skirts rustling like a storm a-coming. Miss Rosebud held a small traveling bag and wore gloves. A lace shawl was swept around her shoulders. She spoke to the saloonkeeper, who didn't bat an eye at her performance. "I'm very sorry to come in here, sir. I know a proper lady should never enter these doors, but I knew I'd find *him* here." She turned to me. If she waited for me to give the next line, I was lost in the imaginary script.

Something came to me. I stood. "I'm sorry, Miss Rosebud." I kept her name, mostly because I didn't know what else to call her. From my lofty stance, I eyed the other men crossly. "Ain't you gentlemen going to stand for the lady?"

They were frozen, somewhat baffled. Then I spoke directly to the baron, loudly clearing my throat. "In this country, we always stand when a lady walks in the room."

"Of course!" he said, standing and bowing to her. The other men stood as well, even though they'd probably seen Rosebud a hundred times playing different roles.

"Charles, you've humiliated me." Her voice was altered, her language more proper. "I'll have to go back to Boston without you. I'd like to leave tonight. Father and Mother will be so ashamed. This elopement was your idea. To reject me now is unthinkable. What will you do with me now?"

Once again, I couldn't generate a single thought. She eyed me to keep the conversation going.

"The coach doesn't leave until the morning," the saloonkeeper spoke up. "You'll have to wait until first light, miss."

Ridiculous! This whole place was Miss Rosebud's playhouse, and all these actors served her and whatever play she was staging.

"Miss Rosebud, I'm heartbroken." I tried putting some feeling into it. "This is more painful for me than it is for you."

"I don't see how that's possible. I've given you my heart, Charles. What more could you want?"

"Don't you see? My father is dead, and Mother controls my inheritance. We'd be penniless, and I couldn't do that to you." I added that trope, and Miss Rosebud went along with it.

"We'd make it just fine, Charles. We're both educated from the finest schools. We'd be alright. The trouble is you refuse to stand up to your mother."

Well, I was downright disgusted with this Charles feller, so I had to give him a good quality to make up for what he lacked. "You know it was my father's dying wish that I take care of Mother till her last breath."

Miss Rosebud didn't skip a beat and said in passionate fury, "Your father would've adored me, and you know it!"

The banker tapped the table to get my attention. "Excuse me, sir, but are you still playing?"

"Have some compassion, man! Don't you see the woman I'm losin'? This here is the finest woman in all the West, probably the entire United States, and I'm forced to cast her aside."

"I'll give you until the morning to come to your senses," she said. "If you don't make good on your promise to me, I'll be forced to leave and, eventually"—she glanced demurely at the baron—"entertain other offers."

If I'd really been Rosebud's intended beau, I would've been embarrassed by her coyness, even angry. But she wasn't my woman to contend with. She and her chaperone left the saloon.

I sat back down in my chair and slumped over the table as only a lovesick man could do. I glanced up at the baron. "What would you do? Would you give up your birthright and all your money for the woman you love?"

"I would consider it," he said, "if I loved someone as much as you appear to love this woman."

"What do you think of her?"

"Of your fiancé?" He seemed confused by my asking. "I know nothing of her, except what I have seen here."

"Based on what you've seen, what do you think?"

"She's a lovely woman."

"Yes, she is. Once you meet a woman like Miss Rosebud, you're never the same again."

Just as I began to suppose my fine acting was hitting its mark, he leaned toward me as if to whisper. "You should come to Munich, my friend. There are swarms just like her."

The words made me flinch. "I beg your pardon, sir, but was that an insult toward my lady?"

"Certainly not." He seemed apologetic. "I only meant that beauty such as hers is equaled only at the court."

"Well, it ain't just the beauty. She's real fine-spirited too and educated with the best of 'em. That's the problem. She's too refined for my mother. True, my mother inherited some money from my father, but she's still a simple woman, no frills about her. She wants me to find that kind of woman too. What kind of lady are you looking for?"

"Discretion is a prized quality in a woman, in my estimation."

"What do you mean?"

He sighed, impatient that he had to spell it out for me. "My problem is not finding a lady. I have a wife. My problem is that I settled down too quickly. My problem is finding ladies who don't make trouble for me, if you know what I mean."

The men burst into laughter, the baron included. I leaned back in my chair and crossed my arms, trying not to show contempt. "I resign this round, gentlemen. Need a little fresh air on my face, you know. Keep my chips as they are." I left my chair, walked out of the saloon, and peered right and left, trying to find the leading lady.

Miss Rosebud zipped from around the corner toward me, without her lady chaperone. "How's it going?" she whispered, eyes bright. This jig was obviously not taking the toll on her that it was on me.

I whispered with a real punch, "The bet's off, Rosebud."

"What do you mean?"

"He's married!"

"How do you know?"

"He just said so. Prob'ly got a couple concubines too."

"Keep up your act," she said. "I'm just getting warmed up."

"Listen, miss, he's a married man. Are you crazy?"

"I can work with just about anything."

"He just insulted you," I said, only because she wouldn't listen. "He said there are swarms just like you in Munich."

"But he admitted I'm desirable?"

"Am I just flappin' my gums? He said you're a dime a dozen. Listen, I can see why you got caught up in the fantasy. He's got money, to be sure. But there ain't no substance to him. You got this one wrong."

"Just keep going," she said. "He may never go back to Germany at all. One more attempt."

"I want no part of it," I said.

"We had a deal."

"Well, it's off."

Her face took on a frightful hardness. "I've got men who'll do anything for me. If you won't cooperate, then I'll dispatch a message first thing in the morning—no, tonight—to that man Torrence, and give him the identities and locations of both you and your sweetheart."

Her hooks were into me good. I couldn't do that to Bea.

"He doesn't even like you," I continued, cruel as I could. "You're a desperate fool."

She spoke sharp as a razor. "Charlie, once you asked me why I don't simply remove myself from this life—as though it's as easy as turning a key—well, I'll tell you. That girl you saw with me tonight? She's my sister. I'm doing this for her. She's only your age, and I don't want this life for her. I won't have men treating her the way they treat me, talking to her in their silky voices the way they talk to me. Our father turned us out cold, but she doesn't have to suffer for it. Any money I take in supports the both of us. Yes, I'd love to escape this life, but my options are not as many as I'd like. The sooner I can find some rich man to take the brunt of this, the better. So get in there"—she drew close to my face—"and do your job."

My body felt like a hanging rug, and somebody just beat me full well with a broom. I waited for a way out, an escape, some other plan to form, but nothing came. Miss Rosebud was determined to make a fool of herself in hopes of winning that pompous clown.

"You better come up with a new tactic, 'cause this fish ain't bitin'," I said.

"Wait and see. *Win the next round,*" she told me.

I entered the room again and took up my same chair. All my chips were as I left them, which was astonishing in itself. When the next round started, I placed a bet.

"The hour draws late, gentlemen," the baron said. "This will be my final round."

"Well." I pressed my hands together. "Better make it count. What've I got to lose?" I played every chip in my possession on my *least* lucky number, three. I was determined to lose this round and ruin Miss Rosebud's game, whatever this was. The baron contemplated his next move before placing a weighty stack on the king.

The other two men cashed out early but stayed to watch the baron and me.

Luck was in Miss Rosebud's favor just then, not mine. I picked the winning card. The door opened. All our heads turned. With a face as blank as an empty page, Miss Rosebud walked up to me and planted herself on my lap. How did I know she'd do that? I'd been here before. Only now, I wasn't proud. Miss Rosebud was playing a sickening game, and I allowed myself to be her pawn.

"Please take me back, Charles. I promise to give up my books and everything about me that your mother despises." She drew close to my ear and whispered, "Push me off your lap."

I couldn't do it. I couldn't fall into her trap again. I knew why she wanted me to—because she thought the baron would rescue her. But who knows what she'd do to me this time?

"Push me off your lap," she whispered, "or your beloved Bea will lose everything, including her copy of *Divine Comedy*, which has been conveniently removed from your room."

Shocked as could be, I stood, knocking Miss Rosebud off my lap and onto the floor. She yelped, just like before. The other two men stood, but the baron remained in his seat.

"You, sir, are a coward!" I pointed to the baron. "You won't stand to help a lady even when she's hurt."

Now he rose. "You are the one who pushed her down!"

"Only to see what you'd do. Proof that nobility is earned, not born. All's you are is a pompous idiot dressed in a lot of shiny duds. I bet the accent's fake too."

I helped Miss Rosebud to her feet. She was baffled at my break in the script. It surprised me too, but wherever it came from, I meant it.

"Are you calling me a fake?" he said, his face scorching. "Is this a challenge to my honor?"

"It would be, if you had any."

"Such irony that you call me a fake. I wonder what kind of professor you are. You speak like a filthy heathen."

My spirit fired up like hot grease in a skillet. How dare he judge me by the way I talk? And with such a sneer. He knew nothing about me. I wouldn't let him have the last word.

"I'm glad you got that fancy title, 'cause that's all you got. You're just a clown with a whole lotta money and no character."

The baron showed me the pistol at his side. "I'll give you one chance to retract your statements, sir. Once you challenge me, I will not back down."

It was far too late to go back on what I said, even if I wanted to. I showed him the pistol at my own side, not flinching nor blinking. "I won't take nothin' back, so I guess it's a challenge. But let's do away with the *sir* business. I ain't flattered by it, and you don't deserve it."

"Fellers, take it outside," the barkeep cut in.

"No," Rosebud said, "nobody's taking anything outside. There's no problem here. Let's not get away from ourselves."

"Excuse me, miss," I said. "There's been a challenge to my honor—and yours too." I stepped away from the table and marched outside. The baron followed. The others came out to spectate, relishing the free entertainment. Nobody could pass up a good, old-fashioned duel.

Miss Rosebud's pleas for us to quit got more desperate. "This is getting ridiculous. I beg you both to come to your senses." We ignored her and lined up in formation in the street, twenty paces from the starting middle. My hand hovered over my pistol. Then I remembered. Damned thing wasn't even loaded. I wished Bea was here. Even though I'd ruined everything, it was her face alone I wanted to see before I died.

"Please stop," Rosebud begged me, shaking me by the shoulders. "This has gone far enough. I never wanted you to do this. You're being a fool. Truthfully, please stop."

"You can contrive any plot you want," I said to her, "but you can't control the outcome."

Having no luck with me, she stood between me and Baron von Klein. "Please, sir, don't go any further. This is not what you think."

"Step aside, miss," he said.

She turned to me again and clung to my neck, her eyes dappled in tears. "Please! I never intended anyone to get hurt. You're taking this too far. You're being a fool."

I didn't fear death, not really. Except something was different. Now it meant never seeing Bea again. I wasn't ready for that. I couldn't part with her forever, especially not the way I left things. Laws, I sure messed things up, and me dying would put the nail in the coffin of my foolishness—literally.

Miss Rosebud must've seen my conviction waver. She must've seen the face of a boy not quite ready to die. At the same time, she knew how these affairs of honor worked. A man couldn't walk away once a challenge was waged, even if the whole setup was a hoax. Me, Charlie Rye, who thought I'd traversed the road of hard knocks enough times, was still no wiser than a fool born yesterday.

"I'll get you out of this with some honor," Miss Rosebud whispered, "if you come back for me in five years."

Even though my heart pounded toward its final beats on earth, I still found myself curious about what she'd say, what she'd do to reverse this. Would she tell the baron that I'm too young to duel?

"Don't tell him my age," I whispered, barely moving my lips.

"No, I won't do that," she said.

"Then how?"

"Just trust me," she said. "I swear on the life of my sister, I'll get you out of this with your honor intact."

I hung my head and heard myself say, "I'll do it."

Her tears stopped flowing. "Do you mean it?"

"Yes, I mean it."

"Everything? Even . . . take me as a wife . . . in five years?" she said, breathily.

"Everything," I said, detesting myself.

She turned toward the baron, blocking me with her body. "You will not shoot this man." She took my gun from its holster and tossed it aside. She walked toward him, each step deliberate. "Give me your gun."

He gave way to a look of confusion but did as she asked. His gun too, she tossed away.

"This was my doing," she said. "I'm a fraud."

The baron said nothing, but his silence turned toward bewilderment.

"You see, this was all . . . a charade. I was laying a trap. I'm not an educated woman. I'm—" Then she paused and called to the bartender, "Willie, tell him who I am."

But Willie the barkeep said nothing.

"Men," she called to the others, "tell this gentleman who I am."

All of them chuckled and shifted around and spoke under their breath. Nobody wanted to outright admit they knew . . . or maybe they just couldn't say the word out loud. Sinning was so much easier without a name attached to it, they figured.

"Never mind, madam," the baron said, an edge of sharpness to his voice. "I think I can guess what you are. No need to shout it in the streets." The baron snatched his gun from the dirt and said, "This is madness," before turning and marching into the darkness.

The observers gave grand applause, like they'd just been treated to the finest performance of the century. "Brava! Brava! Take a bow!"

Miss Rosebud didn't move from the spot of her shame. These gawkers were grating on me.

"Get lost, all of you!" I shouted at them.

They jeered and laughed, but eventually disappeared.

I retrieved my gun and walked to her. Her eyes were closed, overcome with emotion. I wished I could reverse time and do things different. About a hundred things came to me to say, but none of them did justice to everything I felt, so I began to leave.

"You won't regret this," she said, catching the edge of my sleeve. I already did but didn't say so out loud. My anger would've taken hold and manifested itself in unwanted ways. Instead, I said, "You don't have the slightest clue what you made me do."

"I promise I won't disappoint you. Not one single day."

"Well, I got five years to live my own way. I best get started."

Miss Rosebud threw herself down on a nearby bench and trembled with silent sobs. I could have stayed to comfort her, but I reckoned I'd have a whole lifetime to do that, come five years' time.

"I'm leavin' at sunup," I said. "If there's any honor in you, leave that book with the hotel clerk. And my winnings—I'll be takin' those too."

I staggered down the street, defeated. She got what she wanted from me all along.

CHAPTER 23

Beatrice Brannon

Monday, April 16, 1860, minutes past midnight

FUNNY thing about the Cold-Blooded Boys. They'd become a lot less cold toward me after the competition. I'd dreaded my return to the station, expecting to be harassed, but instead I'd found them to be almost jubilant. Maybe escaping accountability had made them so, but after handing me the fifty dollars, they'd seemed to pretend the competition never happened.

We played cards late into the night. Charlie had taught me a couple card tricks over the years, so I mystified them with my skills. Sunday ticked into the wee hours of Monday, as the boys downed their whiskey. A knock at the door sent them into a whirlwind.

"The Colonel's here!" Private whisper-shouted, scraping up the cards and kicking whiskey bottles under beds.

I grabbed my knapsack, ready to take my ride, and opened the door. Charlie stood there, his fake moustache sloping and his arms hanging low.

"It's not the Colonel," I called to the boys. "It's a friend of mine. Be back in a minute." I closed the door quickly behind me.

I tugged Charlie by the arm to a secluded spot away from the Riley boys, who were always loath to mind their own business. "What're you doing here? You can't be seen with half your disguise on."

"Listen," he began, "I . . . *fixed* the situation with Miss Rosebud. She's agreed to keep quiet. You can stay in the Pony Express." The way he'd said *fixed* didn't seem convincing, as if he hadn't really fixed anything but possibly made it worse. I wondered what that woman had required of him. He anticipated my question. "I kept in line with my principles, like I said I would, but I have to go back home now."

Charlie was different. Something had changed in him. A weariness anchored him down like I'd never seen before.

"Why do you look so sad?"

"No, I'm happy." There was an obvious dissonance between his words and the way he said them. It frightened me. Did he really think he could fool me? I kept myself from prying, despite my awful yearning for the truth. Had Miss Rosebud taken advantage of him? Had she hurt him in some way? "I got a couple things to do back at Vict'ry Hills," he continued. "Some affairs to set in order. There may be some noble purpose for me yet."

It was torturous hearing him talk like that. All he'd ever wanted was to make a name for himself—to do something grand and adventurous—and I'd taken away his chance. "Charlie, you would've been so much better at this than me. I'm barely surviving. We should've sent you to the Pony Express instead. They didn't want to send me. We've messed with fate and now we're paying the price."

"Now listen up, Bea," he said, his demeanor still weak but taking on a serious quality. "You were meant for this, OK? Don't doubt yourself ever again. Not to nobody. You've torn this thing up six ways from Sunday. Did you forget you won the shooting expo?"

In fact, that seemed meaningless now. The only things that felt real were the ones going on inside me—my emotions, my nightmares, all my worries. I longed for the day when the things on the inside and the outside fell into harmony again. "It all feels so strange and unsettling," I said, "like I'm standing alone on my own planet."

"I know the feelin'," he said. "But that's how it is blazin' your own trail. Ain't never gonna be easy."

"I suppose not," I said. A quietude lingered, and I felt the doom of our impending goodbye. I couldn't let him go without some proof that he was going to be alright and that his zest for life hadn't vanished. "What will you do back home, Charlie? What are these affairs you need to set in order?"

"Well, first off, I wanna find out what Torrence is up to."

With everything that had happened, he still wanted to solve the mystery of why Mayor Torrence had come to Carson City, and I couldn't have been happier about it. Maybe it would distract him from whatever had happened with Miss Rosebud.

"Yes, we must find out!" I exclaimed with a little too much gusto. "It's all so . . . mysterious."

A grin fish-hooked one side of his lips. He hadn't fallen for my overzealous display. "It's mighty kind of you to pretend to wanna help."

"No, I really do. I'm scheduled for another run to Buckland's in the next day or so. I'll find out everything about Pascoe. You said Mayor Torrence gave him a key, right? Pascoe used a key to unlock all the pouches. He took some papers out and put some in. He's not supposed to do that. He said it was official business, but I know he's lying. Next time, I'll get a look at the papers he's working on."

"That's a tall order," he said. "Sure you're up for it?"

"It'll be easier than your job. Pascoe doesn't suspect me—not yet. But if Torrence sees you in town, following him around, he'll descend on you like a pack of wolves. You'll have to be invisible."

"Don't you worry about me." His smile reassured me some, but his overall presence still lagged. "Speakin' of worryin', you sure got your mama in a dither."

"You spoke with her?"

"No, Cobber showed up at my place before I left for Carson City."

"Did she make any mention of coming to fetch me?"

"Cobber said she wanted to, but I think I gave him the right words to calm her fears. I'm supposed to bring back news of your health and well-being. I ain't even gonna ask about that bruise on your cheek."

"Don't," I said. "But if you're going back to Victory Hills, could you give Mama the money I won?"

"'Course I will."

I took from my pocket the small leather pouch filled with coins totaling fifty dollars and handed it to him.

"Bea, I want you to know nothin' ever happened between me and Miss Rosebud."

"You needn't explain yourself to me. I haven't given it a second thought." My lie hurt him, and it hurt me too. All I'd done since we last parted was imagine what he might've been doing. With such an outright betrayal of my feelings, I attempted to take the focus off my flippancy. "Since when have you cared about the opinions of others?"

His response was much more honest than I had been. "When it comes to you, Bea, I do care."

We stood face-to-face in silence with the subtle glow of the gaslamp down the lane. My mind called up the moment we stood in the river, the eddy tugging at our ankles and the warm sunlight on our cheeks.

"I'm takin' a chance here . . . ," he said.

"Yes?" I said all too quickly, knowing what my answer would be if he asked for an honest-to-goodness kiss.

"Maybe you don't want to wear this no more," he said, drawing from his pocket the silver-button necklace, "but I thought I'd ask just in case."

I pursed my lips, embarrassed for misinterpreting his cue. Never mind the fact that he'd found it in the weeds where I'd tossed it aside. "I didn't understand what I was feeling. I still don't." This small bit of honesty, I hoped, would make up for my lack of it earlier.

"Well, you better take it," he said. "The little rascal did travel a long way to be with you." He cracked another smile as he untangled the twine from it being bunched in his pocket. Instead of handing it to me though, he leaned in close to tie it around my neck. He remained there, taking his time with the knot. Even after securing it, he stayed, his warm cheek touching mine. I closed my eyes and rose a degree to meet his stature. The touch of his lips on mine was ever so gentle, light as a drop of dew.

"I'll never forget you, Bea."

I opened my eyes. "That sounds an awful lot like a forever goodbye."

"Well, you never know what's comin'. From day to day, as mortals, we all live with the risk of never seein' each other again. Life's a gamble, sometimes a cruel one."

What was the meaning of all these final declarations? All this philosophizing about the end of days? That kind of talk didn't suit him, and it might as well have thrown a knife into me. "We've both passed through some tribulation, haven't we?" I said.

"Yes, and I got a feelin' we're both headed for rough waters still."

"Then . . . I'll meet you back at the shore," I said, hoping, praying, leaning upon Providence that this wouldn't be the last moment I ever saw him.

CHAPTER 24

Charlie Rye

Monday, April 16, 1860, dawn

THE sun winked over the hills as I rode up to the Brannons' place. My head was dozy from riding all night, but I couldn't ignore the picture of loveliness before me. The perfect little house, the yellow sweet clover that grew along the porch, the mountain chickadees that fluttered from branch to branch—it all greeted me with a warm familiarity. A voice called out from a tall cottonwood tree, "Ahoy! Who goes there? You! Three points off the starboard bow."

Cobber's head poked through the branches, peering at me through a spyglass and wearing a two-pointed naval hat.

I played along, saluting. "It is I, Charles Rye, Jr., able-bodied seaman."

"Come aboard my frigate, man!" Cobber shouted. "You'll drown out there! Seas will be rough today. The sky is full red this morning. Bound to be squalls."

"Aye, aye, Captain. Allow me to stow the, uh, dinghy, and I'll be aboard in moments." After dropping down and leading Dandy to the barn, I hoisted myself into the tree alongside Cobber.

"Hey, Charlie," he said, breaking character, "look what I got for my birthday yesterday." He handed me the spyglass that appeared to be of decent quality. He showed me how the barrel collapsed and extended and told me to give it a try.

"Well, looky there," I marveled.

"It's a real spyglass from the British Royal Navy. Dr. Pearl gave it to me. He wanted to be a naval captain when he was a boy. Became a doctor instead."

"Dr. Pearl indeed," I said, taking a view through the lens. I wondered about our gallant doctor bringing presents to the Brannon boys. I would've bet my right arm he was making a play for Mrs. Brannon. After all, she was the town's fresh-minted widow and a mighty pretty lady at that. I inwardly chuckled at the sly ol' fox.

"This hat was a gift to JP," Cobber chatted on, "but he didn't want it. Can you imagine? Said it was silly. But it's a bona fide hat from the navy. How can it be silly?"

"I agree. This is no joke, Cobber."

The captain removed his hat and tucked it under his arm. "This is the first birthday I ever had with Da gone. It's the first one we ain't been all together." His words smarted. This family was in the thick of their grief. An ache struck my insides. Luckily, Cobber kept chatting and didn't wait for any words of comfort from me. I had none. "This cheered me up a little," he said, taking back the spyglass. "It can see five miles out. All the way into town."

"It's a fine specimen, to be sure," I told him.

"Did you see Bea?" He seemed eager to hear.

"I sure did see her."

"Don't she miss us?"

"'Course she does."

"I guess she forgot our birthday, though, didn't she?"

"No, not at all," I stumbled. "She . . . was heartbroken to miss it."

"Really? She didn't forget?" His face lit up like a firecracker, and I didn't have the heart to say she never mentioned a word.

"Actually, she sent me here on a special assignment to wish you and JP happy birthday."

"She remembered! She's the best sister this whole world over."

Seeing him come alive, I knew a fib like that wouldn't keep me out of heaven. "In fact, she wanted me to give you this." I reached in my haversack and handed Cobber the silver snuffbox. "You gotta share it with JP, of course."

His mouth gaped open like a wide-mouthed bass. "Charlie, I gotta show Mama. Come on!" He plummeted from the tree and ran for the house. "Mama, Charlie's here!"

I followed behind. Mrs. Brannon opened the door and gathered me up like a mother hen. "Oh, Charlie! How glad we are to see you. Please come inside and give us news of our Beatrice. Have you seen her? How is she?"

"She's great, Mrs. Brannon, you'd hardly believe it."

"Truly? I'm so glad to hear that! Come and sit down. I'll pour you some coffee."

I seated myself at the kitchen table and noticed a few items laid out. The rifle, some china plates, and a couple silver candlesticks. I didn't ask why.

Cobber had the snuffbox behind his back, waiting to spring his surprise, while JP, in a cross mood, played a game of cup and ball in the corner. Before I could break into my report on Bea, Cobber cut in, "Mama, look what Bea gave me and JP for our birthday. It's a snuffbox made of pure silver!"

JP's interest was piqued, and he drew closer. He wrinkled his nose and said, "How're we supposed to split that? Crank the lid off its hinges?"

"We ain't gonna split it," his brother scolded. "JP, how can you be so selfish?"

"I ain't selfish! You got the spyglass and the naval hat."

"You didn't want the hat," Cobber protested. "And I don't want the snuffbox for myself. We're giving it to Mama for the house, of course. Remember what the lawyer man said?"

I looked at Mrs. Brannon to clarify.

"The attorney came again yesterday," she explained. "We owe a good-faith payment on the debt by six o'clock tonight."

"Or what?" I eked out.

"We'll be evicted!" JP stated bluntly.

"Not quite yet," Mrs. Brannon corrected. "I'm sure he'll take these goods as payment." She pointed to the rifle and other fineries on the table.

"And if he doesn't?" I asked, not satisfied.

"Eviction!" JP insisted. "By Wednesday. No sense in hidin' it from him."

She lowered her head, verifying JP's words.

"Wednesday's two days from now!" I said. "Ellerby disgusts me. How can he treat you this way? He pretended to be a friend to Jeremiah—to all of you."

"We can seethe in our anger all we want, but in the end, it was a poor business deal that got us here." I'd never heard Mrs. Brannon speak of it like that—to lay the blame on her husband. It was true, of course, but it would've killed Bea to hear her mama repeat the same words as the town gossips. "Again, I'm sure these items will fetch us something, since we don't have a sum of money, big or small."

"Sum of money," I said under my breath, remembering the winnings from the shooting expo.

"Fine!" JP said. "We'll pawn the snuffbox just like the other stuff."

Cobber leaned in closer to my ear. "He's going through a rough patch."

"Am not! No more'n anybody else. Fine, take it, Mama! Take away our one good birthday present."

"JP, I won't take it from you," Mrs. Brannon said. "Bea intended for you to share it with your brother, and share it you will. We won't sell it with the other things."

"No! Take it. I'm the man of the house now. I'm supposed to provide. Take the money. Use it for the house. That's what Da would want me to do."

"S'cuse me, what makes *you* the man of the house?" Cobber argued. "I'm a man too."

"But I'm older."

"By ten minutes," Cobber scoffed.

JP kept jabbing. "Well, at least I'm not a twelve-year-old still playing pretend nursery games in the trees."

"I'm not pretending. I'm gonna be a real sea captain one day. I'm practicing the jargon and rituals."

"Pshaw!" JP slapped the table.

"Alright, boys, I'm sure Charlie didn't come all this way to hear you two squabble."

JP huffed with his arms folded tight across his chest while Cobber covered his ears.

"Is anybody here interested in what else I got from Bea?" I said, gleeful in what I was about to reveal.

Cobber removed his hands from his ears. Mrs. Brannon sat forward in her chair, and JP, well, he kept his arms crossed, but I had his attention. From that magical haversack of mine, I withdrew the small money pouch and held it out to Mrs. Brannon. "You tell that attorney he can go to hell."

A sort of quiet reverence came over Mrs. Brannon, who opened the pouch and dumped the coins on the table. "Twenty, twenty-five, thirty . . . fifty," she counted aloud. I might as well have given her the moon itself, for all her shock. "Lord-a-mercy!" she whispered. "This is the exact amount we owe. Bea got this from the Pony Express—already?"

"Truth be told, Bea won that money in a shootin' contest."

Now it was my turn to slap the table. I couldn't hold it in. Not with all those stupefied looks pointed at me. From there, I gave the performance of my life telling the story, adding all the right gestures and bang-pop-booms. I watched a gleam return to JP's eye as the story unfolded. Boy, did I have a hog's time giving it the right flourish.

JP and Cobber were bubbled over with excitement. They darted around, mock-shooting and making a playground of the room.

"I challenge you to sudden death!" One of them called.

As I watched the scene, a pin pricked the core of me. *Holy Moses,* I thought. *I'll have to leave them behind.* I always thought I'd belong to them someday, to this family. In many ways, I belonged to them now, but if I uttered the words, *In five years, I'm going to marry a prostitute,* Mrs. Brannon would cast me away from the house. All rights and privileges would be revoked, and they'd never speak to me again. The full weight of my debacle in Carson City didn't strike me till then. And boy, did it.

JP grabbed the rifle. "C'mon, Cobber. Let's see who's a better shot at a moving target."

"Do be careful," Mrs. Brannon called before the boys slammed the door behind them. She sighed with relief.

Could I confide in Mrs. Brannon? Would she understand? Could I abide the look she'd give me? Never. I could never tell them how low I sank. One day maybe they'd find out, but it wouldn't be from me.

"Miracles haven't ceased," Mrs. Brannon said, dabbing her face with her apron. "You see, after the attorney came, I went to the general store to sell my best-stitched frocks, but they wouldn't buy 'em. Business is slow, they said. So when I got home, I knelt in prayer, right there by that fireplace, beggin' the Lord to provide some other means. I was ready to trade those goods on the table, if they'd take 'em, but you showed up with that money from Bea. Fifty dollars! I've always been a woman of faith, but it's been so long since I've seen a miracle. And today, you've brought one here."

I shifted in my discomfort. Of course she had to lay on the guilt like that. I wasn't fit to utter God's name, let alone be his messenger. But she kept going, pouring salt on the gaping hole that used to be my heart. If only I'd never made that promise to Miss Rosebud.

"Charlie, I was wrong before. I thought it was a mistake for Bea to go. Now I know it's exactly where God wants her to be at this very moment. Dear me, I was so wrong. You had faith when I was weak. You've always believed in Bea. You've always been a good friend to her. Thank you. I do believe you love her."

She squeezed my hand. My mouth went dry. I didn't know which kind of love she meant, but it didn't matter. Mine for Bea was every kind possible.

"Are you going back to Carson City?" She patted her cheeks, declaring the crying done.

"Not anytime soon," I said.

"What are your plans, then?" She asked a mighty good question. I couldn't say that I planned on spying on the mayor and uncovering a massive scandal. Surely she wouldn't find that a wholesome endeavor, so I said, "Just figuring out the next thing."

"How's your father? Won't he be anxious to see you?"

I shrugged. "He's long stopped caring about my comings and goings."

"If he's not expecting you, then you're welcome to stay here."

"It's alright, Mrs. Brannon. I wouldn't want to intrude."

"Nonsense! The boys would love your company. I haven't seen JP smile like that in days. And with Bea gone, we've got an extra bed."

"An extra bed, you say?" This caught my interest. Not just any bed—Bea's. Cuss me if I didn't savor that thought. "Thank you kindly, Mrs. Brannon. Maybe I'll take you up on that. I reckon it's a better prospect than sleepin' on the floor at my place."

* * *

Nightfall

I caught up on sleep that afternoon and woke up around nightfall, shifting around in Bea's bed. I buried my face in her pillow. All Bea's scents of maple syrup and lye soap were in my face, like she was right there with me. The torture of it! I sprang from the bed, freeing myself from the covers that twisted around me like a python.

Restless as a caged animal, I paced the floor. My haversack hung beside Bea's mirror. I reached inside for Bea's volume of *Divine Comedy*. A fat space on her bookshelf held its place. I tucked the heavy tome back where it belonged. *There has to be some way out of that contract,* I thought. *Maybe I could buy my way out. A bribe. Anything!*

With no knock or warning, JP shuffled in, shoulders drooping. He plunked down on the floor and wrapped himself in the covers that were heaped there. "I'm glad you're here, Charlie."

"You OK?"

His mouth twisted like he was embarrassed to answer. "I just miss him, you know?"

"I miss him too."

"Is it OK for boys to cry, Charlie?" His eyes watched me for the truest answer.

"Sure it is." There were already tears in the boy's eyes. It took all my strength to fight what my pa ingrained in me. My tears always angered him. "If boys wasn't supposed to cry," I said, "then why was we born with tears?"

He gave a fleeting smile. "Good, 'cause I can't help it. The other boys caught me and gave me a lickin' for it. Said I'm a weakling and a softy. Them boys used to be my friends. Now they won't talk to me no more, 'less it's to tease me and call me names."

"Them weasels," I said. "Who are they to browbeat a kid who just lost his father? And not just any father. Jeremiah Brannon."

"It's true. I'm weak. I'm the weakest person there ever was because I can't shake this."

JP looked so pained, so cast down. I never heard him talk like this.

"You ain't weak, JP. Not at all. You're strong."

"I am?"

"Yes." I wasn't sure where I was going, but I kept on course, hoping the words would come out right. "The love you had for your da was strong. Your bond was strong. That's why you cry. He was the best man that ever lived. Don't let them scamps tell you any different. If he was my father, I'd a' cried a bucketful. In fact, I did."

The tears froze on his cheeks, and hope glimmered in his eyes. Poor lad had really been dealing himself a solid reproof for this crying business. I offered a side smile. "So maybe just cry when they can't see you. Wait till you get home and you can cry your eyes out. Nobody here's gonna judge ya."

He returned the smile. "You're like a brother, Charlie."

That was a fine compliment. One I was proud of. I wondered how different my life would've been if I'd been born a Brannon.

"Still it don't seem right to speak of the dead that way," he said. "I wish I knew why they keep callin' my da a coward."

"*Your da,* a coward?"

"Yes. Freddy Hartley told all the other boys that my da done something cowardly, but he won't say what. Freddy Hartley heard it from his pa, who heard it from Mayor Torrence."

I drew in a long breath. Mayor Torrence indeed. He seemed to be the source of everybody's contempt these days, not just mine.

"Well, we know that ain't true, JP. Your da was no coward, and Mayor Torrence knows that better than anybody."

"I asked Freddy if it was about the Peregrine mine, but he said no. He said it's something else. They won't even give me the chance to set 'em straight."

"Aw, JP, leave it be. If they're the kind of boys to like you one day and hate you the next, what does it say about their character?"

"I have to find out, Charlie. They're trampin' on his good name, and I won't stand for it. Help me find out. Please?"

I sighed. Why couldn't the poor boy just give it a rest? Losing a father was hard enough. Why add the weight of what the town youngsters thought? But that earnest face told me that this matter *was* the weight of it—that JP was nothing without the pride of his father's good name.

"How do you propose to find out? What'll we—"

"We'll search his house," he said, his answer ready to shoot.

"Whose house?"

"Mayor Torrence's! He and Da always butted heads. I bet we could find out why. Maybe in a diary. All's I know is I can't sit here lazy as a lemon while they drag his memory through the mud."

"It's risky, JP. Very risky."

Mrs. Brannon opened the door at that very moment and stuck her head in the doorway. "What's risky?"

JP was wide-eyed and guilt-stricken.

"Stayin' up late on a night before school," I answered.

"Indeed." Mrs. Brannon smiled. "Come on, JP. Let's get some sleep and let Charlie do the same."

"Yes, Mama."

"Well, it's right nice to hear some obedience come from your mouth, JP. Not often I do."

JP gave me a wink and mouthed the words, "Think about it."

"Good night, Charlie," she said. And they left the room.

* * *

Poor JP, I thought, a couple hours later as I crept past the fireplace to the back door. *He'll be cross when he finds out that I left without helping him.* As much as I would've enjoyed finding out why the kids were calling Jeremiah Brannon a coward, I couldn't let this Rosebud business go any longer. The contract would overpower me if I didn't get out of it soon.

The door squealed on its hinges like a high-strung violin. Haversack over my shoulder, I slipped into the barn, took Dandy by the rope, and led him out. JP appeared like a ghost in his glowing nightshirt.

"Deuces!" I said, spooked.

"Where you goin'?" he said, taking no care to be quiet.

"Shhh, you'll wake your mama. There's something I gotta do. It's really, really important."

"What you gotta do? You said you'd help me!"

"Keep it down, OK. You don't understand."

"You promised."

"No, I said I'd *think* about it. And I can't do it now, JP. I'll only be gone a couple days. We'll get them bullies when I get back. Trust me, they won't know what hit 'em."

"Don't go!" he cried. Before I could hush him again, he planted his knees on the ground and sobbed like he was praying to the Almighty. "You can't leave me! Everybody leaves and nobody cares about me. Everybody spoils sweet little Cobber, but nobody cares about me."

Lord, what could I do? The ways and means of comforting folks didn't come natural to me. "It's OK. I won't go. I'll stay."

He kept crying and carrying on like he didn't even hear me. "My da was no weakling. He was no coward. How can they say those things? He taught me everything I know. I'll never get him back. Please don't leave me."

"I'll stay." I took his wet cheeks in my hands and said, "I'll stay, OK? Do you hear me? I'll stay."

Slowly, his sobs ceased. To leave him in that low state would've been wrong. I ignored the impulse to go back to Carson City to get myself out of that mess. If only I could get Mrs. Brannon praying for a miracle on my behalf, 'cause that's what I needed. All's I knew is I couldn't leave JP like that; nothing could've been plainer.

CHAPTER 25

Beatrice Brannon

Tuesday, April 17, 1860, early morning

I tossed and turned with a hundred things on my mind. Never too distant from any particular thought was the moment, exactly twenty-four hours ago, when I'd said goodbye to Charlie. It was then we'd shared a kiss. Mama would've firmly objected, but that didn't stop the moment from playing and replaying in my mind. I didn't regret the kiss. *This is life,* I thought, *and I know too well how short it can be.* If I were to never see Charlie again, I would've regretted *not* kissing him all the more. I smiled to myself, the secret kiss still lingering on my lips.

Now to prepare my mind for the ride back to Buckland's. The east-bound rider was expected any moment. Laws, how I dreaded seeing the faces of Squires, Oscar, and even Jim. But I wrapped my fingers around my lucky silver button and called to mind a fierce remembrance of why I was doing this. *I can do this for my family. I can do this for Da.*

The first sound of disturbance were the horses. They began nickering and clomping from their quarters on the other side of the wall. Then from down the street, I heard the rapid clanging of a bell. Voices shouted. One screamed. I sat up. *Has the war come?*

The Cold-Blooded Boys didn't stir. I put on Mr. Gallagher's boots and stepped out into the night. An orange haze glowed above one of the shops.

Fast as my legs could carry me, I ran toward it. *No, it can't be.* I should have known. Mercy, I should have known they'd go after Tucker's Printing.

Enormous flames swirled skyward, and plumes of smoke floated every direction in the breeze. I clutched my sick stomach.

Hotel patrons and saloon goers trickled out into the street, some screaming, some putting themselves to work, and others staring in disbelief. Two men dropped down from a horse-drawn fire engine, unrolled a long hose, and pumped water onto the burning building.

Mabel rushed toward the flames. Bucket in hand, she threw a splash of water onto the blaze. I grabbed a bucket from a person handing them out. I drew water from a nearby trough and pitched it as hard as I could. When the trough was emptied, Mabel yelled, "To the well!" A group of us ran farther down the road.

I held the bucket as Mabel's arms pumped up and down, the water spurting out. Another helper took over the pump when she scurried away.

"Maybe the equipment can be saved," Mabel called through the chaos. "It's our life!"

I carried my bucket to the blaze. The shape of a man emerged from the burning building, hefting a piece of printing equipment in both arms. It was Mr. Tucker. A fireman barred him from returning for more.

I hurried back to the well with my bucket and filled it again. On my way back to the fire, I saw Mabel standing motionless in front of her shop when it collapsed on itself, flinders falling, the second floor caving into the first.

Mabel stood in the road and sobbed. Nothing more could've been done. Mr. Tucker, his nightclothes covered in soot, took his daughter in his arms and held her.

Nobody returned to the well. The fire brigade had extinguished most of the flames, but not in time to save the Tuckers' beautiful print shop. A few people joined their circle of embrace. Some of them were the abolitionists, but there were others too. I joined them.

One of Mabel's friends shot out of the group and faced the other side of the street. "This is on your hands, *Gazette*!" he shouted.

Another man stepped forward. "My paper had nothing to do with this! Miss Tucker might as well have done it herself, printing all those reckless political tirades."

Some folks gathered on one side with Mabel and her father. Others lined up alongside the man from the *Gold & Silver Gazette*. The shouting turned to shoving, then shoving back, and soon the fight was full blown. Men lobbed hits, threw each other to the ground, wrestled, and kicked. I was pushed out of the path of the fighting and fell to the ground.

Civil war hadn't come, not today, but seeing what I saw and feeling the palpable animosity, I knew it soon would. Nothing less than a war could undo these passions.

Mabel clambered onto the back of a wagon and shouted. "All of you stop! This is my shop burned down—my father's and mine. Now it's my turn to speak, and you will listen to me, if these are the last words on my breath."

Folks listened, quieted down. She appeared so singularly impressive beneath a streetlamp, shouting into the hazy morning like an impassioned warrior.

"I do not ask you to take pity on me. I will not attempt to change any ignorant minds. But I will say that *this* is what comes of hate. Destruction. That's all it will ever bring. It is not capable of anything else. It does not build anything. It only tears it down. My father built this shop out of pure love. You don't know what he went through to make a life for himself in this bitter, bitter world—that he scraped together every cent he had to buy his way out of slavery and, in the end, still had to escape. But he did it for me, his baby daughter. He came West, taught himself to read. Taught me to read at three years old. Earned wages far less than a white man makes but, little by little, had enough to buy this shop and everything in it. By Jesus, he wanted us to be free! Not enslaved again. Do you not see that you are chained to this slavery too? Every one of you. If we are not all free, then we are all enslaved. We are yoked together in this bondage. And if we do not work as one, we will all be burned to ashes with our own hate."

"Amen!" someone shouted.

"We have supported you from the very beginning, Miss Mabel," one woman said. She stood on Mabel's side but spoke contrary to it. "There are those of us who have bought your papers and treated you kindly. Condemnation upon the person responsible for this! But you're dividing this town with your articles, and I cannot contribute to your paper any longer."

"Yes, Miss Mabel, go back to writing about town celebrations and barn raisings!" one of Mabel's supporters said in satire. "You rile us up with your truth!"

The woman defended herself. "You mistake me, sir. I am every bit an abolitionist, but I don't support war."

Mr. Tucker stepped forward and broke his silence. "I'm afraid, Mrs. Lockwood, that soon there will no longer be such a luxury."

His words created a simmering silence, as though each person were forced to contemplate their own convictions and weigh them against all that was happening here and now.

At the most inopportune moment, just as the mob was waiting for a target at which to place their blame, a carriage rounded the corner.

"Look who shows up: Sheriff Lassen," a man from Mabel's group said, sneering. "Late for the party, as usual."

All stood quiet as the mayor's carriage drew near. He pulled back on the reins, aghast at the smoky wreckage as well as the stares fixed on him. He was dressed head to toe in clean, crisp linens, his face glaringly absent of soot and sweat.

"You're late, Sheriff," Mabel said from her wagon.

He acted and spoke very much like a gentleman, a fact that didn't give him much credence in this setting. "Miss Tucker . . . I'm shocked. This is madness. Surely this is the work of an outsider. Nobody in our town could have committed this tragedy."

"We both know who did this, Sheriff. The perpetrators sent me a warning near a month ago—in the form of a note. You chose to ignore it."

"I did *not* ignore it, Miss Tucker," Lassen said, his voice defensive. "I've been deep in my investigation ever since you showed it to me. This group works in the dark. They won't betray each other. In fact, somebody here knows more than they're telling." He turned to the crowd. "If you're harboring their secrets, you're as guilty as the one who committed this crime. It's a brotherhood. A secret organization. Tell me, who in this group is a member of the Vipers for Peace?"

Silence was the only safe reply. Nobody was going to admit to being a member. And for those who'd never heard of this organization, like me, well, I figured we were just taking it all in. They had a name. The *Vipers for Peace*. What did any of this have to do with *peace*?

"Who's this group, Mabel?" someone asked. "What note did they give you?"

"One morning, the lock on our door was broken," she said. "Our papers were scattered. The note said, 'Cease printing your warmongering opinions. Slavery must stay. Union be damned. You've been warned.' There was no name signed, only a symbol that looked like an open-mouthed snake." She jumped down from the wagon, took up a charred stick, and drew the symbol on a plank of wood.

Indeed that was the symbol they'd smeared in ink on Mr. Hobbs's floor. His shop had been broken into and vandalized, just as they'd done to Mabel's. I was forced to reconcile that these violent crimes were done by the same group of people who had dealings in Victory Hills, Carson City, and probably Buckland's.

"Someone in this group started the fire, no question," the sheriff said. "But they all get their orders from the man at the top. They call him the Viper King. If we can nab him, we'll stop them at the source."

Mabel pointed her question back at the sheriff. "Since law enforcement had its chance and failed, we must take a new approach. This Viper King, as he calls himself, must be brought to justice. I call on you, Sheriff Lassen, to offer a reward for his capture."

Vocal support arose. One could see the pressure mount on the sheriff to make a hasty decision. Even those who opposed Mabel's group and the abolitionists were in favor of a reward.

"Fair enough," the sheriff said. "I'll offer a reward. Five hundred dollars for the capture of the Viper King."

"They're not gonna give him up so easily," Mabel said, curtailing a rise of ovations. "That's a pittance to trade for their loyalty. I say double it!"

The mob sang out in jubilation. These penniless fellows who counted flecks of gold had probably never had the chance at so much money.

Sheriff Lassen must've been stunned at the lady's audacity. Even so, before the cheers died down, he pointed his finger to the sky and declared, "One thousand dollars for the capture of the Viper King or for anyone who can lead us to his capture. Bring him back alive!"

For a moment, I couldn't move, like a heavy stone in the midst of a rushing river. The townsfolk bustled around me, forming crews, preparing to ride out. Others saddled up to search on their own. Maybe they knew who they were looking for; maybe they didn't. But I knew everything in that moment.

Back at that saloon meeting, the mayor was clear on his anti-war stance, and this society claimed to be for peace. Then I saw the symbol on Mr. Hobbs's floor, a man who opposed Torrence. Adding to it, Charlie had seen Torrence give a key—or something like it—to Pascoe, who took the key to Buckland's, where, instead of behaving like a station manager, wrote up some documents, probably pushing their cause, and used the key illegally to put them in the mochila. They had infiltrated the Pony Express, and I knew who.

But am I absolutely certain that Mayor Torrence is the one in charge? The Viper King? A scene snapped into my consciousness. That fateful day at

Torrence's ranch, I'd shouted at Torrence to shoot the horse. He'd countered with, "*I don't take orders from nobody. I give 'em.*"

Mayor Torrence would never belong to an organization that didn't have him at the head of it.

A one-thousand-dollar reward. Was this the whole reason I'd come to the Pony Express? Was this why my mind had hummed with curiosity at the words *Pony Express*? Not only would that money pay off the debt, but it would give us something to live off while we got our feet under us. We'd be respected again. We'd stay in the house Da built for us and not be driven out like mice from a barn. They'd remember Da for more than his one failure.

"What's goin' on here?" I heard to my left. The Colonel had arrived from the eastbound run, with his pony in tow, in the middle of this hubbub. "When I landed at the station, the boys were still asleep. They didn't have a clue."

Before I could answer, Abram and Elias accosted their father, trying to jump and speak at once. In that short time, they'd educated themselves about the reward.

Elias couldn't get the words out fast enough. "Colonel, we request your permission to take the horses."

"Slow down, I'm still learnin' what happened."

"Colonel, sir, we wish to make a run for the reward, sir," Abram added, then drew closer to his father's ear. "We know who the Viper King is. Remember that man Pascoe? He tried to recruit us. If we turn him in, we're a thousand dollars richer."

Jealousy and even panic set in. They wanted my reward. Well, I wouldn't share any of the intelligence I'd gathered.

The Colonel asked, "What crime did this man Pascoe do that's worth a thousand-dollar reward?"

"He burned down the print shop," they said, pointing to the wreckage almost gleefully, as if the shop hadn't belonged to anyone.

"I don't know about you takin' the Pony Express horses for your treasure hunt," the Colonel told his sons. They bickered loudly. With one of the cantinas left unlocked, I took out a pencil and a small scrap of paper and secluded myself behind a post to write down my findings.

The Viper King is Oliver Henry Walter Torrence. Find him in Victory Hills. Follow Rocky Pass trail across the Truckee and all the way to the north plateau. He will be armed.

My hands trembled as I folded the paper and made my way to Sheriff Lassen. I walked briskly but didn't run. The sheriff was conversing with two men. I waited. His back was to me. One of the men peered at me and caused the sheriff to turn around. "Something I can help you with, lad?"

I swallowed. "Yes, I'd like to speak with you. I have some information you'll find helpful."

His brows rose. "Alright."

"Privately, if you don't mind."

The two men left, and the sheriff gave a perplexed stare. I glanced down at the paper in my hands.

Trouble was, I couldn't say a thing. It wasn't right.

His face grew impatient. "I've got business here, so if you've got some information, let's have it."

"It's nothing. Sorry to trouble you." I darted in another direction, abandoning the sheriff.

The crowd had dispersed some. Those still there kept to their circles, plotting, deducing, figuring out which way to ride.

Mabel and her crew stood near the smoking rubble. She seemed removed from their discussion—quiet, dispassionate—very different from when she'd given her speech.

It took courage to approach her. Did she even want to speak to anyone after such a loss? After I'd lost Da, I hadn't wanted company, yet I'd hated when they ignored me.

"Mabel, I'm so sorry."

She didn't look at me. "What took him years to build is gone in an instant."

"I want to help. I know who the Viper King is."

Her eyes drifted toward mine. "How do you know?"

"A friend and I have been"—I searched for how to put it—"delving into possible theories. Tonight when I heard about the Vipers for Peace, it all clicked."

I held out the paper. She was reluctant to take it.

"It's OK, go ahead," I said. "Everything you need to find him is in there."

"Alright," she said, opening the note and skimming it. "Thank you."

For a moment, she considered something new and searched my face for an answer. "Why aren't you going for it?"

"I can't," I said. "I've got the Pony Express. The mail goes out tonight. In fact, I'm due to leave right now."

Never mind that five minutes before, I'd deemed the reward for myself.

"Will you ride out tonight?" I asked.

She took her time, gathering her thoughts. "Not tonight. I'm a little tired."

"Of course you are. First thing in the morning, then. I hope you get to him first. Once he gets wind of the reward, I'm sure he'll flee."

"Lafayette, I don't mean that kind of tired."

"What kind of . . . ?" My voice trailed off.

"I've been fighting this war a long time."

"Yes, I heard your speech. It was—"

"What I mean is, I feel the need to step away from the fight, maybe for a little while."

To me, it seemed abolitionism itself died at these words.

"I've got to take care of him," she said, motioning toward her father, who walked to a bench and sat, head hung low. "He's not in the best of health, and this won't help matters."

"Mabel," I said, my nose stinging and eyes clouding. "Please don't give up."

"Not forever, no. Just a little step away to see if it carries on without me."

"It will. It does."

Her despair was profound. Somehow, I could feel it, not just see it. She was tired from trying to remain a pillar of strength against all the harshness.

We said goodbye, and I couldn't help my tears from flowing. I stumbled toward the station. Mostly, I was upset at myself for wanting to claim a reward that was never mine. My desperation had blinded me to the pain of another. Mabel needed the reward to rebuild her shop and her life; in fact, the reward wouldn't have existed without her. I had to believe that if she couldn't ride to claim it herself that her friends would go for her.

There would be no easy answers, for Mabel or for myself. I knew that now. Any that presented themselves as such could only be distractions. I'd done my part to help, as I thought Da would've done, and now I'd carry on with my original plan, though it meant I'd have to ride back into the inferno.

CHAPTER 26

Charlie Rye

Tuesday, April 17, 1860, just before dawn

DAYLIGHT hadn't broke yet. Somehow, I got myself roped into helping JP find the answer to his burning question. I let JP take the lead, as I couldn't see how this search would bring about any answers. The fact that the town rascals were calling Jeremiah Brannon a coward, even after his death, said more about them kids than it could ever say about Jeremiah.

"We gotta beat that sun," JP told me as we hunkered behind some shrubs, spying on Torrence's place. "Mama can't know I was even gone."

"She's smarter'n you think," I said, keeping my voice low. "Mamas ain't stupid . . . or so I'm told."

Torrence came out his front door, locked it, and stowed the key in a potted plant. He was one of the few Victory Hillers who bothered to lock his door. He strolled to his barn, and a couple minutes later, rode out on his horse. He lived alone. Some said that his wife left him long ago and that his daughters got caught up in some seedy practices out in Californy. Who knew if the gossip was true. Either way, his house would be empty.

Torrence was scarcely out of sight when JP made a run for it. I trailed with less enthusiasm. The boy-detective snatched the key and, with no hesitation, wrangled the door open and stepped inside.

A crust of bread and the last dregs of a cup of coffee rested on the table, which I helped myself to.

"Keep to the mission," JP barked. He reached high and ducked low, impatient for clues of any kind. "You keep watch while I search his bedroom."

"Gettin' a little bossy," I mumbled as I moseyed to the window.

I heard a series of rattles, bangs, and crashes from the bedroom. Some stealthy mission this was. I watched a row of ants climb down the windowsill and got thoroughly absorbed in their doings while waiting for something to happen.

"Charlie, I found somethin'," JP declared. "It's about your pa."

"Oh?" I said. "I thought we was here for *your* pa."

"But I think you'll be interested. Did you know he ran for mayor?"

"*My* pa? Nah, I don't think so."

"Come see," he said.

JP had pulled out a small trunk from under the bed. The letters and papers were now scattered everywhere.

"Better put all this back the way you found it."

"Just look at this." He handed me a paper.

It was an early issue of the *Victory Hills Voice* with the headline, "Ellerby Edges Out Rye in Tight Race."

"I'll be darned," I said.

"See? And you thought this mission was pointless."

"Keep lookin'," I told him, my eyes fixed on the page. There in print, it said my pa gave it a go for mayor back in the early days and lost by only a handful of votes. The paper was dated October of 1850, the same year my pa and me moved here from Chattanooga.

"Your pa musta been respectable back then," he said.

Victory Hills was just a tiny town when this took place. It must've been a small election. I was six years old at the time, but I didn't remember a thing about it. I did, however, remember a time when he was more respectable.

I folded up the clipping and gave it back. "Goes to show how far he's fallen. Now get all this cleaned up."

Galloping hooves sounded close. I peeked out the window. Torrence was riding back up. "JP, get that put away *now*!"

He crammed the papers into the trunk and shoved it back under the bed. We darted out the back door and ran through a field until we were safely out of sight.

"Why do you s'pose he's comin' back so soon?" he said, gasping for air.

"Musta forgot somethin'."

"Charlie, we gotta go back. Soon as he's gone."

"No."

"But I know the answer's back in there. Torrence is one of them fellers that holds on to evidence. It's a gold mine."

"No, I won't do it."

"Why not?" he whined.

"'Cause I got a better idea. More to the point."

"What is it?"

"I'm gonna confront him. I'm gonna ask him straight to his face. None of this sneakin' around. If Torrence has somethin' to hide, I'll find out what it is. I got ways of gettin' folks to talk."

"You do?" His trusting eyes put all their weight on me.

"Sure I do. And if I don't . . . well, it's better than tryin' to piece it together with bits of paper."

"I liked my plan," he mumbled.

"It's fine, I'm sure, but if you want my help, JP, I gotta do it my way."

"Alright, well, when do you confront him?"

"Tonight. I'll see him at the saloon. But you're stayin' home for this one, understand?"

"You can't be serious, Charlie! It was my idea to go after him. Now you wanna make me stay home for all the action?"

"Is this a sport? A fun little adventure? Or do you really want the answer?"

He shrank. "I really want the answer."

"Then stay home, or I swear I'm gonna tell your mama about this whole thing."

"Alright," he said. "No need to make threats. I'll stay home."

"Good, 'cause I won't have you gettin' hurt on my watch. Things could get ugly."

CHAPTER 27

Beatrice Brannon

—

Tuesday, April 17, 1860, late afternoon

DARK clouds swelled in the afternoon sky and rumbled like a doleful drum. My pony galloped hard toward Buckland's through ferocious winds, dodging a steady onslaught of tumbleweeds. The bandanna may have shielded my nose and mouth, but my poor eyes watered like rain. *This is good,* I told myself. *This battle against nature will harden me and prepare me for the torment at the station.*

We'd gotten a late start, my pony and me. Two horses at the station had gotten sick, so not only did this prevent the Riley boys from using them to pursue the reward, but I'd waited for the Colonel to acquire this new horse. Poor thing had never been out in such conditions. I'd need to have enough grit for the both of us.

I was done mystery-solving, done interfering with the dealings of evil men. For Charlie's sake, I was glad he had something to occupy himself, but as for me, the Vipers for Peace were not my problem. I'd done my part. Indeed, there was nothing more I could've done. Whether or not Mabel would try to nab Mayor Torrence and get the reward money was not in my hands. I hoped to never come face-to-face with Torrence ever again.

A thick coat of alkali dust covered me, head to toe. Just when I thought the dust could've swallowed me whole, I reached Buckland's.

My mood soured even more, seeing Jim at the point of exchange. I trotted to a slow walk, dropped down, and set the mochila on Jim's horse.

One glance at my appearance and Jim nodded, saying, "I gotta admit, Miss Bea—"

"Professor," I corrected, glancing back at the cabin.

"Professor," he restated, "you lasted a lot longer out here than I thought you would."

"And I care a lot less about what you think than I thought I would."

He mulled this over as though he didn't know quite what to make of it. "You sure know how to hold a grudge. Can't we just be—"

"Friends?" I finished.

He must've felt the irony because it took him a while to recover. "I was gonna say respectful, but I can see you're determined to hate me."

"I don't hate you, Jim. But if you feel I'm lacking respect, then I confess I don't know how to act. I've never been in the position of pretending not to notice when a friend is attacked and held under water to die. When is the precise date that forgiveness should be granted? I won't go a day beyond it."

"I didn't know he—" He cut himself off. "I'm sorry, Professor. At some time in the future, I hope to win your respect back."

"Thank you. A pleasant ride to you." I held out my hand to be shaken.

He shook it and said, "I'd wish you a pleasant stay at Buckland's if I thought it'd make a difference."

Something about his salutation made me wonder if the state of affairs here had gotten worse. "Well, should we get Pascoe out here to record the time?"

"Nah, I wouldn't bother him." He kicked off and charged into the storm.

I sighed deeply, bracing myself for whatever might come my way. Pony in tow, I started toward the barn.

A figure crouched in the corner of the barn startled me. The bearded youngster looked up.

"Jairus, how goes it?"

He looked away, lost in thought, perhaps, and didn't return my greeting.

"Has it been that bad here?"

He tucked his head into his chest, which gave me ample reply.

I began untacking, while trying to artfully glean information. With Jairus, a degree of precision would be required, or he'd close up like morning glory.

"Anything you want to tell me?"

The shake of his head was so subtle, it could've been a shiver.

"Mind giving me a hand?" I said, trying a new tactic. Maybe if he got his hands moving, his mouth would start moving too.

He stood and lumbered to the horse, arms hanging low.

"Jairus, I know you well enough to tell when something's wrong. You can tell me."

He breathed a discontented sigh and reached down to unbuckle the horse's girth. That's when I saw it. The symbol. The open-mouthed snake with fangs, right there in black ink on his wrist. I snatched his arm, all precision to the wayside. The surrounding skin was pink; the wound was fresh. Our eyes connected. "What's this?" The question was instinct. I knew very well what it was.

"Can't tell you." He yanked his arm back.

I lowered to a whisper. "Jairus, I know about the Vipers for Peace."

This helped him let some of his guard down. "I hate this place."

"Did Pascoe recruit you?"

He nodded. "Said he'd get a hired gun to kill my mother if I didn't join."

That threat would've sounded empty if I hadn't seen what the Vipers had done to Mabel's shop.

"Jairus, there's a reward out for their leader. Everyone's looking for him—even your brothers."

He pondered this, probably wondering what the Colonel and his brothers would do if they knew he was a member. He checked the barn doors before saying, "Pascoe wants me to deliver a message to somebody in Carson City. I'll take the next westbound run."

"What's the message?"

"Don't know. Some document Pascoe's workin' on."

"Whatever it is, you can't deliver it. Somebody'll get hurt."

An awful question touched my mind. If I would've endeavored to see Pascoe's documents before, would I have been able to prevent the fire at Mabel's?

"I wanna get out of here," he said. "This ain't what I signed up for."

"Who are you delivering the message to?"

He shrugged. "Some woman. A prostitute."

My arms prickled with chills. How artfully Charlie and I had been played! The woman who Charlie called Rosebud was an informant for this organization—maybe even a member—if they let women into those sorts of things.

"How are you supposed to find her?"

"He said to find her at a place called Jolly Spirits."

Yes, that would've been Rosebud alright. I had an idea, I just hoped Jairus would be keen for it.

"Let's convince Pascoe to send you out early. He doesn't care about the Pony Express. He only cares about his schemes. When you get to Carson, tell the Colonel everything that's going on."

"You must be joking. The Colonel would toss me out of a runaway buggy if he found out."

"No, Jairus. You're a victim of their plot! The Colonel is reasonable enough to see that."

He shook his head violently in dispute.

"Well, you have to pretend to go along with it. Pretend you're going to deliver that message. It's your ticket out of here. Is it better to have them kill your mother?"

His thoughts turned over before he met my eyes, agreeing with me.

"Let's get you riding out today. Not a moment to lose. I'm afraid of what that Jolly Spirits lady's gonna do. We need to get a look at that document. And you need to tell the Colonel what's going on so she can be stopped."

"There's one more thing," he said. "It has nothin' to do with Pascoe or the Vipers. Just don't judge."

"You're back, Professor!" Pascoe said, striding into the barn.

I nearly choked. "Yes. I just got here. Jairus is helping me untack."

"Well, he's needed inside, and you're to put a kettle on." Pascoe chucked the kettle, and it landed at my feet. Jairus sallied forth to obey, leaving me stranded in a biting curiosity.

I was about to hang the saddle in place when the thought came to me that I better tack up the other horse, the fresh one. If Jairus refused to ride out of here soon, I would. The fresh horse plodded over to me, as if needing attention, so I patted his neck and withers. I whispered to him, "You up for a ride tonight?" He flicked his ears and swished his tail, which I took to mean yes.

He set his relaxed eyes on mine, and I felt we were instant friends. I didn't know his name, but I decided to call him Dante. I tacked him up, fast as I'd ever done, and as if nothing happened, I left the barn with the kettle in hand.

I knelt at the creek, sank my face in the cool water, and drank until my belly could take no more. I scrubbed the dirt from my hands and face. The cover of the red willows gave some reprieve from the wind.

My eyes lifted from the creek. Some out-of-place greenery jutted from the far side of the cabin. I dropped the kettle and moved closer. The sight seized me, body and soul. *It can't be,* I told myself. *No, I'm not seeing this.* Five cut trees lay stacked on their sides, the scent of fresh pine weeping from their felled corpses.

Squires lounged on a nearby stump, an expression of malicious glee on his lips. "We'll be warm tonight." His scratchy voice rubbed my skin like sandpaper. "Roasty, toasty warm." He kept his gaze northeast on the Paiute village.

"How'd you get them?" I said, my chest trembling. "Were they not guarded?"

"No." He puffed on his pipe. "Turns out they ain't guarded 'round the clock, as you said. Perhaps they don't care as much as you let on."

How could a human being, I wondered, who seemed to be in possession of his brains, have done something so stupid? I'd warned him. I'd told him about the significance of the trees to the Paiutes—that if we took more, they would retaliate. I couldn't share any of these thoughts with this smirking man. He'd done it knowing the warnings. He had something to prove. He was angry and vile, and all of us at the station would pay the price.

No tiptoeing for me. I burst into the cabin, my pulse thrumming in my ears. Pascoe sat at his desk, and Jairus stood close by, waiting for Pascoe to finish a document. Oscar was seated at the table, playing a game of solitary checkers.

"Who knows about the pine nut trees? Who chopped 'em down? Did Squires work alone or did you help?"

Jairus's normally pale complexion beamed like a hot pepper. "I helped."

"What about you?" I stared Oscar down.

"Sure, I helped. I did most of the work."

"Do you realize those trees belong to the Paiutes? They're a source of food for their tribe year after year. Did Squires tell you this?"

"No." Jairus's voice cracked in its reply.

"I gave him a warning," I said. "One of those trees takes sixty years to grow to maturity, and you just wiped out five of them."

"Seven," Jairus admitted, swallowing. "We already burned two."

"We dragged 'em out with Jim's pack mule," Oscar added. "Squires made us. He kept watch with his rifle. Why? What's gonna happen?"

"Mercy! Are you hearing this?" I said to Pascoe, who'd been ignoring me and scrawling away at his paper, as usual.

"Don't look at me," he said. "I know nothin' about it."

"Isn't it your business to know?" I said.

"They said you was impertinent," he said, giving me a side glance. "Now I seen it firsthand. If they pillaged some trees, what can I do? Stick 'em back in the ground?"

He resumed his work. A pit formed in my stomach, so severe I nearly doubled over.

In walked Squires, offering his usual jeers. "Is this boy's doom and gloom rubbin' off on the rest of ya? We ain't in danger, by the by, seein' as you boys chopped 'em down two nights ago. If they was gonna retaliate, they'd have already done it."

No, I didn't believe that. I believed Tso'apa when she'd told me this would be cause for retribution. "For all we know," I said, "it's part of their strategy to take us by surprise."

"How he talks!" Squires said, gesturing at me like he was tossing something worthless aside. "Nobody need give this boy another thought."

"We made an oath," I said.

"No, *you* made an oath, and it was foolhardy. Why'd you do it? You don't speak for this station."

His argument weakened my resolve. Had I the right to speak for the others? If only I hadn't given my word to Tso'apa . . . No, I wouldn't let him challenge me. *He* was in the wrong.

"Because . . . it was the right thing to do," I said.

Squires gave a grimace that reeked of abhorrence. "See, it's that kind of high-and-mighty talk that really gets my blood to boilin'. The world could use a whole lot less of you sanctimonious saps. You think it's your duty to buzz about, givin' a little sting here and there to the wicked ones, settin' us back on the straight and narrow. Hell's sake, I can't abide the likes of you."

I could feel his words begin to saturate my soul. Why did I feel like crumbling?

Pascoe stood from his desk, restless as ever, mustering the courage to speak. Only now, as a last resort, would he involve himself in the dealings of the station.

"Why'd you order the trees to be cut down?" Pascoe trod gently, but Squires took offense.

"Now *you're* comin' after me, runt?"

"I'm simply askin' why. We got plenty of trees here. Why go after theirs? 'Specially after the boy warned you."

"I'm in a roomful of idiots! This impudent kid told me the trees was guarded. Well, they wasn't! The boys and me worked a full hour, and nobody came after us. Didn't see a soul. 'Sides that, I didn't hear nobody complainin' about the warmth last night. Everybody simmer down. This scamp just wants to stir up trouble, and frankly, I don't wanna hear another word about it." He lugged himself to his bed and heaved down upon it, as though he'd put in a hard day's work.

Pascoe gave me a glance that said, "What do we do now?" Jairus, too, sent cues, begging me to say or do something. And Oscar, well, he began whimpering and pacing, the front of his trousers wet. His tough exterior had cracked like an eggshell, and he was nothing but a runny yolk inside.

At last, my eyes went to Squires, who seemed to say, "I dare you. I dare you to defy me."

I may have been a know-it-all, but by heaven, it was all I had. I drew a step nearer to Squires. "So you think I'm being ridiculous that the Paiutes would retaliate?"

He shrugged as though it was the most absurd notion in the world.

"Then I have one question for you, Squires. If the Paiutes had come and chopped down seven of our trees—the ones here in our camp—would you sit back and do nothing?"

His eyes danced over the question and landed back at mine. Now I had him. I'd shined a light on his broken logic. If he maintained that he'd let such an offense slide, he'd admit to being weak. No part of his rough character would allow for that. He'd load up his gun and set out for blood. But if he declared he *would* retaliate, he'd be admitting that the Paiutes had reason to retaliate—that I was right, he was wrong, and that he'd be culpable if the Paiutes attacked.

After a considerable amount of time regaining his traction, he gestured toward the Paiute village and said, "Them trees is on public land—American soil, I might add. Them's fair game, same as any fish or fowl."

Miss Mabel's speech came to mind. Our conversation. I was an abolitionist now, which came with some responsibility. When I'd asked her how I might become one, she'd pressed her hand over her heart and said, *It starts in here. And then, be willing to speak up when the occasion warrants.* If I were to call myself an abolitionist, I must abolish every pigheaded and ignorant way of thinking and be willing to back my opinions, even if I was afraid.

"Some of those trees you heartlessly chopped down have been here hundreds of years." I might as well have poked a sleeping bear with a fire iron, the way I taunted him, yet my mouth kept going. "The Paiutes were here long before it could even be called American soil."

Hate swept across his face. Like a battering ram, he charged for me, pounding me to the ground. My backside hit hard, while he remained on his feet. Who knew he could zip across a room so fast?

"Easy, Squires!" Pascoe said. "We signed a contract not to quarrel. Besides, you agreed not to interfere with my operations. You was paid handsomely for your trouble. I wouldn't exactly call this keepin' to the agreement."

"To hell with your agreement," he said, huffing from the exertion. "I ain't gonna be disrespected by this mouthy little jackass. And I'm done bein' be bossed around by some fake station manager."

Pascoe didn't deny being called a fake, but what surprised me was that Squires seemed to know nothing about the Vipers for Peace or have any prior connection with Pascoe at all.

"All's I asked of you was to turn a blind eye," Pascoe said, bringing a slow hand to his hip, where a six-shooter was holstered. "Instead, here you are pickin' fights with the fellers, and you've got us on the bad side of the Paiutes, to boot."

"Don't show me that pistol 'less you plan to use it on me," Squires sneered. "'Cause I know your guts ain't equipped for that."

The two of them went back and forth with their big talk. I needed to get out of that cabin. I spied the door. I could scoot my way there, inch by inch. I'd have to work slowly on my approach and fast in my escape.

Out of the corner of my eye, I saw Jairus deftly pluck the paper off Pascoe's desk and, with the noise as a buffer, slip it between two boards.

"The problem is him!" Squires shouted, pointing at me. "At least we agree on that." Both of them peered down at me, as if I'd better offer up a reason not to kill me.

"I have an idea," I said, standing with pretended confidence.

Squires leaned back and crossed his arms, ready to hear it.

"I have a friend . . . a Paiute." I'd promised myself to keep my friendship with Tso'apa a secret, but Squires had left me no choice. "I'll go and talk to her—beg her, really, for her people to show us mercy."

Squires relaxed his stance, immersed in what I'd said. "The little Paiute gal," he mused. "I knew you was holdin' out on me."

I did my best to ignore him. "First, I'll convince her that we mean to take *no more* trees. Maybe she'll believe we didn't fully understand the crime."

"Crime," Squires muttered.

"Second, we'll need to give them something of value to us."

"You can't mean the horses," Oscar cut in.

"Maybe a gun," I said. "That way, we'll show them we mean no harm."

Squires threw his hands up. "You gotta be jokin'. That's your brilliant plan? I say we give 'em you! That'd solve all our problems."

Pascoe made an appeal to Squires. "It's a decent plan the boy has."

"I ain't givin' 'em a gun, plain and simple." As he considered something anew, his face altered, even softened. "But maybe a peaceful talk ain't such a bad idea. I've been known to negotiate a deal or two. We'll ride to their camp." He spoke to me. "You summon that gal, and we'll take her someplace private. I'll do the talkin' and you interpret."

"No!" I said with all the disgust and horror one word could produce. "She's afraid of you, Squires, and rightly so."

"She said that, did she?" he asked with warped delight. "She knows who I am?"

No words would surface. I couldn't let him know how repulsed I felt. I knew all too plainly the motive behind his so-called negotiation. "I'm going alone," I restated. "It's the only way this will work."

Squires fixed his massive body in front of the door. "That ain't gonna happen. I don't trust ya no further than I can throw ya. Either I go with you, or nobody goes."

No one spoke or moved, except Oscar, who began wheezing and turning figure eights. "We ought to leave," he said. "We ain't safe here."

Squires stood immovable, barring our exit. He'd set forth his rules.

"You gotta let me go," Oscar said. "I never wanted to come to this place. Let me go!"

Of course, Squires was undeterred, and nobody dared lay a finger on him. Not even Pascoe, who was armed, would challenge him.

Oscar was desperate, on the edge of a frenzy. Alas, he still had a card to play. "If you let me go," he said, speaking to Squires, "I'll tell you somethin' about Professor."

My face sprang into a fever. This could not be good.

"If you know somethin', you best tell it, boy," Squires warned.

Oscar eyed me, and I eyed him right back. How did he know? *What* did he know? Now was the worst possible time to expose me. My heartbeat thrummed in my ears.

"If it's a gal you're after," his mouth kept going, staring me down the whole time, "we got ourselves one right here."

Squires whipped his head toward me, armed with this information, and surveyed me with a wholly new regard.

"It's true," Oscar said, adding evidence. "I suspected it that time we fought in the creek. 'Sides from that, I never seen him take a piss. Not once. Always goes off somewhere private."

Squires lumbered to me, slowly this time. He stood close enough for me to smell his odor like rancid onions, and he ripped off my hat. I wouldn't look him in the eyes. "You was holdin' out on all of us, I see."

"Leave him alone," Jairus mumbled.

"How do we know he's a *him?*" Squires said. "Sounds to me we got some conflicting evidence. I'd like some proof."

"Lord, Squires, give it a rest," Pascoe said.

"No, no, no, I can't ignore this. We got ourselves a real problem. This kid's a deceiver. A traitor in more than one way. No, I ain't lettin' this go."

Blocking the door, Squires stood far from his rifle. A rarity, to be sure. I knew he kept it underneath his bed, which was across the room from him. He could either block the door or grab his rifle, but he couldn't do both. Did I dare go for the rifle?

I took two steps backward, away from Squires. A couple more steps and I sat on his bed. Every set of eyes was on me. I reached a shaky hand underneath my legs and snatched the rifle.

"Git your varmint hands off that!" He leaped toward me, pushed me to the ground a second time, and wrangled the rifle from my hands. Jairus jumped on Squires's back, an arm around his neck, like a racoon trying to overpower a bear. Oscar joined, trying to seize Jairus and pull him off Squires. In the scuffle, my elbow knocked firmly into Squires's eye. He howled in pain. With that one blessed second of freedom, I weaseled out of the brawl, yanked open the door, and ran. Jairus was close after me.

"The horse is tacked up," I told him. "When you get a chance, go."

I ran toward the river.

"Devil curse you!" Squires called.

Thick, dark clouds hid me temporarily. At any moment the dusky sky could appear through them. For now, nothing but faint, wispy shapes could be seen. I flattened myself in the reeds, holding as still as I had power.

"Don't think for a second you can outrun this rifle!" he yelled.

As soon as I heard him tread in another direction, I sprang up and hastened along the river's edge. Shrubs and stones riddled my path, but the gurgle of the river obscured the sounds of my trips and falls. I had nowhere to go, yet I kept running.

Once my lungs could take no more, I slowed down. My eyes had adjusted. I'd gone some distance, but I couldn't be sure how far.

A shape appeared some yards ahead of me, like a specter.

"Tso'apa!" I whispered in surprise. She didn't react upon seeing me. In fact, she hardly moved.

"Paddoo," she said. I was glad she'd used my Paiute name, but that was as far as the olive branch extended. Her manner was stoic, impassive. "The loud noise from your camp travels a great distance."

The sound of gunfire made us jump. "Git back here, boy!" Squires shouted. He must've been yelling at Jairus this time. "You ain't takin' that horse." Another shot fired. The sound of hooves pounded and kept going until they were heard no more. Jairus had gotten away on Dante.

"My people, we talk." Tso'apa restrained her voice to a quiet but urgent tone. "We fight about what to do. The elders say we will come soon. Could be tonight. Could be in three nights. They will not tell me.

The elders gave the order to kill the bison man. They know he is the one to make trouble."

Squires's shouting sailed across the plain. "You varmint! You traitor! The end's comin' for you, and you can't outrun it. You ain't worth the air you breathe. Give yourself up."

"We best go," I said.

Tso'apa didn't run. Not yet. She had something more to say. Her hand reached out and touched my arm. "I must tell you . . . there are other tribes, other offenses from your people, some far worse than taking trees."

No part of me wanted to know what those offenses were. What Squires alone had done—and wanted to do—was more shame than I could bear.

"The council says the tribes will reclaim the area. It will take time to gather. Before the next full moon rises."

The knowledge that a full-scale retaliation would be coming, bringing together all the region's tribes, brought an awfully bitter taste to my mouth.

Squires's outbursts caught up with me again, getting closer. Every vulgarity was hurled my way. "I know what you want, you little tease! You can come and get it. Don't be—"

His words stopped—caught in his own throat. A groan followed.

Tso'apa's frame stiffened. I froze too. Was he dead? I ran toward the scene, and Tso'apa followed. I clumsily fought through the brush and into the clearing. Only shapes were visible, in hues of gray and black.

Squires was hunched over his knees on the ground. His light-colored shirt stood out in the dark. A knife protruded from his back. Blood flowed from it. He fell on his side and, from that moment, didn't move or speak. Pascoe stood behind him. *Pascoe.* Tso'apa seized my hand.

Pascoe's head pointed my way. I couldn't see his eyes, but they bored into me just the same. Never had I thought it was in him to kill. Pascoe's stature changed; it rose. I wished I hadn't witnessed this and that he hadn't seen me. "Don't tell me you didn't want to see him dead."

I said nothing, for nothing could have prepared me for this.

"Girl," he said, as though all Squires's disdain had transferred to him, "you answer to me now." He picked up Squires's rifle.

I charged the other direction. Tso'apa ran too. Neither of us turned back; we only kept running until our breath was ragged and all used up.

Tso'apa led me across the river to a rocky place. We climbed up and over the largest boulder. Once inside this alcove, she told me, "Wait here until the light comes."

Our friendship, however short-lived, would soon be coming to a close. I didn't know if I'd live to see the morning, let alone another Pony ride.

"Goodbye," I said.

"Paiute don't say goodbye," she scolded gently. "There is no word for *goodbye* in Numu. No final partings. I will see you again."

I said back to her, "Yes, I will see you again."

And she clambered over the rocks and disappeared.

What will I do in the morning? I wondered. *What comes next? How will I get out of this place? Did I really just witness that?*

Jairus had gotten away on Dante, and Pascoe had access to the other horse. Surely, Pascoe would want to finish me off, after I'd witnessed him murder Squires. All I could do was wait for morning light and pray Pascoe wouldn't find me.

I settled on the ground and hugged my knees. *God, please let me see my family again.* This whole endeavor had been foolish, impetuous. Instead of helping my family, I'd taken a horrible risk, and if I didn't make it out, I'd leave Mama to mourn another death.

CHAPTER 28

Charlie Rye

Tuesday, April 17, 1860, evening

JP was none too pleased about staying home during my inquest, but I had my reasons. Mostly 'cause I'd never be able to face Mrs. Brannon if he got hurt or even if he witnessed something ugly. Besides, my hands were trembling something awful, and I still had my pride.

Just off Oliver Street, I slipped down from Dandy and surveyed the scene. My hunch was right. Torrence's horse was tied to a post outside the saloon, and I knew he'd be in there. Most nights, him and Shorty the bartender were the last to leave.

JP had his burning questions, and I had mine. He wanted to know why kids were calling his father a coward. I wasn't sure I'd get a satisfactory answer for him, but I'd still try. And me, I wanted to know what Torrence was mixed up in. What were his dealings with that Pascoe feller? And the most important question: why?

I strode at an easy pace toward the saloon, feeling my trusty Colt revolver at my hip and the bullets jingling in my pocket. I slinked into the alley to load her. I hoped I wouldn't need to use her, but I'd have her with me just in case.

The alley window gave off a little light—just enough to see my doings. I listened as I loaded the chambers. Two men's voices carried through the wall, jabbering about this and that. The hammer clicked as I closed her up.

Hearing the name Charles piqued my interest. There were only two Charleses in town: me and my pa.

"How's that workin' out?" Mayor asked.

"Like a house on fire," Shorty said. "I give him the Sabbath off, where he drinks himself silly. Then he shows up bright and early Monday morning, ready to make deliveries. Never had a trustier employee. He knows if the trek ain't made, his supply'll be cut off. Genius idea of yours to pay him in booze."

Mayor chuckled and added, "Was that my idea? Lord, the poor feller showed real promise early on of being a credit to this town, but he let himself sink lower and lower."

"Question is," Shorty said, chuckling, "did he sink or was he drowned?"

"How do you mean?"

"Come, Torrence, no need to mince words with me. You were the one bent on destroyin' the poor feller. Always undercuttin' him every chance you got. Did you forget about all that? Everybody knew he was your rival in the early days. You found his weakness and played on it. Next thing we knew, he was out of the running."

Mayor Torrence took a swig of whiskey loud enough that I heard the gulp go down. "I forgot about that. Been so long. Had too many rivals since then to remember."

"You sure got a way of keepin' 'em down," Shorty said.

"Ha! Well, I've learned to be more artful as the years have gone by."

"Lord help me if I ever go up against you."

"I'll drink to that," Mayor said. Glasses clinked.

Nothing could've fanned the flame quite like this did. My chest burned. I nearly choked on my own hot spit. I never expected to hear nothing about my pa. I was no defender of him, but to think Mayor had a hand in keeping him down. I might've not believed what I heard, except for that article JP found—the one that said he ran for mayor. No more listening. No more thinking. Time to act.

I stood in the saloon doorway, calm on the outside but thundering within. I strolled up to Torrence and leaned on a stool beside him. He took a quick glance my way then back to his drink. "Well, Charlie Rye."

"Can I pour you a sarsaparilla?" Shorty said, in a tone meant to mock. The two of them busted into bits over this, I wasn't sure why. Maybe it was a jab at my youth. Maybe they was just drunk, thinking anything they said was funny.

Instead of showing offense, I said, "Sure."

"Look who's *not* at the Pony Express," Mayor said, not fazed seeing me.

"Just takin' a little sabbatical," I said.

"After so short a time in the service? That's a generous employer, I'd say."

"Not as generous as Shorty here." Neither knew what I meant, and I was in no humor to bring up my pa. "Saw you in Carson City when I was there," I told Torrence. "I was gonna say hello, but you seemed . . . busy."

Mayor kept his eyes on his glass of whiskey, drained it, then tapped for Shorty to pour him another.

I persisted. "Seemed downright sneaky, if you ask me. What was you about?"

"Go home, Rye. My comings and goings are none of your affair."

"I saw you switch over that key to Mr. Pascoe, and I know what he used it for—something about unlocking mail pouches." I hoped my bluff was right. I never actually saw if it was a key, but it made sense when Bea and me put the facts together. "Pretty sly, I must say. You had us all believin' that your interest in the Pony Express was some patriotic endeavor for the good of the town."

He waved his hand like I was no more than a pesky fly. "That's exactly what it was, Rye."

I had to press harder, dig deeper for his touchy point. Whatever it was, there'd be a reaction. Then I remembered JP's burning question, the whole reason for my inquest.

"Tell me why the town youngsters are callin' Jeremiah Brannon a coward. Word has it you're the source. That's fairly low, even for you, tearin' up the reputation of a dead man."

Torrence let down his glass midswig. For the first time, he turned and made eye contact with me. His long legs elevated him to his full and bewildering height. I stood too. I wasn't short, but Torrence still towered over me. "What do you want, boy?"

JP was right. This was the agitator. Mayor didn't break his stare for nothing. I squeezed harder, like juicing a tomato. "You couldn't break him down in life, so you thought you'd break him down in death. Just knockin' down your rivals, as usual."

He grabbed my collar, backed me up, and thudded me against the wall. Through gritted teeth, he said, "I don't know what you're gettin' at, but this is your warning to leave it alone."

I sent my knee forward, busting his crotch. He groaned, dropped me, and swung something fierce at my ribs. I struck back at his jaw. The hit sent his coonskin cap flying off. He came at me, landing another punch at the same spot on my ribs. I fell backward to my elbows. On the floor, I grabbed my gun from its holster, sprang to my feet, and aimed at him. Slowly, he raised his hands. A hint of terror flashed on his face.

"Act smart, Charlie," Torrence said in a breathy voice, trying to cool himself.

But I didn't act smart. I ran my mouth. "There's a twelve-year-old boy torn to pieces that you're callin' his pa a coward. If you wanna do right by this town, you best go apologize to JP Brannon. All's I can see is the coward standin' in front of me."

With a twitch of his nostrils, Mayor reached for his pistol. I fired mine at his hand. He yowled something awful. His pistol dropped. Gunpowder plumed in the space between us. Mayor doubled over and crashed to the floor.

"Worthless fool!" Torrence gasped, blood trickling from his hand. Shorty ran to his comrade and took a quick look at the injury. "I think it's just a graze," he said a couple of times, to reassure his friend.

"It's more than a graze, Shorty. He's shot clean through it!"

I bolted to leave, but there stood Sheriff Hartley, blocking the doorway with his own gun aimed at me. "You best cooperate, Charlie," he said, as if trying to coax a wild animal. "Come with me now."

Cornered, there wasn't much I could do, so I raised my arms in surrender. "It was self-defense! You saw it, Hartley!"

"I saw no such thing. You fired; he didn't."

"'Cause he was pullin' for his weapon!"

"Just keep your mouth shut," Hartley said. "You're bound to say somethin' stupid like your pa always does. And speaking of him, I got some news for ya."

"What news?"

"Oh, never you mind," Hartley said. "More of a surprise, really. Just waitin' for you."

Hartley prodded me along the dim street to the jailhouse and forced me into the cell. I tripped over my feet. My bad luck caught up with me at last. Lying on a cot was my pa, drunker than a peach orchard sow.

CHAPTER 29

Charlie Rye

Wednesday, April 18, 1860, after midnight

FATE finally caught up with me. The two Ryes—father and son—captive, side by side, living the family legacy. Laws, how it gutted my insides, almost to the point of vomit. No . . . no . . . *actual* vomit rose up like a volcano and splattered on the cell floor. This wasn't the first time a Rye puked here, for certain. Just a way of signing my name in the books of some detestable initiation.

Pa's shoulders shook. At first, I thought he might be coughing, but he was laughing.

I wiped my mouth on my sleeve. "What's so damned funny?" I knew the answer, of course, but my taste for suffering must've been severe.

He was in such a fit he could barely answer. "Fell hard off that high horse, didn't ya?"

Those imaginary iron anchors pulled me down, down until my breath was scarce. I clung to the bars and shouted, "Get me outta here! I give up! You ol' brutes found the chink in my armor. Do anything else to me. Drag me from the back of a bronco for twenty miles, just get me away from him!"

"Looks like you're stuck here with me," he said, chuckling. He sat up and slapped his hands on his legs. "Say, we might as well make the best of it. How 'bout a round of 'Turkey in the Straw.' I'll clap while you dance a rousin' jig."

The smell of my own vomit was getting to me. "At least get me a mop to clean this up . . . or a rope to hang myself with. Either one."

Sheriff Hartley came back with a mop, a bucket, and—for courtesy—a bag of sawdust to reduce the smell. "Stand back," he said, "far enough that you won't be sneakin' out."

"Tell me, Hartley, how does a person sneak out when fate's caught up to him? How does a body escape the hand he's been dealt? I mean, a robin lays an egg and it turns into a baby robin, don't it? Nature repeats itself again and again, don't ya see?"

"Scoot back."

I did as Hartley said. He twisted the key in the lock and swung open the iron door on its rusty hinges. He placed the mop, bucket, and sawdust where I could get them and was quick to lock up again.

Pa had a deck of cards that he shuffled as he watched me work. With every dip of the mop, my misery swelled. This was the end of me. I'd never do a scrap of good in my life. Corruption was in my blood. Sixteen years old and I already shot a man. The town mayor, no less. All the neighbors would nod their heads and say, "Yes, sir, it was only a matter of time before ol' Charles Rye's boy did something like this."

I finished mopping and curled myself into a corner.

Pa set the cards aside and leaned forward, his paunch pressing hard against his buttons. "So, what'd you do to wind up in here, anyhow?"

I couldn't say nothing.

"Oh, come now, it can't be that bad," Pa continued like it gave him real entertainment. "Let me guess. Cheated at the card tables? Stole something? There's the most obvious guess: disorderly conduct."

"Let's call it that," I said. "What else could it be with you for a father?"

"Whoa, son, easy."

"You done me wrong, Pa, and that's the long and short of it."

"What's your crime? Come on, you're already in here. What could be worse?"

"Shot a man," Hartley shouted from the other side of the wall.

Pa whistled in surprise. "I never shot a man. Looks like you got yourself into that fix on your own. Can't blame me for your sins."

"Give me one good reason why not. You never taught me *not* to shoot a man. You never taught me to love my neighbor. You never taught me nothin'."

"Yet you're so well versed in what's right and wrong."

"Aw, hang you! I deserved better."

His degrees of drunkenness were all too familiar—dangerously easy to trigger while still possessing enough wit to make a punch stick. "Now, son," he said, trying to assume an air of honor. "I set out to raise a boy so strong and sturdy that the world could never shake him. And look at you, I done it."

Repulsed, I shook my head. "That's a beautiful speech. Just warms me from head to toe."

All he did was shrug. "I'm no angel and I don't lay claim to it, but when it comes to bringin' up a child, there's more'n one way to skin a cat."

I sprang up. There'd be no sitting down for this. "I'm the cat you skinned, you low, mean, no-good . . ." I couldn't deliver a harsh enough pejorative. If all the pain of sixteen years could've been balled into one punch, the force could've knocked him to the moon.

"This wallowin' and whinin' don't become you," he said. "That's one thing I know I taught you. Anyhow, I done my best with you, son."

"We both know that ain't true," I said, my voice cracking under the tightness. *I'll never tell my pa about the plot to keep him down,* I thought. *He doesn't deserve to know.* He probably would've become the same old buffoon, plot or none.

I returned to my corner and stared up at the ceiling, trying to imagine a sky full of stars or any place besides here. The cell got quiet, but before long Pa's snoring began.

My eyes closed, my body relaxed, and my head bobbed down toward my knees. My thoughts dragged me far away. Whether I was asleep, passed out, or simply dead, I didn't know.

I walked along a winding pathway with trees on both sides. To my right, the Truckee River flowed, wide and placid. A woman sat along the banks, busy with some needlework on her lap and a candle close by.

She felt familiar. She turned toward me, and our eyes met.

"Mother," I said, stunned, frozen.

She stood, the task in her hands falling to the ground. Her hair was long and pulled back behind her. A deerskin dress adorned her with intricate beadwork along the edges. She came forward and embraced me tight. How could this be a dream if it felt so real?

"The last time I held you . . ." she said in my ear, not finishing her thought.

We stepped back a bit and I took in her face, smiling at me, full of love. I knew exactly why my pa had fallen in love with her, but it stumped me as to why she'd fallen in love with him.

Her gaze went to the project she'd dropped, so she picked it up and held it before me: a deerskin coat, of the same quality as her dress, with fringe and beading along the chest. Instinctively, I knew it was for me, so I held out one arm then the other as she fitted it on me.

"This is the coat of a warrior, even though you are only my *usdi tawodi*."

I didn't know the words, but they sounded familiar enough, and they made me smile. Not just from my mouth but from my whole insides to my outsides. This woman loved me. More than anything.

And that was the end of it. That was all the joy my heart could muster before I awoke to my pa coughing and hacking from his cot. Again, the thought plagued me: how could a woman so marvelous love a man like him? What had he done to deserve it? But then, what had I done to deserve her affection? I'd probably only pestered her with my cries for the short time we had together. Well, they must've been cute, endearing cries.

"Hartley, I need a drink," Pa shouted, adding another salvo of coughs.

"Not for you," he called back.

"Of water, you ninny," Pa protested.

Hartley took his time bringing back a flask. Pa stood and Hartley handed it to him through the bars.

"Lord, I'm choking to death," Pa said.

Hartley checked his pocket watch. "I think that's enough time for you."

I stood, ready to fly at the open door.

"Not you," he told me. "The *elder* Rye is free to go. You're to stay."

The deputy readied the key to let Pa out.

"Wait," I said, "where you gonna go, Pa?"

Pa grimaced as if to ask why I cared. But I had a question for him. Lots of questions, about my mother, about when I was little, and about when he almost won sheriff back in the day. And I knew that Pa, momentarily sober, would be leaving for a whisky run soon and would be gone for a couple weeks.

"Pa, I need to tell ya somethin'." And I thought for a second that I might tell him about Torrence's plot to hold him down.

Hartley stepped back, holding the key close to him, as if curious about what I might say. Pa waited, too, but nobody could've been more shocked than me at what came out of my mouth. I skipped all the questions and said, "I love you, Pa."

Hartley let out a soft gasp and held a hand to his mouth, as if to hush a cry.

Pa seemed annoyed at first, but his face softened. No such words had ever passed between us.

I kept on, "I wanted you to love me too. Maybe you did, but I never felt it. You provided some necessities after my mother died, and for that, I thank you. But I needed more. I needed you to show me a good way to be. Show me a decent path to follow. Anyhow, I'm my own man, and I can't look after you no longer even if we are blood kin. I got my own path now. Only you can shake your demons. I clearly got my own."

A sniffling Hartley stepped back farther into a shadow trying to hide his emotion.

It was the single bravest thing I ever done. Funny how light I felt after saying it. Pa, however, drooped like a sunflower in the shade, staring at the floor. He didn't rage or laugh or make fun. Instead, he said, "See, I did raise a good boy."

I wasn't angry when he said it this time. The way I saw it, some fathers taught their young 'uns how they should be. Others, like mine, taught me how I shouldn't. Either way, I figured I'd arrived at roughly the same place.

"I'm off to Californy," he said, as a peer would speak to another. "This time for good. They got whiskey wagons there too, I judge."

"Just make sure they pay you in real money," I said.

He cocked his head, probably wondering what I meant, but he didn't ask.

"Pa, did my mother used to say *usdi tawodi*? Have you heard that?"

He scratched his chin. "That's the name she used to call you. I did, too, back then. Means 'Little Hawk.'"

I was delighted. It must've shown in my face. Pa said, "Don't say I never gave you nothin.'"

Hartley, clearing his throat loudly, finagled the key into the lock and opened the cell door. Pa gave me a nod. I gave a nod back. As unrehearsed and raw and pitiful as that goodbye was, there couldn't have been a more perfect one. Any more or less would've been false.

CHAPTER 30

Beatrice Brannon

Wednesday, April 18, 1860, early morning

I awoke in my rocky fortress, miraculously still alive, but riddled with mosquito bites. I'd become accustomed to waking up in unfamiliar places. The image from last night hit me hard, a knife jutting out of Squires's back and Pascoe standing behind him.

A hint of morning light cut along the deep indigo ridgeline. I needed a horse—or another way back home. If last night had taught me anything, it was that I couldn't give up. Mabel had given me the courage to oppose Squires, and I'd done it. I knew I could do more. Torrence would pay for his crimes. Pascoe too. I'd see to it myself, if necessary.

By my calculations, there should've been one mule left. Jairus had taken the first horse, Dante, and Pascoe had likely taken the other. Oscar could've taken one of the mules, which would've left one for me. That is, unless they'd frightened it off, trying to hinder my escape.

I climbed out of my shelter and scuffled along the creek toward the station, nerves frayed, perusing my field of vision all around.

When I reached the corral, sure enough, there was Molly the mule, long ears pointed skyward. I released a sigh of relief. She stood outside the fence, indicating that Pascoe had scared her off, but she'd come back. I clasped grateful arms around her neck.

With no saddle, I'd have to ride bareback for nearly thirty miles. I could do it. I filled my canteen and readied myself to leave.

A thought sprang to mind. Last night, Jairus had waited for Pascoe to finish a document. And during the argument, Jairus had slipped it between a crack in the boards. *Could it still be there?*

The cabin door had been left open, flapping in the wind. The place already looked abandoned by fifty years. Still, I crept inside with caution. I knelt near the spot where he'd cached it, and I traced my fingers along the wood. Nothing. Pascoe must have taken it.

"Hey there."

I sprang backward. Jairus stood in the doorway.

"Jairus, what are you doing here?" I was grateful as ever to see him, although a bit shocked. "I was sure you'd gone."

"I did go," he said in his usual mumble. "I hid in the hills a couple miles up, but I reckoned I better see if you was OK. Where'd you go?"

I told him about my rocky hiding place and how I'd witnessed Pascoe murder Squires.

His reaction was barely visible. "Pascoe kept tellin' me he was gonna do it. Squires must've pushed him to the breaking point."

"Which way did Pascoe ride?" I asked.

"I didn't see," he said.

"No matter. I know where I'm headed."

"You're gonna stop the Viper King, ain't you?"

"Yes," I said with resolve.

"Then take this." He pulled a document from his waistcoat, sealed with red wax in the Vipers' symbol. "I tried to get a look before he sealed it. I think it's a list of members. I was supposed to deliver it to the prostitute in Carson City."

I secured the document inside my boot. "You're coming with me, aren't you? To get the Viper King? He's in my hometown. I know the way."

"No," was his rapid answer. "This ain't for me. This ain't for me at all. But I want you to get him." The next part he said with a smirk. "You getting the reward means my brothers won't."

In addition to giving me the incriminating document against the Vipers, Jairus insisted I take the horse, and he take the mule. He reasoned that I'd need to go faster and that he'd have relief stops on his way to Carson City.

"Jairus, I owe you."

"Not as much as I owe you," he said.

"What did I do for you?"

He thought for a moment. "Last night, when it came down to life or death, you gave me the horse."

He nodded, shook my hand, and the two of us rode our separate ways.

Just ride, Bea. The words came from inside me and spurred me forward. I'd ride to Victory Hills and to Torrence's ranch. I wouldn't quit until I'd cornered him, confronted him. And at that moment, I didn't care what it cost me.

CHAPTER 31

Charlie Rye

Wednesday, April 18, 1860, early morning

Now that Pa was gone, the jail cell was a whole lot quieter. Sheriff Hartley took a seat on the bench outside the bars and got cozy, like he was warming up for a chat. "Charlie, I downright hate seein' you in here."

"Then release me and we won't say another word about it."

"Ain't that simple."

"Seems pretty simple to me," I said. "You got the key, don't ya?"

"Listen, in case you didn't know, you're in real trouble, kid."

"So Mayor Torrence's hand got grazed by a bullet. He didn't die, did he?"

"I think it's more than a graze, Charlie. We don't know the damage. You heard that howl."

"Sure did," I said, knowing full well it wasn't beyond Torrence to make it seem worse.

"Anyway, shootin' a feller's a crime. One you gotta pay for."

"I'll get a lawyer." I threw it out there, doubting the reality. "I still claim it was self- defense."

"Lawyers cost money. You got any?"

"Not much. But I could win some quick enough. I got pretty good luck with the old coppers. Some days, all's I have to do is *think* about 'em and they come to me."

"Well, unless you can spin sawdust into gold, I think your luck's run out." His face took on a sinister quality. "But . . . there's another way to work this out, you know."

"Let's hear it, man. I'm fresh outta ideas. Thanks to you, I ain't goin' nowhere."

He quieted his speech and leaned close to the bars, though nobody was in the jailhouse but us. "I belong to a brotherhood."

That caught my interest, true enough. I'd long heard of brotherhoods and secret societies. They were a growing trend in other parts of the country, but I never heard of nothing like that in Victory Hills. And here was this respectable member of the town, letting me in on it.

"We look out for each other," he said with a sniff of pride. "We pledge solidarity. And if you joined...well, maybe I could pull some strings to drop the charges."

"They'd let *me* in?" I said, agog. Most the men in town counted me for worthless, but they'd let me join their club?

"Sure we would," he said.

"You swear you could get me out of my charges?"

"It's a real possibility."

"You been holdin' out on me, Hartley." I grinned. "There's gotta be a catch. Gimme the pitch."

"There are certain deeds we do for a cause we believe in. You'd be expected to carry out plans given by your superiors, and in turn, they pledge their life to you. Just think, the very man you shot would be your brother."

And *there* was the catch. "Damnation, Hartley! What you tryin' to pull? I can't join no organization with Mayor Torrence. If he didn't hate me before I shot him, he does now. 'Sides, I ain't too fond of him neither."

"Calm down, Charlie. When you join the brotherhood, you take an oath. The cause is greater than your grievances. You're bound to each other. He'd have to protect you with his life, and you'd pledge the same. We take the oath very seriously. Two men can hate each other, but when it comes to the brotherhood, the hate disappears. We're like a family. Gives you a real sense of belonging, ya know? Now that you're estranged from your pa, who's gonna look after you?"

"Let me clear somethin' up. My pa never looked after me. What's more, Torrence has never treated me with an ounce of respect. There's no way he'd ever wanna be in a brotherhood with me, let alone protect me."

"Torrence would be the main source of your protection. He's the man in charge. He asked for you specifically. Believes you can do us some good."

"Torrence is in charge?" I rubbed my forehead. "You're wastin' your time, Hartley. I can't belong to a brotherhood with him at the head of it."

"You're at a crossroads, Charlie. Torrence can either be your friend or your enemy. It's up to you. Remember, you shot *him*. He's willing to forgive that, but you gotta give your loyalty to the brotherhood. Seems easy to me. What would stop you?"

"Self-respect, I imagine."

"Charlie, there's no finer self-respect than to stand up for a righteous cause."

"What's this righteous cause, then?"

Hartley drummed his fingers, like he was about to up the ante. "We believe in peace at any cost. That's our motto. We oppose any war being fought on America's shores. Brother against brother—they call that a *civil* war, but there ain't nothing civil about it. Tell me, do you give a lick about states leaving the Union?"

"Never thought much about it."

"Then you side with us. We refuse to spill our own blood because of mindless politics. We want to stop the abolitionists from gettin' too much power. There's this politician, Abe Lincoln, who's become a real firebrand on behalf of the abolitionists. We want to stop him and others like him.

He wants to offer up the souls of the men and boys in this country just to keep it one piece. Lincoln's hell-bent on war's what he is. Wants to abolish slavery. But the South would rather leave the Union than give it up. If he becomes president, we're going to war. You wanna die on some battlefield and never be heard of no more?"

"No, but are the only choices slavery or war? I mean, slavery's a cruel practice. It ain't right to enslave a people based on the color of their skin." I thought about my own skin color and that of my mother, God rest her soul. We weren't so white as the predominant race in those parts and somehow, because of that, we were "less than."

"Oh, I agree with you there," he assured me. "Slavery's an abomination in every way. But there's nothing so abominable as war, Charlie. Nothing. That's why we call ourselves the Vipers for *Peace*."

Hartley folded back his sleeve to reveal a tattoo on his wrist: the same coiled snake in a strike pose, like Pascoe had. The urge to jump out of my skin nearly overpowered me. A closer look showed me that the open mouth formed the letter *V*. *Vipers, of course.*

"How 'bout that? Does that catch your fancy?"

"Sure does," I said, barely able to speak. A couple more cogs were fitted into place. Pascoe asking me all those probing questions. Him and Torrence conspiring about something. This had to be it.

A wicked thought perched in my brain, and I let it stay. What if I joined the brotherhood—not as a real, viable member, but to get myself out of the charges? What if my heart wasn't in it and I took the first chance to run? I had to get out of this cell. I had to see the light of day and breathe fresh, non-vomit air.

I shooed the thought away. As a man of honor, I couldn't.

"Lemme think on it, Hartley," I said, taking my pa's former spot on the cot.

"I can see you got your misgivings," he said, "but if I can't convince you, then I'm sure the Viper King will. He's coming here in the morning. This is the rendezvous point. You can meet him then. We got one job here in town, then a bigger job out East."

"Viper King? I thought you said Torrence was in charge."

"He's second-in-command, but there's somebody even higher up than him. The Viper King's got a real presence. You'll wanna join once you meet him, I know it." He drew a pocket watch from his vest. "Time's not far now. You turn all this over in your mind."

He began to make his exit, but I had one more question, one that I'd watch skillfully as he answered. "Hartley, do you Vipers ever . . . hurt innocent people?"

"Come on, boy, give me some credit. Would I join an organization like that?"

"Alright, just crossin' my t's, as they say."

He left me in the quiet, muggy cell to mull things over. What about that dream I had, seeing my mother? It seemed to give me a second chance. Did I really have some value I needed to discover? Deep in my heart, was I a warrior? I still felt as worthless and confused as when I got here. *If I could just get out of this place, I might be able to put a couple rational thoughts together.* I needed to revive myself, just like Dante coming out of that dark wood.

CHAPTER 32

Beatrice Brannon

Wednesday, April 18, 1860

DANTE and I arrived at Victory Hills around six o'clock in the morning. Making our way up Rocky Pass kept me alert, but now my lack of sleep was catching up with me. I began to doubt my plan. How was I supposed to confront Torrence while I was sleep-deprived and weaponless?

Reconnaissance first, I thought. *See if he's here.*

My breaths shallowed as I got closer to Torrence's ranch. This was where Da had died, where the devil horse had slaughtered him. Trembles worked their way from my chest to the ends of my fingers. No, I couldn't let my emotions get the better of me. Night after night, my dreams had dragged me to this place. But this morning was different. Today, I came here willingly and with a purpose.

I tied Dante's rope to a tree and crept to a spot behind the large, A-framed barn. From there, I had a sufficient view of the house. Torrence's horse stood with bulging saddlebags, prepared for a journey. Had someone told Torrence about the reward and now he was skipping town?

The man himself emerged from the house. He added a few things to his saddlebags and made sure the cinch was tight. Where was he going? It didn't matter. I'd have to follow him.

As I turned to make my way back to Dante, a noise stopped me: a murderous, piercing cry coming from inside the barn. I peered between two planks and saw nothing but darkness. The wood beat against my cheek with a kick. I drew back. The shriek echoed again.

"I figured you'd come," a voice said beside me. I turned. Torrence clamped his arms around me, tight as a vise. I writhed and kicked to free myself. He dragged me backward toward the barn doors, the heels of my boots scraping the earth. I squirmed out of his grasp, but Pascoe appeared and gripped me, using the same tactic. I flailed and fought back. Still, they wrestled me like a wild pig and tossed me into the barn. I landed hard on my back, gasping for air. Before I could draw another breath, they slammed the doors and fixed a wood plank across them. I was locked in.

"Word has it, you're a connoisseur of poetry, miss," Torrence called. "How's this for poetic justice?"

That same shrill cry, sharper than the edge of a razor, sliced through that small space. The horse, the devil of my nightmares, thrashed about, beating the walls with his hooves and kicking dust in my face.

I scrambled to my feet to get away from him. My hands went tingly, my head light. I backed away, stumbling over my own clumsy footsteps.

How could it be? Surely I was hearing things, seeing things, in the throes of a sickening nightmare. There could be no other explanation. How could I be trapped in a barn with *that* horse? He'd been shot. Hadn't I seen it happen?

My eyes partway adjusted to the dark. The horse reared up and propelled his hooves out in front of him. I darted to a corner to find safety, but he followed me, snorting and squealing in my ears. I fled to another corner, but nowhere was safe from his terror.

No, I hadn't seen him get shot. I'd only *heard* the shot ring out. I never did see the horse go down. Fog had surrounded the area. I'd left for the doctor. *Could he yet be alive? Impossible. Impossible.*

"Bet you thought he was dead," Torrence hollered, his voice edging out the horse's cries.

"You botched the job, it seems," I shouted back.

"Oh, I shot him good, alright—squarely between the eyes, just like you said, crass girl. He went down fast. But perfect as my shot was, it didn't take. The horse duped us. Pretended he was dead. When I came back later, he was gone."

"You missed the mark, plain and simple," I shouted with an eleventh-hour kind of bravery. As long as I was going down, I'd make an impression.

"Fate let him survive," he said, "and I couldn't have planned it better. We'll see which of you gets out of this alive."

Had I just haplessly waltzed into my own murder? I'd made it so easy for Torrence. This horse had killed before. It could kill again. Torrence would bury my body, and nobody would know. They'd think I got lost on the trail.

"Do you really plan to kill me? The town mayor, a murderer?"

"Let's not assume the high road, shall we? I'll wager your intentions comin' here weren't to pay a social call."

"I came here because there's a reward out for you." I shouldn't have told him, but I couldn't help myself. I wouldn't let him twist my words around and turn me into the criminal. "I'm acting on behalf of the Carson City sheriff. I have undeniable proof you're the Viper King."

"You hear that, Pascoe? She's got undeniable proof." He heckled. "I think you better check your facts."

He'd said it like I'd fallen for a trick. Had I misjudged? Could the Viper King have been someone else?

Like a game of cat and mouse, I stayed in constant motion to keep away from the writhing horse. Running to another corner, I tripped over a long-handled tool and took it into my hands. It was a pitchfork.

"You shoulda thought twice before goin' to the Pony Express, defyin' my rules," he said. "Too late now. You and the Indian boy thought you could fool me. Nay, not so. Not to worry about Charlie, though. He's got a whole new life for himself as our newest recruit."

"Charlie would never join the Vipers."

Torrence forced a chuckle. "He's taking the oath at this very moment."

No, it couldn't have been true. Charlie had better sense than that. But they did have ways and means of getting people. Jairus had joined by way of blackmail.

"He's got a family now—a brotherhood. Poor boy can't resist that. Did I mention it's a lifetime membership and the only way to leave is death?"

Charlie did have weak points to be exploited. What if he did take the oath? He'd been feeling so low the last time I'd seen him.

"Pascoe," he said, loud enough for me to hear, "enjoy the show. I'm headed to town for the job. Gotta make sure Charlie goes through with it."

I didn't know what this job was, but Charlie didn't have it in him to hurt anyone. Shame on them for trying to take advantage of him. What job in town would they try to make him do?

The Viper document had come out of my boot when I tripped. In the faintest light, I saw it lying on the ground, the wax seal depicting the Vipers' symbol. The enemies of the Vipers were the pro-Union printing presses. They wanted to suppress the truth. They'd gone after Mabel, and they'd go after Hobbs too.

A torrent of anger flooded my veins, preparing me for one last onslaught.

"Do you really want to see the champion come out?" I shouted, drawing up the pitchfork. "I'll kill this beast, and then I'll kill you."

Both men laughed, taunting me. They didn't know I had enough rage to do it.

"This'd be great fun to witness, Miss Beatrice. Alas, I'm called another way." He said aside to Pascoe, "She doesn't come out alive."

Torrence rode away with a "ya!" while I still felt the presence of Pascoe lurking outside.

CHAPTER 33

Charlie Rye

Wednesday, April 18, 1860

A jangle of spurs came heavy with each step back to the jail cell. I held my breath. By now, I was so eager to know the identity of this Viper King, I almost couldn't think straight.

A woman walked in, and I couldn't have been more stupefied if somebody'd struck me in the head with a fire iron. Along with the spurs, she wore trousers, a wide-brimmed hat, well-made vest, and a self-important grin. "Mornin', Charlie," she said, more coy than friendly.

"Miss Rosebud!" I gasped. My thoughts leaped every which way like grasshoppers in a field. "How'd you get to be Viper King? *King?*"

"Clever, eh? If they always refer to me as a man, then I'll stay hidden."

"All those times pretending to be a . . . lady of easy acquaintance—was that just an act?"

She came close to the bars and whispered, "How do you think I got most of my recruits?"

"Honey, you wear more hats than a saloon on a Saturday night," I told her.

After a chuckle, she said, "Maybe so, but this one"—she tweaked the hat on her head—"is my most favorite."

"You are a force to be reckoned with, miss."

Her smile gave off an air of satisfaction. "It's time you called me by my earned title: Viper King." She put her hand through the bars, revealing the symbol on her wrist, only hers had a crown. It must've been covered up before with a glove or a sleeve. I refused the handshake.

"Of all the tricksters," I said. "You been feedin' Torrence information this whole time."

"Not the *whole* time. I was the one who discovered you. Found you at the faro table. I've got a good eye for recruits. So I sent Pascoe to find out more about you. We rendezvoused with Torrence that night, who was able to figure out who you are."

"Very clever," I said. "Why, the three of your brains might just equal one decent one."

"What'll it be, Charlie? You have a choice to make: to join or not to join."

"I think the choice is yours, miss."

"How do you mean?" Her eyes narrowed.

"If I join this brotherhood, then you, miss, will let me out of our . . . contract."

"Certainly not!" She stiffened. "Of all the deals I've made this year, that's the one I'm most set on."

"But . . . look at you. I made that deal when I thought you was some damsel in distress. You ain't in no trouble—nothin' you can't get out of yourself. Why, you're the most resourceful woman I ever did meet. What do you need me for?"

"Do you want to know the absolute truth of why I intend to hold you to it?"

"More than ever."

"You speak of resourcefulness, Charlie, 'cause you've got it yourself. Think of what we could do—the worlds we could conquer. I'm convinced it would be madness to let you out of that contract."

I couldn't believe what I just heard. Nobody ever gave me a compliment like that before. Why did I feel like mud?

"Charlie, I do believe that one day . . . you'll come to treasure your experiences in the Vipers and with me by your side."

The outside door opened. Two sets of footsteps clattered back to the cell. Miss Rosebud's words hung over me for a while.

Torrence and Sheriff Hartley appeared. This was the first time I'd seen Torrence since I shot him. He held up a bandaged hand and said, "Greetings, brother," in his self-assured drawl. Bona fide resentment was there, even if he tried to keep it hidden.

"Howdy," I said.

"There's no time to lose," Torrence said to Rosebud. "Is he ready?"

"Almost," she said. "He hasn't taken the oath yet."

"What's the delay, Charlie?" Torrence asked, an imposing gaze on me.

"Miss Rosebud here can tell ya." I sauntered to the cot and sat.

"Who's Miss Rosebud?"

"That's what he calls me," she said, lowering her voice.

"Well, what's the holdup?" Torrence said to her. "We got a schedule to make. You said he'd leap at the chance."

"That tone won't get very far with me. We agreed, that, in the presence of the brothers, you'd treat me with proper deference."

"Don't give me the proper deference speech—the one I taught you," he said. "When it comes to respect, there's a certain degree I've earned. And when I see unnecessary delays . . ."

On and on they went, as it smacked me what was going on here. I leaned back, crossed my arms, and watched the volley more amused than I'd been in a long time.

"Why are you smirking like that?" Rosebud said, distracted from their spat.

"No reason. Just seein' what it looks like to 'outshine your father.' Lord-a-mercy, I should've known you're Torrence's daughter. Little wonder you're so deranged."

She was hopping mad that I figured it out. "Listen here. You're gonna join this brotherhood. You know why?"

I raised my eyes, unable to kill the smile.

"Because you shot this man. You have no defense, no family, and no money. You'll rot in here forever unless you agree to join."

"Not quite forever." I held on to the word as long as I could. "Hartley here can keep me company for five years till you come back to fetch me."

"What's the meaning of five years?" Torrence said, annoyed at the wasted time.

"The way I reckon, *you* have a decision to make, Miss Rosebud. I'll join the Vipers for Peace as long as you let me out of the, er, contract," I said with a wink.

Mayor Torrence was relentless. "What does he mean? I agreed to let you be in charge as long as you didn't do anything stupid."

"You agreed to let me be in charge," she clarified, "because I had all the recruits."

"What's this contract?" Torrence demanded. "You don't make deals with the subordinates!"

"Don't ya mean *brothers*?" I added.

Plain as day, Miss Rosebud didn't want her father knowing about the contract. I rose from the bed, seeing a swell opportunity. "I'm happy to spill it, Miss Rosebud. Old Torrence here'll get a laugh out of it, I'm sure."

"Fine!" she snapped. "I'll release you from it. Only if you join the brotherhood *and* you won't say another word about it."

My trick worked. She released me from the contract so easily. Too easily. She'd caved at the very mention of me joining the brotherhood. Perhaps it wasn't my trick, but hers. Was *this* her ultimate purpose for me? Well, I dropped that hundred-pound pack only to heft another. The lesser of two evils, maybe. The thing that'd hurt Bea less to find out.

"On with the oath," Torrence demanded.

"Alright, raise your right hand," she said, which I did. As she prattled off a number of decrees, I felt myself sinking deeper into some kind of lethal quicksand, especially at the end when she asked for loyalty unto death. They didn't really mean forever, did they? Nevertheless, I heard myself agreeing to it.

"You won't regret it," she said, smirking.

"You keep sayin' that, but it don't make me feel no better."

Her glare morphed into a smirk. "Alright, let's get the marking on him. Hartley, bring me the candle."

The sheriff did what she asked. Miss Rosebud removed an iron ring from her index finger. Its face had the snake symbol on it. She heated it in the flame.

"What's that? You gonna brand me like a cow?"

"This is the quick version," she said. "It'll hold until we can get the tattoo."

I soured. A tattoo had a mysterious quality to it, but a big old burn spot? This woman was one trick after another. She circled the thing until it was good and hot, then planted it on my arm. It hissed a hole in my skin. I howled like a coyote and shook out my arm. A pink circle of flesh was all that remained. If it was supposed to look like the snake symbol, it failed.

As she whooped it up with the others, something hit me, far more stinging than getting branded. *She's enjoying this. She takes pleasure in my pain.*

"There now," she said. "This'll guarantee you're with us till the end."

"I'm a man of honor. You know that."

"You are, and it's served you well."

But it hadn't served me well. Not when it came to Miss Rosebud. She was as double-dealing as they came. In fact, she was downright using my honor against me. She didn't see nothing special in me, other than a fresh piece of meat to pound into whatever she wanted.

As the pain from my wrist lessened, so did the sting to my soul. *A contract is only binding if both sides have honor.* She could brand me and bind me to whatever soul-crushing endeavor she wanted, but she couldn't use my honor against me no more.

"Unlock him," Rosebud said.

Sheriff Hartley tinkered with the key until the lock released and the door swung open. We shuffled outside. The fresh air revived me some, but I couldn't imagine what they planned next. Hartley pressed his pistol between my shoulder blades.

"Where's the trust?" I said.

"Quiet!" Sheriff Hartley whispered. "Just making sure you follow through on your first assignment."

"Which is?"

Mayor Torrence intervened. "Put down the gun, Hartley. This here's a man of honor. He ain't gonna break with us." Torrence wrapped his arm around me so I could see his bloodied bandage. A slick of sweat covered his face, and his speech got noticeably slower. A certain glazing of his eyes made me think he'd taken a dose of some pain-killing tincture that was just kicking in. "It goes like this," he explained. "You're gonna knock on Old Man Hobbs's door and persuade him to come outside."

"What for?" A nip of terror came through. They better not lay a finger on Old Man Hobbs.

"Don't you worry," Torrence said. "You just use them talkative skills the Lord done gave you. Keep him away from his shop till we give you the signal that we've finished our business."

Every one of their faces was keen on mine. None of them was bluffing. "You gonna burn his place down?"

"No, son," Mayor said, tightening his grip. "*We're* gonna burn his place down. You're one of us now." He pushed me toward the old man's place. My footing was as wobbly as a new foal's. I marveled, once again, at how in blazes I got to this point.

CHAPTER 34

Beatrice Brannon

Wednesday, April 18, 1860

"I'LL finish this, Da," I said, lunging a couple warning jabs at Havoc with the pitchfork. This agitated the beast. But I kept my reflexes sharp. The weapon was sharp too. The tines hummed like a tuning fork as I thrust it toward him. Havoc evaded my jabs. One of these would stick, and when it did, I'd impale him as many times as it would take to kill him. At last, I'd bring an end to my persistent nightmares. If I could just slay the giant.

With a sweep of my weapon, the prongs grazed his chest. He halted and looked at me like a child whose wrists had been unjustly slapped. I could not account for what followed. I heard my father's voice as if he stood in the barn beside me. "What're you doin'?"

"Shouldn't I do it, Da?" I spoke aloud. "Shouldn't I avenge your murder?"

"You're bein' ridiculous, Honey Bea," I heard. "A horse cannot be a murderer, no more than I'm the merchant of Venice. A horse reacts to his world from the day he's born. Something bad must've happened to make him this way."

"I should pity the horse? Is that what you're telling me? That I should drop my weapon and let him kill me because the poor thing's been mistreated? He killed you, Da! He murdered you, and I saw it with my own eyes. I can never forget it. Every night when I close my eyes, I see it anew."

My weapon dropped. My knees buckled and sent me to the ground. I pressed my hands into the dirt and sifted through it. I needed to feel something real to stop my thoughts from spinning. My insides beat at me, as if some other Beatrice was pounding, yearning to be set free. I knew the truth, and it had been inside me all along. My task was not to kill the horse. I'd tame him instead.

No, I can't tame this beast! I thought. *If Da couldn't do it, then surely I can't.* I'd rather lie on the ground and let the horse stamp me to death than tame the horse my father could not. No, even if I could muster up the ability, I could not outshine my father. I wouldn't! How dare I presume to? How could I live with myself if I completed the task that had killed him? I'd set out to free his name, not exceed it.

"Don't let your courage fail ya now," I heard him say. "You can do it."

Yes, I did know. I knew I could do it. To save my life, I could do it. I'd seen him do it many times. I'd handled horses all my days. The know-how was in me, if I could only summon the courage.

"Please don't make me do this," I said, speaking to Da—or to the God who had taken him from me. "I'll do anything but this. I won't trample on your pride, Da."

A reply came that was equal parts fierce and gentle. "You *are* my pride, Honey Bea. How could you doubt that?"

Unrelenting tears fell from my eyes. They squeezed me dry. Yet I knew in my heart that the task had chosen me. How else could circumstances have brought me to this very place?

I stood. The horse went into fits again. I tossed the pitchfork aside so he could see me do it. "You're OK, Havoc. I'm not gonna hurt you."

He bucked mightily at this.

"I know. I've already hurt you. But I won't hurt you again. I'm going to ride you. You're alright with that, aren't you, boy? You're a fine horse—majestic. Just think of what you could do with all that power inside you. You could do some good in this world instead of lashing out at it."

I had to let go of my hatred of him. I had to release that image of him kicking Da. If I were to speak affectionately to this horse, I'd have to mean it.

"We could be friends, you and me. What do you say? I could ride you."

He gave a disapproving squeal but didn't buck or twist.

"That's not such a bad thought, is it?"

I inched near him and let him sniff my hand. He sniffed all the way up my arm until his hot breath was at my neck. I remained perfectly still, even when he blew a loud huff. He stepped back as if to get one more good look at me. My eyes must've deceived me because the horse was in a full tremble. Maybe he'd gone too long without food or sleep, like me. Maybe this creator of nightmares did have a sliver of fear in him. In fact, maybe it was fear that had made him this way.

"It's OK, boy. Making friends with the world is a far greater challenge than simply hating it." Finally, I saw up close the hole in his head that had grotesquely closed up on its own.

"What a lovely melodrama," Pascoe said. He waited outside to kill me if the horse didn't. Torrence had told Pascoe not to let me out alive. To rile up the horse, Pascoe clapped the walls with his hands. Havoc drew backward at the sound.

"Don't worry about him," I said to Havoc. "He can't abide the thought of us getting to be friends. I suspect lots of folks will feel the same. Maybe even my own family."

I was making progress, but Pascoe wouldn't have it. "Where's that roster?" he said. "Where's this undeniable proof you got?"

I said nothing and kept my attention on the animal and my attempt to mount him. If I could get on his back, maybe I could get him to kick open the doors.

"I got ways to make you talk," Pascoe said, but the threat was empty. No torture was worse than being locked in a barn with this horse and all the truths it had made me face. "I'm warning you, what I got next, you ain't gonna like. Where's the roster? I know Jairus stole it from me. Where'd he put it? Did he give it to you?"

I said nothing.

"Tell me and I'll open this door," he shouted, attempting the most obvious trick.

Still, I remained silent.

A guzzling sound spilled, glug by glug, around the perimeter of the barn. The strong scent of kerosene filled my nostrils as it oozed into the dirt and boards.

A match flared. "This is your last warning. TELL ME! 'Cause I think you got it, so maybe I'll just have to burn all the proof together."

I peered through the slits. He let the flame travel until it reached his fingers. He dropped the match. It struck the base of the barn. The flame was shy at first, bobbing along. Then it found strength and, like a fire-breathing dragon, spread an inferno over this box—this would-be coffin that held me captive.

Smoke touched my throat and threw me into a fit of coughs. The whole barn was consumed by fire. It baked me inside it, as though I stood in the pit of hell. I picked up the pitchfork and, with the blunt end, beat at the doors and walls, pleading for weak spots. Any effort to free myself seemed to push back harder at me.

Dropping again on all fours, I swept my hands over the dirt in search of the roster. If these flames were to eat me alive, at least I'd let the world know the names of the Vipers for Peace. I wanted them held accountable—those who'd burned down Mabel's shop. At last, I felt the paper fold under my knee. I dug a trench with my fingernails into the dirt, stuffed the paper inside, and patted the dirt back in place.

At my neck, I felt for Charlie's button. Dear Charlie! I clasped a tight fist around the button. I'd want them to see, whoever should find my charred bones, that this emblem meant something to me.

The horse stopped thrashing, and we met eyes. He communicated with me, but what was he saying? I stood and backed away from him. He began doing what he did best, which was kick and buck. With the force of his hind legs, he kicked the center post, knocking it out of place. The whole barn shifted as if one more breath of the devil's hot air would bring it down. The center post fell and dashed against the barn doors. The hinges were knocked loose, and the doors went down like some fateful drawbridge.

The smallest window of time and space opened. I yanked hold of Havoc's mane and hoisted myself up. I charged him forward, keeping my head low. He leapt. I closed my eyes. Like a child who has jumped from the highest branch, the lake below her, I waited to land—that feeble, weightless feeling tugging at my insides. A clamor of boards tumbled behind me, and at last, Havoc's legs hit the ground. I breathed. I breathed in whole gulps of cool air. I did it. I'd gotten out of that fire *on the back of the devil horse.*

Pascoe gaped at me like he'd witnessed a body come back from the dead. That's when I heard my father's voice one final time: "You've got a heart of grit, Bea. Go and use it."

CHAPTER 35

Charlie Rye

Wednesday, April 18, 1860

HOBBS would be awake soon if he wasn't already. His shop was always the first to open.

"You told me we don't hurt nobody," I said to Hartley. "Old Man Hobbs don't deserve a thing like this."

"We ain't gonna hurt him," Hartley said. "Your job is to get him outta there so he *don't* get hurt."

Hartley disgusted me, and my face showed it. How could he do a thing like this? Adding to it, I was confused why they needed me at all. Couldn't Mayor Torrence drum up some reason to get Hobbs out of there himself?

"Peace at any cost," Hartley added, like he rehearsed it whenever his conscience got to bothering him.

"You took the oath," Miss Rosebud reminded me. "And you're not to question your assignment. The place has already been doused in kerosene. Now . . . carry on."

Here was a pickle if I'd ever been in one. I couldn't be part of this, but at the same time, I didn't want to get shot. My mind floundered, hoping for a delay.

I asked them, "What if he's asleep? What if I can't get him out? Any number of things could—"

"Let me put it this way," Torrence said. "The second you rap on that door, the clock starts a-tickin'. You got two minutes to work your magic."

"Or what? You'll just burn him up?"

"Charlie, brother," Torrence said, "don't let it get to that point. Understand?"

I faced toward the task. Somebody'd have to warn him. But how could I keep them from burning down his place? Was it too late now? They'd already saturated it in kerosene.

I kept walking, itching for a way out—a way to save Hobbs *and* his shop. I was trapped. There was no foreseeable way they *wouldn't* set his place ablaze. If I shouted for help, they'd shoot me and set it burning. If I did what they asked and got him out of there, they'd still set it burning. Whether I cooperated or not, they'd burn his place down. Man alive! I'd done so many idiotic things to get myself here; I had to fix this.

Wait a minute, I thought. *Why do they want me to remove him from the premises? If they don't care if he lives or dies, as they say, then why is my job to get him out of there? If he refuses to leave, will they still burn it down?*

I thumped at the door, loud as I could, knowing the poor feller was hard of hearing. Soon, I heard the clatter of him coming down the stairs. Glancing behind me, I noticed the other Vipers had gone—taken cover already. Not a one of 'em was in sight, but they were there, sure as ghosts in the graveyard.

"Alright, confound it, I'll be there in a jiffy. Got the rheumatism, ya know. Don't move so spry as I used to." His voice got louder as he moved to the door. He checked through his side window. His saggy eyes gave a look of undeniable shock. I gave him a friendly salute.

"Charlie Rye," he said, opening the door, his gaze full of questions.

"Mornin'," was all I could manage. My voice may've been tighter than his, my throat constricted like that.

"Somethin' wrong, Charlie? I thought you's gone out of town."

"I was." I cleared my throat. "But I'm back now. I need your, um, help with somethin'. Can I come in?"

Old Man Hobbs picked up on the danger scent like a hound. I winked at him slowly. "Sure, come on in. Glad to help with whatever you need."

After he shut the door behind me, the imaginary clock was already ticking. My fellow Vipers wouldn't approve of me stepping inside where they couldn't see or hear me.

"Listen up, Mr. Hobbs."

"It's the Vipers for Peace, ain't it?" he cut in.

"You heard of 'em?"

"They sent me warnings aplenty, so I been askin' around. It's safe to say I know more about 'em than you do." His ink-stained fingers held up a copy of his latest work, the headline reading, "Vipers for Peace: Rearing Ugly Heads."

I looked away from the paper, sick as sour milk in the belly. "I'm a member. They recruited me."

"Don't give yourself a lickin'. They work by blackmail and coercion. Must've had somethin' good on ya. I been gatherin' facts for a while. They must've got wind my article comes out today, sneaky devils. Well, what's it gonna be? They gonna shoot me? Burn down my press?"

"Them generous souls already doused the place in kerosene," I said.

The thin skin of his gullet tightened as he swallowed hard.

"My job," I told him, "is to lure you out without tellin' you what's going on."

"Well, well. Mighty kind of 'em to spare my life."

I'd been holding back a thought I knew sounded crazy, but it pestered me and pestered me, so I let it loose. "That's just it, Mr. Hobbs, I don't think they'll do it with you in here. Mayor Torrence is high up in the Vipers. He'd never kill you. They ain't in the business of killin' innocent folks, just rufflin' some feathers is all. Would they send me here to fetch you if they didn't care if you lived or died? Something's hittin' me over the head with this. If you leave, they'll burn the place down. You stay here and stand your ground, they won't do it."

"Charlie." He caught my shoulders and spoke like he was giving a lifesaving tonic. "I don't care what they told ya. They paint a purty picture of themselves to their recruits, but I know different. They'll squash anybody who stands in their way—and I got proof. It's all in the article."

A voice boomed from outside. "CHARLIE! Game's up. Come on out now."

"That's Torrence!" Hobbs said in a violent whisper. "The jig's up if he's willing to open his mouth. He's shown his cards now. He's in this to the end."

"Don't be fooled, Mr. Hobbs. The thought that keeps comin' back to me is why haven't they done it yet? They keep giving warning after warning."

Hobbs glanced out the window and whispered, "Torrence has a lantern, and he's fixin' to throw it! My place is all wood, no bricks. It'll flare up like summertime straw."

"That's another thing," I added. "They *said* they doused it, but I don't smell no kerosene. Do you? That stuff's horribly strong, and I ain't smelled a whiff of it."

"Save yourself," he told me. "Leave now. If anybody's to stay, it's me. My revolutionary ancestors wouldn't abide me standin' alongside 'em in the hereafter if I abandoned my post."

"I can't go," I said. "If I walk out that door without you, they'll kill me."

"You just said they wasn't in the business of killin' innocent folks."

"I ain't innocent no more! I took the oath. I defied 'em, so I'm fair game now. And I'm Indian, besides. Torrence has always hated me for that. But you're a respectable man in town. Trust me, their mercy extends to you, not me."

"Poppycock! I'm no more respectable than a peddler of fake cures. I've always been a nuisance to Mayor. Listen, I got two muskets." He pointed to them on the mantel. "You take one. I'll cover you from here while you make a run for it."

"No, sir, I won't leave without you," I said.

"You got lots to live for, Charlie. Don't try to be a hero."

"I ain't! The only way to save both of us *and* your shop is to stay put. You watch, they'll turn tails the minute they see you stand your ground."

Mayor Torrence hollered his second warning, louder this time. "This place is goin' down, Charlie! You got to the count of ten to get yourself and that ol' fogey out of there or you'll be burned down with it!"

I waved away Torrence's hollow words. "Pathetic! He thinks we're gonna fall for the old count-to-ten trick!" I began laughing maniacally. Maybe I *was* going mad. Before I could shut myself up, I shouted out the window, "I'm callin' your bluff, you ol' turkey buzzard! We ain't goin' nowhere."

"Don't tempt him!" Hobbs shout-whispered.

"ONE!" Mayor Torrence's counting only brought out more laughs from me.

"There he goes, shoutin' off numbers. Let's see if he really has the guts to do it when he gets to ten. I tell you, Hobbs, I'm insulted!"

"TWO!"

Hobbs brought down the two revolutionary muskets, the bullets, and the powder.

"We don't need them guns, Hobbs. They'll never burn you down in your own shop. It makes no sense."

"THREE!"

"Torrence helped build this town," I tried to reason. "He wouldn't want a stain on his reputation, not in the town he claims to love so well. He'll never do it."

"FOUR!"

Hobbs loaded the bullet and powder into the musket with a ramrod as he spoke. "Charlie, that's *why* he's doin' it. Don't ya see? He thinks the Vipers can stop war from ever comin'. He thinks if war does come, then *all of it* will be destroyed. My shop's a small sacrifice in the bigger picture."

"FIVE!"

"I hate to tell you this, Charlie, but that's why he had it in for Jeremiah Brannon—'cause he wouldn't join."

The madness that had gotten hold of me loosened its grip.

"SIX!"

"That's right, son," Hobbs said, now seeing he was getting through to me. "Torrence wanted to turn this whole town to Vipers. Jeremiah was the only one standing in his way."

JP and his quest, I thought. *His instincts were a dead shot.* He knew something was amiss, Torrence calling Jeremiah a coward and destroying his reputation. Jeremiah had the popularity Torrence needed. If he didn't have Jeremiah's support, he wouldn't have gotten far with the rest of the town.

"SEVEN!"

"Think about it," Hobbs said. "Why did Jeremiah agree to tame that wild horse? It was a duel. Jeremiah took the bait. He thought it would get him his respect back. He didn't know it was an unfair fight. He was up against the devil. Torrence was never so happy as when that horse killed him. Saved him from having to do it himself."

"EIGHT!"

Son of a biscuit. I could scarcely believe what I just heard. Jeremiah purposely put in harm's way? Killed? It couldn't be true. Hobbs handed me the musket and began loading the other. I couldn't wrap my head around it, but then, I knew how Torrence had a way of knocking out his rivals.

"NINE!"

I turned to Hobbs and declared, "Torrence is gonna kill us, ya know."

"I BEEN SAYIN'!" the old man chided.

At last, the final number was uttered. "TEN!"

"STOP!" I hollered out the window. "I invoke the rights and privileges of the brotherhood!"

"Alright, then both of you come out with your hands up. Now!" Torrence shouted.

"They got us cornered, Hobbs. Let's play their game. Then when they least expect it, we'll turn on 'em."

"No, I won't go. This shop is everything my ancestors fought for. This is the freedom of the press, right here. If it goes, I'm going with it."

Mr. Hobbs's hair was full white, and his hands were knobby and ink-stained, but he was every bit a soldier.

"You go, Charlie," he repeated. "Take that article with you or it'll never see the light of day."

I folded the paper and tucked it in my breast pocket. Where were all the neighbors? We needed witnesses. I thought of an idea. "You got a way I can get on the roof?"

His brows shot up. "A spry one like you could climb out my bedroom window." He pointed upstairs.

"Alright, we can use these muskets. If anybody gets close to throwing that lantern, take a shot at it. I'm gonna get as close as I can to that bell and ding it. Best we can do to stop 'em now is get witnesses."

"That's good thinkin', Charlie. Listen, you only got one shot. You won't get a chance to reload."

"I know," I said, drawing a breath of courage. "Off I go."

Musket in hand, I rushed up the stairs. The window gave a crack when I pulled it open. I stepped out onto the windowsill and threw the musket onto the roof. I clung to the eaves and hoisted myself up. I ducked behind the square front of Hobbs's shop. *Beautiful,* I thought, noting my excellent view of the fire bell.

Below me, the Vipers were getting fidgety, impatient. Torrence tried to pass the lantern to Hartley, urging him to do it, but Hartley shook his head. Wouldn't take it. During their spat, Miss Rosebud came up from behind and whacked Hartley on the back of the head with her pistol. He dropped like a fly. Hobbs was right. They were in this to the end.

I focused on the bell, had it in my sights, and was ready to shoot when . . . BOOM! The sound came from *inside* the shop, followed by a howl of pain. Curses! I bet that old musket of Hobbs's misfired.

Torrence swung back his arm and tossed the lantern toward the shop. Without a second thought, I aimed and fired. The lantern burst midair.

"He's on the roof!" Rosebud shouted. A pepper of gunfire hailed around me. Torrence and Rosebud were taking shots. I scaled the rooftops toward the fire bell, taking cover behind the storefronts, bounding from roof to roof. The last one's pitch was high. I jumped far as I could and grabbed the ridge, feeling splinters slide into my hands. I hurdled over the pitch and slid down the other side, dropping to the ground. My legs hurt from the drop, but the momentum kept me going.

I ran hard. Bullets whizzed past my ears. The tower was a few feet away. I pumped my legs harder, at last reaching the ladder. Rung by rung, I raced up it like hickory dickory dock, almost to the top. Thank God Torrence's aim was affected by that medicine. But my luck ran out. Pain struck the right side of my back and knocked me clean off the ladder. I thudded to the ground, hard as a lodgepole pine.

My sight got blurry, and my head spun like a top.

"What have you done, Father?" I heard Rosebud say.

Then Pascoe shouted, "Ride out!" and the two of them got on their horses and took off.

I gasped for the final breaths left in me. Not enough air would come. A shadow slipped over the morning sun in my eyes. Mayor Torrence stood above me, come to finish me off.

"You're done, boy." He pointed his gun at my head.

I still had Hobbs's newspaper in my pocket. I wanted to say, "You haven't won," but only a groan came out.

"You and that little gal of yours thought you could hoodwink your ol' mayor. Well, who done the hoodwinkin' now? I'm about to blow your brains out, and she's locked in a barn with the horse that killed her father. I told her it was poetic justice, but I don't think she was amused."

A hard whinny, like the ripping of canvas, interrupted his speech. From down the lane, it came barreling our way. That horse. The one that killed Jeremiah. I'd a' known it anywhere by that shriek Bea described. Here it came, galloping toward him. Praise the Almighty, was that Bea on his back? I couldn't see too clear, but I sure hoped. Didn't Torrence know by now that Bea couldn't be held down?

If I could've spoke, I would've asked him how much he liked poetic justice now.

CHAPTER 36

Beatrice Brannon

Wednesday, April 18, 1860

MAYOR Torrence stood as though he'd been struck by lightning at the sight of me riding in, but I took no joy from it. He'd shot my Charlie and, from the looks of it, wanted to shoot him again.

I had no weapon—none but the one I rode upon. I had no plan in my head. Forward I charged toward Torrence with everything in me. Maybe I'd knock him over. Maybe I'd get thrown or trampled. I didn't know. This was reckless and crazy, but I had to show Torrence that I wouldn't back down. And I couldn't let him shoot Charlie a second time.

Torrence glanced over his shoulder and back at me. He noticed the smoke rising from his property, probably wondering how Pascoe let me get away. He changed the aim of his gun from Charlie to me. Still, I pressed forward, hurtling toward him, all my senses vanishing. Havoc didn't back down. I squeezed my eyes shut as I got closer. Surely Torrence had me locked in his sights by now. I opened my eyes at the last second.

A shot rang out. Torrence collapsed like a rag doll. Havoc reared up on his hind legs. My hands slipped from his mane, and my body slid down his back. There was nothing to grab. My arms reached behind me to catch my fall. I landed hard on my left arm. Havoc bounded down in a fit. I rolled out of his way, trying not to get trampled. He turned a couple circles before charging away down the street.

As the dust settled, I caught sight of my deliverer. At the edge of Oliver Street, Mama stood on the seat of our wagon, lowering Da's rifle, JP and Cobber planted fearlessly by her side. I'd never seen anything so terrible and majestic in my life. *Lord, have pity on us.* Mama just shot a man.

All became hushed and still, like that brief lapse of time between lightning and its imminent thunder. And thunder it did. A woman wailing, "Nooooooo!" rode into the scene. She dropped from her horse, stood above Torrence's body, and looked down at him, shaking her head. I'd seen the woman before. Her clothes were different, but sure enough, it was Miss Rosebud. Miss Rosebud raised her pistol in Mama's direction.

"Mama, down!" I screamed. Rosebud fired a shot, but Mama ducked herself and the boys in time. The woman switched her target to me and pulled the trigger but was out of bullets.

Pain surged in my left forearm from my fall, but I managed to get to my feet.

The woman walked toward me as she shouted, "My father has finally given his life for this stupid, ungrateful town. War is sure to come now. He was the only one willing to protect you all from it, but you didn't deserve him. Now the abolitionists will destroy it. They'll destroy the West and everything we've built, town by town."

I should have known Miss Rosebud was a Viper too. I gave her an icy glare before turning away to help Charlie.

"You don't deserve *him* either," she sneered as I staggered away. "Ask him! Ask Charlie about the pact we made."

I did my best to ignore her and used my good arm to help myself down beside Charlie.

"Charlie, you're going to be OK."

He'd taken a hard fall, not to mention a bullet in his back. He fought to breathe, like an accordion with a hole in it. "Bea . . . she's getting away." He motioned his chin toward Rosebud.

"I don't care about her." I gently moved Charlie from his back to his stomach. I ripped the sleeve off my shirt and pressed it to the hole where blood oozed out. He groaned. The bullet was probably still lodged inside.

The fire bell clanged madly. JP had climbed the tower and gave that bell more use than it was likely to see in its lifetime.

A man blew past me on a horse. It was Pascoe, riding Dante, who I'd left at Torrence's place. He stopped beside Rosebud and reached out his hand. "Miss Opal," he said, throwing his gaze right and left, "we gotta go. We got a job to do."

"We'll go when I say," she snapped. "Never mind the job. This man was my father. We're obligated to help him. Somebody's got to see he gets a proper burial and not leave it up to these people."

"But Miss Opal," Pascoe said, "there's folk comin'!"

"Bea, you gotta stop her," Charlie said, struggling. "She's the . . ." His words got caught, but I knew.

"Viper King," I finished.

Miss Opal noticed a few spectators gathering from here and there. She grabbed hold of Pascoe's hand and flung herself onto the horse with him. They charged west for a quick exit.

They didn't get far. A group on horseback rode toward them, blocking their escape. I couldn't believe the sight. Mabel and her crew had come, and she was riding at the foremost of them. In seconds, the two scoundrels were surrounded.

Cobber ran toward me and Charlie, saying, "Mama's gone to fetch Dr. Pearl."

"You hear that, Charlie?" I said. "Dr. Pearl's coming. Not to worry now. You're gonna be OK."

"Cobber," he said weakly, "Hobbs is shot. He's . . . in his shop."

"Cobber, run and tell Mr. Hobbs that help's on the way," I said, which he hurried to do. "He'll fix everybody up right, you hear?" I kept my hand pressed to Charlie's wound.

His voice crackled. "Beatrice." He hadn't called me that in ages. To him, I'd always been just Bea. I leaned my head close to hear him. He said something I never would've expected, quiet as a whisper in a church pew. "Beatrice. Sweet and precious guide. Who cheered me with her comfortable words."

Somebody might as well have stopped my mouth with a cork, for all my lack of speech.

"It's *Divine Comedy*," he eked out, the faintest smile on his lips. "Don't look so surprised."

* * *

After arriving home, JP, Cobber, and I waited outside on our porch during Charlie's surgery. Dr. Pearl was in the process of removing the bullet from Charlie's back. I'd tried to convince Mama to let me help, but she'd refused. My arm was likely broken, and in Mama's words, I'd "run the gauntlet" in recent days and needed respite. Maybe she was right about that.

At least I was at home though, and nothing could replace that comfort. Our house had been converted into a temporary hospital, as Dr. Pearl's clinic only had one patient bed.

We three sat on the porch, huddled close. Cobber got extra squirmy when Charlie cried out in pain. I wouldn't allow myself to flinch, hard as it was.

Mama cracked open the door to announce, "He got it out."

My brothers sighed in relief, but I held on to my concern. "Is he going to be OK?"

Mama sighed. "He's having some trouble breathing, but Dr. Pearl is hopeful. And we must be too. You three stay put while we get him bandaged up."

Cobber, at least, felt comfortable enough to embark on a one-way conversation. "Charlie saved Mr. Hobbs's shop, you know, and probably his life too. I saw the whole thing with my spyglass." He held up the shiny brass object. "I woke up early to check the seas and went up to the forecastle—I mean fo'c'sle—and looked out. There was Mayor Torrence pressing a gun against Charlie's back and pushing him out to the street. Next thing I know, Charlie's climbed up on the roof of Hobbs's place. And when Mayor Torrence chucked the lantern Charlie shot it right out of the air. That's when I ran to get Mama."

"Remarkable," I said, musing over all the things that had happened since Charlie and I had said goodbye. We'd have so much to catch up on. I prayed I would get the chance. "I'm glad you were vigilant."

"It was nothin' more than my duty. A good seaman is always vigilant when he's on lookout. And this spyglass can see up to five knots."

I cocked my head toward my brother, now using all these peculiar terms.

"While you were gone, he's decided to become a naval captain, in case you haven't guessed," JP said, annoyed. "Also, the kitchen is now called the galley."

Cobber gave a playful smile.

"How very exciting," I told him.

"Dr. Pearl gave us all kinds of naval stuff for our birthday," Cobber said.

"About that," I said, "I'm sorry I missed it."

"That's OK," he said. "The gift you sent made it extra special."

"What gift?"

"The silver snuffbox," he said.

"Where would I get a silver snuffbox?"

Confusion bounced back and forth between us.

"It has a bee on the top, and it pops open with a spring. Charlie said you felt bad that you couldn't be here, so you sent it with him."

My eyes widened, finally understanding what had happened. What Charlie had done.

"Now do you remember?" he said.

"Oh, *that* silver snuffbox."

"He also told us about the shooting competition," JP spoke up. "Wish we could've seen it, Bea. Cold-Blooded Boys indeed! Well, if we *must* be cursed to have a sister, I reckon you'll do."

I stood and peered inside the window. Charlie lay on the sofa, shuddering to get air in his lungs.

Oh God, please let him stay. Mama had been right to bar me from the surgery. I could not bear this moment. Not for anything. I ran—down the porch and onto the road, fast as I could.

"Where you going, Bea?" JP shouted.

I kept running. I wished I could've run forever and not felt the pain inside me ever again. I stopped only when my legs gave out. My arm hurt more than ever. I held it close to me. My father had been killed before my very eyes, now my dearest friend might die, and I still was no closer to keeping my family under our roof than when this whole misadventure began.

In the distance, someone approached on horseback, waving at me. It was Mabel. It did my heart good to see her.

She swung down and noticed my tears. "Lafayette, you OK?"

"My radius bone's seen better days. Just waiting my turn to see the doctor."

"Lord, I don't envy you," she said. "I broke my arm a couple years back. It's devilish painful."

"I'm glad you came," I said. "I thought you were stepping away."

"I said only for a little while, and as it turned out, I needed to jump back in immediately. When I figured out who the Viper King was, I couldn't stay away."

"How did you figure it out?" I asked.

"Miss Opal is a friend of mine," she said. "She used to attend our services. I know, it wasn't exactly good for business to have a soiled dove among our congregants, but Father makes it a point not to deny anybody."

"*She* was an abolitionist?" My hate for the woman called Opal thawed a little, replaced by an unexpected pity.

"She appeared to be. After a while though, something changed, and she stopped coming. Whatever she was hoping to find, she didn't find it with us. Anyhow, the night of the fire, shortly after I'd seen you, I saw her charging out of town like Pharaoh in his chariot, and I rode after her. She turned back and saw me, and she looked ashamed, but she didn't stop. I just knew."

"Did she start the fire?"

"It's a strong possibility. Either way, she's responsible."

"Well, she'll serve her time," I said. "And you'll get the reward. Now you'll be able to rebuild your shop."

"I hope we see the reward."

"Why wouldn't you?" I asked.

"Well, Mayor Lassen's been known to make a promise and not follow through."

"Oh, he better!" I said, working myself up. "We have witnesses."

"Calm down now," she said. "I'll do my best to keep him honest. You know me."

"Yes I do."

"Question is," she said, "do I know *you*?"

I shrank, lowering my gaze, knowing what she meant.

"I have this suspicion, you see. Is it true?"

My silence was confirmation of it.

"Why didn't you tell me? On we went, pontificating about politics and literature and abolitionism, and all the while, you can't tell me you're a girl?"

"I should have. I'm sorry, Mabel."

"Well, I'm all too mindful of why you felt it was necessary."

"It was," I said. "I won the qualifying race, but they refused to send me."

Mabel nodded, with keen understanding. "Just so you know, I would've kept your secret."

"I see that now," I said. "It may be late in coming, but I'm Beatrice Brannon. Pleased to meet you."

"We've not heard the last of you, Beatrice Brannon."

"Nor you, Mabel Tucker."

CHAPTER 37

Charlie Rye

Wednesday, April 18, 1860

DEATH'S doorstep was a cruel misery. Minute by minute, I forced air into my lungs, hoping I'd make it to the next hour. The good doctor gave me laudanum to dull the pain, but nobody else could do my breathing for me. I wasn't willing to die just yet.

I almost found it funny, in a tragic way, wondering how things would turn out. How would foolish ol' me get myself out of these scrapes? Was I still bound to the Vipers? Would the Brannons find out I'd made a marriage pact with a prostitute? Would I find a venture to lose myself in? How would my pa fare without me? Foul man that he was, he was still kin. Most of all, would I ever tell Bea everything she meant to me?

Bea was right beside me, holding my hand. The minute Dr. Pearl let her come in to see me, she took hold of it and wouldn't let go. Even now, she was asleep in her rocking chair beside me with her hand in mine, while I was face down on the sofa. I must've been dreaming 'cause I woke up calling to Bea.

She bolted upright. "I'm right here." She squeezed my hand for proof.

"I got . . . a confession," I labored to say.

"There'll be no confessions," she whispered back. "All purging of your soul will have to wait until you're recovered. Let *that* keep you alive."

"But Bea, it'd ease my sufferin' some to tell you."

She twisted her mouth sideways. "As long as you promise to keep fighting."

"It's about . . . the cow incident," I said.

"Yes?"

"Well, I milked it."

"The cow?"

"No, the incident," I said. "I wasn't that offended. Maybe at first . . . but it wore off. I kept acting hurt so that . . . you'd have to win *me* over, not the other way around. It was my fault we didn't speak for two years."

She leaned in close. "It wouldn't have mattered if you'd milked it or if you hadn't. I was the one who treated you so abominably. I was so intent on my ill-fated quest that everything got mixed up in my head. I coveted the shiny counterfeit thing, but you are the true article."

Now I hadn't expected Bea to go on like that, but I was mighty flattered. And a little speechless too. I let my lungs have a rest from so much talking, because, well, Bea just called me the true article.

I'd need courage now for the deeper confession, the one regarding Miss Rosebud. Sure, I was out of the contract now, but the thought of Bea finding out from somebody else what I done, I couldn't abide that.

"Bea, there's something else," my voice croaked. "It's about Miss Rosebud."

"I told you, I don't care about Miss Rosebud."

"But what if I told you . . . we made a pact." Bea was right. Now was not a good time for confessions. My heart started going faster. My breathing got shallower.

"Do you need more laudanum? Shall I wake Dr. Pearl?"

"No, Bea, no."

"OK, then, please believe me when I tell you that I don't care what Miss Rosebud made you do. If I had to venture a guess, I'd say she took advantage of your blinding sense of honor."

A little shame rose in me when she called it *blinding*, but hang it if she wasn't right. My heart calmed down.

"It's unforgivable what she's done . . . to more than just you. That whole brotherhood was founded in hate. Why would she start a thing like that?"

"She said . . . it was to outshine her father," I said, "but I'd say it was to gain his love. A person does a fair amount of foolishness in that pursuit."

Bea sat quietly for a while, then said, "You're right. She didn't care about the politics. It was Torrence who cared about the politics, not her. She wanted to do something grand that her father cared about—to gain his acceptance. Seeing his angst about a possible war coming must've given her the idea to form the group."

"And I bet it didn't hurt to be in charge of all those men." I chuckled, but the tightness in my chest turned it into a gasp.

Bea squeezed my hand again.

For the first time since I fell from that bell tower, I thought that if I lived through this, my prospects might be alright.

"Charlie," she whispered, "how did you know that quote from Dante?"

"Cobber loaned me your book."

"And you read it?"

I took her jab in stride.

"Cobber thought it'd help me understand you better."

She smiled. "And how did you fare?"

"None too good. That Beatrice . . . she's too perfect. Nobody *always* knows the right thing to do."

All the sunshine left her face, and she patted my hand. "There, there. That's only the laudanum talking. I'm sure you'll think the better of it in the morning."

"Read it to me," I said.

"Right now?"

"Sure, just pick any part."

"Good idea." She tiptoed around sleeping bodies and returned with my old friend, that thick book, and opened to the beginning. "In the midway of this our mortal life, I found me in a gloomy wood, astray . . ."

Her voice eased my tension. I didn't know if I was falling asleep or dying. I only knew I had no fear of the place I was going.

CHAPTER 38

Beatrice Brannon

Thursday, April 19, 1860

My dream that morning represented a hodgepodge of the past few weeks. One particular image burned in my mind and woke me up for good: smoke rising from the woodpile that used to be Torrence's barn. I wanted to put all this to rest, but something still felt unresolved.

The Viper King had been captured. The second-in-command had been killed. And Pascoe, whatever role he'd played in the Vipers, was also behind bars. But what if others were involved and hadn't been captured? What if they, too, had committed crimes but would never face penalty because of the secrets they kept? I wanted to see that roster, if that's what it was. Could it still be where I'd left it, unburned?

The clock struck seven chimes. Nothing would wake this crew anytime soon. Charlie was asleep and breathing loudly. Thank the Lord he'd made it through the night!

With my broken arm in a sling, I knew I'd need help, so I enlisted the person who'd appreciate it most, aside from Charlie.

JP lay on the floor in a mess of blankets. I knelt beside him and gave a nudge. "JP," I whispered. He grumbled, probably assuming I awoke him to complete some household chore. "Shhh. We've got to be quiet."

He rubbed his eyes and tried to focus on me.

"I need your help," I said, hushed. "How about helping me solve one more mystery?"

A mine blast might as well have jolted him awake. He nodded. I pointed to the door. He put on his boots and followed.

Out in the barn, I told him to get a pair of Da's work gloves. To my surprise, JP did what I asked without question. He saddled up Thundercloud, and we rode together out to Torrence's ranch. By now, there'd been enough conversation in our house about the Vipers for Peace, that JP needed no briefing.

A cloudy haze covered the sky as we arrived at the charred skeleton of Torrence's barn. A few boards held the shape of the pitched roof, now level with the ground. Flecks of ash flurried in the breeze. JP awaited my instructions while I surveyed the perimeter, at last finding a good spot to enter.

"You'll need to go in there. I buried something in the dirt. We need to get it out. Can you do it?"

JP nodded again, eyes wide with interest. He crawled inside on his knees and elbows.

"There should be a small mound in the center. Feel around."

"There's a lot of boards in here. I can't even get to the center."

"I didn't say it'd be easy."

JP grunted and boards clattered as he moved around in the shell of the barn.

"Be careful."

No sooner did I say that when there came a thump. "Ouch! Hit my head."

"One of these days, you'll listen to my advice."

"This is harder than you think! And I just tore my sleeve. Mama's gonna kill me."

"Keep going. I know you can do it."

"I'm in the center," he said, "and I feel something. Could be a mound."

"Start digging."

"What am I digging for? Better be gold."

"It's a paper."

"Paper! Should've known."

"It's sealed and very important. Trust me, it'll be worth it."

After another few minutes of digging and grunting, he said, "I got it!"

"Is it burned?"

"Nope. It ain't in the best shape, but it's still in one piece."

I couldn't believe it. My silly idea of burying it in the dirt had worked. "You've done it, JP."

He scuttled out the same way he'd gone in, now ragged as a marooned pirate. He handed me the paper, dirty but not scorched. The red wax seal was still in place, but the Viper symbol had become obscured.

Whatever secrets remained would soon be available to me. I cracked open the seal and unfolded it. Jairus was right about it being a roster. Titles were listed in one column, while the names of people who filled those positions were on the other. The first position, of course, was Viper King. To the right of this said O. Torrence. Just below it was the position Viper Deputy. To the right of that was the same name, O. Torrence. This was intentional, to protect Opal Torrence and Oliver Torrence and to make it ambiguous who was in charge.

Other men from town were listed. My mood sunk a little reading each one. Farther down, all the way at the bottom, was the title Financier. Listed in this position was a name that prickled every pore on my body. I pointed to the name. JP's mouth dropped open. Why hadn't I considered this before? Surely Mayor Torrence's most devoted follower had played a part in this too.

I wasted no time. "Let's go."

"What are we . . . ? Are we confronting him?"

"Yes."

JP conveyed fear, disgust, and exhilaration all at once. We mounted Thundercloud again and rode to the Ellerby estate. The time must've been about eight o'clock.

"You wait here," I said.

"No! I dug the darn thing out of the rubble. Besides, you'll need a witness."

His answer impressed me. He was probably right.

"OK, but let me do the talking."

He agreed. We marched up the steps. I raised my hand to knock but heard my name called to my right.

"Miss Beatrice, is that you? And JP?" George Ellerby had come from the side of his house with his horse in tow. He glanced at the sealed paper in my hand and quickly back to my face. "I'm headed to town, but is there something I can do for you?"

He'd caught me off guard, and the words I'd prepared were gone.

"I'm glad you've come," he said and motioned us closer, as though wanting to speak without the risk of his family hearing.

JP and I descended the stairs, and we stood face-to-face with him. I gathered my courage. "I'm gonna ask you a question, and I'd appreciate an honest answer."

"Absolutely, anything you want to know," he said.

So many questions plagued me; I struggled knowing where to begin. I blurted out one that he was directly responsible for. "Why are you so bent on seeing my family leave town?"

"You're mistaken. I never wanted that."

"Then why are you holding us so mercilessly to this debt? Our father's only been gone a month, yet—"

"I know," he interrupted. "I know. I've treated you poorly, and I own that. I allowed myself to be influenced by a vindictive, cruel person."

"My da told me you wanted to make an example of us. Why?"

"It was Oliver Torrence who wanted that."

"Because my da wouldn't join the Vipers?"

"Yes. Torrence was hitting him hard so he'd join."

"Not just Torrence. It was you too. On the very day of my da's service, you sent the lawyer over to our house to tell us our days were numbered."

"It was wrong of me. I was convinced that the Vipers would keep our town safe—keep war from coming. Your father held out, and because he held out, others did too."

"I'm proud of him for holding out, for standing his ground. That's the kind of man he was, yet now all he'll be remembered for is his failure in that stupid Peregrine mine and this cursed debt."

"That's not what I want," Ellerby said.

"Well, neither do I! I've been to hell and back to rescue his name that's been dragged through the mud."

"We'll fix that."

There was nothing, in that moment, that frightened me. I could've said anything and not felt the least bit uncomfortable.

"Was my father murdered?"

Ellerby hesitated to answer, eyeing JP.

"If you've got somethin' to say, you can say it," JP said, rising in stature, taking on a toughness, like Da used to do when demanding the truth.

Eventually, Ellerby answered, "No."

"Did Torrence put our father in harm's way on purpose?"

His eyes met mine. "Yes."

"Then it's the same thing," I said. "Why didn't you stop him? Why didn't you tell my father not to go through with it?"

"He was determined—the same way men are determined when they're challenged to a duel. Your father knew the risks."

"I don't think he did. I don't think he was ready to die. He would've never left his family in this predicament. He wanted to join the Pony Express. He told me that before he died. All this because of a ridiculous brotherhood, which, come to find out, you helped pay for." I held up the paper.

He squinted to get a look at it. "What's that?"

"Proof of your guilt," JP said.

"Please destroy that. And not just for my sake. There's no point in laying blame on men whose jobs and reputations were at stake if they didn't join. Torrence was determined to get his way. He would've stopped at nothing."

The notion that the town elders had all the answers and did all the right things was long gone—capsized and drowned. That's when I hurled the most painful truth at him. "Doesn't it make you wish you'd followed your conscience instead of cowering to fear?"

"I'll make it up to you and your family, I promise," he said, "but please burn that. Destroy it. It's dead now that Torrence is."

From there, we made an agreement that I could live with. Him coming clean to the whole town would've been preferable, but I did what I felt Da would've wanted me to do, which was, of course, the thing that suited our family best.

CHAPTER 39

Beatrice Brannon

Saturday, November 10, 1860
(Six months later)

OUR wagon descended the highest peak of Victory Hills. There, we got our first glimpse of the Ellerbys' big red barn, decorated for the highly anticipated Election Ball. Clouds loomed low, and the autumn air smelled of deep burning cedarwood. Festive bunting was draped the length of the barn, and an enormous wreath hung from the pitched roof. Lit torches outlined the path to the open barn doors. My, how pretty everything looked!

With a gentle "whoa," Mama halted the wagon. The boys sprang from the back, eager to make their guesses in the sugar-drop contest. Mama reined them back, reminding them to carry pies to the refreshment tables.

"Mind you don't drop them!" I called.

My gown was Mama's own design made from indigo silk with a handmade lace collar. For years, she'd held on to this fabric for an extra special occasion, but after Da's death, she'd stopped saving things for later, determined to enjoy them now.

The presidential election had occurred Tuesday night, but here in Victory Hills, we would wait for a special courier to bring the news of who had won five days ago. We in the territories didn't vote, but our patriotism ran just as deep as in the states. The contenders were Lincoln, Breckinridge, Bell, and Douglas. I hoped for a Lincoln victory, knowing full well what it would mean if he won. The Southern states were waiting with bated breath to secede from the Union if he did. A change, for good or ill, seemed forthcoming.

"One day, women will be able to vote in this country," I told Mama as we walked down the path of torches. "Folks always say that women don't need to vote because their households are represented by their husbands, but what about us?"

Mama took it in and let it sit awhile. "True indeed."

"Injustice in this country will end, Mama, first by freeing all enslaved people. Lincoln can help with that. Do you think he'll win?"

"I do hope so," she said.

Mr. Ellerby greeted us warmly at the entrance. "The Brannons! Now the festivities can truly begin." Mr. Ellerby's effusive delight might have been overdone.

We Brannons were to be the guests of honor. George Ellerby, now serving as mayor, had chosen tonight to unveil his charitable foundation, the Jeremiah Brannon Fund, which would raise money for families who'd come West with the promise of wealth in the mining business, but whose dreams hadn't "panned out." The first donation had come from his own pocket, which was to pay the debt Jeremiah Brannon had incurred. So . . . our land was our own again. And Mama would serve on the governing board.

Delilah and Daphne Ellerby, standing regally in red tartan plaid, the seasonal print of choice, both greeted me with a curtsy and a, "Welcome, Beatrice."

Daphne spoke in a bubbly whisper. "Where on *earth* did you get that dress?"

Delilah added, "I must say, Beatrice, it's stunning."

"Thank you," I cleared my throat for emphasis. "My mother made it."

Every Ellerby in the line bounced the awkwardness along like a hot coal, until finally Mrs. Ellerby caught it and spoke up. "Ellen, you've outdone yourself with Beatrice's dress. The delicate lacework on that collar." She touched Mama's arm and leaned toward her. "Dear me, I hope you'll reinstate us as clients."

An uneasy smile swept across Mama's face as she fought for the right words. "I'm still unsure as to why my services were discontinued, but—"

"I hope you'll accept my humble apology. My husband was simply convinced . . ." She didn't finish. The words made her apology sound hollow, and she knew it. Da had been right about Mayor Torrence pressuring Mr. Ellerby to cut us off, and she'd gone along with it blindly.

"Of course, I accept your apology," Mama said, in her unfailing forgiveness. Also, a widow such as herself was in no position to refuse the work.

"Be sure to make your guesses," Mrs. Ellerby said, pointing to a small table situated at the entrance where the jar of sugar drops stood, mottled in red, white, and blue. I scrawled my name and a random number on a paper and folded it twice; Mama couldn't be bothered with such frivolities. She did, however, take a dance card and handed one to me as well. We strolled into the barn, arm in arm. The band played a lively reel, and dancing was in full swing.

I glanced across the room and, at last, spotted Charlie. My stomach flip-flopped. He'd say I was putting on airs and would never let me hear the end of it.

Mama stripped the quilt from my arms. "I best take this to the raffle table. Have a marvelous night, Honey Bea." She kissed my cheek and left me standing there, unprotected and alone.

My proverbial soft underbelly thus exposed, who should approach me but the Ellerby girls again, this time out of their parents' earshot.

Daphne spoke up on behalf of her elder sister with a crafty grin. "Delilah has a question for you."

"It's not so much a question as it is a thought," Delilah corrected. "You see, Charlie signed my dance card." She held it before me as proof. "Well, I wondered if you'd be bothered if he danced with me."

"Certainly not," I said. "Charlie may dance with whomever he pleases."

"Well, what if," she hesitated to finish, "he were to set his cap towards me?"

Now I was annoyed. Delilah interested in Charlie as a beau? Unfathomable.

"I'm surprised you'd be interested," was all I could say, considering her complete about-face.

"Well, he's always had a sort of rugged charm. Earlier, he told us the story of how he shot that lantern straight out of the air then ran through a storm of gunfire for the fire bell. Anyway, it's so old fashioned to reject someone based on class. After all, Romeo was beneath Juliet's class."

On and on she went. I summoned the muse of scathing retorts to inspire me, but alas, she'd set me up for it herself.

"Actually, Delilah," I cut her off midsentence, "Romeo wasn't beneath Juliet's class. The Montagues and the Capulets were both wealthy families."

"But I thought—"

"One only need recall the first line of the play to settle this: 'Two households, both alike in dignity.'"

"Oh . . . I thought that's why their love was forbidden. She was rich, he was poor—star-crossed lovers and all."

"Their love was forbidden because the two families were locked in a bitter feud. They were considered star-crossed lovers because the fates had supposedly conspired against them. It had nothing to do with class distinction."

Delilah blinked again and again, trying to rescue her pride.

"It's been far too long since we've met for tea, hasn't it?" I added that quip in honor of Da, who always told me that the best kind of insults were masked as compliments.

Delilah chuckled nervously, while her sister outright laughed.

What completely astounded me was Delilah's response. "We'd love to have you over for tea again, wouldn't we, Daphne?"

Daphne squelched her giggle and said, "Yes, we would. Very much."

They curtsied and made their way to the throng of people our age.

I whisked myself to the cider table, grinning, sipping my warm, spiced cider. For once, being a know-it-all had offered a small dividend.

Now I needed Charlie's thoughts on this whole liaison Delilah had cooked up. Did he share her enthusiasm? I doubted it. Either way, I felt my grudge toward the Ellerby girls lessen its grip on me. They may have steered me away from Charlie's friendship, but I'd allowed myself to be steered. I knew I'd never let it happen again.

Every so often, Charlie's gaze flew across the room, never for very long, before returning to his jolly banter. Was he looking for me?

For heaven's sake, I told myself, *I can't hide forever. I've been through the inferno and back. Facing my best friend should be easy.*

I drew in a deep breath and marched toward the group, wringing a pair of clammy hands. Seeing him there with Delilah and the others, I almost turned back. Instead, I said to Charlie, in front of everyone, dance cards to the wind, "Do you know the waltz?"

"Bea!" he said, surprised. "I mean . . . Miss Beatrice. I don't know the waltz, but I'm a quick study. You taught me how to read. I'm sure you could teach me the waltz too."

An elated laugh tumbled out of me. I couldn't believe he'd just let out one of his best-kept secrets.

"Consider it returning the favor," I said, "for encouraging me to join the Pony Express."

"Well, long as you don't laugh so hard—"

"That's enough stories for tonight," I said, pulling him toward the dance floor lest he regale us with the urine anecdote.

The waltz was a hilarious episode of missteps and syncopated footfalls, crushing the other's toes.

After the song ended, Mr. Ellerby took to the stage. "Folks, me and Polly are tickled pink to see everybody. You know, I could search the world over and not find better neighbors nor a better town. Thanks for comin' out."

Folks showed their delight with proper applause.

"Still no word on the outcome of our highly anticipated presidential election," he continued, "but there is one contest that's been tallied, and we're ready to announce the winner."

More eager applause followed, which was pointless, of course. I knew my name would be called—mine or one of my brother's. The numbers we'd guessed didn't matter. One of the Brannons would be taking home the candy jar. It was part of Mr. Ellerby's predictable charade to spoil us and put us front and center.

"Without further ado," he said, "the winner of our sugar-drop contest is none other than . . . Miss Beatrice Brannon."

Applause erupted. My face glowed red-hot with embarrassment, not because I was taken by surprise, but because I wasn't. Could I fool everyone that I hadn't known this was going to happen?

My neighbors cleared a path for me to take the stage. Mr. Ellerby handed me the heavy jar. I began to return to anonymity when he took my shoulders and faced me toward the crowd.

"Before you go, I've got a little something to say. Folks, we've got ourselves a right hero. As you know, Miss Brannon participated in the very first—and very successful—Pony Express ride."

My neighbors offered a rousing cheer. "I recall somebody saying," he continued, shaking his head in chagrin, "that the Pony Express was no place for a girl. Guess Miss Beatrice showed us different. And I'll tell you what. When I see the kind of pluck this gal has, there's one person I think of."

His voice quieted, and he turned to speak directly to me. "That's your father, Miss Beatrice. No doubt, he's beamin' with pride from where he is now."

Could Mr. Ellerby have been speaking from his heart? Were those genuine tears in his eyes? Was that quiver in his voice real?

With all the rapt attention on me and with Mr. Ellerby's mention of Da, the tears welled. I tried to hide my face, but Mr. Ellerby kept turning me toward the audience.

"A couple other folks ought to be recognized. Where's Charlie Rye? Charlie, come up here. Mr. Hobbs, you too. Ellen Brannon. The Brannon twins. All of you, please come forward."

Mama and Charlie supported Mr. Hobbs up the steps, as he'd slowed down considerably since his musket had misfired.

"These folks brought down a criminal organization," Mr. Ellerby said.

A soberness settled over the proceedings. Instead of cheers, there was a collective nodding of heads and respectful murmurs. Most of them were mourning Mayor Oliver Torrence's death twice—once for his actual death and once for the man they thought he was.

"How 'bout a word, Miss Beatrice?" Mr. Ellerby prompted. "Won't you?"

I wondered what he wanted me to say. Was I accepting an award? Was I thanking him on behalf of my family? The last time I'd felt this much pressure was at the shooting contest. Then I remembered Mabel. Her speech.

I stepped forward and said the first words that came from my heart. "I'm an abolitionist."

The room was still. I bet nobody expected me to say that. "My friend, Mabel Tucker, taught me about abolitionism. She and her band came out of Carson City and helped take down the criminals too. They also deserve our thanks."

I knew I had more to say, but the words weren't coming. I caught glances with Mama and then Charlie, who both nodded me to continue.

"What does it mean to be an abolitionist? It means you stand against slavery, not just in word, but in deed. It means you support our Black brothers and sisters. You help them build their shops and their homes. You stand up to anyone who mistreats them. You strive to live peaceably together. My father was an abolitionist. He never said this to me, but I know it because he refused to join the Vipers for Peace. This he did at great risk to himself. And because he refused, this gave others the courage to refuse. His bravery was infectious. Da wasn't a saint. He made mistakes, as we all do. But he's still the most decent, honorable person I've ever known."

Before my voice choked up entirely, I added one more thing so unpredictable I wondered where I came up with it. "For all who love freedom!" I opened the jar's lid and placed the cylinder down on the stage floor. Children came forward in a throng, wanting to take a piece. In the bustle, the jar got knocked over. Sugar drops cascaded, rolling off the stage and into the audience. All the children squealed and pecked like chickens at seed.

Mortified, I stared at the pandemonium I'd just created. Someone took my hand. Without looking, I grasped it and ran. Charlie and I were running off together, down the stage, out of the barn, and through the corridor of torches until all the chaos was behind us.

At last, we slowed down at the edge of the Ellerbys' land. Charlie bent over, wheezing.

"Have you outdone your lungs?"

"No . . . I'm fine," he said.

"You're certain? I could get Dr. Pearl."

"I'm OK . . . I promise."

After a moment to regain his regular breathing rhythm, he straightened up tall again. His face offered that expression I'd seen before—one of wonder and pride and pure love. "Miss Bea, that was the finest speech I ever did hear."

He held out a hand. I stepped forward and took it. He tugged me toward him, gently, and wrapped his other arm around my waist. The only thing left to do was close my eyes. Our lips touched—mine cold, his hot—in a kiss more delicious than the warmest, spiciest cider I'd ever tasted.

Thunder cracked loudly in the sky, and I was grateful for some other place to divert my attention. It was a bizarre feeling indeed to feel so awkward and yet so comfortable in someone's presence.

Neither of us noticed at first when JP and Cobber came running, calling to me.

"Bea, I saved you a piece of candy!"

"Bea, they're starting the bonfire now!"

"Hey, what are you two doing out here?"

"Yeah, what's going on?"

We ignored their interrogation, each took a sugar drop from Cobber, and walked arm in arm through the torch-lit corridor. The boys snickered as we found our way back to the crowd.

A little way off from the barn, the bonfire was prepared. Broken barrels and crates were stacked in a heap with dried weeds and shrubs as kindling. Mr. Ellerby used a torch to set it ablaze. Everyone cheered. Folks stared at the rollicking flames, wrapped in shawls and cloaks. Some children played tag, while others ate slices of pumpkin pie with their bare hands.

All manner of merrymaking was taking place when the moment of anticipation hit. A tall man on a sleek stallion rode to the bonfire, another rider trailing close behind. It was Colonel Riley! And with him, Jairus wearing a snare drum around his neck.

Jairus dismounted alongside his father and drummed a percussive solo as an overture to his father's words. "Ladies and gentlemen, I bring news that is most important in nature." His shouts were sharp, as though we were his troops. "I am Colonel David F. Riley of the United States Army. I am on a special charge to bring news of our presidential election. The man who will assume the office of the president for the next four years is Mr. Abraham Lincoln."

Wild cheers broke out. Others gasped. Loud discussions erupted. If anyone had doubted whether war would really come, Colonel David F. Riley was there in uniform to confirm it.

"Small townships such as this one are necessary for the preservation of the Union. We need active, informed citizens. More importantly, we need volunteers—able-bodied men, ages eighteen and up—to bolster the army for Lincoln. The future of our nation is at stake. Indeed, this is your chance to prove your devotion to this great country of ours, to prove your gratitude to our forefathers who gave their lives in the great War of Independence. Did our fathers spill their blood on the battlefields of Bunker Hill and Yorktown only to leave us cleft in twain? As for me, I'm going to help Mr. Lincoln save the Union. War is coming. Gentlemen, come and talk with me. Ladies, send your man off to glory. If you're willing to defend your country, now's the time to act."

The Colonel's words nibbled greedily at my insides as I watched Charlie receive the news. In all my professed opinions of the necessity of war, I had never considered it taking Charlie.

An electrifying verve set Victory Hills a-humming. I looked around at the animated discussions taking place. Our days of quiet, small-town innocence, it seemed, were drawing to a close.

Lost in somber reverie, I turned to Charlie. "Good thing you're only . . . seventeen." But my words dropped, unheard. Alas, he was already in line to speak with the Colonel.

CHAPTER 40

Charlie Rye

—

Monday, November 12, 1860

TWO dozen men from Victory Hills answered Colonel Riley's call to join the US Army. I was determined to do my part, since war would be coming, sure as sparks fly. South Carolina was threatening to secede from the Union, and some other states too. As far as ventures to give me the sense of purpose I so ached for, this was the mother lode.

This morning, the soldiers and me would ride out to Carson City with Colonel Riley. The war secretary called on him to train a company of men to guard the overland mail from Carson City to the Great Salt Lake City. Funny how things worked out. Here I was, off to help the Pony Express and the Army at the same time.

The Colonel provided us with military uniforms. I fastened the brass buttons down my long blue coat and looped in the belt that flashed a shiny "US" on its buckle. Next, I combed my head of hair and fixed the cap on top. The best part was my last name that I stitched myself onto the side of the cap. "Rye" was getting tired and didn't seem like me no more, so I switched it out for "Little Hawk." From that day on, I would be Charlie Little Hawk. I wanted my company, and everybody else, to know I was Cherokee.

I had no mirror to see the whole picture but knew I'd appear soldierly in the presence of Miss Beatrice. When I told her I joined, she'd made her displeasure known, but seeing me in this getup would set her mind at ease. It would give her a proper lasting image of me for when her heart started to grieve. And perhaps, I dared myself to think, we'd share another kiss like on the night of the Election Ball.

A silvery white blanket of snow greeted me outside. I saddled up Dandy and took a slow ceremonial walk toward the Brannon place. Up ahead, JP and Cobber waited outside and summoned Mrs. Brannon to come out. The three of them waited on the porch, the boys waving wildly.

Where was Bea? This wasn't good. In my mind, I saw her tucked in bed, not speaking to anybody, just like when her da died. I should've known. This was the wrong time to go. The wrong time to leave her bereft again.

After allowing the Brannons ample time to admire me on horseback, I hopped down to commence the farewell.

JP and Cobber assailed me with hugs.

"We're gonna miss you, Charlie."

"We're sad to see you go."

"Look at you—a soldier!"

"Are you gonna kill anybody?"

"Enough questions, boys," Mrs. Brannon intervened. "You've had your hugs. Now I get mine."

I embraced her, the closest thing to a mother in recent memory. The rims of her eyes were red, and when she blinked, tears fell. "You take care of yourself, you hear?"

"Yes, ma'am. I want you to know that if I do any good in the Army, it'll be 'cause of this family and the influence you've had on me. You've raised 'em right."

She gave my hands a tight squeeze before letting them go.

"Where's Bea?" I said after a spell. "Is she a bit forlorn today? Maybe I should've . . ."

The door opened, and Beatrice stepped out, bringing rays of hope and happiness with her. "Charlie!" She wrapped her arms around me, and I did the same to her. Neither of us let go too soon. Her delight startled me at first—a rebuke to the high opinion of myself, for certain.

"To think, I imagined myself leaving behind a swooning young lass."

She laughed. "I'll leave the swooning to Delilah Ellerby. Or better yet, Miss Rosebud."

Joking about Miss Rosebud was a bit low so I shook my head.

"I couldn't help myself," she said. "I'll miss you, Charlie, more than you can imagine."

"And I'll miss you." I nodded.

And I'll miss you. These were to be my parting words? This was my big, monumental goodbye?

Adding to my defeat, I hoped to have a small window of time alone with Beatrice. I couldn't have this girl forgetting me. I waited for Mrs. Brannon to gather the boys inside, but nobody moved. Beatrice never requested a moment alone, and it would've been ungallant for me to ask. I'd have to do my best with an audience.

I took a deep breath and tried to imagine the others gone. "Miss Bea, the other day I had this dream." All these blank faces stared at me. This would definitely be harder than I thought. "It was more of a nightmare, actually. And you were there."

"In your nightmare?" she asked.

"Yes, but you weren't part of the nightmare . . . you were the good part." Oh, boy, I'd have to do better than this. "Miss Bea, you're everything good about this world. Every day, I'll be thinking of you—every memory we ever shared: climbing trees and splashing in the Truckee River, running wild and free, growing up alongside you, seeing you sprout real nice."

Mrs. Brannon cleared her throat, but I kept going. "And you introduced me to the splendor of Dante. You bring light to my life, and you chase the demons away with your warmth and kindness and honesty. Every night, I'll fall asleep to the sweet remembrance of our first kiss."

Bea's eyes widened, and she glanced toward her mama and brothers. I forged on, no longer caring what they thought. If I didn't do this now, I might've never gotten the chance.

"And Miss Beatrice, I can promise you that when this country of ours goes to war, I'll call upon every miracle in the heavens to keep me alive so I can come back to you. And if I might be so bold as to request a parting kiss, I'd be ever so complete."

Bea didn't wait for her mother's approval. She stepped toward me, and I toward her. I pressed my lips against hers in a sweetness I wouldn't soon forget.

JP and Cobber giggled. I dared not look at Mrs. Brannon, who gasped. Instead, I watched Beatrice. Hers was the only response that mattered. In earnest shock at her behavior and mine, she said, "What are we doing? We're standing in front of my mother!"

Finally, I turned to Mrs. Brannon, whose stern expression forced more confessions. "Mrs. Brannon, you may's well know—I love your daughter. I've loved her since we were children. With every fiber of my being, I—"

"Charlie." Mrs. Brannon stopped me cold. "I think you're gettin' a little ahead of yourself. You're seventeen years old. Mercy! How they let you in the Army, I'll never know, but to be kissin' at your age. It's unthinkable! Why, I was *good and married* before I did any kissin' at all."

"You're right, ma'am, I'm sorry." But with Bea's face illuminated like that, I continued, "I'll do anything to make this girl happy, Mrs. Brannon, anything at all."

My wit had gotten to Bea, my audacity. I went in for another kiss, which Bea had anticipated and returned with pleasure.

"Beatrice!" her mother chided. "This is quite unseemly—and right in front of the boys. Charlie, you must go!" Mrs. Brannon took me by the shoulders and sent me toward my horse.

Beatrice was laughing so hard by now that I couldn't help but congratulate myself. Leaving my girl with a smile would be a fine memory for the both of us.

I mounted Dandy and was about to take off when Beatrice stepped toward me. "Wait! I almost forgot." She untied the silver button from her neck and handed it to me. "Keep it with you. It's bound to find its way back home."

CHAPTER 41

Beatrice Brannon

—

Tuesday, November 13, 1860

FOLKS had said that a saloon's no place for a lady of refinement. In that light, either refinement eluded me—along with the others who'd come to today's meeting—or a new era for Victory Hills had begun. One that would include the women and girls as part of the town's discussions. Our voices and opinions proved to be as boisterous and animated as the men's.

Mr. Hobbs whistled to quiet everyone down. "The question is," he said, "what do *you* think about it, Miss Beatrice?"

I stepped forward and took a deep breath. "I'm honored by Sheriff Hartley's invitation to serve as his deputy, the first female deputy of our town. Either I'm as skilled at taking down criminals as he says, or he's gotten a lot more desperate to find good help."

Everyone snickered, even those who opposed the idea. This time, however, most did support Sheriff Hartley's proposal. They supported me.

"As flattered as I am," I said, "I can't accept it."

Those who had championed the idea gave murmurs of disappointment.

"I appreciate that," I said. "The truth is, there's another endeavor calling to me. The Vipers have done untold damage. I wasn't able to stop them from burning down my friend's shop in Carson City, but I can help rebuild it. She's finally been able to purchase the bricks, and now she's ready to start building. I'm sure it will take some months to finish."

"How about take the job when you get back?" Daphne Ellerby said, who'd become an advocate.

"Well, I'm sure Sheriff Hartley will need to hire someone else."

The sheriff himself nodded at this.

"And not to shorten the list of contenders, but anyone who wants to join me in Carson City is welcome. I ride out in an hour."

They continued their animated discussions while I left to go pack my things. Being a deputy would've been exciting without a doubt, but I was bent on choosing for myself, even if it meant the possibility of letting someone down.

"Honey Bea," Mama called after me. She too had been present at the meeting. "Are you sure?"

Nobody, not even Mama, could ignore the perfect denouement it would've been to our family tragedy: the former sheriff, gone too soon, begets a daughter who becomes the deputy, continuing his legacy. But, for me, the only way to honor his name was to be the kind of person who made her own decisions, no matter the forces at work.

Mama placed her hands on my shoulders. "My, my, you do blaze a trail."

Seeing the implicit trust in her eyes awakened something in me—not boastful, but not exactly modest either. It was true. I had blazed a trail. I had crossed my bridge. In a moment of peril, I had done what I thought to be impossible. I was more than Dante's Beatrice or Shakespeare's. More than my father's daughter or my mother's. I was a living, breathing me.

HISTORICAL NOTE

(Contains Spoilers)

The American West in 1860 was a time and place in history brimming with hope and progress, but also with tension and unrest. Within this context of growing pains and shining light into shadows, I bring you the stories of two teens involved in a similar process happening inwardly. Here is a sliver of the historical backdrop on which I place my fictional elements.

The Pony Express

The Pony Express remains one of the most iconic features of the Old West and embodies the fiery spirit of the age. It ran from April 1860 to October 1861, a mere 18 months in existence, and ended when the transcontinental telegraph connected the East to the West.

It never achieved the financial success the owners hoped for and, in the end, lost a great deal of money. What it lacked in revenue, it supplied in legend. The Pony Express motto was "The mail must go through," and the brave riders delivered on that. They risked their lives riding through all manner of weather and conditions, and as fable has it, only one mochila was lost in the entire duration of the enterprise.

Another testament to its success was that it met a genuine need. Not only did the Pony Express provide quicker communication from East to West, but the state of the Union was tenuous, and California was crucial to the Union's survival. California was rich in gold that the Union desperately needed. It had been admitted to the Union as a free state in 1850, though it had citizens loyal to both the Union and the Confederacy. The Confederates in the South regularly sent anti-Union propaganda to California in hopes of swaying them to join the Confederacy. The government used the Pony Express to counter these communications. In many ways, it was a battle of information.

According to my research, there were no known females who rode for the Pony Express but given the accounts of women fighting as men during the Civil War, I feel it's worth imagining.

Locations

Victory Hills is a fictional town inspired by real boomtowns that sprang up over the American West during the California gold rush of 1849 and later the Comstock Lode silver discovery in Nevada in 1859 (which was part of the Utah territory at the time). My fictional town is situated along the Truckee River, about 30-40 miles north of Virginia City.

Virginia City was the actual site of the Comstock Lode discovery, causing its population to explode. This bustling, vibrant area yielded millions of tons of gold and silver in its "bonanza period," which ended around 1880. While many boomtowns were abandoned after all the gold and silver ore had been extracted, Virginia City endures and is a charming tourist attraction rich in history.

Buckland's was the name of an actual Pony Express station. Samuel S. Buckland built a sizable cabin in 1859 which functioned as a ranch and trading post. The Pony Express acquired it in 1860 to use as a home station as well. For the purposes of my storyline and characters, I made the cabin small and rough-hewn as if it had been thrown together in a day (as were many stations along the western route). Buckland's was only used during the first few months of operation.

The Pyramid Lake War

In the Pyramid Lake region in 1860, a significant conflict arose between the white settlers and the Indigenous people of the Paiute and Shoshone tribes. Tensions had been on the rise for more than a decade, as hordes of miners, hunters, and ranchers made their way out West, depleting the limited resources relied on by the tribes. This included chopping down pinyon pine trees for firewood and hunting on ancestral grounds. There were also accounts of sexual assault and murder. The tribe members countered these offenses with their own acts of violence, and hostilities reached a critical point.

In late April of 1860, a council representing all the region's tribes gathered to debate the possibility of waging an all-out war with the settlers. My fictional character Tso'apa alludes to this impending war when she says that the council will reclaim the area. My book does not follow the progression of this event, but in May of 1860, war did break out, halting Pony Express operations from Carson City to Salt Lake City until July. The war's outcome led to a tragic loss of life on both sides and further strained relations.

The Copperheads

The "Vipers for Peace" is my own creation, based loosely on the fraternal organization called the "Copperheads." The most notable difference is the timing. The Copperheads originated in 1861 after the Civil War had begun, as a means of protest. My fictional "Vipers for Peace" surfaced before the war started in an effort to prevent it. Both the fictional and the actual groups purported the same anti-Union sentiments.

The Copperheads, also referred to as the Peace Democrats, believed a war against slavery was unconstitutional and not worth the cost. They were anti-war, anti-Lincoln, and aimed to thwart the abolitionists' cause. They were not, however, against committing covert acts of harassment and violence to make their messages clear to their rivals. Abolitionists before and during the war faced severe opposition; I created the "Vipers" to illustrate this. Not all the Copperheads were violent, and generally, they did not keep their affiliation with the group a secret. In some cases, members even held political offices. Abolitionism also had supporters with organizations of their own.

BIBLIOGRAPHY

Alighieri, Dante. *The Divine Comedy: The Vision of Hell, Purgatory, and Paradise.* Translated by Henry Francis Cary, 1814. (To download a free copy, see The Project Gutenberg at www.gutenberg.org.)

Brown, William Wells. *Narrative of William W. Brown, a Fugitive Slave.* Written by Himself. Boston: published at the anti-slavery office, No. 25, Cornhill, 1847.

Corbett, Christopher. *Orphans Preferred: The Twisted Truth and Lasting Legend of the Pony Express.* New York, NY: Broadway Books, 2003.

Di Certo, Joseph J. *The Saga of the Pony Express.* Missoula, MT: Mountain Press Publishing Company, 2002.

Douglass, Frederick. *Narrative of the Life of Frederick Douglass.* (Originally published in 1845.) Mineola, NY: Dover Publications, Inc., 2016.

Hermann, Ruth. *The Paiutes of Pyramid Lake.* San Jose, CA: Harlan-Young Press, 1972.

Hopkins, Sarah Winnemucca. *Life Among the Piutes* [sic]*: Their Wrongs and Claims* (1883). Arcadia Press, 2017.

Nevada Bureau of Land Management. *The Pony Express in Nevada.* Carson City, NV: Harrah's, 1976.

Stowe, Harriet Beecher. *Uncle Tom's Cabin.* (Originally published in 1852.) Mineola, NY: Dover Publications, Inc., 2005.

Weber, Jennifer L. *Copperheads: The Rise and Fall of Lincoln's Opponents in the North.* New York, NY: Oxford University Press, 2006.

ACKNOWLEDGMENTS

Recently I received this message in a fortune cookie: "Your biggest battle will be won with the help of others." The accuracy, as it pertains to me and this book, is spot-on. This 15-year project has indeed been a battle, and I certainly do not stand alone on this parapet.

To my readers of much earlier drafts, Ellie Jenkins, Destiny Gutke, and Karen Smart. Thank you for wading through the weeds. May you enjoy the super-evolved finished product. To the finest equestrian I know, my horse advisor and reader, Abigail Sivert. And to Marc Nielson for your horse expertise as well. To my writing friend, Lexie Hill; I wish you massive success in your endeavors. And to Jessica Ball and Karena Lapray, members of my first writing group, who pushed me in critical ways to bring this manuscript to fruition. To my readers of later drafts, Marianne Firth and Megan Sivert. Both of you brought me and my manuscript to the home stretch with your invaluable feedback and endless encouragement.

My editors are the very best. To Jolene Perry for your masterful developmental editing. To Jennie Stevens, a copywriting warrior, in whom I have absolute trust. To AaLeiyah DeSimas, for your insightful sensitivity reading; if any errors or blind spots remain, they are mine, not yours. To my proofreader, Sana Abuleil, for your crisp and thorough final pass-through. Again, any remaining errors are mine.

To my friend and accountability partner, Julie Smith. I'll always remember to experience, wonder, and savor. To Brandie Siegfried, for your lifelong dedication to inspiring college students. To the singer,

Cara Dillon, whose Irish melodies sustained me during many a writing session. To all my supporters, newsletter subscribers, and blog readers. You are my people.

All my love and gratitude to my parents, Glen and Thelma Thomas, for encouraging my writing and for your unfailing nudges to keep going. To the world's greatest siblings and their spouses, Laurie, Ken, Jeff, Nancy, Sam, Amy, Kevin, Karen, Paul, Viv, Joe, Jenni, and Kristi. To my incredible bonus family, Dale and Esther, Ben, Erin, Bill, Megan, Becky, Bruce, Jake, Marianne, Buffy, Sam, Bethany, Hardy, Juli, and Braden. Thank you all for your contributions to my book and more importantly to the person I am. To Lisa Freshley and Katy Hogan, the women I can never truly thank enough.

To my boys, Jed and Gunnar, for your love, hugs, and antics, some of which may have made it into the text. And to my pup, Luna, for your love and licks.

Finally, to my sweetheart and greatest supporter, Bob, who has proven to be unshakably dedicated to me and this project. You are my right-hand man, my consultant, the one with whom I share all my epiphanies. You can breathe a sigh of relief as deep as mine now that this project is complete.

The list goes on in my heart. Many thanks!

SHELLI SIVERT grew up minimally supervised in a small town called Pleasant Grove, to which she credits her wild imagination and storytelling spirit. As soon as she learned to write, she began putting stories on paper. She hails from the Bookmobile era and relishes the days when it rolled into town bearing literary treasures. Studying English in college deepened her love for literature. She has a special affinity for a well-crafted essay and has helped hundreds of college-bound students learn the self-reflective process of writing and revising personal essays. She lives in the Arizona desert with her husband, two sons, and dog Luna. *Heart of Grit* is her debut novel.

You can visit Shelli at shellisivert.com